The Duplicity

by Nina Martineck

Chapter One

Hush, hush, the world is quiet.
Hush, hush, we both can't fight it.
It's us that made this mess.

"Animal"
Neon Trees

My phone rings at one-fifty-six AM. Granted, I'm awake, and I was waiting for it. I'm already dressed, my purse has been packed since dinnertime, and I made sure to leave the back door unlocked before my parents went to bed because I've never heard a lock more keen on making everyone in a thirty-mile radius aware of its existence.

For good measure, I go up to my glass room, throw a pillow over the opening, and curl up like an armadillo under a blanket before answering my phone in a whisper. "Are you outside?"

"Down the street," Hunter replies. "Outside the house with all the gnomes."

"The Gnome House," I say. "Perfect. Give me five minutes, please?"

"You'll beat Hallie no matter what, so take your time."

This isn't even close to the first time I've snuck out of my house in the middle of the night, but regardless of how many times I've done it, it never gets any easier. It isn't *supposed* to get easier. You get complacent, and you get caught.

I know all the spots that creak on the staircase. On my tiptoes, I avoid them. Then I hug the wall of the foyer all the way to the kitchen, since the middle of the floor sounds like an actively occurring shipwreck. That's the curse of extremely old houses—you are always able to tell exactly where its occupants are situated.

Once I make it to the kitchen, I'm mostly safe. The house doesn't groan as much when someone's in the kitchen, as long as they don't touch anything. I gingerly open the door, slip out onto the back porch, and slowly close it behind me, mitigating the *click* as well as I can. Then I walk around the side of the house and down the sidewalk towards the Gnome House. Fortunately, I don't see any lights in any of our neighbors' windows. Here, people can tell who someone is by the length of their shadow.

I see Hunter's car, practically sprint to it, and climb into the back seat, since I'm sure Jacob's already taken the front.

"Are you wearing a dress?" Hunter asks me as I buckle in.

"Are you judging me?"

"Hunter? Being judgmental?" Jacob says. "I can't imagine."

"Did you specify the Gnome House when you called Hallie?" I ask Hunter.

"Yeah," he says. "Unless your street has multiple gnome houses?"

"Three-and-a-half," I reply. "But this one has the most varied collection."

Hallie opens the other door and slips inside. "Damnit. Skylar beat me again? You called her first, didn't you?"

"We called *you* first," Jacob tells Hallie. "Skylar's just more prepared than you."

"Skylar has five fewer people in her house to accidentally wake up," Hallie says.

"Do you have the tickets?" I ask Hallie.

She pulls an envelope from her pocket and sticks it in my purse. "Printed in color, even."

"Fancy."

"Everyone buckled up?" Hunter asks. He doesn't wait for a response for pulling out of his parking spot and heading towards Alex's house.

Hunter doesn't *really* have his driver's license, but he has a learner's permit, access to a car his parents won't notice is missing, and Orion attempted to teach him how to drive over the summer in the high school parking lot (which I would have paid an exorbitant amount of money to have witnessed). And every chief of police in the tristate area owes his father Praxis a favor for one reason or another, so we're pretty much in the clear. Which is good, because being pulled over—or dying in a fiery explosion on the side of the road—seems inevitable when Hunter is driving.

He hits the curb as he tries to park a few houses down from Alex's. "That's the third time tonight," Jacob says.

"Would you rather drive, Mr. That's-the-third-time-tonight?"

"I cannot think of something worse than Jacob driving," Hallie says.

"I can," I say. "Hunter driving."

"Skylar, you are welcome to take the wheel," Hunter tells me as Alex climbs in the car.

"Please, God, no," Alex says. I slide into the middle. "I'd rather Jacob drive than Skylar."

"Thank you, Alex," Jacob says.

"You don't even have your permit," I say to Jacob.

"I'm really good at Mariokart."

"No, you're not."

"Put me in Moo Moo Meadows, and I'm really good."

"The real-life open road is not Moo Moo Meadows, Jacob," Hunter grumbles.

Once we get Lexie from her house—where Hunter hits the curb again—we head towards the bridge. I get especially nervous on the bridge; it's not the actual bridge that's scary so much as the merge to get on. Even though there are literally no other cars out, the turn is at an awkward angle and you have to accelerate as soon as you get out of the turn or else you'll be hit by oncoming traffic. Fortunately, there isn't any oncoming traffic. There never is whenever Hunter drives us around, since it's always in the middle of the night.

"Who's navigating?" Hunter asks once we're off the bridge.

"I can," Hallie volunteers.

"No," we all say, pretty much simultaneously.

"Come on. My sense of direction has improved."

"From complete shit," Alex says. Hallie pokes him in the shoulder.

"I'll do it," Lexie says. "The address is in the group chat?"

"I sent it this morning," I say. "Unless Andrea wiped our group chat from afar again."

"I told her not to do that anymore," Jacob says. "Whether she listened or not, I have no idea."

"It says we'll be there by three," Lexie says.

"Good," I say. "I told Everett we'd be there by two-forty-five, and he'll inevitably be late."

"Jacob, are you on aux cord?" Hunter asks.

"Jacob got to do it last week when we went to the prison," Lexie whines.

"I have excellent music taste," Jacob says.

"Make him run through a Meeting," Alex recommends.

"Hunter, make Alex walk."

"Jacob, put on some music, or we let Skylar play Vivaldi again."

"You liked my Vivaldi," I say. "Don't pretend otherwise."

Jacob puts on Neon Trees, which everyone can always agree on. Reminds us of middle school, maybe, when things were easier because we never had to drive two cities over in the middle of the night to talk to corrupt congressmen—congressmen, of course, that we've corrupted.

"Jesus, Hunter!" Hallie yelps when Hunter almost misses a turn and takes it way too sharply.

"I'm sorry!" Hunter shouts back. "It snuck up on me!"

"I told you it was coming a mile ago," Lexie says.

"A mile is not a lot of time."

Miraculously, Hunter gets us to the Wash N' Fold Laundromat without killing us all. There's a Lincoln in the parking lot, so Everett Caldwell is most likely here already. Hunter and Jacob turn to face the rest of us.

"Okay," I say. "So. Plan A *should* work. If not, we have Plan A-point-five, which *really* should work. Alex brought the baking soda for Plan B. And Hunter? The contingency plan?"

Hunter grabs his tiny silver handgun, Eradicator-issued, out of the glove compartment. Good Lord, I hate that thing. One look at it and Harlow's splattered out on the floor again, and the spot on my arm that was nicked by a bullet burns as if I were still cut open. But God only knows what lurks in this town at this hour, so it's better to have a contingency plan.

"Okay," I say. "Everyone, keep your ringers on in case we switch plans."

"I'll go do recon," Hallie says. "Alex? You coming?"

"Yep. We'll be right back."

"Good luck, guys," Lexie says. "Be careful."

They grab the load of laundry at Lexie's feet and slip into the building. A few minutes later, we get a text: *The chicken is in the henhouse.*

"Okay, Skylar," Lexie says. "That's your cue. Please be careful."

"I'll be fine, Lexie," I say. I give her hand a squeeze for good measure.

"We'll be right behind you," Jacob tells me. Per usual, I linger on his brown eyes just a bit too long. Just enough to make it weird. But it's not my fault they look like mid-November. He should have less alluring eyes.

"Thanks," I tell him. Then I climb out of the car, pull my coat tighter around me, and enter the laundromat. I know Jacob and Hunter follow behind me a few seconds later, leaving Lexie to watch the car (and pick any music she wants).

The bell on the door languidly jingles when I walk in. The place is almost completely empty, except for a woman folding mangled towels in the corner, Hallie and Alex loading clothes from Hunter's bedroom floor into a dryer, and a man in khakis and a rumpled blue button-down standing at the back counter on his phone. Jacob and Hunter follow me across the chipping linoleum, weaving between rows of creaking machines, until we find our-selves in front of Representative Everett Caldwell, D-20 of New York State.

"Hello," I say.

He looks up at us, and for a second, I'm thrown off. My gosh, this guy is hot. I wasn't expecting that, and I don't like when I don't expect something. Sure, I'd seen pictures, but I guess I overlooked the floofy gingerbread hair, piercing jade eyes, and a mouth that must form the most vivacious of smiles. I see why he keeps winning his district over. "Hi?"

"Representative Caldwell, I presume." I hold my hand out, and he shakes it haphazardly, like he's afraid he'll break my arm off if he gives it any more strength. "I'm Skylar Rawlings. These are some associates I brought along."

"You're Skylar Rawlings?" Predictably, he seems perplexed. "I knew you were young, but . . . not like this."

"I'm older than I look," I say. (Which is true—I'm sixteen and look eleven at best.) "Thank you for coming all the way here. I do think it's best for us to not have met anywhere near your dis-trict."

He's quiet for a minute before saying, "I'm sorry, I just was not expecting to be meeting an actual child."

"And I was expecting someone in such a precarious cir-cumstance to be a bit kinder," I say.

He seems a bit taken aback but recovers quickly. "Well, I'm here now. You brought what I asked for in return for meeting you out here?"

I take the envelope out of my purse. "Four tickets to open-ing night of *Pokémon the Musical: Gotta Catch 'Em All* at the Winter Garden Theater on Broadway." Thank goodness Orion goes to school with Stephen Sondheim's great-step-nephew, or else the whole plan might have fallen through.

"Orchestra seats?" he asks.

"Sixth row."

He opens the envelope and checks over the tickets. "How did you get these? They're impossible to find."

"I have resources," I say. "And so, it seems, do you."

"Not enough."

"Good thing we can help each other."

He leans against the counter. "You can make the whole thing disappear? Make all the protests in Redway stop and some-how make people think I should be reelected come November?"

"Yes," I say. "The protests will most likely last for a week or so more. That's unavoidable. But we can get the bus operators back on your side. Build them a new bus garage."

"That's why they've been protesting in the first place. Federal funds were rejected."

"Then get them the federal funds."

"Didn't I just say that's why they're upset? Because I *can't* get them?"

"You did. But we can work around whatever you believe to be true."

Jacob hands him a flash drive. "Here are some building plans for a new bus garage, complete with a recreational space and full-service kitchen for the operators. It should cost a little under twenty-five million dollars to build and take about eight months. Also, it's environmentally-conscious, which should make your constituents happy, and fits in the vacant lot on the corner of Cherry Street and Main Street in Redway, away from most residential areas, and intersecting with seven of your bus routes."

Everett looks at the flash drive as if he can already see the garage. "This needs to be vetted and approved by the Redway municipality. It might not fit their zoning laws."

"It's been approved by the municipality," Hunter says. "We had it checked over before sending it your way."

"And it definitely fits all their zoning laws," Jacob says. "The architect triple-checked."

Everett looks more and more confused by the second. (Not that I blame him. We're a confusing bunch.) "Fine. Then how do we get the money for it?"

"There's a representative you can talk to." I take a business card out of my purse and hand it to him. "Navid Rashimi, from Maine's second district. He can attach your funding to a health code bill that hits the floor in two months. All he asks is that you support the bill."

"So I do all this, and you think I'll be reelected."

"Certainly," I say. Quite honestly, there is no way in hell Everett Caldwell is getting reelected after this disastrous term. His constituency suffered a less-than-stellar harvest last season, and even though Everett does not control the weather, he is one of the easiest people to blame. And now the budget cuts, and this drama with the bus operators—he would need a miracle to win November's election. However, he doesn't need to know that. I'm quite surprised he hasn't come to terms with it already. "Does that solve your problem, Mr. Caldwell?"

"It starts to," he says. "So, what did you want in return?"

"Get Cécile Kettering out of office."

He laughs. "That's impossible. She's been the incumbent for going on eighteen years. No way she's heading out. No one *loves* her, but her district tolerates her, and that's almost harder to come by. She'll be reelected, no doubt."

I take a folder out of my purse and hand it to him. "Here's some information that might help you. Her district needs funding, and you, being in the position you are in the party's funding committee, can cut her off. Her campaign runs out of money, supporters back other candidates, and she'll be out of office come November."

He turns his head to the side a bit, and I notice a line on his cheek. A scar, maybe, or just a strange birthmark. It's hard to tell in the fluorescent lighting. But I only notice it now. He's forgotten about it. He holds his head differently when he's forgotten about it.

"I think I know some people I can talk to," he says.

"Thank you, Mr. Caldwell. It is very much appreciated."

"Why do you kids want her out of office?"

We want her out of office because she's dealing with some messy stuff that includes a shit ton of Eradicators and Robin Hood-esque embezzlement. (We take money from places that don't really need it—like the US military—and give it to the Knower Treasury Board, which will distribute it to causes that do. And Cécile gets to keep about three percent, which is how we got her involved in the first place.) She's almost slipped up a few times now during press conferences or media encounters, mentioning names of Eradicators she's working with or things of that sort. (Not that she knows what an Eradicator is, but we don't want someone smarter than her starting to connect any dots.) We have to get her out of the public eye before we can extract her from the embezzlement operation. So it's either removal or assassination, and the slight majority of us think the former would be better.

But I say, "She doesn't connect with the youth."

"I'll keep that in mind. And you're sure I can get that funding for the bus garage? If I don't get it, I'm out."

"We helped Mr. Rashimi out of a similar pickle just last month, so he owes us this," I say. "If you don't get your funding by mid-June, call me. I'd be happy to share some pictures from his hunting trip last year."

Seemingly despite himself, Everett smiles. "Thank you."

"Of course. Now, if you'll excuse us, we have an early morning obligation, so we'd best be on our way."

"It's a school night?" Everett asks, eyebrows raised.

"Something of the sort," I reply. I give him one last smile, and Jacob, Hunter, and I head back to the car. Hallie and Alex come a few moments later.

"Jesus, he's hot," Hunter says. "I wasn't expecting that."

"Tell me about it," Hallie says.

"No wonder he keeps winning," Hunter says. "I'd vote for him on that hair alone."

Once we're all buckled in and ready to go, Hunter tries to back out and misses a lamppost by a few inches.

"Can someone else learn to drive before our next outing?" he asks.

"Skylar." Evan wakes me up by jumping on my bed. I almost chuck a stuffed whale at him, but I notice he's in his school uniform already. I turn on my phone on my nightstand and see that it's almost seven.

"Shit," I say, jumping out of bed. I get up too quickly and fireworks frame my vision. When I try to put my glasses on, I poke myself in the eye. "Good God, Evan. How is it already seven?"

"You didn't hear your alarm go off?" Evan asks me.

"I might have in a dream," I say, pulling an evergreen polo and khaki skirt from my closet.

"Hallie's on the porch. You have about seven minutes before the bus gets here."

"Wonderful," I say. "Go tell her I'll be right there."

I manage to get ready in three and a half minutes. I mean, I pull my hair into a shitty braid to excuse myself from brushing it, and I don't put on my red flower necklace that I usually wear with my uniform, and my socks don't match (one seahorse, one R2-D2), but all things considered, I'm pretty proud of myself.

"You look like you didn't sleep well," my mom says as I grab a granola bar from the pantry.

"Stomachache," I say. "I should watch my citrus intake so close to bedtime."

"The kettle's hot," my dad says. I pour some hot water over an earl grey teabag into my travel mug. "You shouldn't eat oranges before bed, Skylar."

"I know. Just wanted a healthy snack."

"Try a pear next time," my mom recommends. "Are you coming home after school?"

"Rehearsal," I remind them. "For the musical. Then maybe my friends can come here for homework?" *Or running a practice Meeting since Jacob hasn't practiced in almost five days now?*

"Of course," my mom says. "As long as you're actually doing homework."

"Of course, Mom. We don't do much else."

I give them a wave before sprinting to the front porch, where Hallie stands on the steps, arms crossed, eyebrows furrowed.

"Skylar, it's freaking cold out," she grumbles.

"You could have come inside," I say. "You're not banished to our front steps."

"I was hoping you wouldn't take that long."

"The bus isn't even here yet, Hallie."

"Yeah, but it *will* be here any second now."

Sure enough, the school bus meanders up our street within a few seconds, the sickly yellow stark against the snowdrifts. It hasn't snowed substantially in a few weeks now, so the big drifts at the end of each driveway are streaked with dirt. Which is normal for early March. Soon they'll start to melt and the incessant rain will begin, and honestly, I don't know which is worse. But at least now there is limited precipitation, which makes traversing the island a bit easier.

We climb on the bus, and Hallie lets me take the window seat, as always. As if you can actually *see* out the window. It's frosted over with steam and third-grader spit, but I get the general sense of the outdoors.

As I do every morning, I use this time to check all the messages on MeetingGround, the Knower/Eradicator app Andrea designed, and thank goodness, there aren't too many. Ms. Parkins talked to that cobbler she wanted help from, so that's groundbreaking news. Cristobal says that, globally, there were only three deaths from the Winther strain this week, which is half as many as last week, so we're doing much better than before. Cristobal's friend who runs a research team in Londrina, Brazil has found something concerning that seems to be affecting Brazilian free-tailed bats. I don't like thinking about bats—I believe them to be Satan's own children—so I push that away. Orion has EmMarked all three posts, but Jacob has yet to mark any.

Surprisingly, the world has been relatively quiet lately. The Winther strain pandemic, started intentionally by Freja Lundquist last September, is just about over. Cases still pop up, but it's no longer a pandemic, and it's been out of the news cycle for nearly a month now.

As for Freja, she's back in Sweden, dethroned from her position at the Uppsala Clinical Research Center. Orion forced her to destroy all traces of the virus and the ineffective vaccine, lest she try something like that again. She now teaches at a university in Uppsala, but Orion keeps a close eye on her. People who know the Knowers and Eradicators exist but *aren't* Knowers or Eradicators are a different type of dangerous, if they don't have every ounce of your trust. She, needless to say, has none of ours.

The Mechanism is totally fine now—evident by how often Orion freezes time just because he can. (Seriously, he'll stop the world from turning for the most ridiculous reasons. He definitely could have told us that the prime minister of Germany died from a heart attack with the clock still ticking, especially because Mr. Hallawin, our global teacher, told us before Orion even knew.) Eula, Dakarai, and Orion (as he claims) were able to fix it in about four days, so it was up and running by the end of September. They stayed in New York until it was done, and then they tested it about six times a day for the following week, which might have been the most annoying week of my life. We'd be in class, or sound asleep, or, once, all in Lexie's bedroom running a practice Meeting for Jacob. It was weird, watching Alex freeze like that. It's only in those moments that I remember he's not actually one of us, since he adjusted to Knower life so quickly.

It takes about twenty minutes to get to school on the bus, which aggravates me to no end. If Hallie and I walked, it would be seven, eight minutes at most. But we might freeze before arrival, so we relegate ourselves to the bus until the green starts showing itself again.

Jacob and Alex are already in homeroom when we get there, but God only knows where Lexie and Hunter are. Hopefully not still sleeping, though I wouldn't be surprised. Hallie and I take our desks right next to theirs.

"You look dead inside," Hallie tells them.

"And you look beautiful, Hallie," Alex says.

"So nothing's changed, then."

"You didn't EmMark anything on MeetingGround," I remind Jacob.

"I always forget," he says, taking his phone out of his pocket and opening the app. He puts in his login info and reads the messages other Knowers and Eradicators have posted, and he marks them so they know that the Eminences saw them. Orion, as always, beat him to it. "It would help if Andrea would allow notifications."

"Your phone would never stop buzzing," Alex says.

"True," Jacob says, scrolling through the posts. "Free-tailed bats. Ew."

"Coira commented underneath and she could handle it," I tell him.

"I don't trust Coira near living things. Her solution is usually massacre."

He looks to me, and I look to him. We look away at the same time. Of course, it was just a bit too long, as it usually is. If it's enough time for me to catalogue the color of his eyes (hazelnut brown) and feel a tiny little firework in my chest, then it was too long.

We made a mutual agreement after getting home from New York that whatever had happened between us, it just couldn't happen again. (Not that he would have another opportunity to be forced under oath to confess being in love with me in front of two secret societies of geniuses, and not that I'd ever have the nerve to kiss him again.) It would be a horrible idea to date someone you'll be forced to know for the rest of your life, especially if that person is sort of the leader of the universe. Double-especially if he really doesn't know how to lead the universe yet. Triple-especially if you have the same group of friends and multiple classes together.

Did this agreement really change anything, though? It's been six months, and I would still say *definitely not*. Which is worsened by the fact that we seem to have lost all ability to have a conversation with one another without the presence of other people. He doesn't send me whale memes anymore, he hasn't called me Bubble in months, and I don't ask him about his buildings because I know that his eyes would light up and he'd tell me about the things he builds in his head, and I would be back at square one and in love with him all over again.

So this arrangement works for now. We should be past it in another month or so. (I said that last month. And the month before. And the month before that.)

Hallie yawns. "Hopefully that was the last late night for a-while."

"Should be," Jacob says. "If I have any say."

"You should," Hallie says. "You're, like, the Eminence."

"I try my best."

Lexie practically sprints into the room before throwing herself into her desk. "Thank every God there is. I'm not late again."

"Two minutes to spare," Hallie says. "Not bad."

"Way better than Hunter," Alex says.

"Are you surprised?" Being late for homeroom isn't exactly unusual for Hunter.

Jacob sighs. "I'll call him."

He doesn't have to, though—Hunter walks in right as the bell rings. "Nailed it," he says.

"I wouldn't say that," Hallie mutters right as the morning announcements start.

"I'm here, though, aren't I?" Hunter counters. "That in itself is a miracle."

Chapter Two

"Moscow"
Autoheart

As soon as the bell rings, signaling that the school day has come to an end, the six of us head across the quad to the auditorium. I'm exhausted from a particularly draining chemistry lab and getting approximately thirty seconds of sleep last night, so I don't really *want* to go to rehearsal, but the show's in just two weeks, so I can't skip now.

I gave into Lexie, Alex, and Hunter pressuring me to audition for the musical, which, despite all the rumors, ended up being *Lightning in His Hands*, the one and only musical about the life and triumphs of Nikola Tesla. That's mostly why I relented—Tesla was a Knower. Of course, that's not why Mrs. Darner picked the musical. She has no idea what a Knower is and that there is quite the sizable population of them at her school, but it nevertheless feels especially important for us all to be involved. Besides, we're one of the first high schools to put on the high school version, which would be quite the honor, if the show were any good.

The show kind of sucks. I'm not going to sugarcoat it.

Lexie and I were both cast as Girl Ensemble Members, like most underclassmen, which is entirely fine by me. Though Alex and Hunter were appalled that I didn't get cast as Marica Tesla, I don't think I could have handled any lines and being in more than five scenes for my first time being in a musical. Hunter actually has four lines, since he's playing Assistant to Westinghouse Number Two, which is very impressive for a sophomore.

But when the cast list was posted online, Alex surprised the entire theater department by getting the part of Mr. Charles Batchelor, who has solos in two songs and twenty-three lines. Damn, that boy can *sing*. I had absolutely no idea until his audition in January, when everyone (most of all, his friends) were completely floored by his rendition of "Grow for Me" from *Little Shop of Horrors*. You would never be able to tell by looking at him, since he has the appearance of a heartthrob hockey player (which is his winter sport season gig). But he is one of the most talented people in the show, second only to Wyatt Farrington, who plays Tesla and is committed early-decision to NYU's drama program. If Alex were a senior, he'd have given Wyatt a real fight for that part.

Jacob's working on sets. At first, he thought he'd be too busy with Eminence stuff to help out with the show, but he took one look at Mr. Hallawin's sketches for the set pieces and pointed out twelve historical inaccuracies and eight structural concerns. Mr. Hallawin practically handed him the job of designing all seven sets and directing their construction. Set Production Assistant is his title, but Jacob Connelly is no one's assistant. He'd build the whole thing himself if he had two more weeks and one fewer planet to run.

Hallie outright refuses to have anything to do with the show, often referring to it as "geeky," yet whenever we have rehearsal, she sits in the ninth row in the auditorium, pretending to do her homework. She'll usually give us notes on the way home, letting us know when we entered too early or when we were off-beat on dances.

"Can we please run 'Parisian' from the top?" Mrs. Darner calls out.

Lexie grabs my hand. "Alex's number! Let's go watch!"

We tiptoe out from backstage and watch as Alex, Wyatt, and Rachel Kwan take their places on stage. This is the scene when, in the middle of the night, Tesla meets Edison and his manager, Mr. Charles Batchelor, for the first time. (Of course, Edison is played by Rachel because not enough boys do theater here, so Mrs. Darner had to gender-bend most of the male roles if she wanted people who could actually sing.)

"This is the best song in the show," Lexie whispers. She's completely correct. The three part harmony is so cool, even if Rachel's part had to be adjusted to accommodate a soprano instead of a baritone. And the three of them nail it every single time. I think Mrs. Darner likes running it so often because it's the only number in the show that isn't currently a total mess.

"I find it so funny that the real reason they were tense with each other was because Tesla was a Knower," I whisper to Lexie, "and Edison was an Eradicator."

"Team AC all the way," Lexie whispers back.

"Next year," I say, "we should do Romeo and Juliet—"

She sees where I'm going. "With one Knower and one Eradicator?"

"Yes!"

"*West Side Story* but with Andrea and Eula."

I laugh so hard that Mrs. Darner turns and glares at us. We shut up.

"Let's run 'An Alternate Path!'" Mrs. Darner calls.

"Uh oh," I say. "That's us." Lexie and I stand up and sprint backstage and make it to our places right before the lights go back on. This is the song when Tesla leaves Edison's company and creates alternate current. It's a super long scene—it's over ten minutes—and it's impossible for everyone in the company to get every bit right. We average thirty-eight percent correctness.

"Mr. Edison," Wyatt says. "I regret to inform you that I will be taking my leave of your company."

Rachel jumps up from her desk. "Mr. Tesla," she says, trying to deepen her voice to sound more like a man. (It never works.) "We will be sad to see you go. May I ask why you are leaving us?"

Wyatt looks out over the audience as the orchestra begins the song, and he starts to sing. "I must take an alternate path, it's time I find an alternate direction."

I try my best to remember all the words to the song and all the dance moves, but it's not as easy as it looks. Every time I mess up, I'm thrown off and I mess up again. It's a vicious cycle. Lexie can't sing at all, but she's a wonderful dancer. Which is strange, since dancing depends so much on having a good sense of rhythm, something at which Knowers are notoriously horrible. But Lexie's also a drummer and a swimmer, so she's had lots of time to practice pretending she knows how long a beat is.

We make it through the scene without too large a catastrophe, but Mrs. Darner still declares it to look like "if you taught a pack of zombies Fosse combinations in exchange for brains." We run it twice more before she dismisses us a half-hour late.

"Your house for Meeting practice?" Lexie says as we pack up our character shoes and scripts.

"Yes," I say. "I'll grab Alex and Jacob. Get Hallie and meet us up front?"

"Coolio," Lexie says.

"Alexander Summerheld," I say, finding him waiting to fill his water bottle at the water fountain.

"Skylar Rawlings," he replies.

"You have a very long name," I say.

"My middle name is Montgomery."

"I mean no offense, but ew."

"My mom needs to take a breath halfway through yelling my name when I'm in trouble." The person in front of him moves, and he starts filling his water bottle. "Meeting at your house?"

"Yes," I say. "It's been five days since Jacob's practiced."

"That's a long time," he replies. "What type are we running?"

"I'm thinking a Type B," I say. "We haven't done a Type B since February."

"Please, not a Type B," Jacob says, joining us at the water fountain. "They're my second-least favorite."

"You've only been doing Type A Meetings for the past two weeks. And if they're your second-least favorite, you should practice them more."

"Or I could *not* practice them more and pray we'll never have to call one."

"Or you *could* practice them more and be prepared for when you inevitably have to call one."

"Or I could *not* practice and just *choose* to never call one."

"You can't just *choose* not to call a Type B Meeting, Jacob. Not when the world is in mortal danger."

"Depends on how mortal the danger is."

"My bottle's filled," Alex says, holding up his water bottle. "Are you two ready?"

"Yes," I say, turning around and walking towards the front of the auditorium, not turning to see if the others are following me because I already know that they are.

"Objection." Hallie points to a line in her book. "You're not supposed to mention a motion until the first thought has been stated."

"So I can't even say we're going to take one eventually?" Jacob asks.

"Guess not." Lexie shrugs. "Just don't say the word *motion* until you finish the whole intro, and you should be good."

"Just start the whole thing over," Hunter says. "I don't feel like calling Lexie into prosecution for improper speech out of turn."

"If we must," Jacob says.

As of today, this year's Meeting is in a month and nine days. That means Jacob has a month and nine days more to learn the Meeting format. When he and Orion run the Meeting, they will have nothing in front of them—the entire thing needs to be memorized. From the Opening Statements to the Comments of Conclusion to every irritating and pointless nuance in between, they have to be ready.

Knowers and Eradicators don't really do approval ratings like normal populations do to see if people actually like their leaders. But that's because we don't have to. Regardless of how good we are at hiding things, we don't do well hiding things from each other. We're too perceptive. Which is usually nice, except for the fact that Jacob and Orion know that pretty much everyone hates them.

It isn't really their faults. They are very unequipped to lead the world's geniuses. No one wants to listen to them because they think they're just children. People rarely get approval before setting out on missions or starting projects, so proper motions are almost never called, and proper protocol is seldom followed. When Jacob and Orion advise people not to do something, people do it anyway, sometimes just to spite them. Treasury rarely gets verification before allocating funds, and there are definitely other things that they don't even know about because no one has bothered to tell them.

There is no way to recall an Eminence—they're stuck with the position until half the pair dies—so the best hope our Eminences have is to win people over. And the best—and probably only—way to do that is by running a flawless first Meeting. It's a lot of pressure, sure, but Jacob has dealt with worse than a few angry smart people, having spent two weeks in architecture school, and he's been doing pretty well with the memorization, all things considered.

"As Eminences of the Knowers, we commence this Meeting," Jacob says, pacing the width of my bedroom as he does so. (He can't move around during the Meeting, so we'll have to get him to stop pacing eventually, but he might combust if we make him keep still, so we'll soon have to come up with some sort of compromise.) "The date is Monday, March eighth, the time is five-seventeen PM, and the location is Skylar's house. I am Jacob Thomas Connelly, Eminence of the Knowers, speaker. My partner is Orion Priam Athan, Eminence of the Knowers. Are there objections?"

There are almost never objections here unless Jacob forgets what day it is or how to read a clock. (Both happen quite frequently.)

"Okay, good. Moving—"

"Objection," Lexie says. "That's not in the script."

"Objection," I say. "That's not sufficient enough to make him start over."

"I request a citation," Lexie says.

Hallie's on book for Speaker Conduct, so we look to her for the citation. She flips through the pages of *The Practices and Rituals of the Knowers* (by Lady Adelaide Grace Wincott, 1736, language updated by Doctor Maria Ana LaRosa, 1912) until she lands on one and says, "Page three-twenty-nine. Chapter forty-six, section eighteen, subsection Q, sub-subsection ninety-eight. 'Personal additions of fewer than six words or fifteen syllables do not warrant objections in Type B or Type C Meetings of any subdivision.'"

"I override the objection," Jacob says.

"I request grounds for the override," Alex says.

"The objection has been overridden on the grounds of the referenced citation," Jacob replies. "Are there objections?"

There are some days on which we try to throw him as many curveballs as possible. We call them Coira Days after our most difficult colleague.

"Moving forward," he continues. "This is a Type B Meeting, subdivision three—an emergency of the outside regarding a natural disaster. The last Meeting was held on September twenty-second of last year, and the last Meeting of this caliber was held on August twenty-seventh, 2005. Are there objections?"

Nope. He's doing pretty well.

"The primary focus of today's Meeting is to learn why the turtle population of Argentina has dropped and to propose and enact a solution. Are there objections?"

"Objection," Hallie says, keeping in the spirit of the Coira day. "Are we only proposing one solution?"

"Objection," Lexie says. "His language was clear enough."

"Objection," Alex says. "That isn't a citable objection and therefore can't be treated as one."

"I request a citation," Hallie says.

There's a knock at my bedroom door.

"The speaker has been absolved of scripted speaker conduct until otherwise noted," I say before calling, "Come in!"

My mom steps into my room with a plate of muffins. "I thought you guys might need some snacks to help with all the studying. They're apple cinnamon with walnut. No nut allergies, right? Or dairy?"

"We don't have any, Mom," I say, taking the plate from her. Since Evan's allergic to five million things, my mom is very conscious of allergies. (Nearly embarrassingly conscious.) "Thank you."

"Thanks, Dr. Rawlings," everyone says, taking a muffin.

"Let me know how they are," she says. "I tried a new recipe. It was an experiment. You're my guinea pigs." She glances at our books. "Global homework again?"

"Yeah," Hallie says.

"Mr. Hallawin doesn't relent," Alex says.

"Well," my mom says, "I'll let you get back to it. You're smart kids. You'll be fine. Don't stress yourselves out too much. Enjoy the muffins!" She smiles and leaves the room.

"I'm not taking the first bite this time," Hallie says. "I almost cried last time."

"I'm not doing it," I say. "I live with her, so I have to do it all the time."

"We have rehearsal tomorrow, so I can't die," Alex protests.

"I call a motion to make Hunter do it," Jacob says.

"I second the motion," Lexie says.

The motion would pass unanimously if not for Hunter's dissenting vote.

"Fine," Hunter sighs. He takes a bite of his muffin and immediately spits it out. "I don't know what that is, but it's not cinnamon or apple. I think that might be a walnut, but I can't say for sure."

I collect the muffins (except Hallie's, since she claims it's edible) and throw them out in my bathroom. Sometimes, my mother is a wonderful baker, and her creations warrant their own cooking shows. But other times . . .

"The speaker must now resume scripted speaker conduct," I say.

"I request a record of the last thing stated," Jacob says.

"'I request a citation,' stated by Hallie Giovia," Lexie says.

"We can skip it," Hallie says, cheeks full of muffin. "Carry on."

"Moving forward," Jacob says. "There is no end time set for this Meeting because our wealth of information, both known and unknown, has yet to be determined. The achievement by the end of this Meeting is to have proposed and enacted a solution to address the decrease in the sea turtle population. Are there objections?"

Nope.

"You have thirty seconds to collect your thoughts. There will be no talking."

Jacob has to practice the thirty-second timing. When your brain literally cannot comprehend the length of a second, it's difficult to count thirty of them. During practice Meetings, Alex gets out his phone and times him. When we first started practicing, back in September, Alex would have to shout out different time stamps so Jacob could get a sense of what thirty seconds feels like. Which is difficult—if not impossible—for a Knower to do, because thirty seconds always feels different. Sometimes minutes, sometimes hours, sometimes you blink and it's passed four times over.

"The Meeting will now begin," Jacob says.

"That was seven seconds," Alex says. "Closer than last time, though."

Jacob sighs. "Can we just call it there?"

"No," Hunter says. "Finish the Meeting. You usually forget to ask for final words."

"I won't this time."

The Meeting takes too long to end. These things get tedious after awhile, but just because something is boring doesn't mean it's unimportant. After Jacob asks for final words and adjourns it, he asks, "Coira day?"

"You're getting better at Coira days," Alex says.

"I'm trying to, at least," Jacob says. "You guys don't make it easy."

"Why would we?" Hallie asks.

"Should we go over that thing for the Boston Children's Museum again?" I ask. "Doesn't Eula want another draft of the third section by next week?"

"Hell no," Hallie says. "We did enough today. *Parks and Rec?*"

"I second the motion," Lexie says.

Parks and Recreation is the best show ever created, and no one could ever convince me otherwise. Though I've seen the whole series on my own more times straight through than I'd like to admit, we've been watching it in order together when we can't deal with the Knowers anymore. (So we watch it a lot.) Only Hallie and Alex have seen it beyond us watching it together, so I especially love Jacob, Lexie, and Hunter's reactions to it.

We all crowd around my laptop on my bed, therefore evicting most of my whales to the floor. I'm practically on Hallie's lap and she's practically on Alex's lap; Lexie and Jacob squish on either side of the conglomeration; Hunter isn't even really on the bed.

We're a few episodes into season four—we start the one where the cult that believes in the lizard god takes over the park for the night. Season four is one of the best seasons, but in all honesty, I wish I could skip to the second half because the Leslie and Ben plot is a little awkward to watch at the moment in present company.

But it doesn't really matter. I'm never happier than I am with all my friends right here, laughing with me at Andy thinking the Grand Canyon has presidents' faces carved into the rock.

I can't say that, presently, life is easy. I have never been as hopeless or confused or nervous or angry as I've been in the past six months, for a multitude of reasons that always seem to change. But this moment is intangible, stolen from a broken timeline that appears to be against my possession of something as blithe and ebullient as this. Eventually, in a few more fleeting seconds, I'll have to return this stint of happiness and wait for the next one.

Just not yet.

Chapter Three

Oh, why won't you make up your mind?
I think I must confess,
I'm learning to unwind.
I've been tripping over you.
so tell me something new.

"Take It or Leave It"
Cage the Elephant

I wish I could take math tests in a vacuum. Sound waves can't travel in a vacuum. Then I wouldn't have to endure the torture of Meredith Pandey tapping her pencil as if her desk were a timpani. Or of the incessant ticking of the second hand on the clock—they really should make silent clocks for classrooms. Or the continuous stream of pencil scratches, calculator clicking, and page turning. It makes me want to scream. There are only twenty minutes left in class and I've only answered three questions because every time I try to read a number, someone's pencil tip snaps and I forget what all those squiggly symbols mean.

Then, by some miracle—*BANG!* Everything freezes. Including all the scratches and clicking and turning. Pure silence apart from my own breathing and the tapping of my own foot, which somehow doesn't bother me. Ideal test-taking conditions.

"Where is everyone?" I hear from down the hall. Lexie, it sounds like, from the science wing.

"I'm finishing this goddamned math test if it kills me!" I call back.

"Skylar, come on," Hallie says. She appears in the doorway of the classroom. "The world could be ending."

Miss Felding appears behind her, coming from her freshman algebra room across the hall. She's been through the most of these time stops, being a Knower for the longest, so she traipses across the hallway with elegance that only comes with practice. "Besides, Skylar, I'm fairly certain that counts as academic dishonesty."

I set my pencil down and stand up. "In whose handbook?"

Whenever time freezes while we're at school, we meet in the front entryway. There are usually very few students hanging out in the entryway, and it's best to not be around students. Not only is it super creepy to see people frozen as if the world turned into a three-dimensional photograph, but if we accidentally touch someone or something and it moves, people get very confused. Lexie walked straight into Will Harding last December and sent him crashing against the terrazzo. People aren't frozen in the sense that they can't move anymore, just that they stopped moving, so Will ended up in a flesh pile, arms and legs contorted weirdly and face pressed against the floor. We tried to stand him back up, but that's like getting a newborn baby to stand on his legs, so we just left him on the floor. We weren't near him when we unfroze, so I have no idea what became of that situation, but he seems to be fine. Hasn't sued the school yet, so I think we're okay.

Jacob and Hunter are already there. Hallie, Lexie, Miss Felding, and I join just as Jacob's phone rings. He puts it on speaker. "Hi, Orion."

The voice of the one and only Orion Athan suffuses from Jacob's phone like sulfur dioxide. "Oh, hello, my dear fellow Eminence! How are you this fine afternoon?"

"Did you freeze time?"

"Why yes, I did, Jake."

"Don't call me Jake. What's up?"

"We have a slight issue."

"How slight?"

"Remember our phone conversation yesterday evening? With our beloved Coira Findlay?"

"Pretty slight, then."

"What phone conversation?" Miss Felding asks.

"Coira's solution to stopping the spread of the disease thing affecting bats in Brazil," Jacob explains. "Which was to eliminate the bat population so it doesn't infect humans. We told her to hold off. We don't know enough about the thing that's affecting the bats. And also killing is not good."

"She has just petitioned for the funds from Treasury for forty-three gallons of rodenticide and two-hundred jars of creamy peanut butter," Orion says. "And Treasury approved her petition, even though they did not go through the proper channels and did not receive permission from either of us to verify the approval."

"Orion," Jacob starts, "as much as I care about the bats of southern Brazil, was it really necessary to freeze time to talk about them? You could have called me after school."

"It could not wait until after your school day concludes, and you would not be able to abandon your classes to have this discussion unless I were to provide you with a way to leave without being noticed."

"Orion," Jacob says, getting more exasperated by the syllable, "have you ever thought that *maybe* part of the reason people don't like us is because they get sick of us freezing time for stupid reasons?"

"I'm sorry, my dear fellow Eminence, but I did not find this a stupid reason. Southern Brazil's sickly bat population is not as concerning to me as Coira's blatant disregard for our ruling on the issue. We told her to conform to Eradicator animal protection guidelines, and she has neglected to follow them."

"I could try to talk to her," Miss Felding says. "I've known Coira a lot longer than you all have, and she rarely takes advice. I stand a chance, but even then, it is somewhat of a long shot with her."

"Thank you, Miss Felding," Jacob says. "That would be—"

"Lea," Orion interrupts, under no obligation to call her Miss Felding since she isn't his teacher, "with every ounce of respect that is due to you and your very kind offer of assistance, I do believe that this is a matter that Jacob and I should handle on our own. We are the Eminences, after all, and it's high time that our associates learn to view us as such. We will speak to Coira and Treasury, see if we can amend this issue, and prevent further issues in this vein."

Miss Felding looks to Jacob. "If that's the course of action you both would like to take."

Jacob closes his eyes for a second, but then he relents. "Fine. We'll talk to her. And if that doesn't work, we'll find another way to intervene."

"Sounds like a wonderful plan, dear co-Eminence."

"Awesome. Can you unfreeze time now, then?"

"No!" I say. "Give me twenty minutes!" I sprint back to my math classroom, weaving between frozen students and trying to keep every pencil and tissue that litters the hallway completely intact.

I manage to finish the entire test before the clock starts ticking and the pencils start tapping again. I check it over three times and I'm still the first to turn it in.

Before math class ends, as the rest of my classmates finish their tests, my mind starts to wander, as it usually does when there is nothing to occupy it. For some reason, a reason I wish I could thwart, it wanders in the direction of Margaret White.

For all we know, the former Eminence of the Knowers is still comatose in a hospital somewhere. But we *don't* know. We know so, so little about her. Eula, who served as Margaret's co-Eminence, won't tell us anything about her. She says we don't need to worry about her anymore. That doesn't mean I don't ever wonder if she's awake, or if she's still asleep, or if she's even still alive. I guess it doesn't really matter—she'll never be a Knower again. Jacob may claim that he's not a leader, but he will fight anyone and everyone who tries to argue with him on Margaret's status as a Knower. She's out. She's never coming back. Try as she may, there is nothing she can do to get through Jacob and everyone who agrees with him. And I agree with him whole-heartedly. I tend to do that.

Yet I can't help but wonder: If Margaret isn't a Knower anymore, who is she?

Do we really have the agency to recall the most prominent part of her identity? Probably not. There's a reason the verdict was unprecedented. But how are we supposed to let her do something like that without consequences?

Maybe the same way we allow ourselves to do everything we do without consequences.

Margaret White, it pains me to say, is not much different than the rest of us. We all rely on our underground spiderweb, powers of manipulation, and alliance with time to get us out of any pickle into which we place ourselves. Though Margaret certainly crossed a line with the whole attempted mass-murder thing, and another forty lines with the destruction of the Mechanism, her tactics didn't differ too much from anyone else's. Or mine.

Or Orion's.

One could say that Orion did nearly the same thing. Maybe something worse. He prompted Freja Lundquist to have Stellan Winther, a Knower and renowned Swedish pathologist, killed and alter the composition of a flu vaccine, thus starting a minor pandemic in Eastern Europe and rendering the developed treatments useless. The only reason no one has brought it up is because no one knows that's what actually happened. The only two people who know exactly how he came to be the Eminence are himself and me.

Orion certainly knows that I could obliterate his entire existence with a single phone call to Eula, or, even worse, to his mother, but I won't. I didn't even tell any of my friends about his little stunt. Not even Hunter, his brother, or Jacob, his co-Eminence. I debated telling them and everyone else, but what difference would it make at this point? He's the Eminence, and he's stuck that way until the unthinkable happens.

Besides, Orion's ability to pull off something like that just makes him a better Eminence. It's a true talent to lie so seamlessly to literally every single person with whom he interacts, especially to people who are practically human lie detectors. And I'm not concerned about where his loyalties lie—not only are we all technically one group now, but he must have been at least a *little* loyal to the Knowers to want to become one so badly. Now that he can toss the world between his hands, he has no reason to embark on such a scheme ever again. It's just nice knowing his capabilities just in case something like that is needed in the future. In our line of work, it's always a possibility.

Another reason I have yet to tell anyone: Orion told me that I should keep this information to myself.

He called me two days after we got home from New York. Our school day ends at three-twelve; he called me at three-thirteen. I told everyone else I'd meet them in the library—I had a feeling that they didn't need to know about the conversation that was about to occur.

Once everyone else left Hallawin's classroom, I answered. "I cannot possibly imagine what you would like from me."

"And many warm greetings to you, too, my dear," Orion replied. "What makes you believe I have called to ask something of you and not to simply chat with a dear friend of mine?"

"You don't *simply chat* with anyone without some ulterior motive," I said, "and we aren't friends."

"Well, you are certainly correct on both counts, so I might as well cut to the chase, if you don't mind."

"Please do."

"Have you told anyone about my little shenanigans I pulled these previous few months?"

"You mean coercing Freja Lundquist into killing Stellan Winther and altering the vaccine of the Winther strain of influenza to start a pandemic which then would coerce the Knowers and Eradicators into merging?"

"Yes, those would be the shenanigans in question."

"No, I haven't."

"Not even Jacob?"

"He qualifies as *anyone*, so no."

"May I ask why?" He sounded surprised, despite his best attempts to sound as if he knew the whole time.

"I have no interest in making things any messier than they already are," I said.

"Dear Skylar, the faith I found myself regrettably having in you appears to not be so regrettable after all."

"You are too kind."

"So I do not have to explicitly ask you to keep this between us, correct?"

"No, you don't," I replied. "Like I said, things are disastrous as is. Outlining exactly how they came to be so disastrous, and who, exactly, orchestrated the disaster, would do nothing to fix any of the problems said orchestrator created."

"I am so glad that we are on the same page," Orion says.

"That's an overstatement," I say. "I know your motives are mostly oriented in self-preservation, but at least we're in the same book."

"We can't always say that, can we?"

"No, we cannot."

"I won't keep you any longer. Thank you, Skylar, dear."

"I would say any time, but part of me hopes you'll never call me again."

"Darling, that is a promise I wish I could make." He hung up after that.

I will never trust Orion Athan because he has never given me a reason to trust him. He will probably never trust me for the same reason, plus the fact that I shot him once, which tends to put a rift in a relationship. But as long as we keep attempting to fool each other—and ourselves—we'll be just fine.

Besides, when things get to be too much and his fissures reveal themselves, I couldn't say I'm not excited to watch him fall apart.

There's only one problem with that: Jacob. I shouldn't be keeping something like that from him, especially because he hates Orion with a passion (his words, not mine). But telling him would make him hate Orion more, and the more they disagree, the fewer things get done. I honestly didn't think about that when I nominated Orion—he and Jacob so rarely agree on things. Sometimes they disagree with each other just for the sake of disagreeing with each other. There are a lot of things I should have thought through more before nominating him, but that was the worst thing I overlooked by far.

But if Jacob ever finds out, I might lose his trust. I don't keep secrets from him (except for the fact that I could still be some kind of in love with him, but that's besides the point), and I'm pretty sure he doesn't keep secrets from me (unless he's still some kind of in love with me, which is also besides the point). But knowing this, knowing the things Orion did to get where he is, where *I* essentially placed him—my God, I don't even want to think about what could happen if Jacob (or any of my friends, for that matter) found out.

I should have told him months ago, but it never seemed like the right time. Once we got home from New York, we nearly didn't speak to each other until well into October. I had a few different plans to enact, ways to bring it up in conversation, but I never followed through with any of them. It never seemed right. It didn't seem like something I could bring up during homeroom or while sprawled out on my bedroom floor doing math homework. Besides, I'm so rarely alone with him now, by my doing or by his or by a joint effort, and I don't think I should tell too many people at once. And I don't want to break my promise to Orion, since I don't break promises.

So it will just stay this way for now, as it has for the past few months. What I know can't hurt anyone as long as I am the only one to know it.

Chapter Four

Life comes a heart in heart,
it's hard to comprehend.
And it doesn't start making sense
until the very end.
But for you, it all seems to dissolve.
Then I don't care if I break or bend.

"How Close"
Cinders

Because we're all exhausted after an especially draining rehearsal, we decide, in lieu of Meeting practice, to do our homework while it's still light out and actually get some sleep once it darkens. I still haven't caught up on the sleep I missed because of our meeting with Everett Caldwell, or from the global DBQ essay due the day before that took me seven hours in normal people time to complete.

I actually stick to my word that I won't procrastinate and I'll finish my homework before it gets dark. Time must have been on my side, because when I set my pencil down, sunlight still grips the treetops, and the neighborhood's evening cacophony hasn't quite dissipated yet.

I feed Naussie, my hermit crab. She gets some apple with her food pellets today, since she's been a very good crab all week. I let her snip at my finger a bit before she skitters back to her favorite log.

Taking Naussie's terrarium with me so I'm not completely by myself, I climb into my glass room—if there's still daylight, I can still read. It's much cooler up here, since there isn't any insulation, so I curl up with a fuzzy blanket and my pile of stuffed whales, Naussie safely between some larger whales next to me. I have a Nancy Drew book with me, but I check MeetingGround before I dive into it.

Nothing new. Both a good and bad thing. No issues are being solved, but no issues are being created, either. Jacob and Orion have EmMarked every post. I read back through the most recent ones—I usually miss something important the first time around.

It looks like someone got through to Coira—she posted something saying that she will return the materials to Treasury and recuse herself from the bat issue. Jacob and Orion both Em-Marked the post. But now what? We can't have a bunch of sick and dying bats flopping around. That's, quite frankly, gross.

Though—

My God. How did I miss this?

It could be much worse than just *gross*.

I go back down to my bedroom and grab my laptop before climbing back to the glass room. It's so much easier to think up here. I throw a pillow over the opening to the staircase, which cancels out any noise my family might make that will throw me off my rhythm.

It takes a little bit of searching through my freshman year Google Drive folders, but I find what I'm looking for—a reading Mr. Hallawin had us do in global last year. *The Eighth Plague*, it's called, after all those bad things that happened to Egypt in the Bible. It tells the story of a town in Eastern Asia in the eighties, whose wheat crop was lost almost entirely to an influx of Hessian flies. Their pesticides were no match. Why so many more Hessian flies than usual? The question could be answered by the field mice, or the lack thereof.

The field mice had been keeping the flies' larvae at bay. But the mice started to die out. At the time this article was published—1996—no one knew why. Farmers would find droves of dead field mice and swarms of the Hessian flies they didn't eat.

I try to search for an answer, to see if anyone figured it out, but no one did. But it doesn't matter. However those mice were dying, whatever caused them to drop in between the rows of wheat —they didn't keep the Hessian fly population in check, and the flies destroyed the harvest.

Bats also eat insects.

Brazil produces a lot of crops. In the state of Paraná, where Londrina is, where Cristobal has noticed the weirdness, the crops are primarily corn and soy. Corn, that should be okay. But the world barely produces enough soy as it is. It's used in everything from tofu to animal feed, therefore integral to most forms of pro-tein. Their economy could fall to pieces without it, and the rest of the world might face food shortages.

No bats means more insects. More insects means less soy. Less soy means global economic turmoil.

Taking Naussie with me, I practically jump down the spiral staircase and frantically search for my phone. I find it an eternity later. I then take a breath and make a call.

"Hi, Skylar." Jacob seems perplexed that I called him. We aren't exactly on call-each-other-on-the-phone basis, at least not anymore.

"I think we have a very major issue," I tell him.

"How major?"

"That depends. How are the bats in Paraná looking?"

"Pretty dead, according to Cristobal."

"Then exceedingly major."

"Do you want to come over?"

"I—" I'm almost as surprised he asked as he is, judging by the way he trails off at the end, like if he says the last part quietly, the first part never happened. But I think we can set the Awkwardness aside long enough to save the global soybean trade. There are far more important things at stake here. "Yes. Give me ten minutes. I'll bring chocolate."

I hear him smile. I wish I didn't know how to do that. "Sounds good."

I pace around my room a bit. I think I just made a horrible mistake. Maybe we *can't* put the Awkwardness aside for that long. Trust me, we've been trying. It hasn't been working. At least we can form words around each other now, which is better than the first month or so after the Thing happened, when we legitimately did not speak to each other. The one exception was that brief and horribly nauseating conversation in which we determined that a similar Thing should not repeat itself, lest we compromise our ability to work together and, potentially, our friendship.

Are we friends right now, though? It's very hard to tell.

I brush my hair twice, and it's still a mess. Whatever. It's been a lost cause since I was two. I grab my backpack so it looks like we're doing homework, and then I go downstairs. Fortunately, no one's in the kitchen, so I can grab a bag of Hershey's Kisses and slip it into my backpack.

"I'm going to Jacob's house to study for chemistry," I shout to my parents as I put my shoes on. *Please let there be no further questions.*

"Okay," my mom says, poking her head into the hallway. "Be home by dinner, please. It's a school night."

"Of course, Mom," I say.

"Are your other friends going?"

I could so easily say *yes,* but I lie to my mom so often as it is. "That has yet to be determined."

She gives me a smile only an embarrassing mother could
give. "I knew he was sweet on you."

"Mom, please," I say. "Not only is that very far from the
truth, but no one says *sweet on* anymore."

"I'm just saying," she says. "He's really cute. And very polite."

"Mom," I groan. "I'll be back before dinner." I leave before
she can say anything else.

During the eight-minute walk, I almost turn around and go
home twelve different times. I could tell him I sprained my ankle
on the way over. That my parents said I couldn't leave the house.
Or that there was an angry duck on my front porch that wouldn't
let me out. Or that I got lost or I fell in the river or never mind, a
food shortage isn't as imminent as I thought and it could wait until
school tomorrow.

But, alas, things like this don't fix themselves. Time is only
so gracious.

I've only been to his house a few times, since we don't usually do a lot of Knower things here. My house and Lexie's house
are the best for Knower things, since both of us have our own
rooms and families that won't bother us if we say we're studying.
Hers might be even better since her room is so far from her dads'
or her sister's, and the sound doesn't carry well. Alex's mom's
house is nice if all three of his sisters are out of the house, even
though the third floor is usually an ocean of pink plastic and pools
of itchy dress-up clothes. His dad lives downtown in the city, so we
don't go there. Hallie's house is probably the worst, since she has
six siblings, and someone is always eavesdropping or bothering us
because it bothers Hallie and—I'll agree—it can be really funny to
bother Hallie. And I've never been to Hunter's house. He doesn't
have us over.

Jacob shares a room with his brother, and his dad works
from home, making it difficult for running practice Meetings or
revising trade negotiations. His house is great, though, for Mariokart and after-school snacks when there's nothing on the agenda.
But maybe I should have invited him over to my house instead.
Then I wouldn't have to talk to his family or—

Too late now. Things like this don't fix themselves.

He lives on Brighton Street, which is very aptly named. The rows of Gothic-Victorian houses could beat San Francisco's Painted Ladies in a fistfight any day. His is a dandelion: sunny, cheerful yellow with effusive leafy green trim. The molding turns it into a gingerbread house; oriel windows and cute little dormers give it dimension. It's the perfect home for an architect.

After taking a series of seventy deep breaths, I ring the doorbell.

A girl opens it, her face obscured by a mass of nearly-black curls. She immediately turns bright red, as if someone dropped a gallon of red paint on her cheeks. "Hi," she says.

"Hi," I say. I don't really know what to say next. "I'm Skylar. Jacob's friend. I, um, we're studying for chemistry?"

"You can come in," she says, though she doesn't sound like she means it. Especially because she doesn't step aside to let me in. She turns around and in a voice barely above a normal talking voice, she says, "Jacob!"

He comes to the door. "Hi," he says.

"Hi," I say.

"Jacob," the girl says in a harsh whisper, "you didn't tell me you were having people over."

"Last-minute thing," he says. "Skylar, this is Molly. Say hi, Molly."

"Shut up," she says, and she sprints away like a baby bunny.

"She's super shy," he explains, stepping aside to let me in. "Which is why you've never met her. She barricades herself in her room whenever someone who doesn't live here comes over."

"Ah," I say.

"Is that your friend, Jacob?" a voice calls from somewhere inside the house.

"Yeah," Jacob calls back.

His dad appears, apron tied around his waist, bell pepper still in his hand. "Hi, Skylar."

"Hi, Mr. Connelly," I say. Is there any way this encounter could not go terribly? Has an encounter like this ever *not* gone terribly? "Thank you for having me."

"Any time," he says. "Are you staying for dinner? We're having stir fry." He holds up the pepper.

"Thank you, but I have to be home by dinner," I say, slightly relieved for the out. I hope it doesn't come across that way.

"Another time, maybe," he says. "What are you studying?"

"Dad, we really have to go start working," Jacob interrupts. "I'll tell you about ionic bonds later."

"Okay, okay," he says. He gives Jacob a look. "Get some work done. Don't get distracted."

"Since when do I ever get distracted?" Jacob says.

Mr. Connelly looks to me. "He's funny."

"Hysterical." Despite myself, I smile. "I'll keep him on track."

"You're a brave girl, Skylar. Such a challenge that is."

"Okay." Jacob's bright red by now. "We really have to get to work."

"Happy trails," Mr. Connelly says before heading back into the kitchen.

"Sorry," Jacob says as we climb the stairs. "He doesn't realize I can manage my own time now."

"Can you?"

He gives me a look. "I'm just glad my mom isn't home. You'd never want to speak to me again after her interrogation."

We climb another set of stairs—he and his brother are on the third floor. My God, I've never been to his room before. *Sure, Skylar, blow this way out of proportion! It's not like he's in* your *room four days a week or anything.* But still. It's a part of his life I've never gotten to see before.

When we get there, I can immediately tell which side is his. For starters, it's way, *way* neater. Never mind the drawings of buildings pinned to the sloping blue walls, the myriad of Lego models I know he built without looking at the directions, or the stacks of notebooks and sketchbooks shoved in every corner. His bookshelf is at maximum capacity, though it would seem everything is organized in alphabetical order by author's last name, which is kind of hot, I'm not going to lie. His desk is a wreck, riddled with various straightedges and chewed mechanical pencils and different types of graph paper. On his nightstand rests a sketchbook still open to a half-drawn skyscraper, next to a tiny model of the Chrysler Building and a lamp shaped like a dinosaur. On his window seat, tucked into a dormer, lives a family of four stuffed Canada geese. Everything smells slightly of lavender.

My God, Skylar. This was a very bad idea.

"Daniel," Jacob says.

I didn't even notice the other boy in the room, sitting at his desk, nestled among strewn about clothes and sports gear. He doesn't respond—he has earbuds in. A cat sits on his lap, unfazed by the homework. Jacob goes over and taps him on the shoulder.

Daniel pulls an earbud out. "Good, you're back. What's the limit of this thing?" He points to something in his textbook. The cat meows, and Jacob pets him.

"Infinity," Jacob replies. "Can you go downstairs?"

Daniel turns to see me standing there, and he raises his eyebrows. He looks a lot like Jacob, but his eyes are greener, his hair is lighter, and there's an air of confidence about him that Jacob doesn't really have. "Oh. Hi."

"Hi," I say.

"You're Skylar."

"Yes?" It sounds more like a question than I intend it to.

He gives Jacob a look, and Jacob gives him one back. They seem to have a soundless conversation, to the point where I feel like I'm eavesdropping.

"Nice to meet you," Daniel says to me.

"Nice to meet you, too," I reply.

"You guys have fun," Daniel says. He hands Jacob the cat and gathers his homework. "Jacob, I'm coming back if I need math help."

"No, you're not," Jacob replies.

Daniel gives me a smile. It's like Jacob's, but different. More certain he's supposed to be smiling. "Have fun studying," he says. I don't think he believes we will be doing much studying. (And I suppose he's right, just not in the way he thinks.)

"Bye, Daniel," Jacob says.

Daniel gives him one last look before disappearing down the stairs.

"You two are telepathic," I say.

"We know each other way too well."

"Who's this?" I say, reaching out to pet the kitty.

"Rosie Belle if you ask Molly, Can Opener if you ask Daniel."

"What do you call her?"

"It depends on my mood, but mostly Cat."

"Hi, Cat," I say.

We kind of stand there, unsure how to interact with any of the furniture in his room.

"You can sit anywhere," he says. "I— it doesn't matter."

"Thanks," I say. "I'll just . . . I'll sit here." I sit on his window seat, next to the goose family. "I like your geese."

He immediately blushes. How can he turn red so quickly? He's too adorable for his own good. "I— thanks." He sits at the foot of his bed and sets Cat next to him. "I forgot to shove them under my bed."

"No, I like them," I say. "It's cute. I mean, the geese. The geese are cute."

"Thanks," he says again. We're quiet for a second, forgetting how conversation works, before he says, "So, you think the
world is ending?"

Right. "Well," I say, "it seems more probable than usual at
the moment."

"Okay?"

I take my laptop out of my backpack. "Oh, here," I say,
handing him the bag of Hershey's Kisses I brought. "Chocolate."

"Oh, thank you," he says. He unwraps one and hands me
another.

After he connects me to the wifi, I show him the reading
from global last year. "Remember this reading?"

"I definitely did not read that," he says.

"Jacob. It's about a wheat shortage that happened in Eastern Asia because the field mice that ate the bugs' larvae started
dying, and the bugs grew up and obliterated the wheat crops."

"That's not good," he says, skimming over the article. "Especially because—"

"We have an awfully similar situation happening in Brazil."
I pull up the map of crops in Brazil. "See, in the state of Paraná,
the main crops are corn and soybeans. I'm more worried about the
soybeans. The world uses a lot of soybeans and it struggles to grow
enough as it stands. They're used in all sorts of food, and in animal
feed, so they're also essential to the meat industry. If we lose even
part of Brazil as a producer of soybeans—which could very well
happen if this bat thing spreads to more states—then we're facing
a global shortage of at least two main sources of protein, which
could not just lead economic turmoil beyond the agriculture industry, but also start a global food shortage."

He looks at me, his eyes darkening. "So the bats in Brazil
are dying from whatever it is that's killing them. And dead bats
don't eat bugs. And uneaten bugs eat soybean crops."

"Exactly."

"Well, shit."

"Exactly."

He bites his lip and thinks for a second. "Technically
speaking, this is still hypothetical, right?"

"As of right now," I say. "But for how long will it remain
theoretical? This started at the very least three days ago, and think
of how many bats have died since then."

He thinks for another minute before he jumps up and goes
over to his desk. From his backpack, he grabs a notebook. He
comes back to the foot of his bed and hands it to me. "Can you
look for Glaucia Alejo Bardo, please? It's in cursive."

I take the notebook. It's an address book, actually, in which everything is written in not just cursive, but horribly messy cursive. No wonder he can't read it. He has trouble reading normal, pretty cursive. "Whose writing is this?"

"Margaret's."

"This is a cursed object."

"I know," he says. "Orion said he'll type up the information for me over the summer, and then we can burn it."

"I look forward to it." I flip through. They're in no particular order, and most of the people don't have titles, just words scribbled even smaller beneath their names. I eventually find what could be Glaucia Alejo Bardo. "Here. Who is this?"

"Head of some office in the state of Paraná. Can't remember which. I think it's the Department of Health, maybe." He grabs his laptop from his desk. "Could you read me her email?"

I do, and he types it in. Then he types a bit longer and reads it back to me. "Ms. Alejo Bardo, I am an associate of Margaret White—God, it makes me nauseous saying that—and I have a few questions regarding the bat population of Paraná. Does it appear to be decreasing? If so, at what rate? Is this something that should be concerning my associates and me? Thank you." He looks to me. "We should wait to ask more questions until we know what's going on for sure."

"Okay, that makes sense," I say. "But we should call Orion."

He looks at me and sighs. "Do we have to?"

"Yes," I say. I grab his phone from his desk and hand it to him. "We have to."

"Skylar."

"Jacob. Call him."

Maybe I imagine the involuntary smile cross his face. Or maybe I don't. "If you insist," he says.

Chapter Five

I woke up on the ground, and you
were in a cardigan sweater
with your horn-rimmed glasses on.
Can't see the world without them.
Living in the pages of a book she read,
I sewed a farewell letter
with a needle and thread.

"Art School Girlfriend"
Andrew McMahon in the Wilderness

Orion answers nearly immediately. "Oh hello, my dear fellow Eminence! How are you this fine evening?"

"Hi, Orion," Jacob says.

"Oh, you're on speakerphone! Hello, Skylar!"

Jacob and I exchange a look. "Hi, Orion," I say.

"How are you both on this wonderful evening?"

"Orion," Jacob cuts in, "can we skip your weird pleasantries?"

"Of course, dear Jacob. To what do I owe this pleasure?"

"There could be an imminent crisis."

"Oh, wonderful!" I can practically hear him clap his hands. "Skylar, if you wouldn't mind excusing us so we could discuss."

"No way," I say.

"Whatever we talk about, Skylar can hear," Jacob says.

"She is quite trustworthy, I do agree," Orion says. "Wonderful at keeping the skeletons in your closet well-dusted."

Jacob and I exchange another glance, but thankfully, he doesn't think too much of it. "Stop being creepy. There's a chance we could be facing a shortage of soybeans."

"Because of the bats, or lack thereof." I explain to him exactly how a food shortage could arise from the situation.

"Well," Orion says. "That cannot be good."

"No, it can't," Jacob says. "So I'm waiting to hear back from Glaucia Alejo Bardo, and then I'm thinking we could ask Eula—"

"Jacob," Orion interrupts. "I don't think it to be the best idea to involve other people with this."

"What do you mean?" Jacob says. "Eula could contact people who know about wildlife, and Cristobal can keep the research going—"

"My fellow Eminence, people do not like us."

"I'm aware. People would hate us more if we allowed a food shortage to happen."

"Jacob. It is sort of our fault that a food shortage is such a strong possibility."

"No, it's—" He stops himself.

"I do think myself to be correct on this front. If we had been more firm with Coira, if we had allocated more resources for her, different resources, or if we had a stronger grip on Treasury, if we had been more proactive in responding to this bat sickness, or we'd been more adamant that Cristobal report his research to us, or even if we had just been better at preventing situations like these from arising, then we might not have found ourselves in this predicament."

Jacob's eyes darken to nearly black. "My God, you're right. I hate when you're right."

"I do truly think that we should try to solve this on our own. Under the radar, as they say. Please, Jacob—and Skylar, you surely must agree—we aren't in need of another reason for them to root against us. And I am quite sure that very few of them would uphold our ruling on the issue, anyway."

Jacob looks to me.

"I do sort of agree, believe it or not," I tell him, a fact which surprises me most of all. "Since the issue hasn't spiraled yet, and we hopefully have some time before it does, maybe it's best if we keep this . . . under the radar, as they say."

"Do you think we can get away with it?"

"Most of us are extraordinary liars," I tell him. "And you're the one with the contact book."

"And you're the one who can read it."

"Orion," I say. "if you really think this should be done discreetly, we at least need to tell Hallie, Lexie, Hunter, and Alex. You two can't do this alone, however you decide to handle it, and Jacob and I cannot and will not hide anything from those four."

"That should be alright," Orion says. "But, if you will, keep Lea Felding out of it. I have a strong supposition that she would not like the fact that we are not employing everyone we know."

"Fine," I say. "For now. This gets anything above hypothetical, or it inches any closer to danger, or the possibility of people getting hurt or going hungry gets any higher, we get Miss Felding and Eula and everyone else involved. Understand?"

"Yes," Orion says.

"Definitely," Jacob adds.

"Good," I say.

"I am glad this is settled, then," Orion says. "I shall book my flight for tomorrow afternoon."

"I'm sorry, what?"

"Well, I'm not going to allow my co-Eminence and his very dear friends, one of whom happens to be of my own flesh and blood, deal with this on their lonesome. I'll be back on your little island come sundown tomorrow."

"That's not really necessary," Jacob says. "Like, I can't stress how unnecessary that is."

"Jacob, my friend, it is highly necessary."

"You'll miss school," I tell Orion.

"Skylar, my darling, I finished all of my senior year studies over winter break in a fit of boredom. I haven't touched a schoolbook since January. I am far less productive in the confines of my cinderblock dorm room than I am in the embrace of your island."

I look to Jacob and shake my head. There isn't anything that will sway Orion in an opposite direction now that he's decided on this one.

"Fine," Jacob says. "If you must."

"Goodbye for now, my dearest acquaintances," Orion says. "I look forward to seeing you both!"

"I wish I could say the same."

Orion hangs up.

Jacob sighs. "I hate him."

"I know," I say. "But you two have to learn how to not hate each other long enough to make some decisions."

"Yeah, I know," Jacob says. "I just—" He glances at me out of the corner of his eye before he hops off his bed and joins me on the window seat. Cat follows and sits at our feet. There's enough room for both of us, but his knee brushes mine and a million fireflies light up simultaneously in my chest. "I have a bad feeling that once we do this, whatever it is we're about to do, things are going to be different. And I can't tell if it will be a good different or a bad different."

"Let's see what happens next, then."

Subconsciously, almost, he takes my hand. I let him. It's familiar, like a song I used to love but thought I'd forgotten all the words to until I heard it again and sung every line perfectly. His thumb draws circles on the back of my hand instinctively, like I'm built into his movements, his light and his energy. A hurricane. Throws everything around him off-course. Pure, unmitigated chaos. As reckless as a lightning strike.

What is the absolute worst thing that could happen if I kiss him right now?

I pull my hand away. *That was a terrible idea. Now you remember what his architect hands feel like and you were better off forgetting.* "I should go," I say. "Dinner will be soon. Probably. What time is it?"

He checks his phone. "Six-thirty."

"Yes," I say. "I should . . . go."

"Right," he says. "I can walk you out. Not that I'm kicking you out. You can stay."

"I know," I say. "I just . . . shouldn't."

"Right," he repeats. "I'll let you know if Glaucia gets back to me."

"Thank you," I say. "And I'll read up on soy shortages tonight so we're prepared for a worst-case scenario."

"Sounds good, Bubble."

I look at him and feel myself smile against my will.

He hasn't called me Bubble in months.

"Sounds good, Jacob."

As I'm walking home, my phone buzzes. I answer immediately. "Isn't it dinnertime at the Rainer house?"

"Just finished," Harlow replies. "You haven't called me in three days, Skylar Amelia. That is *appalling*."

"I'm sorry," I say. "It's been a wild three days." I take a detour and start heading towards Starlight Cove instead of home.

"Are you walking somewhere?"

"Yes," I say. "I'm on my way home. I was at— I was at a friend's house."

"What friend?"

"Jacob," I say. "So, how was school?"

"Don't you dare change the subject, Skylar Amelia! Oh my God! You went to a *boy's* house?"

"It wasn't the first time, Harlow," I say. "We've been friends for nearly a year now. I've been to his house before, and he's at my house at least three times a week. It's nothing noteworthy."

"Were other people there?"

"Yes."

"People who don't live there?"

". . . no."

She laughs. I wish I could live in the sound of her laugh. It's like a music box—slightly off-key, twinkling and airy, more reminiscent of home than my actual house. "And you still haven't hooked up with him?"

"Harlow!" I push through the trees to Starlight Cove and take my spot on the rock under the willow tree. It's colder here, at the very edge of the island where dissolves into the river, so I pull my coat around me tighter. "We're not— It's not like that." A flat-out lie. One of the many flat-out lies I tell Harlow June Rainer. At least this one's more normal than most of the other ones. "As I've told you hundreds of times before."

"Sure. I totally believe you. Especially with a definitive answer like whatever that was."

I sigh. "Don't believe me, then."

"'Kay, I won't. How's the musical going?"

"It's a lot of fun, but the show is, quite honestly, completely terrible," I tell her. "There's one good song, and I'm not even in it. It's an absolute train wreck. We could rehearse now until opening night, straight through, no breaks, not even for sleep, and it would still suck."

"Especially after not sleeping for two weeks," Harlow says.

"And it's supposed to be some big honor that we're one of the first schools to do the high school version," I continue. "And it should be even *more* interesting to us because Tesla was—" I cut myself off before I say something dangerous.

"Tesla was what?"

"So integral to our society," I say. "They called him the man who invented the twentieth century."

"Riveting," Harlow says. "If you don't mind, can I wait till the show for a history lesson?"

I smile. "Fine. Tell me something interesting, then."

Harlow and I talk for another few minutes, but dinner time is imminent and I promised my mom I would be home, so I say, "I will call you tomorrow. Scout's honor."

"You were never a Girl Scout," Harlow says.

By the time I get home, Jacob's texted me four times. He's sent me screenshots of his response from Glaucia Alejo Bardo, his response to her, and proof of how bad this could become.

Chapter Six

I always find it hard to ascertain
why it is that I feel this way
when my whole life is in disarray.
The future makes me feel alive.
I've always known the romantic side
of not knowing where I'll sleep at night.
I can't stand when my hands are tied
my bed the ground, my roof the sky.

"Wild I Am"
Vocal Few

"So the bats are dying," Hallie clarifies, "meaning that the bugs are increasing? So I have to care about bats now? Gross."

"Basically," I say. "Exactly *how* the bats are dying is still, for the most part, unknown. We know they're getting sick, and we know that most don't survive it. Whether it's some sort of virus or poison or something else entirely is yet to be determined."

"So what are we gonna do about it?" Alex asks.

"Well," Jacob says. "I don't really know yet."

We've gotten some weird glances, having this conversation in the middle of the library, but I'm sure both the librarians and the students here have heard weirder. We still sit at our signature table, the one overlooking the senior parking lot, despite the fact that it was never meant to hold six people. Not that anyone else ever sits here—either because they know it's ours, or because it's quite possibly the worst location for a table in the library. But at least most people don't wander our way, unless they're looking for Kant or Socrates.

"Is that why Orion called last night and said he's coming home for the time being?" Hunter says. "Is this your fault?"

"We tried to tell him he didn't have to come here," I say, "but, per usual, he refused to listen. I'm sorry, Hunter."

"I hate when he's home. You think he's bad when you only have to talk to him on the phone? Try living with him. He never shuts up. Silence just goes *poof!* Out the window." Hunter emphasizes this with a swoop of his hand. He must be upset—Hunter doesn't gesticulate.

"He'll have his hands full," I say. "Because—" I look to Jacob to make sure it's okay for me to tell them the catch to this. He nods, ever so slightly. "Because we're hoping this issue does not leave this circle of seven, at least for the foreseeable future."

"You don't want to get anyone else involved?" Hallie asks.

"Not even Miss Felding or Eula?" Lexie says. "Or Cristobal, who knows all this stuff, or Coira?"

"No," Jacob says. "It was Orion's idea. And I don't know exactly how I feel about it, but . . . But Orion has a point. If we were better Eminences, we probably wouldn't have gotten here. But we're not, and everyone knows that, and if this spirals out of control—which has been known to happen—everyone will blame us and we'll have an actual mutiny on our hands. And I really don't want a mutiny so close to tech week."

"I agree," Hallie says. "Everyone hates you."

"Thank you, Hallie."

"I'm serious, though," Hallie continues. "You keep this on the DL, and no one knows it happened. Or they find out it happened after you fixed it, and they think you're awesome for fixing it. Win-win."

"If it gets to the point where lives are really at stake, we bring in backup," I say. "I made that very clear to Orion, and I'll make that very clear to all of you. If people get hurt, we swallow our pride and call Eula or Miss Felding."

"Okay, good," Lexie says. "That's fine, then. It'll be fun!"

"*Fun* is a generous term." Hallie crosses her arms.

"So, what's our first step?" Hunter asks. "What do you need from us right now?"

I don't mean to smile, but I do. How I managed to find friends so willing to save the world with a second's notice, I'll never know. "Read up on soybeans."

"And find out everything you can about the bat sickness in Paraná," Jacob adds. "If any of you have any contacts that aren't Cristobal, now's the time to use them."

"And when you find something, fact-check it, write it down, and share it with everyone else," I say. "We can't use Meeting-Ground for this, since Andrea and her team have access to everything posted on there, so keep this to our group chat only."

"We'll have to add Orion," Lexie reminds me.

"Okay, we will make a new group chat," I reply.

"On it," Lexie says, pulling her phone from her pocket.

"I came up with a multi-step plan of attack." I look to Jacob. "Is that okay? Do you want to review it or approve it first?"

"I trust you," he says. "Whatever you think will work, will work."

"Thank you," I say. "Should we meet at my house after rehearsal? We end at four-thirty today, so we'll have a lot of time."

"No," Hunter says. "Spare your parents from having to meet Orion. My mother's in DC hanging out with the First Lady until Thursday and my father's in Dublin till April, so come to my house."

"You're actually inviting people to your *house*?" Jacob says. "That's miraculous."

"Desperate times call for desperate measures," Hunter says. "But don't expect this to become a regular thing. I don't like having strangers over."

"We're strangers?" Hallie asks.

"Do you live in my house? If not, you're a stranger. Except Jacob. He practically lives there."

"Thank you, buddy," Jacob says.

"Call me *buddy* again, and I will cut you out of my life."

After rehearsal, Hunter tells us to meet in the lobby of the auditorium once we're out of our character shoes and ready to leave. "I'm half-ready to blindfold you so you can't retrace your steps and find my house again," Hunter says.

"That's a little extreme," Lexie says.

"No, it's not," Hunter replies. "Everyone ready?" He doesn't wait for our response before walking out; we follow behind like baby ducklings.

For the majority of the walk, it's exactly the same route that Hallie and I take every morning. But instead of turning down our street, he continues up Riverway. Every time I expect him to turn off onto one of the residential streets, he keeps going straight, until we get all the way to the Northern Tip of the island.

"You live on the Northern Tip?" Hallie says. "Why haven't you had us over?"

"Because I live on the Northern Tip," Hunter replies.

The Northern Tip is home to the castles: the stately Georgians, palatial Victorians, austere new-builds in bold wood and frosted glass. They stand guard at the tip of the island as if they were its tiara, like the entire island is at their beck and call and in their debt simultaneously. These are the houses of daydreams, the idylls painted by those who have never been here. They still know what they would find should they cross the northern bend of the river. The fantasies are rooted in a certain level of truth.

Hunter's house is perhaps the furthest from an exception. Constructed from faded yellow brick and shrouded in climbing vines, it sits on its own hill as if it were a queen on her throne. White-paned windows flanked by pristine navy shutters line the façade in two neat rows. It breaks for the front porch, crowned with a small yet grand portico lined with columns and sheltered by carved stone and dentil trim. Delicately gabled dormers pop out of the gleaming roof, slightly obscuring four (4) chimneys. An arched loggia runs across the right side, and glass French doors peak out from between the columns.

A castle.

It doesn't feel like I legally should be approaching it—it seems like I should admire it from afar, that taking the path to the front door would be trespassing. But Hunter leads us up the steps, through the front door and into the vestibule, a carved box of crisp white panelling and cheery yellow wallpaper.

"Hunter," Lexie says, "are you actually a prince and you just haven't told us?"

"No," Hunter says. He opens the next door to the rest of the house.

The vestibule's dancing mosaic gives way to fathomless hardwood. Kinetic molding spills towards a staircase that gently creeps up the wall before flourishing against the windows of the back wall and soaring over our heads. Beyond the staircase is a room entirely made of glass, where a baby grand piano waits patiently for someone to play it. A parlor sits on our left—it looks as if no one has touched anything in there since the day all the furniture and breakable knickknacks were placed. Same goes for the dining room on the right—I count twelve velvet chairs expertly tucked in against the long, shimmery table.

A very long dachshund waddles into the room. When he sees us, he starts barking.

"Pickle, be nice," Hunter says.

"Hi, Pickle," Jacob says, and he crouches down to pet him. Pickle's tail waggles in response.

"Hunter?" a voice calls from somewhere further within the palace. She follows his name with a string of words in another language.

Hunter replies back in this other language. Greek, I think, but I can't be entirely sure. I had no idea Hunter spoke another language, but I'm not surprised. Nothing I learn about Hunter really surprises me. Somehow, it all makes sense.

Out from under the staircase emerges a tiny woman. Like, we're talking less than five feet tall. I think I have a shot at being taller than her, and that isn't something that happens very often. Her shiny black hair, streaked with gray and pristinely detained by a silver hair clip, frames a round, weathered face. She wears a plain white blouse and a vibrant floral maxi skirt that drags on the ground a few inches past her feet. Upon seeing us, her calloused hands fly to her hips, and her eyebrows bounce, just once.

"More than I was expecting," she says. "Usually it's just that one." She points to Jacob.

Jacob smiles at her. "Hi, Lauren."

She points a finger at him. "I told you, you tell me before you come so I make you those *loukoumades* you like."

"I'll give you a fair warning next time."

"I *need* a fair warning before dealing with you."

Jacob only grins at her.

"It was a last-minute decision," Hunter says. "I'm sorry."

She waves away his apology with a flick of her hand. "Introduce me to your friends."

"Lauren, this is Alex, Lexie, Skylar, and Hallie," Hunter says. "Everyone, this is Lauren."

"It's good to see Hunter having more friends than this bad influence." She jabs a thumb at Jacob.

"I am a wonderful influence," Jacob says.

Lauren looks to Hunter. "Your brother got home not an hour ago. You should say hello."

Hunter sighs.

Lauren scolds him in Greek. She then looks to us. "You come to the dining room in a half-hour for snacks. Oven's warming up for *amygdalota*."

"*Efcharisto,* Lauren," Hunter says. We thank her in English.

"Say hello to your brother," Lauren says, pointing a finger at Hunter, before disappearing back under the staircase.

"We'll go to the third floor," Hunter says, picking up Pickle and carrying him against his hip. We follow him up the beautiful staircase; I run my fingers along the woodwork of the railing, which looks to have been carved by fairies. Since the century-old glass of the giant is slightly warped and slightly ripples, the sunlight sparkles on the chocolate woodwork and beckons the flaxen walls to sing. My goodness, it's huge. I count six doors from where I stand, not counting a seating area just to the right of the stairs framed by mahogany bookshelves. The six of us, plus Orion and Delia and Praxis and Lauren, could all live in here and we would never have to see each other. We have to go through a door that nearly blends into the wall to find the second staircase—one of the wonders of a house as old as this.

"When was this house built?" Hallie asks.

"1874," Jacob replies.

"You are so creepy," Hunter tells him.

When we emerge onto the third floor, we've practically entered a third house. There are even more doors, leading to even more rooms—I could very easily get lost in here. Hunter hops a few steps ahead of us and pounds on the door at one end of the hall. "Come to the big room."

A few seconds later, Orion opens the door. "Oh, wonderful! Look at all this company! Welcome!"

We follow Hunter down the length of the house to the opposite end. This room is pretty much the opposite of the rest of the house—the Athan boys must have taken the lead on decorating this one. There's an air hockey table and a sectional drowning beneath big fluffy pillows and a TV surrounded by plastic super-heroes. Since we're on the third floor, window seats resulting from each dormer are evenly spaced along the sloping walls. One of the non-sloping walls is a bookshelf which seems to hold hundreds of books. Lauren's already started a fire in the fireplace.

"Since when are you bilingual?" Hallie asks him.

"Since always, I guess," Hunter replies. "We mostly speak Greek here."

"And you never mentioned it?" Lexie asks.

"It never came up," he defends. "We didn't know Skylar could speak French until, like, a few months ago."

"I don't think it qualifies as the same thing," I say. "My summer boredom coagulating into a new language doesn't equate to growing up speaking two languages at once."

"And your house," Lexie says. "It's *gorgeous*." She reads Hunter out of the corner of her eye before asking him, "Why is this the first time we're all here?"

Subconsciously, Hunter shifts a bit before saying, "Never got around to it, I guess."

"Oh, you know our Hunter," Orion says. "He only shares when absolutely necessary. And even then, it depends on the wea-ther."

"Orion, do you want to sit outside by yourself?" Hunter asks.

"No, I do not."

"Then stop."

"Alrighty, then." He looks to Jacob. "My dear fellow Eminence, have you an idea to solve this predicament?"

"Not really," Jacob says. "We have to figure out why the bats are getting sick, first off. And I don't know how you cure a bat of a disease or feed it an antidote to a poison or do whatever else we might have to do to make them not sick, but we can probably figure that out. And in the meantime, we have to somehow keep the insect population in check so they don't eat Paraná's soybean supply."

"As of right now, the farmers in Paraná have noticed something's amiss." I take my narwhal notebook out of my backpack—I wrote down a few things I found by reading Brazilian news all through my lunch period. My Portuguese isn't the best, but I think I got the gist of what's going on. "They've been seeing lots of dead bats in the area, and are starting to get concerned. Seems now they're more concerned if it's a disease that can be transmitted to humans—which we still don't know. I only found one article that mentioned an increase in insects at one particular farm, which has started increasing their use of pesticide. No word yet on the effectiveness of that approach, but it's something to keep in mind. I think our best course of action is to start with the bats. Essentially, they are the root of the problem. We find out what's wrong, we find out how to fix it, and we fix it. If it doesn't get any better, we move onto Plan B."

"Is there a plan B yet?" Hallie asks.

"An amorphous one," I say. "It involves much more bribery than Plan A does and quite possibly a truckload of honey, so we'll stick with Plan A until it proves fallible."

"Sounds splendid," Orion says. "Care to divulge the details of Plan A?"

Lauren calls up from the foot of the stairs. "Your snacks are done. Come eat something."

"You'll have to tell us after snack time, dear Skylar."

Chapter Seven

*We start with small talk but
we know that it's not so.
We take our time 'cause it feels
like we're lying.
We run in circles and
we scrape our elbows so
we know that we're not
the only ones pretending.*

"Small Talk"
Call Security

Once we've eaten every last *amygdalota* and finished the hot chocolate Lauren made for us, we trudge back up to the third floor. I'm glad Hunter and Orion lead the pack—I don't know if I could find the third floor on my own again. This house is a labyrinth.

"So," Hallie says. "Plan A?"

"We start with the bats," I say. I flip my narwhal notebook to the pages on which I jotted the steps down. I got some strange looks from the other girls at my lunch table, but they've all stopped questioning me at this point. It's in their best interest, whether they know it or not. "We need to put proper procedures in place for the safe disposal of the dead bats, first of all. We don't know how this pestilence spreads or what's causing it or if it can be trans-mitted posthumously, to other bats or to humans. The absolute last thing we need is another pandemic."

"I can do the procedural document," Hallie volunteers. "I still have the format from last time we did biohazard disposal procedures."

"Perfect," I say. "After that's done, we get in touch with different wildlife preservation groups and research institutions in Paraná. Send them the procedures, ask for full lists of symptoms, pin down exactly how many bats are affected, and try to gauge how many have died. Since it could take days or even weeks to figure out what's going on with the bats, we need a temporary solution:

"

to allocate more resources to pesticides." I look to Jacob. "Can Treasury do that?"

Orion answers for him. "If we are to keep everyone else out of this affair, we cannot go through Treasury."

"That's a terrible idea," Jacob says. "That's, like, Knower 101. All our spending goes through Treasury, and then through the Eminences. Any spending that doesn't follow that goes against the rules."

"Jacob, my friend," Orion says, "when is the last time Treasury came to us for approval?"

"I don't know, three weeks ago, maybe?"

"And do you truly believe that no Knower or Eradicator has spent a cent of our funds in the past three weeks?"

"Well, if they did, they did it wrong."

"It does not mean that they did not do it, though."

Jacob crosses his arms. "If *we* don't go through Treasury, then we're no better than the people we're complaining about."

"We are the Eminences."

"That doesn't mean anything. We still have rules. We can't just do whatever and justify it later."

"Jacob, I kind of agree with Orion," Hallie says. "In for a penny, in for a pound. If we're keeping other Knowers out of this, then we have to keep Treasury out of it, too. Word spreads. People try to keep secrets, but none of them do it well."

Lexie shrugs. "And Orion has a point. If everyone else is breaking the rules, why shouldn't you? If they think it's okay, they can't get mad when you do it."

"And you won't get in trouble if no one finds out," Hunter says.

"If no one finds out, then no, we won't," Jacob says. "But someone always could. It's risky."

"Do you not deem this to be worth the risk?" Orion asks.

"Not really, no," Jacob says. "If they find out we circumvented Treasury, we could get in a ton of trouble."

"Jacob, my friend, they already despise us," Orion says. "Should they discover this little endeavor one day, what more could a little more bitterness our way do to us?"

Jacob looks to me. "What do you think?"

"It's your call," I tell him.

"I am only proposing what I think is best," Orion says. "I'm only concerned with the betterment and the efficiency of our mission."

Jacob's quiet for a few minutes, pacing back and forth, until he finally says, "We can do it without Treasury, then."

"Thank you, dear fellow Eminence," Orion says. "I believe this was the right decision to make."

"How does Treasury get their resources in the first place?" Lexie asks.

"Bribery and extortion, usually," Hallie says. "Or embezzlement, like what Cécile Kettering and her Eradicator buddies are up to with the Pentagon right now. Highly illegal shit."

"I'm okay with highly illegal shit if you guys are," Lexie says.

Hallie shrugs. "I'm down."

"I don't know about highly illegal shit," Jacob says. "That seems . . . illegal."

"I think that if we're really gonna do this," Lexie says, "then we just have to *do* it. Full send. If no one finds out, there's no harm done, right?"

"I think I know just the way to find some funding without encountering Treasury," I say. "We need to get back in touch with Everett Caldwell."

"I hate that guy," Alex says.

"I'm not a huge fan, either," I say, "but they grow a lot of soybeans in his congressional district."

"They grow soybeans in the US?" Alex asks.

"The US and Brazil alone grow about eighty percent of the world's supply of soybeans," I say. "A lot of them are grown in New York State. And, fortunately for us, Everett's district produces quite a few. The town of Redway—the one Jacob designed the bus garage for—is one of the biggest farming towns in the district. So I'm hoping he could put us in contact with some people there who know what they're doing. We could see what pesticides should be used or what other measures should be taken, or if they've ever encountered a similar situation. There was recently some strife in his area with the poor harvest, so maybe they'll have some ideas on how to combat that. One of us should call him tonight and see if he could be of assistance."

"Does he owe us anything?" Hallie asks, arms crossed.

"He could," I say. I think for a second and say, "Lexie, do you still have Carson Sloane's email address? The town supervisor of Redway? From when you got the zoning laws for Jacob?"

"I should," she says. "I always forget to delete my emails."

"Ask if he'll endorse Everett Caldwell for Congress."

"There's no way in hell Carson would endorse him," Hallie says. "He's a shitty congressman and did his town dirty."

"He might with a little extra incentive," Hunter says. He turns to Lexie. "Ask what he wants in return. We might be able to get it for him. Use those powers of persuasion."

"Okay," Lexie says, pulling out her phone. "I got this."

I look back to Hallie. "We get Carson to endorse him, and he owes us his entire district."

"And if we don't?" Hallie asks.

"We will," I reply. "So, once Everett owes us something, he'll get us in contact with soybean people who are closer to home than Brazil. We can sneak away to upstate New York—especially because Orion actually has his driver's license—but there's no way we could secretly fly to Brazil, especially without making a non-existent Day. The soybean people might have better ideas as to what we can do to thwart the crop failure, and maybe we can even convince them to up their production so a global food shortage becomes less likely. I don't know exactly how that would work with distribution and trade and all that—we'd have to do more research—but it might be an effective short-term solution. Not long-term, or else farmers in Brazil start to lose their jobs, but we can cross that bridge upon arrival."

"Well, Skylar," Hallie says, "that sounds like it might work."

"Might?" Alex says. "Sounds seamless."

"No plan is entirely infallible," I say. "But we have a lot of contingency plans worked in."

"You're an actual genius, Bubble," Jacob says, which wraps me in miles of Christmas lights and sets me on the brightest setting.

"Thank you," I say. "Does that mean I have Eminence approval?"

"Yes," Jacob says.

"By all means," Orion adds.

"Then let's get to work."

It takes Lexie just ten minutes to convince Redway Town Supervisor Carson Sloane to endorse Representative Everett Caldwell for Congress. Turns out Lexie was able to promise him funds for an expanded art program in the Redway elementary school. (That'll take next to nothing—we can get money for kids' finger paints in thirty seconds if we show people stick figures that five-year-olds drew.)

To share the good news, I step out and call the personal phone of Everett Caldwell.

"This is Everett," he answers.

"Mr. Caldwell," I say. "It's Skylar Rawlings. A pleasure to talk to you again."

He tries to hide his sigh, but he does a terrible job. "Hello, Skylar. What can I do for you?"

"You should be getting a very important message from Carson Sloane in about an hour's time."

"Redway's fake mayor?"

"Redway's real town supervisor," I correct. "He's endorsing you for Congress."

"No, he isn't," Everett says. "No way he's endorsing me."

"He's endorsing you," I say. "I wouldn't make that up. Now, because he is endorsing you and because it was our idea, we would like something from you."

He doesn't even try to hide his sigh this time. "You and your AP Gov class don't do nice things for free, do you?"

"Oh, we do. Just not for you. Could you put us in contact with the president of the New York Corn and Soybean Growers Association? And perhaps a few of their associates as well? We're facing a bit of a predicament elsewhere in the world and would love to speak to some experts on the topic."

"Why didn't you just call NYCSGA directly?"

"Because we would like to speak to the president, not a receptionist."

He's quiet for a second before he exhales for ten straight minutes. He mutters to himself before saying, "I'm having a fundraiser Saturday evening. In Redway. Darcy Brecken, the president of NYCSGA, will be there. A bunch of area farmers will be there, too, including a lot of soybean farmers."

"And that event would be this Saturday? As in, two days from now?"

"Yeah," Everett says. "So cancel your Model UN meeting now."

"Excellent," I say, letting his Model UN comment slide, since I would have joined Model UN had it not conflicted with math club. "You'll email me the invitation as soon as possible?"

"Yes."

"And I'll be bringing my associates with me."

"You can have a plus-one."

"I would like a plus-six."

He laughs once, sharply, but says, "If you really need your whole AV club with you, then fine. I don't care."

"Thank you."

"It's black tie, so don't wear your school uniforms."

"Wouldn't dream of it."

"And, remember, it's a fundraiser. So—"

I cut him off. "Carson Sloane endorsed you. That's worth more than any amount of money we could give you."

"I don't know about that."

"The bus garage? The funding for it?"

"That was a different transaction for a different service."

"Depending on if your soirée gives us what we would like to get from it, we'll consider some sort of donation to your campaign. But do not take that as a strong likelihood, let alone a promise."

"Fine," he says. "Let me tell you, I don't know how you kids got mixed up in the cutthroat world of Central New York politics, but I find it amusing."

"I'm glad someone does," I say. "Thank you for your time, Mr. Caldwell. We will see you this Saturday."

I go back into the big room.

"How'd it go, Sky?" Lexie asks.

"Does anyone have plans for this Saturday evening?" I ask. "If so, please clear them."

Later that night, once I'm in my pajamas and the sun has completely set, and after I've called Harlow so she doesn't throttle me next Obligatory Family Dinner Night, I stand in front of my closet. I don't have anything even *close* to being appropriate to wear to a congressman's black-tie fundraiser. The fanciest dress I own is from my eighth grade Snow Ball dance. I actually have grown since then, so it falls just above my knee, and when I Googled "black-tie," it told me I should probably wear a floor-length gown. At first, I was beyond ecstatic. I considered wearing a tiara as well so I could get my whole Disney Princess vibe just right. But it hit me—where can I find a gown that isn't too expensive and that I don't have to tell my parents I got? And that doesn't smell like the corpse of a spinster, isn't ridden with moth holes, and won't make me look like I jumped out of the prom scene in *Pretty in Pink*?

Out of curiosity and desperate need for inspiration, I text Hallie and Lexie: *How should we figure out the gown thing? We need them in two nights. That is nowhere near a lot of time.*

Using Kelsie's prom dress, Hallie replies. She's lucky she has an older sister with impeccable fashion taste and who's away at college and won't notice it missing for a night.

I bought my senior prom dress freshman year, Lexie texts back.

Why, Hallie replies.

Too pretty to leave on the rack. And I wasn't gonna grow anymore.

Skylar, ask your aunt, Hallie asks.

She's right—if anyone I know were to have a dress for a gala, it would be my Aunt Jessamine. And we are roughly the same size, though she's (fortunately for her) a bit taller. I call her.

"Skylar, my darling, is that you?" I hear Jessamine's little smile in her voice—the one that makes you think she has a secret that she's about to tell you.

"Hi, Aunt Jessamine," I say. "How are you?"

"I'm wonderful," she says. "How is your musical going?"

"Well, actually, that's why I called," I say. "Mrs. Darner is contemplating adding a scene where there's a ball. I mean, she isn't entirely sure if we'll need it or not, or if we can learn a whole new scene by showtime, but we're supposed to have gowns for this weekend's rehearsal. Do you by any chance have a ballgown? One that could be considered black-tie?"

"I do," she says. "I have three. You could borrow any one you would like."

"Thank you so much, Aunt Jessamine," I say.

"Would you like me to run them over tomorrow?"

"Oh, no, my friend can drive me," I say. "After school tomorrow." I don't really want my parents knowing about this, and I know Jessamine wouldn't bring it up to them unless they asked first, which they never will do if they don't know about it.

"That would be wonderful," Jessamine says. "What time?"

"Well, it takes about forty minutes to get to your house, and I have rehearsal, so a little after five?"

"Perfect," Jessamine. "Oh, I can't wait to see you, Skylar."

"Likewise, Aunt Jessamine." My God, do I feel guilty for lying to her. "Thank you."

"I'll see you tomorrow." I hear her smile again before she hangs up.

Then I take a deep breath, pre-roll my eyes, and call Orion.

"Skylar, dear," he answers. "What a pleasant surprise!"

"I need a favor," I say. "What are you doing tomorrow evening?"

"Spending time with you all, I presume, but I will most happily help you should you need it."

"Could you drive me to my aunt's house in the city?"

"Most happily," Orion repeats. "You would like someone with an actual driver's license to drive you?"

"Yes," I say. "Jessamine would know in a second that Hunter isn't actually licensed, and I would rather not get into that with her."

"I agree," he says. "May I ask why we will be journeying to your aunt's house?"

"To get a gown for Everett's gala," I say. "Do you own a tuxedo?"

"As a matter of fact, I own three." Of course he does. "I do not know which one I should wear. Perhaps during our drive together, you could help me choose. One is more obsidian, whereas another has more of an onyx hue—"

"Please don't make me regret asking you to take me," I say. "I'll be at your house at approximately four-thirty, depending on when we get out of rehearsal."

"Excellent. I look forward to it immensely, Skylar, dear."

"I wish I could say the same." I hang up.

Chapter Eight

I lost all sense of what I had intended,
I can't remember where this song began.
But maybe jubilation
led to youthful procrastination.
So I bought myself
a plane ticket
and ran.

"California"
LaPeer

Per usual, rehearsal is not going well today. Half the cast misses its entrance for the opening number, which is legitimately the easiest entrance in the show. Just be in your place when the curtain comes up. They even give you a cute little countdown of the minutes you have *until* that curtain goes up. And they start at ten. Now, I'm not one for knowing what a *minute* is, but Lexie, Hunter, and I were all on stage, so there's no excuse for anyone who can count at a reasonable pace.

And this is our first run with costumes, which is a battle all in itself. We were supposed to be rehearsing in our character shoes this whole time, but did people take this recommendation to heart? Goodness no. I'm surprised how many of the girls try wearing their high heels for the first time today and topple during the dances.

It took me *ages* to learn how to walk in high heels. And my character shoes are only two inches tall. I wore them around my house for the entire week after I got them, practicing journeys up and down the stairs and re-learning the dances in my bedroom to make sure I could do them all while being two inches taller. (I'm approximately five-four in my heels, which makes me pretty happy.) Now, I'm just as coordinated in heels as I am out of them, which isn't very, but at least the heels aren't a factor in further un-coordinating me.

"My goodness, Sofia!" Mrs. Darner screams in the middle of "Mountain Time". Sofia Cargotti missed her line once again, for the third time today and the millionth time ever.

"He will go and explore the mountains," Sofia sings.

"You are a minute and three months late," Mrs. Darner replies. "I'm sorry, but I'm going to have to give this line to someone else."

"Yeah, that's fine," Sofia says with a shrug.

To my abject horror, Mrs. Darner looks at me. "Skylar."

"Hi," I say.

"Can you take over Sofia's line?"

"That's okay," I say. "She can keep it."

"I don't want it," Sofia says. "Please. I don't want this line anymore. It keeps me up at night."

"You're never late, you work hard, and you can dance in your shoes," Mrs. Darner says to me. "Have at it."

"He will go and explore the mountains," I sing.

"Beautiful," Mrs. Darner says. "I forgot you sounded like that, or Sofia would have never had the line in the first place."

"You know, that's completely fair," Sofia says with a nod. "You sound like an innocent baby Barrett Wilbert Weed who is still teething."

"Thank you?" I say.

"Run the number from the top," Mrs. Darner calls out, "so Skylar can practice her line."

"We don't have to run it just for me," I say. "Really."

"Well, we should run it again anyway, since the number is just not good," Mrs. Darner says. "Like, it's very not good. Not one thing about that last run was good. Except for you, Wyatt. You were acceptable."

"Aww, thank you, Mrs. Darner," Wyatt replies.

"But I wouldn't call you good. Places!"

Through the entirety of the number, I try to remember my line. It would seem that it has already slipped out of my head. Something about mountains? The whole freaking song is about mountains, since Tesla avoided being drafted into the army by going on a huge mountain expedition, which, honestly, is such a Knower thing to do. Avoid problems by hiding.

Oh, God, that was Karina Bepal's line, which means—

"He will go and explore the mountains," I sing.

"Yes!" Mrs. Darner calls from the audience. I must have done it correctly, then.

She makes us run the number another two times through because the featured dancers in the dance break have no clue what they're doing. It's because our leading dancer, McKenna Sterran, left our show to do a professional show in the city that she'll actually get paid for being in, which means our other dancers don't have anyone to watch and copy off anymore and need to actually learn the dance for themselves.

We end late, per usual. As I'm taking off my character shoes and packing them up, Lexie, Alex, and Hunter run up to me.

"You have a line!" Lexie cheers, jumping up and down. "Oh my God, you *actually* have a line! You're going to be famous! You'll definitely get a lead next year!"

"Congratulations, Skylar," Alex says. "You killed it every single time."

"You were awesome," Hunter adds with a nod.

"Guys, stop," I say. "It's just a few words. And you two—Mr. Batchelor and Assistant to Westinghouse Number Two—have no reason to congratulate me. Neither do you, Lexie."

"No, it's so, so exciting!" Lexie says, starting her jumping again. "Now the whole school will know how good of a singer you are!"

"From one line? In the key of B-flat?"

Jacob comes over, a splotch of white paint on his cheek, still holding a screwdriver. "Did I hear from backstage that you have a *line* now, Skylar?"

"Unfortunately," I say. "It isn't a big deal."

"It *sounds* like a big deal."

"But it isn't."

"But it *is*."

I stand up and sling my backpack onto my shoulder. "You have paint all over your face."

He touches his cheek. "Oh."

"Are you going on your secret mission now?" Hunter asks.

"Unfortunately," I say.

"What secret mission?" Jacob asks, trying to get the paint off his face but just making it worse. Dear God, can he give me a *moment* of sanity in which he isn't endearing? Is that a possibility in the slightest?

"My mission to get a black-tie appropriate ballgown before the gala tomorrow and without spending a million dollars or looking like it's prom night in 1985," I tell him. "I have to go to my Aunt Jessamine's house to pick one up."

"Sounds riveting," he replies. "I still don't know what I'm going to wear."

"Orion has three tuxes," Hunter says. "You can borrow one. He's wearing the onyx one, but the obsidian and the ebony ones are up for grabs."

"I thought I was going to use the ebony," Alex says. "Since I haven't worn my tux since my First Communion in third grade."

"It probably wouldn't fit me anyway, since I'm taller than him," Jacob says.

"You're exactly the same height," I say.

"No, we're not."

"Yeah, you are," Lexie says.

"No, I'm definitely taller."

"How tall are you?" Hunter asks. "Five-ten?"

"Yeah."

"You are literally the same exact height," Hunter says. "The obsidian one would look better with your hair." He turns to me. "Ready?"

"Ready," I say.

"Skylar, send pictures on the group chat if you need help choosing a dress," Lexie says.

"Or don't do that," Hunter says.

"No, please," Alex counters. "I want to see Jessamine's whole collection."

"And we have to start deciding what we're going to do with your hair sooner rather than later, and we need to see your dress to decide that," Lexie says.

"I'm thinking an updo?" Alex says.

"With little curls coming off the side!" Lexie claps her hands.

"Like Audrey Hepburn in a windstorm," Alex says with a nod.

"My God," Hunter groans. "Skylar, I am leaving with or without you."

"I'm coming," I say.

The walk with Hunter is nice in the fact that we don't talk to each other. Not in an awkward way, like it used to be when just the two of us happened to find ourselves together. That only changed within the past few months. Maybe because of Jacob, maybe not. It might have been our own doing.

I was never friends with Hunter; not until maybe late June of last year did I consider him to be any more than a person in my class that I knew on occasion. Sure, we've gone to school together since kindergarten, and we were lab partners all through seventh grade, but I knew nothing about him. Absolutely nothing. I didn't know he had a brother, or a dog, or that he spoke Greek, or even that he lived on the Northern Tip, a fact difficult to hide from anyone. I mean, I *still* don't know that much about him. Not nearly as much as I know about all my other friends, including Alex. But I don't mind. I don't take it personally. Hunter chooses to share parts of himself with different people, and sometimes two people don't get the same parts.

He warmed up to me the quickest, compared to Hallie and Lexie and most of all Alex. I don't know why. I'm not particularly likable, especially when compared to Lexie. (Hallie can be stand-offish at times, but I thought Hunter might vibe with that before he vibed with whatever it is I've got going on.) But we were at Lexie's house once, and it was just the two of us in her backyard around the fire pit when everyone else went in for snacks, and he actually initiated a conversation about something I can't even re-member. I don't have to, since whatever it was, it worked. Then we were friends. It wasn't that hard.

I'm expecting him to say silent until we get to his front door as he usually would, but then he says, "You didn't tell Jacob about your secret mission." He states this as a fact—he doesn't need to ask something to which he already knows the answer.

"I didn't," I say. "It didn't come up."

"Okay," Hunter says.

"You nailed all your lines today during the run-through. I liked the way you said 'But it will never work!' so vehemently."

He side-eyes me, but I pretend not to notice. "Thanks. Darner said I should have more emotion, so I've been trying."

"It shows."

"Acting is hard," he says.

"But you're quite good at it," I counter. It's half-true. Hunter's very good at lying, and acting and lying are practically the same thing. The nuances trip Hunter up, though. He's so good at lying that he delivers his lines with little flourish, and a musical demands flourish.

"I'm not," he replies. He kicks a stone on the sidewalk. "But it's fine. It's four lines. And as long as I'm not the worst actor in the show—and I'm not, thanks to Casey Whitten. As long as I'm not the worst, it's fine."

"I think you're doing wonderfully," I say.

"Thanks."

We settle into the silence again. I think we work best in the silence.

Orion's waiting on the front portico when we arrive. "Skylar, dear! I've looked forward to our adventure all day!"

"Good luck," Hunter says. "Try not to kill each other while on the road. At least pull over first."

"Will do, my wondrous brother," Orion says. He pats Hunter on the head, and Hunter subsequently looks like he wants to bite him. He then turns to me and holds up his car keys. "Ready, my dear Sky?"

"Please stop calling me that," I say. "Only Lexie calls me Sky. It's weird when anyone else does, especially you."

"Of course, Sky*lar*," he says. "Shall we, as they say, hit the road?"

"Like I said," Hunter says, "good luck." He goes inside.

We get into Orion's car, and he starts driving before I finish setting up the navigation. "You don't even know where we're going," I tell him.

"Well, I know how to get over the bridge," Orion replies. "And I do believe that to be the first step to getting to your aunt's house, am I correct?"

"You already know you are," I say.

"Shall we play some tunes?"

"If you want," I say.

Without taking his eyes off the road, he plugs his phone into the aux cord. A few seconds later, a straight-up sea shanty starts playing.

"What in God's name is this?" I ask.

"'Ocean's Majesty' by Pirate John and Crew. Have you ever heard it?"

"No."

He starts singing along. "Oooh, the sea is high, the tide is nigh, the bow shall break the waves!"

"I feel like I should be lusting after a white whale right now," I say.

"Ah, are you a fellow Herman Melville fanatic?"

"More of a whale fan," I say.

"Whales are truly magnificent critters," he says. "The ocean's greatest mystery and loveliest companion."

"That's actually quite true." I wait a second before asking a question I should already be able to answer but can't: "Where are you going to college next fall?"

"Yale," he replies.

I can't say I'm surprised. "I expected as such. You practically go to the Yale of high schools as it is."

"I wanted to attend the University of Southern California, but the decision was not mine to make."

"Oh," I say. Knowing Delia and Praxis, I can't say that surprises me, either. "I'm sorry."

"It's quite alright," he replies, a smile appearing on his face. "I've been afforded such a unique opportunity. It would be a shame to pass it up."

"Not if you don't want it," I say.

He's quiet for a second, the look on his face pensive and unsmiling. I'm not used to seeing him like this. Then, quietly, as if someone were around to eavesdrop on us, he says, "Let it be known, Skylar, that I think Yale is a wonderful school. But my father does business with the husband of the dean of admissions. Neither of my parents know a soul at USC. I was accepted by my own accord."

"I see," I say. "Then you should go there."

"I would much rather avoid a mutiny, my dear," he says. "Besides, to complain about attending Yale is among the most privileged of things for me to complain about." He chuckles to himself. "I should find myself so fortunate." He pauses, as if he were about to say something else, but then he says, "My trifles are of no interest to anyone. Tell me about your recent life, Skylar, dear. Has anything of interest occurred?"

"We're going to a political gala this weekend," I say. "And I got assigned a line in the musical this afternoon."

"A whole line just for you! What an honor, Skylar. I am most happy for you."

Despite his verbal fanfare, he seems genuinely excited for me. Strange, but I can't help but smile. "Thank you, Orion."

"I am very, very excited to see the show next weekend," he says. "My own brother has such a wonderful role, and Alex— my goodness! I've heard from Hunter that he is quite the singer, though I'd always suspected as such, what with the way he carries his speaking voice. And my fellow Eminence, working on the sets while managing the entirety of the planet—and I'm quite certain they are wonderful sets."

"They are," I say.

We stay quiet for a few minutes.

"He does not like me," Orion says.

"Jacob?"

"Yes."

"No, he does not," I admit. "It doesn't take a Knower to figure that out."

"Fully knowing that, you nominated me anyway. So were my perceptions of your emotions incorrect, or—"

"I take it they were entirely correct," I say. "I just thought he would get over it."

"He hasn't."

"You're awfully annoying," I say. "I haven't quite gotten over it either."

"Oh, I'm aware," he says. "I probably annoy myself most of all. You all don't have to live with me twenty-four hours a day, seven days a week."

"Fair point," I say. "I'm sure it'll get better." I mean it enough to pretend I mean it wholeheartedly.

"Have you and Jacob fully recovered from the occurrences of last September?"

I consider my answer, but Orion doesn't ask questions to learn the answers. Just to prove to himself that he's right. So I go with honesty and say, "Not at all."

"Ah," he says. "Young love is such a tricky thing to navigate. Have you spoken to him about how you feel?"

"Orion, there is no way in hell I am talking about my love life with you."

"Alright, then we will talk about mine. Have I told you about Bertha?"

"Bertha?"

"My first girlfriend."

"You had a *girlfriend*?"

"Yes," Orion says. "I've had two. Bertha was quite horrible, but I loved her all the same. We were, as they say, an *item* for approximately eight months."

"Someone willingly dated you for *eight months*?"

"I ended things with her once I discovered that she used my history notes without my permission on a project, thus usurping my research from me. I also reported her to the dean of discipline."

"That sounds about right," I say.

"I then dated a lovely girl named Gretel, and our relationship progressed quite a bit further than it had with Bertha—"

"Please stop," I say. "I don't want to know."

"—and rather quickly, too, if I may add—"

"Please don't add anything else," I say. "Please."

"All I'm saying, dear Skylar," he says, "is that ignoring things of this nature will not do anything but make you upset."

"I am completely fine."

"You may be able to fool everyone else, including yourself, but you are unable to fool me."

"Remember when I said we weren't going to talk about this? We're breaking that rule."

"I only mean—"

"Orion!" I cut him off. "That was six months ago! I kissed him six *months* ago! Do you know how much can change in *one* month, let alone *six*? Why is everyone still on this? So what if there was something there at some point? It is pretty freaking obvious that there is nothing there now, so why does everyone still care? I am so *sick* of people asking about it! It has nothing to do with anyone else, and I'm quite sure there isn't even an *it* to begin with!"

My God, I just told Orion Athan that I kissed his co-Eminence. I haven't told another living soul about that. Not Hallie, not Harlow, not Lexie or Alex or anyone else, dead or alive. Just Orion Priam Athan, of all people.

"I'm very sorry, Skylar," he says. "I didn't mean to upset you." He really, actually sounds like he means it. I know he's a professional liar, but still. It's hard to fake sincerity to someone trained to spot insincerity.

"Thank you," I mutter. "I'm not good at talking about . . . feelings."

"It's quite alright," he says. "I should not have pried into your personal affairs."

"You should not have," I agree.

"Would you like me to tell you a story about our fluffy friend Pickle?"

"Yes, please."

He tells stories about Pickle nonstop until we pull onto Jessamine's street. She lives in an apartment building, an old one with ornate molding and giant windows. She always says how lucky she is to have found this one, since older buildings usually have smaller windows.

"You can wait in the car," I tell Orion.

"But I would absolutely love to meet your relative," he counters.

"But I'm not sure she wants to meet you."

"Have you asked her? Are you *sure* she would not like to meet me?"

"Quite."

"I will get so lonely in the car."

I relent, mostly so he'll shut up. I don't feel like arguing with him. And it's only Jessamine. If it were anyone else, I'd hand-cuff him to the steering wheel before I'd let him into the building.

We buzz in, and she lets us up. I know exactly how to get to her apartment—it's on the fifth floor at the end of the hall. When I knock on the door, Jessamine opens it, smiling as if she knows something no one else in the world knows. "Hello, darling."

"Hi, Aunt Jessamine." She hugs me, gently, and then she sees Orion.

"Hello, Ms. Rawlings," Orion says. "It's a pleasure to meet you. I am Orion Athan, Skylar's friend from her school musical."

"Nice to meet you, too, Orion," Jessamine says. "Please, come in. Who do you play in the musical?"

"Oh, I'm not onstage," Orion replies. "I assist with costumes and props."

"Equally as important," Jessamine says.

Jessamine lives in a studio apartment, but it's sort of like two rooms because her bed has its own alcove-type situation. She leads me over to her closet while Orion lingers near the kitchen.

"Now, Skylar, I have three dresses I think you might like," Jessamine says. She pulls them out and lays them on her bed.

"Oh my goodness." Gossamer tulle, shimmering silk, and kinetic taffeta tumble to the floor in generous waves like vertical oceans. Deep blue, dangerous red, and a scintillating yellow. I hold them up and twirl and run my fingers through the fabric as if the daydream might dissipate if I close my eyes too long. "Jessamine, I didn't know you had these."

"The yellow one was my prom dress," Jessamine explains. "And the other two were made by my friend Cyleigh. You remember Cyleigh, right?"

"The one whose name is a phonetic nightmare?"

Jessamine chuckles. "She sews gowns for fun, in addition to her photography, sculpting, gardening, and metalwork."

"They're beautiful."

"I think I know exactly which one you will choose."

I consider for a second before making my selection. "This one."

"Well, you proved me wrong. I wasn't expecting that one. But it will look absolutely beautiful on you."

I try it on quickly, and it fits perfectly. It's too long, of course, but Jessamine isn't too much taller than me, so with a pair of three-inch heels, I should be okay. I can borrow those from Lexie without a problem—she has at least seven pair of heels. When I emerge from the bathroom, having already taken it off and packed it up, Orion calls from the kitchen table, "Skylar, please come look at this."

I go over, and sitting atop Jessamine's mail pile is a flyer from Everett Caldwell. "Could I look at this?" I ask Jessamine.

"If you'd like it, you can have it," Jessamine tells me. "I was going to recycle it."

"Everett Caldwell is nowhere near your district," I say. "He's in upstate New York. Why on earth would he mail this to you?"

"I thought it was odd," Jessamine concurs. "I hadn't heard his name before, and I didn't think he was my district's incumbent."

"Curious," Orion says, "that he would use funding to mail flyers to people who cannot vote for him."

"Curious indeed," I say.

"I didn't know you were well-versed in upstate New York politics," Jessamine says to me with a smile.

"It's a newfound hobby," I say. "Thank you so much for the dress. I really hope Mrs. Darner doesn't cut the scene."

"I hope not," Jessamine says.

Orion and I are mostly silent for the drive home, our brains spinning around the information we gathered from atop Jessamine's table.

At one point, he looks to me and says, "Skylar, dear, we may have wandered into something bigger than we think it to be." Then he looks back to the road and we drive in silence once again.

Chapter Nine

But when I close my eyes,
I want only to stay
where the farthest you are
is a heartbeat away.

"Bring Me the Night"
Sam Tsui and Kina Grannis

Orion drives me to his house. He takes my dress inside with him—we're all getting ready before the gala tomorrow at Hunter's house so our parents don't wonder why we're heading out in floor length gowns and tuxedos.

I call Harlow as I walk home. The anxiety has been starting to hit me—we're going to a super fancy political gala tomorrow, and the world's economy might be in jeopardy, and I have a line to memorize now—but talking to Harlow infallibly stymies any and all impending anxiety, at least for a little bit.

"Skylar Amelia," she says when she picks up. "How on Earth are you doing?"

"Just fine," I say.

"You sound nervous."

"Harlow, I *always* sound nervous."

"A little more so right now," she says. Of course she can tell. She can always tell. When it comes to me, she reads me like a Knower can. "What's up?"

"I have a line in the musical now."

"A line? That you say by yourself?"

"I sing it, actually."

"Skylar, that is so beyond awesome," Harlow says. "Sing it. Right now. I want to hear it."

"He will go and explore the mountains," I sing.

"Angelic," she says. "Absolutely angelic."

"Can I ask you something weird?" I ask.

"If you must."

"Have you gotten any mail from Everett Caldwell?"

"Is he a politics guy? My mom got like four of those stupid junk mails today, and I'm pretty sure— 'kay, found the pile, I'm just— Yeah, this one's from Everett Caldwell. Holy shit, he's hot. My God, I'm gonna hang this on my wall. He's beautiful. Look at that hair."

"I know, right?" I say. "That's why I asked. He's something else."

"He has my vote."

"But, Harlow, I don't think he represents our district."

"He can represent my district anytime."

"Harlow! Seriously, though, we're in the same congressional district. And we're represented by Mary-Grace Carressy. So I don't understand why Everett would mail us things."

"Probably to grace more people with his wonderful face. Is this what you think about to avoid doing homework?"

I force a chuckle. "I guess. I'm home now, so I'll call you tomorrow."

"Love you bunches, Skylar Amelia."

"Love you more, Harlow June."

I go up to my room and throw my backpack to the floor without a single thought of homework. I throw open my laptop so forcefully I'm afraid I'll snap it, and I Google Everett Caldwell.

Fortunately for me, his website has a pretty sizable section titled "Get to Know Everett," so I can answer most of my questions without a questionable amount of digging. He grew up in a town just a few miles south of Redway, one somehow even smaller, called Sharonsville. (Is it even a town when it gets smaller than Redway?) His wife's name is Luciana, and he has two kids and a golden retriever named Sparky. He loves animals and has adopted a series of rescue dogs and volunteers at the Redway ASCPA at least once a month. (There is a disappointing lack of doggo photos to accompany this fact.) He is a proud alumni of William Beekman High School in Sharonsville, where he and Luciana were high school sweethearts and even Homecoming king and queen. After earning his political science degrees from George Washington University (no surprise there), he worked for a bunch of different politicians before stepping out on his own and running for various positions in state government. He was on state congress for a bit before being elected into the House of Representatives the November before last. He's been doing a somewhat terrible job ever since.

He seems extremely boring. To find something more interesting, I'll have to get creepy.

His sister, Sadie Caldwell-Henderson seems to be a famous blogger in Sharonsville. Her blog is called "Farmer Mommy" and appears to be updated almost daily. She has four kids—Temperance, Hyacinth, Amadeus, and Gix—and roughly two hundred cows. I stalk her posts, navigating through cow crafts and corn recipes, until I see that she mentions that her parents were farmers. Therefore, Everett's parents were farmers. Makes sense, I suppose, since two-thirds of Sharonsville's population are farmers. They grew corn, from what I can gather.

Sadie doesn't mention Everett once. He's in a family photo that appears in one of her posts about the blessing of family (of which she has many), but that's it. No mention of his politics, or that he won the election, or that he stopped by last weekend to make cow patterned tie-dye and eat corn brownies. I look at the family photo again, and there doesn't appear to be a disconnect between Everett and the rest of the family. His wife and Sadie embrace, even, and the kids look as if they're all siblings. This photo was just posted three months ago, at Christmastime, so unless something changed by the new year, I would assume that their families are close.

I zoom in on Everett in that photo. He looks exactly the same as he does now, same floofy hair and infectious smile, wearing a horribly ugly Christmas sweater with a penguin on it. But nothing here answers my question—why is he campaigning to people who cannot vote for him? It's a waste of money. Even if he's planning on running for the Senate eventually, there are better ways to get your name statewide than with a piece of glossy paper that will get shoved into the recycling bin upon reception.

Everything about him gets more and more confusing the more I look. It's weird. I wouldn't expect someone like him to have this many complexities.

I look at the policies he's supported and the things that he's worked on and the stances he holds on certain issues, but none of them do anything but confirm what I'd already believed. I knew he'd be slightly conservative, living where he does and representing the people there, but less so than I thought, I guess. He's empathetic at the very least.

Eventually, I just give up. Everything about him is predictable, to be expected. If I have questions about him, I'll have to ask him directly. Either I'll get an answer or I'll be able to tell he's hiding something.

My door opens a bit. "Are you clunking around in your high heels?" Evan asks me.

I look down at my feet. I'm wearing my pajamas and the three-inch heels Lexie's loaning me for the gala. "Yes," I say. "I have to be able to walk in them without tripping."

"Why are you pacing?" He walks in and jumps on my bed, messing up my perfect arrangement of whales.

"To learn to walk in them," I repeat. Three inches is not too much more difficult than the two-inch heels I've been rehearsing in, so I should be able to last in them. "I'll have to dance in them, anyway. For the musical."

He crosses his arms. "Want to go to the thrift store tomorrow?"

"I can't," I say. "I'm going to Lexie's house to work on our global project. And I'm sleeping over. And then working on it again on Sunday."

"We have family dinner Sunday night."

"I'm trying to get out of it." I asked my parents if I really *had* to go to Obligatory Family Dinner Night this Sunday, seeing as though I would be exhausted from my weekend, but they would not hear of it. They said I'd make my grandmother upset, or make Harlow upset, or that I'd have to go another few weeks without Grandma's chocolate cake. But I know myself, and I know that I would just be miserable the whole time, and it wouldn't make anyone else happy.

"Good luck with that," Evan says. "Have you ever successfully gotten out of it?"

"That time I had strep throat."

"You still had to FaceTime the rest of the family from your bed."

"Maybe I'll misplace my phone this time. Or I'll leave it on silent."

"Look, Sky, I'm on your side," Evan says. "But there is no way you're getting out of it."

"We'll see," I say. "Isn't it your bedtime?"

"It's eight-thirty."

"Please leave my bedroom."

He throws a whale at me.

Lexie sends a text in our group chat. Once Evan's left and has closed the door behind him, I read it. *Went grocery shopping with my dad and he didn't buy tofu because it was like waaay more expensive than normal. So I came home and did some research and soy product prices are like so much higher now than they were a few months ago. Mega yikes.*

That is surely a mega yikes. I wasn't expecting the economy to be affected so soon, but I guess I was wrong.

We'd better find something at this gala to fix this.

I can't fall asleep at all. I must lie in my bed for days with my eyes closed, feeling around for the switch that turns off my brain. I take three times the recommended amount of melatonin supplements (Knowers normally take twice the recommended because our circadian rhythms are legitimately nonexistent), and I drink a vat of chamomile tea, but I'm still not tired. This is common for Knowers, since our brains don't know what *nighttime* means, but I should be exhausted. I've had a hellish week, a very busy day, and I'll have a worse day tomorrow, so if I don't get some sleep, I'll make mistakes. Tomorrow, I can't make a single mistake.

Perhaps that could be why I can't fall asleep.

Eventually, I stop trying and flick on my lamp. I'm only making myself more nervous by lying alone in the dark. I could try to read, but I already know that wouldn't work. I usually try it, and the results always disappoint. *Parks and Rec* is always an option, but looking at a screen can wake you up more.

If I sit idly any longer, the spiraling will start. It feels imminent, like when your throat starts to tickle and you just know with a sense of dread that you'll have a fever in a matter of hours. The longer I think about it, the twistier my stomach gets and the fuzzier my vision becomes.

I look at the clock on my phone: one-twenty-seven. Lexie and Alex are probably asleep by now, and Hallie's definitely been asleep for hours. I have no idea about Hunter. But Jacob sleeps like a dolphin—not very much and not very well. I text him. *Are you awake?*

He responds within seconds. *Per usual.*

Can I call you?

Not even a full minute later, my phone rings.

"Hi," I say.

"Hi, Bubble," he says. "Are you okay? Is there something wrong?"

"Nothing's wrong. I just— I can't sleep, and— I don't know." I give up. "I didn't really want to be alone."

"Well, I'm very much awake," he says. "And probably not going to sleep for a very long time."

"As in tomorrow night?"

"As in whenever I'm not the Eminence anymore."

"That's a tad morbid, considering your circumstances."

"A little bit," he agrees. "Do you want me to bore you into falling asleep?"

"Please," I say.

"I can talk about buildings."

"That wouldn't work. I find your buildings exceedingly interesting."

I can practically hear his blush through the phone. I bite my lip—that probably wasn't the best thing to say. But he moves on and says, "How was your secret mission earlier?"

"It was fine," I say. I don't want to bring up Orion past midnight, so I say, "My Aunt Jessamine had a flyer for Everett Caldwell. Got it in the mail. We're miles away from his district, yet she still got a flyer from him."

"Weird," he says. "Why would he send one to her? Or to anyone not in his district? He does know how districts work, right? He should."

"No idea," I say. "Seriously. I've been contemplating all night, and no reason makes enough sense. I'm planning on outright asking him tomorrow."

"Think he'll tell you?"

"If he doesn't, we'll still know he's hiding something. Win-win."

"I don't like him," he says.

"I like his hair," I say. "But not much else."

"He does have nice hair."

I smile. We're actually having a conversation. A real, actual, back-and-forth conversation. And it's easy. Wonderful, even. Like it used to be, before all the shit happened. Maybe everything really *will* be okay, and we can actually escape the holding pattern.

"Are you still awake?" he asks.

"Yes," I answer. "Sorry. I was just . . . thinking."

"About what?"

I can't tell him now. Not right when we're starting to talk to each other like functioning humans again. We can just pretend all that stuff never happened. Because given the choice between never talking to him again or never kissing him again, I would take the latter, and it would seem the two are mutually exclusive. "Everett," I reply.

"And his beautiful hair?"

I chuckle. "No."

"That's not very convincing."

"Is Daniel awake, too?" I ask. I don't have the energy to lie, which is a good sign that I'm getting tired. "Or can he just sleep through your conversations?"

"I'm on my back porch," he says.

"Jacob! It's freezing outside!"

"It's nice out," he says. "And Cat's sitting on my lap, so it's even warmer. And I can be as loud as I want and no one will wake up."

"You're insane."

"Are you only figuring this out *now*?"

"Oh, I've known since the day I met you," I say.

"Was it the orange juice?"

I laugh. "Yes. Who buys orange juice in plastic containers?"

"My mom, actually, not me. I would've gotten the carton."

We're silent for a moment, and for the first time in ages, the Awkwardness doesn't creep up through the floorboards and suffuse through the space between us. This silence is comforting, like the whisper of wind through the trees once the birds have retreated to their nests. A full silence, not an empty one.

I almost say a lot of things. Like, *Are we okay now? Can things stay like this when the sun rises? Can we pretend that September was nonexistent, like it was supposed to be?*

Technically, I don't *have* to love him anymore. Really, I don't. They say that love is a conscious choice, a consistent decision we make before each interaction. Building a something on feelings alone is like building a skyscraper on a sand dune—shifty, erratic, susceptible to windstorms and dry spells and collapsing with the slightest inclination. So what if the sand feels warm, like an embrace from every direction, or if the chaos and the energy of the winds lured you in and trapped you and now every time you think you're safe, the wind rustles through you like leaves on a tree once the birds have flown away and you wish with parts of your heart you didn't know could wish that it would start storming again—

"I think I've gotten tired now," I say. "I'm sorry if I kept you up."

"Not at all, Bubble," he says. "I like talking to you."

"I like talking to you, too," I say.

"See you tomorrow?"

"In my beautiful princess dress, too."

He laughs. "I can't wait to see it."

My God, I miss him. I miss him beyond words. He's right there, just a phone screen away, and I miss him. I wish he were here, that I ran all the way to his house or he came here and his arms were around me, his steady architect hands keeping me grounded, my head on his chest and my heart beating with his, as if they were harmonizing. He isn't close enough to me. Three miles away isn't close enough to me. Three seconds away would still be too far.

I technically don't *have* to love him. It would be better for the both of us if I stopped.

"Goodnight, Jacob."

"Goodnight, Skylar."

I fall asleep within seconds.

Chapter Ten

> *I threw my voice into the dark,*
> *but the dark had no remark,*
> *just repeated what I said.*
> *Claustrophobic at first,*
> *struck by hunger and thirst,*
> *I stood up and looked around.*
> *There was nothing to be found,*
> *just a world*
> *I couldn't see.*

"Underground"
Cody Fry

Redway is about an hour and a half drive from the island, not accounting for traffic. Not that there should be a lot of traffic midday on a Saturday, but we're giving ourselves two hours for the drive. I should be at Hunter's house by one o'clock so we can get ready (which Lexie claims will take two hours at least), which means I should leave my house by twelve-forty-five.

It's six AM now. I guess I could have slept in longer.

But there is absolutely no point in me trying to sleep anymore, so as quietly as I can, I get dressed and slip out the back door, leaving a note on the kitchen table telling my parents and Evan that I went for a walk.

I love walking around the island before it wakes up. Saturday is the one day a week the island sleeps in. It's awake by six-thirty on weekdays and seven on Sundays, before the church bells ring for eight o'clock mass. Practically everyone here follows the same exact schedule as their next door neighbor, but Knowers are excluded from this, of course. We aren't very good at following schedules.

The sun has just barely crept out from behind the trees, and the birds haven't returned from their migration yet. It's near silent, I guess, besides the trains just across the river that never seem to rest or the mirthless wind chimes dangling from a porch roof somewhere. A wind darts across the river before slamming me in the side, making me wish I wore a warmer coat.

Some people seem to think our river is pretty, and on mornings like this, I tend to agree with them. The river is religiously ambivalent, but when it settles on this nearly splenetic gray, forgoing all notions of the color blue, it stops pretending and you see it for what it is. Harsh. Unforgiving. Indifferent to every-thing and everyone that bends to its will. It beguiles you, tricks you into believing it to be melted sapphire, or liquified forget-me-nots, or the irises of love poems. When it looks like anger, if ice were kinetic, then it's far simpler to remember the danger it so graciously conceals.

I follow Riverway all the way to the Northern Tip. I take my time with the castles, absorbing each little detail and hypothesizing what their interiors could hold. At the end of their reign is their sovereign—the Rathcliffe Manor. Daydreams aren't opulent enough to reach the Rathcliffe Manor. It was spun from clouds and tinted with seawater and sheathed in intricacies beyond human comprehension. It breathes, its diaphragm expanding and contracting as it tiptoes towards the river, daring it to come closer. Even the river stays away. A veranda snakes around it, cloaked in lacy railings and gingerbread trim. The ruddy peaks of the roof pierce the sky like a mountain range. Bay windows and oriels and corbels and balconies protrude from the house, rejecting any notion of symmetry and—seemingly—gravity.

Jacob says some guy named Auden Callaway designed it for Mr. Florian Rathcliffe and his family back in 1882, but I don't believe him. It must have been fairies. And it has existed since the fairies said it may begin to exist. Unless something drastic has changed in our chemical composition over the last hundred or so years, I don't think humans are capable of imagining something this elegant.

It sits completely empty. The doors are all locked, the gate around it is sealed, and no one has legally gotten closer than this since Florian Rathcliffe's great-granddaughter died in 1963. The town took it over, since no one was set to inherit it, but they've done nothing with it. They never put it on the market, they refuse to sell the land, and they haven't undertaken any renovations or revival projects. There was a movement quite a few years ago, spearheaded by Delia Athan, to turn the mansion into a museum of some sort, but it never got enough funding to get off the ground. It would make a beautiful museum, I think—they did it with Cooper Hewitt in New York, turning the Carnegie Mansion into a museum, and it worked wonderfully. Granted, I don't know enough about the interior layout of the Rathcliffe Manor to know if it would make a good museum or not, but I imagine it would. Even if they left it as is and just cleaned it up, it would be magical.

I keep walking, wandering to the west side of the island. I don't really go to the west side unless I'm just wandering like this. All the schools are on the east side except for West Island Elementary (but I went to East), and all of my friends live on the east side, except for people whose houses I never visit. The east side looks like the set of a film adaptation of an Edith Wharton novel, and the west side looks like a traditional seaside town. It comprises straight streets of cottages with screened porches and creaky weathervanes and clapboard siding in seashell tones. They look as though their floors would be incessantly coated in sand, regardless of how many times you've swept, and that the screens in their windows let in the sound of the ocean when the tides are high, lulling you to sleep. Granted, we have very little sand and even fewer oceans, but the west side remains optimistic.

At least you can walk on the shore here. Some may even attempt to call it a beach, since the rocks are smaller than your average kindergartener, unlike those on the north and east coasts. In the summer, seagulls croon overhead, and the sun likes you enough to burn you, and if you're lucky, you can find shells the size of a fingernail nestled between the smoothed stones. Venture out a few feet, and only the minnows will find you; venture out a few more, and you're at the mercy of the tide. It doesn't care if you're a newborn baby or an Olympic swimmer—once the tide has you, you belong to it.

We can always tell when a storm is on its way because the river will warn us. It'll be extra choppy for a few days, brandishing whitecaps and taunting the docks and challenging stilted houses to come closer, just a step closer. Then it will go completely still. Like glass. A mirror. Look down and see your reflection. That's when you close your shutters, reel in your awnings, cancel any outdoor plans for the next three days.

We don't do rain showers here. Those are too easy. You can recover from a drizzle too quickly. When the island rains, it storms. Thunder rattles the buildings, wind tests our trees. The rain converses with the river as if it were its mercenary—it'll help flood the areas the river can't reach yet. The island is a bowl, and the rain loves to fill it. I find myself thanking God too often that I live close enough to the edge that our street is on a hill and that we don't flood. Center island isn't so lucky.

And then there's the lightning. One might suppose it's harmless. It strikes the tallest trees or the river, not us, since it's as drawn to water as everyone else who lives here. But our lighting is spite. It tricks us, only for a millisecond, into believing in daylight. It blinds us, just for a moment, before we blink and it's only all darkness once again. Lightning is nothing but cruel deception. At least our river has the decency to show its true color every so often. Lightning doesn't even have one.

In the summer, when the air is hot and stale, we'll get lightning storms. Sometimes no rain, sometimes no thunder—just continuous lightning. There isn't any counting between strikes to see how far away the storm is—its epicenter is everything. The sky is just gash after gash after gash, lie after lie after lie, bleeding electricity, soundlessly screaming as if something could stop it. As if something could challenge the sky itself. The flashing glues us to our windows, sends photosensitive people into their basements, makes children wish for the monsters under their beds because at least they can't see them. Each time it happens, we claim that we have never seen anything like it. Nature's wonder, we say. It'll happen again in a month, so don't fret if you didn't have your camera with you. The storm will lie to you again. You'll undoubtedly let it.

I should probably at least start in the direction of home, since I can see the sun now. It's only a matter of time before the lights flick on and the coffee gets made. I cut down a street transplanted here from Maine and over onto Main Street.

Unless it's a school, a church, or a house, it's on Main Street. Our Town Hall, our only grocery store, post office, library, any medical practice (including the psychology practice where my mom works), a few shops of knickknacks and secondhand treasures (like Twice Loved), two restaurants, a bed-and-breakfast, an ice cream parlor, a pharmacy, a drug store (not a pharmacy), and a café. If you need anything else, the bridge at the end of the street can direct you to the mainland, which is far more accommodating than we are.

Main Street hasn't seen an addition since 1918, so each building is built from clapboard and gingerbread and frosted in white trim and wrought iron. Our zoning laws are actually quite lax, since there's only one: Don't even try, nothing gets zoned. Our street must always look like an illustration from Samantha the American Girl's books. They don't make these types of materials anymore, and even if they did, would people want to use them? Would that be seen as regression? This is how we reconcile with that: You can't regress if you never progress in the first place.

The Café on Dove Street should be open by now. It's really on the corner of Main and Dove, but everyone knows it as the Café on Dove Street. That's not even what it's actually called—it has some stupid name like Riverside Coffee or something in that vein —but islanders make up their own names for things. We don't play by our own rules.

It's busier than I expect it to be at seven-fifteen AM on a Saturday, but everyone in here is quietly reading or gazing out the window or chatting in whispers. No one is quite awake, though they may pretend to be. Islanders aren't good at pretending and could stand to learn something from our river.

I get one of three orders every time I come here: earl grey and a blueberry muffin in the morning; jasmine green tea and chocolate cake in the afternoon; hot chocolate with extra marsh-mallows and whipped cream after dinner. I order earl grey and a blueberry muffin now and take my favorite table, nestled between a bay window and a bookshelf. I usually bring a book or choose one at random from the shelf to my right, but my brain is far too occupied now to even attempt to distract it. Instead, I gaze out over Main Street.

I feel like I should be more nervous than I am, which conversely makes me nervous. Am I going about this too blasé? Is this nonchalance just apathy? With apathy comes mistakes. You get complacent, and you get caught.

If the soy people at Everett's gala are of no use to us, then I'll have to think of a next step. Logically, it would be to call Eula. If I trusted us less, that would have been move number one. But now, that's the last resort. Not only do Jacob and Orion have to learn to handle things on their own, but we've gotten ourselves too deep into this without adult supervision to ask for it now. We'll just get in trouble for all the phone calls we've already made and the emails we've already sent. None of us *really* know all the rules, so there-fore we can't break them. If you chuck a vase across the room thinking it's plastic, and it hits the wall and shatters, is it still your fault for breaking it? Even if you did your research and a full examination and you still believed it to be plastic? Then who's breaking the rules: you, or the vase? Were there rules to begin with?

Tonight is all about getting information directly from the sources. We find out how soybean farmers deal with pests from the soybean farmers themselves, and we implement those pro-cedures. We ask NYCSGA if they know anything about what's going on in Brazil, see if they have ideas. Maybe try to shake some funding out of them, too, if we're feeling confident. There will be seven of us, after all, so we can split up the work.

Worse comes to absolute worse, I'll get to live out my *West Wing* fantasy and wear a ballgown at a fancy political gala. If I were any shallower, that would outweigh anything pertaining to a soybean.

I walk back home once I've finished my tea and my muffin. The sun is no longer as shy, though it still lingers behind the haze of late winter, and more people meander up and down Main Street, talking themselves into being productive. It would seem the island is awake as it will be for now.

The river winks at me as I pass it, once again flimsily blue.

Back to pretending, it would seem.

I'm trying to get all my homework done now so it doesn't hang over my head this weekend as I deal with an impending world crisis, but that isn't enough to guilt my brain into paying attention. Even as I blast Tchaikovsky to drown out every other atom of the world, my brain is slipperier than a wet fish.

I eventually give up and pack my overnight bag, since I'll be staying at Hunter's house after the gala. It takes me a minute to choose my pajamas, but I go for a button-down beluga set, and I throw in a few stuffed whales to help me sleep in a strange place. Then some clothes for Sunday, my toiletries and melatonin supplements, and—most importantly—my heels. The dress, which is already at Hunter's house, won't work without those extra three inches.

My phone starts to buzz, and I'm slightly surprised to see that it's Jacob. Not as surprised as I would be if he'd called before the occurrences of last night, but surprised enough that I answer right away without allowing it to ring a few times first, as I usually would with him. I wouldn't want to seem too eager. "Hi, Jacob."

"Skylar, I— Coira and— I don't know what to do." Uh oh. I can tell by his voice: He's on the verge of spiraling. Badly.

"Take a deep breath," I tell him. "I'm right here. What's wrong?"

"I don't know what to do," he repeats. "We told them not to, and— I don't know what they— what they want from me."

"Jacob. It'll be okay. Can you explain what you mean?"

"No, I— I don't— I can't—"

"Do you want me to come over?"

"I— Yes."

"Okay, hold on," I say. "I'll be right there. Can Hallie come, too?"

"Yes."

"We're on our way."

"Okay." He hangs up.

I throw on my Converse without lacing them and slip on my dress coat because it was the first coat I could reach in the closet. Then I run to Hallie's house and make it there without seeing any of the houses between ours go by.

Her brother Stephen opens the door. "Yo, Skylar," he says. "What's up?"

"Where's Hallie?"

"Hi, Stephen. It's nice to see you, Stephen."

"Stephen, I'm dead serious. Where is Hallie?" Usually I like talking to Stephen, but now is not the time.

His smile falls when he sees how upset I am. He turns around and calls, "Hallie!" He looks back to me and says, "I hope everything's okay."

"Me, too."

Hallie replaces Stephen in the doorway. "What's wrong?" she asks.

"Jacob," I say. "Something's wrong and he's panicking and I have to go talk to him but I can't go alone because I know he's scared and that scares me and—"

"Skylar, calm down," she says. She slips on her shoes and grabs a coat. "Let's go."

Usually, I have to jog to keep up with Hallie because her stride is nearly four times mine, but I walk so quickly that she's the one jogging.

"Skylar!" she calls. "Is it really that bad?"

I stop and wait for her. "Hallie, he—" I almost stop myself, unsure if it's my place to tell her. But she'll find out eventually, in as soon as five minutes. "He spirals. Like I do. Sometimes worse."

She kicks a lump of dirt and snow off the sidewalk. "I figured."

"And he's been under a ton of pressure lately and whatever he just learned is really not good and it's freaking him out and there isn't really a good possible outcome and—"

"Skylar," she says. "He'll be okay. He's pretty tough."

"I know he'll be okay," I say, "but he isn't okay *now*."

We get to his house and knock on his front door. Daniel answers, still in his pajamas, hair a mess. "Hi." I can't tell if he's perplexed or amused by the fact that we're here, especially this early.

"Hi, Daniel," I say. "Is Jacob home?"

"He's upstairs," Daniel says. "But he's kind of a mess. He's freaking out about that giant math test he has this week. I'm just giving him some space right now."

"We know," Hallie says. "We thought we could calm him down a bit. Or help him study, if that would make him feel any better."

"You can try," Daniel says, stepping aside and letting us in. "But you know how he is when he gets like this. It's hard to convince him the world's not gonna end."

"I know," I say. "But the world isn't going to end just yet, and we're here to reassure him of that fact."

Daniel looks at me for a second, and then he says, "You're pretty brave, Skylar."

"I try my best."

"You guys can go up." Daniel gives us a smile. "Good luck, though. He's a stress ball."

"Thank you," Hallie says.

As we ascend the second set of stairs, I call, "Jacob?"

"Skylar?" I hear him reply. His voice sounds like an earthquake, which confirms all my worst suspicions.

"I'm here," I say. "So is Hallie. Can we come up?"

"Yeah." When we go into his room, he paces back and forth like a pinball stuck between two of the little pegs off of which they bounce. He's still in his pajamas, his hair sticks up at odd angles, his hands fidget with a mechanical pencil, and he's not breathing so much as hyperventilating. He sees us, drops the pencil, and rushes over. His eyes are nearly black. "Guys—" His breath catches.

I hold my arms out, and he falls into them, burying his head into my shoulder. His whole body shakes. "It's okay. You're okay."

He starts to cry then. I stand there with him, holding him, rubbing his back, trying to make this better in any way possible. Eventually I sit him down on his bed because I'm afraid he's going to collapse, and he's so much taller than me, so I couldn't catch him well enough. Hallie and I sit on either side of him. He keeps his head on my shoulder, so I hold onto him and run my hand over his head. He really can't breathe, and it really freaks me out. I genuinely think he's not getting enough oxygen. I keep reminding him *in, out,* just like he does for me, but he doesn't listen. Not because he doesn't want to, but because he can't.

"I— I've never been this scared in my— my entire life," he says.

"It's okay," I tell him. "We're right here."

"I can't— I can't do this. I just—"

"Jacob. Whatever it is, we can fix it. Think about everything we've fixed before."

"They won't listen. We told them no and they won't listen."

"What happened?"

"Coira."

"What did she do?"

"Everything we told her not to do," he says. "And Treasury authorized it. And it made everything worse. And I don't know what to do."

"Coira went ahead with the plan to get rid of all the bats?" I ask.

"Yeah."

"She said she wouldn't."

"She didn't listen to herself."

"How far did she get?"

"I— I don't know," he says. "Orion texted me and then— then I don't know."

"What a bitch," Hallie says. "I'll handle this."

"No," Jacob says. "Then we'd have to tell her why we don't want her to deal with it."

"We don't have to tell her anything," Hallie says. "She did *not* have Eminence approval, so she shouldn't have done anything. You don't need to give her a reason. She needs to follow your verdict anyway."

"But she doesn't listen," Jacob says. "None of them do. They expect me to lead, and when I do, they don't follow. They say I have to tell them what to do, and when I do, they don't do it. I don't know what to do anymore. I don't know what they want from me."

"Give me ten minutes," Hallie says. "I'll call Anastasia from Treasury and nip that in the bud, and then have a nice chat with Coira."

"You don't have to," Jacob says. "I can handle it."

"No. Stay with Skylar and take some deep breaths and talk about buildings. I'm really good at scaring people." She goes into the other half of the third floor. Before she wanders too far in, I hear her say, "Hi, Anastasia, this is Hallie Giovia, calling on behalf of Eminence Jacob Connelly. I think there's been a misunderstanding with Coira Findlay's request."

"Bubble, it feels like the world is exploding," he says. He rests his head on my lap. I remind my accelerating heart that this isn't the time to blow things out of proportion. "All of it. Just— on fire."

"I know," I say.

"I— I just—" He takes a breath and starts over. "I seriously don't think I can handle this."

"That's not true at all."

"No, it— I have no idea what I'm doing. None."

I realize I've been absentmindedly playing with his hair because my hands need to do something or else I'll chew off my fingernails, but this is absolutely not the time to worry about our superficial suppression of feelings. It doesn't matter right now. Besides, his hair is soft and smells like lavender. "No one ever really knows what they're doing. We're all just at various stages of pretending."

"I should know, though. I should at least have an idea. It's been six months, so I should at least have an idea. And I don't."

"Tell me about the Chrysler Building."

"I— Why?"

"Because you have a little one on your nightstand."

"It's— it's one of the best buildings ever built. It's Art Deco. William Van Alen . . . he designed it. I like the— the loopy things. I don't think they have a real name. Daniel got that for me on his sophomore trip."

"What makes it Art Deco?" I ask.

Although I have absolutely no idea what he's saying, I can tell that it distracts him, so I don't mind it at all. When he can't think of anything else to say about the Chrysler Building, I ask him to tell me about another one.

"You'd like 8 Spruce Street, Bubble," he says. "It's Frank Gehry. It— it's like he froze a waterfall. It looks like your eyes. En-chanting."

Regardless of the situation, I find it very difficult not to read into that.

He proceeds to tell me all about this building I've never seen before. But now, I suppose I don't have to see it—with his descriptions, he might as well have taken me there. I can tell that this method helps him—he seems to be calming down a bit, his sentences slowly become more coherent, and he isn't shaking as much as he was earlier. So when he finishes building that one, I ask him to tell me about another.

"My grandma took us to this library in Concord once. It had this green atrium that went up three stories, and dark wood shelves with hundreds of books. The door was a time machine. The ceiling seems to be a thousand feet high, and it's bright white and has these beams that don't sit at right angles. It's like someone zoomed in on a spiderweb and copied its lattice. Everything is deliberately connected. Like—"

Hallie comes back into the room. "So I talked to— Sorry to interrupt."

"You're fine," Jacob says. He leaves his head in my lap, so I keep playing with his hair. The odds of Hallie caring are very slim. "Who did you talk to?"

"I called Anastasia from Treasury first," Hallie says, hopping onto the window seat next to the Canada goose family. "I asked her if Coira's petition was verified by the Eminences. She, of course, said that they weren't, and I asked a million questions until she broke and admitted that yeah, there's no way that shit's allowed. She canceled the approval and sent Coira back to stage one of the petition process. Even posted on MeetingGround and said that the petition was not approved, contrary to what some people have heard."

"Thank you," Jacob says.

"No problem," Hallie says. "She was pretty easy to talk to. But then I called Coira."

"That must have been wonderful."

"Coira was *pissed* at me," Hallie says, "but what else is new? I told her that if she doesn't have Eminence approval, she doesn't just do whatever she wants anyway. I told her to recuse herself from the bat issue for real this time, focus on something worthwhile, and get Eminence approval if she wants to do something. I also offered to call Eula and tell her what had happened with Treasury, and she didn't seem to want that. I don't know if she'll listen to me, to be honest, but it might shut her up for a little bit, at least."

"Thanks, Hallie," Jacob says.

"Only you could stand up against Coira," I say.

Hallie shrugs. "She's all talk. Really. She has no more power than the rest of us. She's just outspoken. Which isn't a bad thing. Being outspoken is great. But not when you don't have Eminence approval."

Footsteps start to ascend the stairs. Jacob takes his head off my lap but doesn't let go of my hand. Molly pokes her curl-covered head in, the few visible parts of her face almost completely red. "Hi."

"Hi," Jacob says. He holds his breath because he knows Molly will notice his irregular breathing.

She walks into the room, her footsteps almost entirely soundless. Without making eye contact with anyone, she hands Jacob a handful of mini Kit Kat bars. "Mom told me to give you these."

He actually smiles, just a little bit. "Thanks, Molly."

"She also wanted me to tell you that it's okay and not to freak out. And everything will be okay. And Daniel wants his earbuds."

"You're the best."

"Shut up." After turning an even brighter shade of red, she runs over to Daniel's desk, grabs his earbuds, and runs back downstairs.

"My mother thinks chocolate cures everything," Jacob says, unwrapping a Kit Kat.

"She's not wrong," I say. He hands me one without asking if I want one first. He already knows.

"We might need a little more than chocolate to fix this one."

"I'm not sure," Hallie says. "I think we'll be okay."

"Hallie, would you like a Kit Kat?" Jacob asks.

"You know it."

Hallie and I stay a little longer, just to make sure he's okay. Then, when I'm fairly certain he won't spiral again, at least not right now, we leave him to finish (or start) packing his stuff for our journey and sleepover at Hunter's house.

He walks us out, onto his front porch. Hallie bounds down the steps right away and checks out Mr. Connelly's garden gnome, but I linger just a bit longer. So does he.

"Thank you," he says. "For . . . you know. Everything."

"Of course," I say. "Any time. I'll see you later."

"I'll try not to panic until then."

"If you don't succeed, you know where to find me."

"Good to know you have so much faith in me."

"My faith in you is actually quite endless."

"Skylar, come on," Hallie calls from the garden. "I haven't packed, either."

"See you later," I say.

"See you later," he repeats.

"Tell your dad this is a dope gnome," Hallie tells Jacob.

Chapter Eleven

"Nicely Done"
Wild Party

I'm planning on going upstairs and sitting on the floor of my glass room until my brain stops spinning, but as I walk into the house, I hear my mom call, "Skylar!" Judging by her tone of voice, I already know what's coming.

"Yes, Mom?" I go into the living room.

She crosses her arms upon seeing me, and my dad looks up from his book and mimics her. "When were you planning on telling us you were leaving the house?"

"I'm sorry," I say. I could lie, or I could *not* lie. I take the middle path. "Hallie and I just went to Jacob's house to help him with something for math team."

"Jacob needed *math* help?"

"Not with *math* math," I say. "Logistical things. Like running meetings. Making sure all the members are doing what they are supposed to be doing. Harder than it looks."

"Can you tell us where you're going next time? At least leave a note, like you did this morning, if you can't find us?"

"Of course," I say. "I'm sorry."

"When are you heading over to Lexie's?" she asks.

I inwardly sigh in relief—I was sure that she would say I couldn't go anywhere until I learned to tell her my every move. "In an hour-ish."

"And you're sleeping over?"

"Yes."

"And you'll be home Sunday morning?"

"Maybe Sunday afternoon?"

"We have family dinner," Dad reminds me.

They're already on the verge of being angry with me, so it couldn't hurt to ask. "Is there any chance I could skip? I'll be so tired."

"Skip? Family dinner?"

"Yes?"

"We'll talk about it tomorrow," Mom says. "Go make sure you have your things packed."

"Thank you. I'm sorry about leaving without saying something. It won't happen again."

It definitely will happen again.

I double-check my bag, throw in another whale, and—at the very last second—toss in a pair of contacts. I almost never wear my contacts, only during the three or four times a year I go skiing with Harlow and the rest of the Rainers, and that one time Hallie and I tried to learn how to skateboard and both sprained something. They're so old, I don't even know if they're my prescription any-more. But without my glasses, I do look a *tiny* bit older. Maybe actually sixteen instead of my usual eleven.

Hallie's waiting on my front porch at exactly twelve-forty-three. "Ready?" she asks.

"To live out my dream of being in *The West Wing*? Hell yes, I'm ready."

She chuckles and shakes her head, a genuine Hallie Giovia smile sneaking onto her face. "Honestly, if that's the only thing we get out of tonight, it still will have been worth it."

When we get to Hunter's house, Lexie answers the door before Hunter gets there. "Thank God you're here! If I had to wait another second to start getting ready, I might have actually died."

"We're here now," Hallie says. "Wait till you see my dress. Kelsie bought it for her half-boyfriend's prom her junior year—you know, the one who got expelled from that reform school in the city?"

"Ah, Spike," I say. "I remember."

"She never wore it because Spike dumped her, like, three days before reform school prom, and I don't know if she really ever got over it, but I have the dress now, and no attachment to reform school Spike."

"Oh my God, I can *not* wait to see it!" Lexie grabs both of our hands and pulls us into the vestibule. "Come on!"

"Finally, you're here," Hunter calls from the dining room. He, Jacob, and Alex sit at the twelve-person table, eating Lauren's *loukoumades*. "She's been trying to do our makeup for the past ten minutes."

"Don't you think Alex would look good in eyeliner?" Lexie asks.

"Alex, you would look so hot in eyeliner," Hallie says.

"I'll try anything once," Alex says with a shrug.

"Come on come on come on!" Lexie jumps up and down, still holding our hands. She has the grip of a vice. "We have to start getting ready right *now* if we want to be ready by the time we have to leave."

"It's not even one, Lexie," Jacob says. "And we're not leaving until at least four."

"That only gives us three hours! I am *appalled* that you think that's a lot of time to get ready for a *gala*. What kind of Eminence are you?"

"I've been asking myself the same question for six months."

Lexie holds up her duffle bag. "I was so ready for this, I actually packed last night."

"That's dedication," Alex says.

While they're talking, I go over to Jacob. "How are you?" I ask quietly, so only he can hear me.

"I'm fine," he says. "Thank you."

"If there's anything you need, please let me know."

"I'm okay, Bubble," he says. "Really. But I appreciate it."

Lexie turns to Hunter. "You said you know which room we should get ready in?"

"Yeah, I'll show you," Hunter says.

"Give us a tour!" Hallie demands.

"Yeah, Hunter," Alex says. "Give us a tour."

"You've already seen most of it," he says. "This is the dining room. Kitchen's through that secret door. Various living spaces over there."

He leads us up the stairs, not bothering to take us through the fancy-looking parlor or anything that must be behind it. We get to the second floor and stay there, so I can soak in each motion in the wood and fleck in the walls and shimmer in the metalwork. Hunter skips the first door on the right. "My parents' room. Nothing too interesting in there."

"I beg to differ," Jacob says. "They have the coolest judge paneling and a tiled fireplace and an epic chandelier."

"Can you not be weird for one minute?" Hunter opens the next door. "Here's the green bedroom. Usually Lauren stays here when she stays the night, and she'll be here tonight since my parents are still away. It's kinda boring."

"*Boring*?" Lexie repeats. I'm with her on this one. Even if ornate, embossed floral wallpaper isn't your thing, you couldn't deny this selection's intricacy. It's a bit toned down by white wainscoting and light wood furniture, but it certainly is exuberant for such a little room.

Hunter closes that door and opens the next one. "This one is the blue bedroom. It's pretty cool."

It's *really* cool, actually. It has the same white wainscoting as the green bedroom, but on the top, instead of a loud floral, is a delicate, muted periwinkle print. The two twin beds are dressed in fluffy white duvets. Across from the beds is an archaic roll top desk that looks as old as the house itself.

"Jacob and Alex, you'll probably stay in here," Hunter says. "Jacob, everything you've ever left here is in the dresser."

"Which drawer?" Jacob asks.

"All four."

Hunter skips the next door and goes to the one straight across from it. "Hallie, Lexie, Skylar, you guys can stay in here tonight. I think you'll like it. Besides mine, it's the best one."

He's right—this *is* the best one. The walls, embellished with intricate band molding, are a jubilant lavender. Gossamer white curtains flutter beside both of the giant paned windows. A fireplace takes up one whole corner; two chairs and a little table sit in front of it. But the best part: It has built-in bunkbeds. One wall has four beds subtracted from it and a little staircase running up the middle. Each bed has its own glass sconce and poofy purple bedspread.

"All my girl cousins stay in this room when they come for the summer," Hunter explains. "They nearly kill each other over who gets the top bunks."

"I call a top bunk," I say.

"Me, too," Lexie says.

"Not fair," Hallie complains.

"You have a loft bed," Alex points out. "You sleep elevated every night."

Hallie sighs. "Fine. You have a point."

"Which one's your room?" Lexie asks Hunter.

"Across the hall," Hunter says. "But it's not that interest-ing, so we—"

"Of *course* we have to see it!" Lexie protests. "You've seen all of our rooms. I'm to the point where I don't even clean it before you guys come over anymore."

"There was a point where you *did* clean it?" Jacob asks. Lexie elbows him.

"I mean, I guess, if you want," Hunter says. "Don't judge me." We cross the hall and go into his room.

Instead of white wainscoting and molding like the other three rooms we've seen, Hunter's is all dark, rich wood. The rest of the walls are deep—hunter, if you will—green. His desk is an absolute disaster—I can't even see it under all the stuff piled on top of it. Clothes litter the floor, his bed is unmade, and the books on his colossal bookshelf aren't in alphabetical order by last name of author. There is, however, a fire in his fireplace, a meticulous shelf of labeled rocks, and two cushy armchairs draped in thick woven blankets. It feels like we've stepped into the quarters of a tortured British writer from the late nineteenth century.

"I'm not neat," Hunter says.

"Couldn't tell." Hallie picks a granola bar wrapper off the ground.

Hunter picks up a pile of green uniform polos and khakis and throws them into a hamper. "I wasn't expecting company, or else I might have neatened up a bit."

Jacob crosses his arms. "Really."

"Really!" Hunter protests.

"How were you *not* expecting company?" Alex says. "You had, like, three days to get ready."

"I wasn't expecting people in *here.* And I'm a procrastin-ator."

"You are quite correct on the latter front." Orion appears in the doorway. "Welcome, everyone. Jacob, Alex, shall I show you the tuxedos you will wear tonight? They're just up a flight of stairs, in my bedroom."

"Okay," Alex says. "Good luck getting ready, girls." He and Jacob follow Orion, with Hunter close behind.

Hallie, Lexie, and I go back to the purple room.

"Can you even *believe* this?" Lexie cries, twirling around the purple room like a dizzy ballerina. "This is the coolest bedroom *ever.* Look at those beds!"

"They are quite awesome." I take the ladder up to the top bunk. "Hello, down there."

Hallie and Lexie clamber up the ladder and join me. "Can this one bunk hold three of us?" Hallie asks.

"It seems to be doing okay," Lexie replies, but she shifts across the staircase to the other bunk anyway. "Now can we *please* start getting ready? I cannot *wait* to do your makeup."

"I wasn't planning on wearing any makeup," I say. "I just brought some lip gloss."

"Oh, hell no," Lexie says. "I brought all of mine—and I mean *all* of mine—so I can do both of your makeup. And there's no arguing. I even brought my sister's foundation and concealer because I knew mine wouldn't match your skin tones."

"Does Nari know about that?" I ask.

"No, and she doesn't need to," Lexie replies.

"I'm down," Hallie says. "Usually the twins do my makeup since I'm shit at it, but I clearly couldn't ask them for this."

"Yay!" Lexie claps her hands and turns to me. "Come on, Sky, it'll be awesome!"

"Fine," I say. "But nothing extreme."

I climb down the ladder and then notice that Orion left my dress hanging on the door to the bathroom. I go over to it.

"Oh my God, that dress is a daydream," Lexie says. "It must be Delia's, and she just keeps it in here."

"Actually, it isn't Delia's," I say. "It's mine."

Lexie came with everything we could possibly need to get ready, including things I A) didn't think we would need and B) didn't know existed. She even brought a speaker so we can jam out as we get ready. Her playlist may be the audible equivalent of a sugar high, but it manages to succeed in hyping us up.

"Oh my God, Hallie, please try on this lipstick," Lexie says, shoving a tube into Hallie's hand.

"It's a little pink for me," Hallie says.

"With your dress," I say, "it'll be perfect."

"Foundation first, though," Lexie reminds her before she puts it on. "And eye makeup and blush and highlight. Lips are last. Have your sisters taught you nothing?"

"I just let them attack my face," Hallie admits with a shrug.

"Can I attack your face, then?" Lexie asks, too eager for us not to laugh at.

"If you want to, go ahead," Hallie says.

I watch, intrigued, as Lexie paints Hallie's face. My goodness, am I a terrible girl for not knowing how to do any of this? I can apply lipgloss and chapstick (though lipstick has too much color for me so I tend to shy away from it), and that's literally it. Lexie is an actual artist when it comes to this stuff.

She and Hallie are both so beautiful, it's insane. Forget princesses—they're actual goddesses.

"Skylar," Lexie says, "it's your turn."

"I don't know," I say, suddenly wary. "I think I'll be okay with my lipgloss."

"This is a *gala*, Sky! Lipgloss won't cut it!"

"Yeah, come on, Skylar," Hallie says. "It'll be fun."

"Just a little bit," I say. "Nothing too intense. Do the equivalent of riding a bike with the training wheels on, please."

"Okay," Lexie says, "but we have to take *some* risks."

"My dress is a risk in itself, Lexie. I would be fine if you made my face the least noticeable you could."

"Hell no. Red lipstick—"

"Absolutely not."

"Skylar, it'll look so good on you," Hallie says. "Seriously!"

"Yeah, Sky, you have to!" Lexie adds.

"Lips are last," I remind her.

She laughs and starts my foundation. It takes her a lot longer to do mine than it did for Hallie's because I keep flinching and making her mess up.

"Now for blush," she says.

"I don't need blush," I tell her. "Give it five minutes, I'll step on a congressperson's foot, and I'll have a nice healthy glow for the rest of the night."

She doesn't listen to me and applies it anyway. Next, she does highlight, which just makes your face sparkly, which is quite possibly my favorite thing ever. Seriously, where has this been all my life? I could have spent every day with a sparkly face, and no one told me?

"Eye time," Lexie says.

"Eye makeup with glasses is pointless," I say. "No one can see it, and it just smudges the inside of your lenses, and the whole thing is just a mess."

"Did you bring your contacts?" Hallie asks.

Lexie throws her hands to her heart. "Skylar Rawlings has *contacts*?"

"Only for emergencies," I say.

"This qualifies as an emergency. My *God*, this is the biggest emergency ever!"

I sigh. "They're at the bottom of my bag."

It takes me several tries to get them into my eyes, Hallie and Lexie over each shoulder, cheering me along. Six hours later, they're in, and I *really* don't think they're my current prescription. A headache feels imminent. Lexie pounces on my eyes almost immediately.

Hallie uses her own curling iron to pull her hair into a mass of strawberry curls, and she pins it away from her face with a series of silver barrettes. Since Lexie's leaving her hair as is, she works on mine, going off of nothing but a black-and-white printed-out-from-the-library picture of Audrey Hepburn.

"You can thank Alex for this inspiration," Lexie says as she yanks at my hair. I try to fight my instinct to swat her hand away, but it does happen a few times. "He found the picture and everything. And he didn't even see your dress yet!"

"Lucky guess," I say.

It takes her over a half-hour, but when she's done, I don't even look like myself. All my hair is pulled atop my head in a series of braids and twists, held together by at least fifty bobby pins. (That is no exaggeration. I honestly think there are fifty bobby pins in my head.) Two tiny pin curls fall just behind my ears like kite tails. My goodness, I look like a princess.

"You're a fairy godmother," I tell Lexie.

"That is the best compliment I could ever hope to get." She smiles and hugs my shoulders. "Now, red lipstick?"

"I don't know," I say. "Lipstick seems very intense. Especially red."

"With your dress?" Lexie's hands fly to her hips. "You *need* red lipstick. That is non-negotiable."

"What if it smears?"

"Tell Jacob to bring some baby wipes, and it should come off of him just fine."

"Lexie!"

She laughs. "You were right. You really didn't need any blush." She puts the lipstick on me without a second's hesitation.

Hallie claps and cheers when she sees my hair and makeup completely done. "Is it dress time?"

"Hell yeah, it's dress time."

Lexie immediately runs over to her bag and withdraws an evergreen dress. She picks it up, skirt swishing towards the floor, and I realize that the entire thing is coated in covert, subtle sparkles. It is not a disco ball but an icicle: dangerously blinding. The skirt starts off nearly black where it touches the floor, becoming lighter and lighter like a sunrise until, at the tips of her shoulders, emerges a vivacious emerald.

Hallie drifts in a rose garden of lace and organza. The dress centers her in a pink meadow floating on a cloud of whispered pink and intricate roses that dance across her skirt and up her body. The neckline's convoluted lace twists around her collarbone and almost disappears entirely, melting into her until she is just another flower in the fallow. I wouldn't expect something so delicate of her, but it suits her perfectly.

And then there's mine. The neckline falls off my shoulders in two dramatic swaths. It cinches right below that, just above my belly button, before cascading down to my feet like snowfall. When I turn, the dress responds, fluttering around me as if I had my own flock of butterflies comprising my skirt. My favorite part: It is unapologetically red.

I don't wear red. I don't think I own anything red. It's so . . . *there*. It usually makes my skin look pink or it brings out weird tones in my hair or doesn't help the mess of my eyes, but when I slipped into the dress in Jessamine's apartment, all I could hear in my mind was *yes*. I'm supposed to be someone else for the night anyway, so why not commit to being someone else?

We twirl until we're dizzy and sing until our throats hurt, and I manage to forget about everything going on behind the door to the purple bedroom. Who decided that thwarting a global food shortage had to be serious? Why can't we smile as we save the world? It's supposed to be happy, keeping the economy from tanking and people from starving.

There's a knock at the door. "Are you guys almost ready?" Alex calls from the other side.

"Go away!" Hallie shouts. Lexie and I burst out laughing.

"We're supposed to be on a secret mission!"

"So?"

"We're leaving with or without you."

"Without, then," Lexie says.

Alex eventually gives up. "Just meet us downstairs when you're ready."

"So, never, then," Lexie says, and we burst out laughing again.

We do, however, attempt to clean up our mess and give each other final touches before going downstairs. I'm so, *so* happy I spent so much time rehearsing for the musical in my heels—they don't seem to affect my walking at all. Even on the stairs. And in contacts, too, when everything looks like it has six dimensions and colors look like someone bumped the saturation all the way up on Photoshop. I'm pretty proud of myself for not collapsing by now.

The boys wait for us at the bottom of the stairs, and when they see us coming, their conversation drops and hits the floor with a shatter. It's like they've never seen girls in dresses before. Though I can understand that maybe—

Who in God's name allowed Jacob Connelly to wear a tuxedo?

My eye catches his, and I swear on my life, that should be illegal. He should be forced to wear a tie-dye potato sack and Crocs at all hours of the day, lest someone be horribly thrown off their game and forget every play in their masterplan. I can't even look at him. But he's like a lit flame in a pitch black room—I physically cannot pull my gaze away.

"Your glasses are gone," he says.

"They're in my eyes," I reply. "Contacts, I mean. I'm wearing contacts. I didn't stick my normal glasses into my eyes. That would hurt."

"I kind of guessed that much," he says, a dangerous smile surfacing on his face. Is it going to be like this all night? It better not be, or else this entire plan might fall apart. Surely, he can't expect me to stay focused if he looks like this. His eyes are far too brown and his hair is far too on-purposely messy for my brain to work.

"I like your suit," I say. As if that does anything to help the situation or to remove me from it.

"I like your dress," he replies. "I didn't know you knew what the color red was."

"Only when it's in my best interest to recognize it as part of the spectrum."

"Are you two coming?" Alex says from the vestibule. Only then do I realize that everyone else has already gone outside.

"Yes," I say. "Just let me double-check my purse." Phone, wallet, school ID, vial of vinegar, small plastic dinosaur (diplodocus), jar of ibuprofen, pocket-sized narwhal notebook. "Okay, I'm good."

"Are you taller?" Jacob asks me.

"By three inches." I put my coat on and start towards the door. "Are you ready?"

"Bubble, you're a princess."

I turn back and try to glare at him, but I end up smiling instead since my mouth so rarely likes to listen to my brain. "We're going to be late."

Chapter Twelve

Don't spend your money
on a broken jar of honey, man.
It's sweet,
but it sure won't last you long.

"Relimerance"
The Happy Fits

"Our first black-tie event," Hallie says, "and we're taking a freaking mini van."

"This was the vehicle we had at our disposal that could safely and legally transport the seven of us," Orion says from the driver's seat.

"It smells like old milk."

"I do apologize for the ancient dairy odor," Orion says. "Regardless of how many times this car has been detailed, the milk scent remains."

"It'll go away in a bit," Hunter says from the front passenger seat. "You'll become nose-blind in another five minutes or so."

We've only been in the car for fifteen minutes at most, so we still have a long way to go, but I'm already ready to get out of the car. I'm squished between Jacob and Lexie, which is so far from being the best situation. Lexie dances to whatever song comes on and tends to elbow me in the arm, and being next to Jacob is abject torture. I keep *trying* not to look at him, and I'm very sure he's trying not to glance my way, so I end up forcing myself not to look to my right for any reason, and his hand keeps accidentally brushing mine and vice versa, and the whole thing is just horribly awkward. I don't know who picked this seating arrangement, but I blame Hallie and Alex. They took the back-backseats, contently sharing memes and giggling. They only *giggle* when they're together.

"Has anyone visited the town of Redway before?" Orion asks. My God, even Orion looks good in a tux, as much as that pains me to say. It brings out his blacklight and makes his white shirt turn purple.

"No," Alex calls from the back. "Never heard of it until we started chilling with Everett."

"I did some research on our destination before departing," Orion says, "and I learned some extremely fun facts if you would like me to share."

"No," everyone says at once.

"If you've all elected *not* to learn something new today, that is fine by me," Orion says.

I imagine driving through Central New York is beautiful in the springtime or the summer, when the rolling hills look like emeralds and the trees undulate like an ocean, or in the fall, when everything is on fire. Now, all the trees are dormant, and I suppose it's pretty because it isn't. It's a tentative graveyard. Only half-committed to death.

"Let's play a game!" Lexie says.

"Lexie, I swear to God," Hallie says.

"I'll play a game with you, Lexie," I say. If it means I don't have to look to my right, then I'm down.

"I will, too, Lexie," Alex says.

"A game sounds most delightful!" Orion says.

"Did you bring spies?" Jacob asks Hunter.

"No," Hunter says. "I didn't even think to bring spies. I should have brought spies. I've never been more upset with myself."

"We could play Alphabet Soup," Lexie suggests.

"No," the rest of us say at once.

"What is Alphabet Soup?" Orion asks.

"Something we will never do again," Hunter says. "Never."

"It was like communism," Hallie says. "A fantastic idea in theory, and a shit show in modern practice."

"I had another nightmare about Alphabet Soup only last week," I say.

"I'm calling a motion with an override next Meeting to globally ban Alphabet Soup," Jacob says.

"It was fun!" Lexie claims.

"Nothing about that travesty was *fun*," Hallie says. "I'd take a blunt knife in the side over Alphabet Soup."

"I would quite like to play," Orion says.

"You need both your hands, feet, and elbows to drive," Hunter says. "You couldn't play anyways."

"And we don't have a dictionary," I say.

"We can just use someone's phone," Lexie says.

"That's how the first fistfight broke out."

"I thought the first was the use of *clementine*," Hallie says.

"No, that was way later," Jacob says. "At least third."

"Sing the song about all the cartons of milk," Hunter says. "That's less painful than Alphabet Soup."

"I mean, I'll agree, Lexie," Alex says. "It was kinda cool to see all your brains working in hyperspeed."

"What a waste," Hallie says. "Of any time, especially the fast kind."

"I love how they'll be nice and fast during games, but not during math tests or the PSATs," Lexie says.

"Very helpful, I know," Jacob says. "I was at church for four days last Sunday. I shit you not. Four days."

"There's no way to control that?" Alex asks.

"No," Hallie responds. "God, I wish there were. That'd be freaking awesome."

"Like Doctor Strange," Jacob says. "That would be so cool."

"I believe it to be possible," Orion says. "With enough practice, if your mind is strong enough, and perhaps your genetics allow for it."

"Can you do it?" Hunter asks him.

"No," he replies. "I cannot. I would be telling a fib if I implied that I haven't tried, however. I have, out of sheer curiosity."

"Did it ever work?" Lexie asks.

"No," Orion says. "It never did. But that is completely understandable. Time is no one's mistress, though we may attempt to court her and fool ourselves into believing we have won her hand."

"Orion, you need to stop," Hunter says. "Seriously. You make people uncomfortable."

"I only mean to say that time allows us just enough control to lead us into a false sense of security," Orion says. "When you teach a dog to sit, it still does not know how to roll over or let you shake its paw. When you teach a child to read, they still cannot write. When you determine how you could reach the stars, you still must build the rocket ship. The Knowers have taught time how to ring the bell on the door handle when it wants to go outside and not much else. Time is not interested in learning things."

"Aren't we interested in learning, though?" Jacob asks. "That must count for something."

"Well, of course we are," Orion says. "Most humans are. Time is not human."

"Neither are dogs, and some of them are pretty interested in learning how to roll over when there are treats and belly rubs."

"Time has no interest in treats," Orion says, "and you cannot rub its belly."

I don't agree with Orion. (Then again, I rarely do.) If time had no interest in knowledge, it would work better. See, people seem to think that time is some linear thing. A double-page spread in a history textbook with interesting dates in chronological order on a line with thumbnail pictures and vocabulary words in bold. Maybe to some people, it works like that, at least in their perceptions. But time is not a line. It isn't a spiderweb. It's liquid. Moves in a thousand directions at once, trillions of atoms with a connection so weak to other atoms around it that they will slide past each other in an instant and never see each other again. Dictated by nothing but itself, it forms limitless arrangements. It is unpredictable. Irrational. Sporadic and impulsive and serendipitous.

Time doesn't work for Knowers because unlike most, we see it for what it is. That rhythmic ticking can't deceive us.

It isn't interested in learning how to deceive us.

The Athan brothers are horrible at navigating and even worse at cooperating. I'm so glad we left a half-hour early, since we circle the town of Redway maybe three whole times before we even find the right street, which is Main Street, straight through the center of the town. The two of them argue in Greek in the front seat, and the rest of us, knowing that we're doing okay on time, collectively and silently decide to sit back and watch, stifling our laughter. We pass the Princess Alice Hotel once, and we don't point it out, seeing if Hunter or Orion might notice, but neither of them do.

"How long do you think we'll circle the town?" I whisper to Jacob.

"With the way these two fight?" he whispers back. "Maybe forever."

"That wouldn't surprise me," I say.

"It would be faster if we got out and walked."

"I would consider it if I didn't find this so amusing." I gesture to the two of them bickering in front of us.

We pass the Princess Alice Hotel twice more before Hunter finally sees it. He looks to Orion and shouts, "You said it was blue!"

"I believed it to be blue," Orion replies.

"Look at that building and tell me it's blue."

"Perhaps it's been painted."

"In the past thirty minutes?"

Orion has to find a parking spot, which sends the two of them off in Greek again. But he manages to find one, thankfully, so that we're technically here before the sun has completely set.

"Okay," I say. "We're going with Plan A first. It should be infallible, as long as everyone remembers their targets." I take my mini narwhal notebook from my purse and give it to Lexie. "You can pass this around and review if you need to. If we haven't gotten where we need to be by eight-forty-five, we transition to Plan A-point-five. Anyone can call transitioning into Plan B if someone says something suspicious. You hear the word 'Knower,' and we drop everyone but Darcy Brecken."

"When do we employ the contingency plan?" Hunter holds up his tiny silver handgun. Goosebumps crawl across my arms and bile splashes in the back of my throat.

"If someone else shoots first."

"Alright, let's go, team!" Orion says.

"Don't call us *team*," Hallie says.

"Gang? Group? Compatriots?"

"Orion, please turn off the child locks," Jacob says.

The Princess Alice Hotel looks like a daydream amid a wash of beige. Redway is far from an interesting town—all of these buildings are tan concrete boxes with neon-lit lettering, selling the same things as their neighbors. The Princess Alice must have been transplanted; either that, or she stood here and watched her neighbors die. It's Victorian, like everything back on our island, but somehow more ostentatious. Maybe because it's so foreign to the rest of the street, or because it looks like home to me, or because people just spent a ton of time on each detail. Still, it could use some help— scarlet paint flakes off the clapboard siding, parts of the veranda's trim have snapped off, the glass of the windows has scratched, some mosaic tiles have chipped. Though, in a haunting sort of way, I like her more because she's disheveled. I like her fortitude. Although her crown has slipped, she stands as regally as if it hasn't.

Fortunately for us, it seems we've picked the perfect time to arrive—we swim into the building among a school of bright silky gowns and dashing tuxedos, and no one pays us too much notice. They'll deal with whom they know first and then move on to strangers.

The current guides us through the main lobby, past a tearoom, beyond a row of golden picture frames. It's all too much too fast too all at once for me to catalogue anything to remember for later, and when we emerge into a ballroom, all other minutia falls away. We are in a *ballroom*. Like, a princess-level, gold-leafed, azure-tiled, airy, ebullient ballroom. I feel my own pulse to make sure I'm still alive. Yes, I think so, but this surely must be a dream. Places like this only exist in storybooks.

Though it may be a bit mean, this is the only coherent thought I have: What on earth is a room like this doing in Redway?

"Should we disperse?" Hallie asks.

"Hush," I say. "I am having a moment."

"Jesus, Skylar."

"Let her have her moment," Alex says.

For only a second, or for what I perceive to be one, I close my eyes and listen, to fifty pairs of high heels clicking like telegrams against the tile, coughs and chuckles and effusions that fall somewhere in between, chairs shrieking as they're scraped across the floor, distressed clinks of glasses, and voices. So many voices. So many conversations to peer into, autopsy, and probe for information. Anyone at any time could say something that could become the reason we came. What if they say it and we aren't there to catch it? How on earth do we stretch seven pair of ears across a group of a hundred-fifty people?

If we need it, it will find us. Information finds Knowers like pollen finds a bee—if it is your purpose for being, then your paths will cross. The universe isn't cruel like that; it won't let you circle a garden until you hit the grass without finding a single flower. Rather, it's cruel like this: It has no qualms about suffocating you. There's so much pollen that all you can see and breathe is gold dust. It fills your lungs eventually. You know too much.

This is not actually that different than our usual gig, if you disregard the costumes. We're illusionists, fluent in manipulation and sycophancy. Look at a person and see what you can learn from them now or get from them later. Take their phone number and their email now, and bring it to the hive and turn it into honey later.

I shouldn't feel guilty. Everyone here is a gilded sycophant. Bees flirting with flowers.

I open my eyes.

You're definitely in the right dress.

"Okay. Disperse."

Chapter Thirteen

"Wicked World"
Matt Jaffe

Hallie and Alex take off in one direction, towards the left of the ballroom, where they'll try to find some soybean farmers. Their job is to feel out who knows about what's happening in Brazil, see firsthand what farmers might do in a situation like this, and have a lot of conversations about pesticides. They're hoping to have a solid short-term solution drafted by the end of the night.

Lexie and Hunter go in the opposite direction, attempting to find people who can find us some funding for intervention in Brazil, and for an expanded arts program in Redway schools for Carson Sloane in exchange for the endorsement he gave Everett.

Orion's off doing his own thing, networking for future projects or dilemmas. There are a lot of politicians here, and Knowers never know who we might need as a pawn in some future game, so we tend to recruit them wherever we go.

Jacob and I have two targets—Everett Caldwell and Darcy Brecken, president of the New York Corn and Soybean Growers Association. If there's anyone in this building who can help with knowledge, or with funding, or with contacts to more people with knowledge or funding, it's Darcy. I studied her picture on the NYCSGA website and tried to envision her with her hair down and black-tie apparel donned, but she seemed inextricable from her plaid shirt and strangled braid.

Let it be known that I did not intentionally choose to work with Jacob. I just knew I needed an Eminence at my side and would choose him over Orion for literally any reason. Had I known how much of a distraction he'd pose in that tux, I might have done this by myself. But regardless of anything superficial, we work together pretty well. That is, when we actually manage to work together. Jury's still out on how well this will work.

"Everett first," I tell Jacob. "He'll make it easier to find Darcy, and I have a few questions for him anyway."

"About his weird campaign mail outside his district?" he clarifies.

"Yes," I say. "And to check his progress on the removal of Cécile Kettering."

"I forgot about Cécile," he says.

"Me, too," I say. "She's slippery like that. It's dangerous."

"I am so not used to you being this tall."

"I should wear heels all the time. Especially if it makes you this uncomfortable."

We circle the room once and a half before I even spot Everett. As expected, he's completely surrounded by people. He's the sun, after all, and we're all just planets caught in his orbit. At least that's what he appears to think. Whether or not that's true has yet to be determined. I haven't been here long enough.

"Do we just go talk to him?" Jacob asks.

"I don't see why not," I reply. "Everyone else does. What do you think?"

"I trust your judgement."

"As you should."

Everett and his wife Luciana chat lightly with whoever passes by them. Fortunately for us, we can tiptoe up and pass by them. Once we reach them, I say, "Hello, Mr. Caldwell. And Mrs. Caldwell, I presume, it's a pleasure to meet you."

"Hello, Skylar," Everett says. I'll give him credit—he masks his annoyance quite well. I guess that's a necessary skill for a politician to have. "Hello, Skylar's date."

"He isn't my date," I say.

"I'm not her date," Jacob says.

"This is Jacob Connelly. He's my . . . he works with me."

"It's very nice to meet you, Skylar and Jacob," Luciana Caldwell says. "I *love* your dress, Skylar."

"Thank you," I say, genuinely smiling. She says it as if she means it, not as if it were small talk. I look back to Everett. "Is now a good time for us to discuss a few things?"

"No," he replies. "There will never be a good time for us to discuss things. I have actual people to talk to."

"Hear her out," Luciana tells her husband. With a huff, he obliges.

"Why did you send campaign mail to people multiple districts over?" I ask.

He gives me a confused look. "Why would I do that?"

"I don't know. That's why I asked you."

"I didn't send mail to anyone but the people in my district."

"I know of at least two families in Mary-Grace Carressy's district who received campaign mail from you."

"That's impossible," Luciana says. "How would Everett's mail end up there?"

My God, they like to turn questions around. "I wish I could answer that," I say.

"It must have just been a mailing mistake," Everett says.

"Two mistakes?" I ask. "At the very least?"

"We'll look into it," Luciana assures me. She reaches out and touches my forearm, and once again, I believe her. Maybe it's the sincerity in her intricate hazel eyes, or the firm line into which her mouth sets, or the slight, nearly imperceptible nod of her head, but something makes me believe her.

"Thank you," I say. "It's more curiosity than anything. Mr. Caldwell, have you come across Mrs. Brecken yet this evening?"

"Just spoke with her maybe ten minutes ago," Everett says. "So unless she got sick of me and left already, she should be here." He chuckles as if he were funny.

I play along and chuckle, too, and it sounds pretty convincing, I won't deny. I'm getting quite good at this. Maybe I should go into politics, too. "Would it be too much trouble to ask for an introduction?"

"Oh, I would be happy to introduce you," Luciana says. "I haven't seen Darcy in much too long. Everett, you can stay here and wish our guests the best, and welcome them for me, too. I'll help these kids find Darcy."

"Sounds good," Everett says. "Thank you for coming," he says to Jacob and me in lieu of a dismissal, and Luciana leads us away.

"Darcy likes to hide somewhere up front when people come in." Luciana says this through the side of her mouth, as if it were esoteric information and we should be so lucky to be privy to it. It makes me smile, just a bit, to see someone so excited about something seemingly so mundane. "She likes to see who comes to these things without anyone seeing her."

"That would make sense," I say. "To see to whom you'd like to talk."

"Or whom you should avoid," Luciana says with a giggle.

Even as the crowd gets thicker as more people trickle in, it proves easy to pick Luciana apart from the crowd. Her taffeta grape popsicle gown sticks out regardless of whom she stands near, and the miles of mahogany hair piled atop her head has yet to be surpassed by any other guest. She's beautiful, of course, but it's not that difficult to be beautiful at an event that requires it. Luciana is enchanting. She says hello to nearly everyone we pass, gently touching people on their shoulders as if she's known them her whole life and complimenting their appearances, meaning it wholeheartedly every time. It saddens me momentarily when this thought pops into my head: She makes a wonderful accessory for any congressman.

"Ah, there she is!" Luciana says. "Straight ahead, guys!" She follows this with another giggle before she turns to Darcy Brecken with her arms flung open like a butterfly. The two women hug and kiss before Luciana turns back to us. "Darcy, this is Skylar and Jacob, and they would love to talk to you."

"Talk to *me*?" Darcy throws a hand to her heart. "My goodness, aren't they just the two cutest things to walk planet Earth!"

"Thank you, Mrs. Brecken," I say. "And thank you, Mrs. Caldwell, for helping us find her."

"Of course," Luciana says with a wink. Somehow, she doesn't make it unnerving or tacky. Just instinctual, as if this interaction were nothing more than another secret for her heart to guard. "I have to get back to Everett, but it was wonderful to meet you both. Thank you for coming." She's absorbed back into the crowd, but she doesn't disappear. I track her amethyst gown all the way back to Everett.

"Well!" Darcy exclaims, a smile appearing on her face as quickly as a firefly. In her nearly golden gown, graying blonde hair tangling down her neck, and blinding green eyes drawn out by emerald jewelry, she *is* a firefly. Outrageous, jubilant, a little bit jarring, but she strikes something comforting in your heart, like lemonade on a hot summer day, or a flash of daylight in a fit of darkness. Refreshing, I suppose. "It is *so* nice to meet you two! We *never* have kids come to these things, which is why they are so darn *boring*. It's too wonderful to see youthful faces here. Though by the looks of you, I'd say you can't even vote yet!"

"No, not yet," I say.

"Two more years," Jacob adds.

"But we would like to talk to you about a few things."

"Well, sweeties, I'm all ears." She takes a seat at the table behind her, and we follow suit. "Shoot me."

"We know that you're the president of the New York Association of Corn and Soybean Growers," I say.

"Right I am," Darcy replies. "For seven whole years now. A darn blessing, that is."

"How did you get involved?" Jacob asks. "It seems like such an interesting job."

"You are right on the nose, Jacob," Darcy says. Luciana only said our names once, so I'm pretty impressed that she remembered. I can only imagine how many names swim around her head. "Well, you see, my mama and daddy were farmers, and their parents before them, and even their parents before them! Long line of farmers in my clan. My husband is a soybean farmer still, working on passing the business down to my daughters and son. And I get to work for NYCSGA! Great way to make farmer voices heard, it is, and I get to meet all sorts of people from around the state and help 'em get the stuff they need."

"Are you familiar with any soybean growers outside the state?" Jacob asks.

"Well, of course, I've met a bunch over the years," Darcy replies. "Can't say any are dear friends, but I do have quite a few acquaintances in some of our sister states."

"So, if I may ask so bluntly," I say, "are you aware of the troubles going on with farmers in Brazil?"

Something shifts in her face, ever so slightly. I can't exactly put my finger on it: maybe the color, maybe the expression, maybe just her aura. "Dear me. Troubles? With soybeans? Oh no."

Jacob and I explain what's going on with the bats, and how that's leading to more bugs and fewer crops. "We're already seeing an increase in soy prices," I conclude, "and we're wondering if you have any inclination to intervene."

"My gosh." Both of Darcy's hands fly to her heart. "Oh, I hate to hear stuff like that. Farms failing, people losing their livelihoods, all those poor plants getting demolished. A true shame, that is. Dear me."

"I'm sorry to have to share such upsetting news," I say. "But we could really use your help, or at the very least your guidance."

"Sweeties, I wish I could do more," Darcy says, throwing her hands up, almost in surrender. "But it's so hard to deal with unions outside the country, and I don't know the first thing about growing soybeans in the climate down there, and I'm stretched so thin in our state as it is."

"Well, if something similar were to happen in New York State, how would you go about solving it?" I ask.

"I can't believe you young kids are even concerned about something like this," Darcy says. "You should be worried about your schoolwork and spending time with your friends, not farmers in Brazil."

"We have time to worry about all three, Mrs. Brecken," Jacob replies. I try to ignore the little grin he gives her, lest I'm thrown off again and jeopardize the entire operation. He's too cute for my own good. "So, since we've already got this on our plate, how do you think it should be handled? Do you know of any other resources we could try to obtain, or of anyone we could get in touch with, or where we could find someone who knows anything about bats or pesticides?"

"You two are too much," Darcy says, laughing to herself. "If most kids were half as dedicated as you two— well, then, we wouldn't live in *this* world, now would we?" She digs through her purse for a bit, but she pops back up and says, "You have anything I could write something down on?"

"Yes," I say, taking out my narwhal notebook and a pen. I open the notebook to a page towards the back so she won't see any of the other strange things I have written in there, because then she'll *really* get suspicious of us.

"Thank you, sweetie." She scribbles down three phone numbers and a Sharonsville address before handing it back to me. "Top one's mine. Next one's for a man you might be able to talk to about bats. Last number is for a woman called Cécile Kettering."

"Cécile?" I say.

"Yeah," Darcy says. "Real pretty French name, with the fancy accent and everything. She's the representative one district over. She's got a lot of soybean farmers in her midst, too, so she might be able to help, or at least have an idea or two for you. She could be here at this gala tonight, but I can't say for sure. She and Everett don't get along much."

"Why not?" Jacob asks.

"Oh, you know," Darcy says. "Politics this and politics that. They think Central New York should be run like two different places. I try not to get involved in all that gunk. Do what's best for me and my farmers, and you get my vote."

"I see," I say. "And you think Cécile is here."

"Have yet to see her with my own eyes, but she did get an invitation. Luciana invites all the reps from neighboring districts to these shindigs. Courtesy, you know."

"Of course," I say. "And the address? What's that?"

"That's mine. You two'd better send me Christmas cards this season!"

"Of course," I repeat. I'll consider it, definitely. She seems like the type to tape a cardboard evergreen to her pantry door and hang Christmas cards from it like ornaments. And I'll bet she has an extensive porcelain Christmas village, too. "Thank you for your help, Mrs. Brecken."

"Any time, sweeties," she says. "Now, you two listen to me good. Don't you try to grow up too fast, you hear? You don't need to be poking around in all this. All this stuff—the hardship, the arguing, all the people being mean to each other—that's all for grown-ups. Be kids a bit longer."

"Thank you, Mrs. Brecken," I say.

"We'll try our best," Jacob says.

If only anything she said was actually true.

"So?" Jacob asks once we're on the opposite side of the ballroom than Darcy Brecken. "You think she'll actually be any help?"

"I was expecting her to already have been of more use," I admit, "but I'm having my doubts that we'll get much more from her tonight."

"There are a lot more people here," he says. "If she wasn't the one, maybe someone else can help."

"But she *should* be," I say. "She should care, don't you think?"

"Yeah," he says. "I thought she'd have more ideas. Though we did get her phone number, which counts for something. We can call her later when she's less distracted."

"Yes, she's probably just distracted." I gaze out over the party. "There are quite a few distractions here." I try very hard not to glance over to him when I say that, but I fail miserably.

"That is true," he says. I think (maybe hope) he looks in my direction, but I can't be sure. "We'll have to call her another time and talk to her when she can actually think."

"The problem with that," I say, "is I'm afraid we don't have a lot of time. How many bats died yesterday alone?"

"Six-thousand, four hundred, by Paraná Wildlife Preservation's latest count," he says. "Glaucia emailed me again before we left."

"A few more days of numbers like that, and the problem could become irreversible," I say.

"We're well on our way."

There's a tap on my shoulder. I jump a little bit and turn to see a woman, gauzy blue dress fanned around her as if it were made of nothing but translucent air. Dark, cylindrical curls cascade down her back as if she were a painting. No one's hair should behave that well.

"You're Skylar Rawlings," Cécile Kettering says.

Huh. I can't say I was expecting that to happen. I don't like when unexpected things happen. "And you're Cécile Kettering."

"I wasn't expecting you to be so small."

"I'm sorry to disappoint you."

She drily chuckles. "You didn't. I'm impressed." She looks to Jacob next. "You know what your girlfriend's been up to?"

"I'm not his girlfriend," I cut in.

"She's not my girlfriend," Jacob says, "but yes, I know, like, seventy percent of what she gets up to."

"Maybe sixty," I say.

"Everett told me that some kids thought I shouldn't run for reelection, even recommended I don't finish the term." Cécile tilts her head a bit to make up for the fact that she has to lift both eyebrows. (I feel you, Cécile.) "Something about not connecting with the youth. Which I have no reason to do. My district is sinfully geriatric. I'd thank gerrymandering for that if it were something to be thankful for."

"There's always a little youth in a district," I say.

"Well, I'm not running again anyway."

"Oh," I say. I didn't know that. I hate when I don't know things. "May I ask why?"

"I'm bored with Congress," she says. "Nothing interesting seems to happen."

"In . . . in federal government?"

"After this term, I'm retiring," she says. "It's been almost eighteen years of this fuckery. I'm out."

"Oh. Well. That's . . . good."

"So I'm not gonna bother asking you why you *really* want me gone, because it doesn't matter. Everett—and maybe you guys —are right. I should quit of my own volition, not because people decided they didn't want me anymore. Eighteen years straight, they wanted me, and I'm going out on top."

"That's very noble," I say.

"How are things in your district, anyway?" Jacob asks.

"Fine," Cécile says.

"Anything interesting happening?"

"Why in the hell do you care?"

"Curiosity," he says. "We're very curious as to the state of Central New York."

"Nice pun."

"It was unintentional."

For the first time, she boasts something that could, in some circles, be considered a smile. It doesn't *look* like one, but it has the vibe. "No, nothing *interesting* is happening in my district. Nothing interesting *ever* happens in my district. That's why they keep electing me. Do they *want* something interesting? Hell, no. They would have gotten rid of me years ago if they did."

"How are the farmers?" I ask.

"Grand," she says. "Planting more crops now than ever before. It's nice, I guess, to see them happy."

"More crops?"

"Yeah," she says. "They plant all sorts of stuff. Corn and soybeans, mostly, but we have a ton of wheat, too. And that's not including the dairy people. We have more cows than we have people. If they could vote, we'd have a cow in the House of Representatives."

"That would be awesome," Jacob says.

"She would be the best congressperson in the House." She looks back to me. "Why are you here?"

"Why are *you* here?" I ask.

"I asked you first."

"I don't answer questions. I have no reason to. You, however, with one foot out the door and therefore nothing to lose, shouldn't be asking questions. Why are you here, Ms. Kettering, if your days are so numbered?"

Cécile's somewhat-smile comes back. She looks to Jacob. "Is she always like this?"

"Always," he says. "It's best to roll with it and do what she asks."

She looks back to me. "I have a few old friends to say hi to, then thank Everett and Luciana for inviting me, and I'm out before dinner. I hate these things, and I know Luciana invites me out of pity."

"Luciana does the inviting?" I ask.

Cécile throws her arms around, gesturing to the entire ballroom. "She sets all this up. Everett isn't that interesting or co-ordinated."

"And your old friends?" I ask. "Who's lucky enough to see you tonight?"

"Mary-Grace Carressy is the only person here I genuinely like. Love, even. We have lunch once a month, and I'd trust her with my life. I'm also the godmother of her children."

"She sounds wonderful," I say. "Anyone else?"

"Joachim Winston and Darcy Brecken."

"Darcy Brecken," I say. "We just spoke with her."

"I take it you're exhausted now."

I laugh. "She's very sweet."

"She is," Cécile agrees with a nod. "She's a doll, and she does a lot for my district. I owe her a lot, for her kindness alone."

I take a second to analyze any possible outcome of what I'm about to do. Nothing that could be irreversible. "We spoke with her about the tragedies happening in Brazil."

She gives me a look that I can't quite read. "Why in the hell would you ask her about that?"

"Again, Ms. Kettering, just pure curiosity." I look back to her, catch her sunset eyes. "Are you aware of what's going on in Brazil? With the soybean crops? It's quite terrible."

"I don't know the first thing about Brazil besides the big Jesus and the Portuguese," Cécile says. "There something else I should know about Brazil?"

Once again, Jacob and I explain what's going on.

"You kids are something else," she says.

"Mrs. Brecken mentioned that you might have an idea of what to do," Jacob says.

"Brazil is not in my district. Now, it was great to meet you two, but I'm checking off my list of people I have to acknowledge and I'm heading home before the sun fully sets. Pleasure to meet you both."

Before Jacob and I can reply, she's evaporated. I can't even tell into which direction she's ventured.

"Well," Jacob says, "I take it she loves talking about Brazil."

"I didn't mean to offend her," I say.

"I don't think you did," he says. "I think she's, as she said, bored."

"Hey, she came to us first," I say. "She can't be upset with us."

"Was that a weird reaction, or am I paranoid?"

"Some combination of both," I say. I look back to him without meaning to. "I don't trust her."

"That's because she's a politician." He smiles just enough to make my brain go fluffy. "They're not supposed to be trusted."

Chapter Fourteen

Afraid to light the fuse again,
start a fire, lose a friend.
But when your heart opens,
it's like I'm ready to fall again.

"Timebomb"
WALK THE MOON

As Jacob and I walk away from Cécile's vacated spot, we see Orion walking towards us. "There you two are!" he says. "Do you have anything of interest to report?"

"All reporting will be done later, off-premises," I say. "Everyone here has prying ears. It's part of their job descriptions."

"Have you talked to anyone named Joachim Winston?" Jacob asks Orion.

"As a matter of fact, I just met Mr. Winston," Orion says. "What a bland, bland man. He is like mashed potatoes without a hint of butter or salt. Sleep nearly took me hostage whilst I talked with him."

"Is he someone important?"

"That would depend on your definition of important. He owns and manages the Princess Alice Hotel, and he happens to be a dear friend of Luciana Caldwell's, and he is in an a cappella hymn group at the local church called Lift Your Voices, but that would be about it."

"Oh," I say. "Maybe we should talk to him, then, and see if he has any interest in helping us, which seems to be a rather uncommon trait around here."

"If I recall his visage correctly," Orion says, "I believe him to be the one talking to Luciana Caldwell right now."

"Okay," I say. I turn to Jacob. "Are you coming?"

"Skylar," Orion says, "Jacob would follow you through every circle of Hell and back again without you having to ask him first."

"Go network," I tell Orion, and I set off for Joachim Winston.

Jacob, of course, follows me.

I succeed on keeping my eye on Joachim, which makes me wish the three inches that came with my high heels were permanent. This is how averagely-heighted experience the world? No wonder short people are so full of spite. We're so much farther from the stars down here.

Luciana and Joachim start to walk away, leaving Everett and a few others behind. They leave the ballroom through a back hallway.

I look to Jacob. "We're following them, right?"

"Oh, totally." His eye color shifts, just a tiny bit, to freshly baked brownies. "You should wear red more often."

"Because it exacerbates my impulsivity and guides me towards questionable decisions?"

"Because it looks really pretty on you."

My brain goes *kerplut* for a bit. Like, it stops working. Hiccups. Why must he say things like that and make my brain stop? Especially when I need my brain the most? I'm sure my face matches my dress now—valentine red—but I pretend it doesn't. I'm quite good at pretending. "Shall we explore that sketchy hallway?" *SHALL? Good God, Skylar.*

"Yes, we shall," he replies.

I need a new partner. My current partner makes it impossible for me to look into a crowd and see anything but noise or hear anything but his laugh in my head like a recurring nightmare. Nonetheless, we move nearly silently down the hall—I mastered mitigating the *click* of a high heel during musical rehearsal, since we have floor mics and, according to Mrs. Darner, *you guys aren't auditioning for* 42nd Street.

The two of them disappear down another hallway that intersects this one, and we follow. They go down one more hallway —this place is misleadingly big—before we open up into a second, smaller ballroom. I can't see any of them before Jacob takes me by the wrist and pulls me into an alcove, out of their sightline. I scream at the butterflies under my skin to stop flapping, but they don't listen, especially because the alcove is so small, I can practically feel his heart beating.

"Oh, Lord, she *is* here," a voice says.

"You sound disappointed." I'm pretty sure this comes from Cécile Kettering.

"Trust me, he is," says a third voice. Maybe it sounds familiar, but maybe not. I can't tell.

"You told me you wouldn't do it," Cécile says. She's upset, clearly, but not like someone lied to her. More like they took a knife to her chest and gashed her open. Her voice nearly doesn't sound the same as the voice we heard earlier as she griped about boredom. Now, she's in pain.

"You agreed to it," the last voice says.

"I agreed when it was hypothetical," Cécile says. "I guess I didn't think it would actually ever happen."

"Well, it happened," the last voice repeats. "So are you onboard to reap the rewards of seeds you didn't help plant, or are you out?"

The room is quiet—Jacob and I hold our breaths. Then someone new replies, "You should be in, Cécile. It really is a great opportunity." This person is undoubtedly Luciana Caldwell.

"Is Everett okay with this?"

"Of course he is," Luciana replies. "Why wouldn't he be?"

Someone new chuckles, just once, as dry as a drought. "You're either onboard or you're drowning, my friend."

"I'm drowning, then," Cécile replies, before her footsteps come closer and closer to where we're hiding. "Wholeheartedly drowning. Go to Hell. All of you." Fortunately for us, she's too upset to glance to her right, but we see her.

"She'll come around," another voice says. How many people are in this room? At least five, now that Cécile left, and that's just whom we've heard so far. I didn't get a good look at the room before taking cover in the alcove, so there could be hundreds for all I know.

"She'd better," the first voice says. "I'd hate to lose her."

"We won't," Luciana says firmly. "I know we won't. Her heart is too big. This is just a little lapse of judgement. Now, if you'll excuse me, Everett will be wondering where I am." Luciana walks swiftly past us and back down the hall.

"I knew we should have left her out."

"Now, how would we have done that?"

"Shoulda been up to you to figure that out."

"Stop arguing," someone else interjects. "Can we do this later? There's a party going on, and we'd be much more useful out there."

"Take us out the back entrance, then."

"Sure thing. This way, everyone."

We wait until it's silent for at least another few minutes before poking our heads out of the alcove. No one's here, thank goodness.

"What was that?" Jacob asks.

"No idea," I say. "Luciana was there, and Cécile, obviously. Did you recognize any other voices?"

"Two, but I couldn't place either," he says.

This now leaves us with two choices: We leave the ballroom and forget we heard anything and focus on the problem in Brazil, or we could expand our horizons. There is something in the air tonight, or perhaps woven into the fabric of my dress or nestled into my hair, but I'm in the mood to expand my horizons. I can solve multiple problems at once. I've been doing it for awhile.

I look around the second ballroom. It looks like this room is used as a conference center more than a place for galas or weddings; tables and chairs on wheels tangle haphazardly on what used to be the dance floor. But right now, it looks as if it's become one giant office space. Papers litter every table, pens and pencils stick out of nice glassware, and anywhere a pile of books or an orchard's worth of printer paper could be stacked, they're stacked.

"What is this?" Jacob asks.

"No idea," I say. "An impromptu office, it would seem."

"Wouldn't a hotel like this have an *actual* office?"

"I would think so."

"Not that it would have room for all this stuff," he says.

I approach the table in the middle. I look at the first stack of papers, and my brain won't let me read them. The lettering is too small and too dense for me to make any sense of it, and it's hard enough as it is to read things up close with my contacts in, but I stick with it until they start to form something coherent. "It's a contract, I think."

"A contract for what?" he asks.

"It's borderline illegible," I say, holding it up so he can see.

"God, who would intentionally choose that font?"

"Someone who doesn't want their contract inspected," I say as I inspect it. "Seems illegal to me. If someone is signing a contract, all parties should be able to clearly read it." I turn to the end, where I'd presume the signatures to be, and sure enough, there they are. Three of them. All of them look like spaghetti thrown against the wall—I can't for the life of me figure out to whom they belong. And under each line, where you might think the signature owner's name might be printed, it only says "Signer" followed by a number one through three. I take a picture of it with my phone.

"I'll do the rest," Jacob says, taking his phone out of his pocket. "We can read it later."

"Good idea." I finish going through the papers underneath the contract, but it's just a land deed. It's dated a few weeks ago, so someone just recently bought a few hundred acres of land between Redway and Sharonsville. Someone whose signature is once again illegible. It doesn't match any of those on the contract, though. This one is far smaller and much more deliberate and clearly starts with the letter A. I take a picture of that one, too.

"It looks like a nondisclosure agreement," Jacob says, flipping through the contract. "For what, I can't tell. Something sketchy, though."

I look at it, too, and it's no easier to read now than it was a few minutes ago, but now I can see what he's saying. Most of the paragraphs pertain to the "non-divulgation of this material to parties who have not signed this document at the proper time."

"Does that seem legal?" he asks.

"No," I reply. "Nothing about this document seems legal."

He wanders over to another table and says, "This is nothing but farm stuff."

I join him. "What kind of farm stuff?"

"This is tractor insurance, I think." He holds up one of the papers. "Did you know you could insure a tractor?"

"The thought never occurred to me." I flip through more of the papers. "More insurance of farm equipment, another land deed with a name that clearly reads 'Franklin Zerkses,' and plans for a barn."

"Building plans?"

I smile to myself and hand them to him.

"This can't be for a farm near Redway," he says. "The structure system isn't up to code, unless the codes have changed since I did the bus garage, which they definitely haven't. They're not using steel for the primary structure. At least I don't *think* they are, since they could get rid of half these I-beams if they were."

"That's strange," I say.

"Really strange. This barn might be cheaper to make material-wise, if they're not using steel in it, but it'll take at least two weeks longer and a bigger crew of people, so it's ultimately more expensive because of the labor."

"Is there a site listed?"

He reads it over again before saying, "No. No site."

"Weird."

He takes a picture of the plans—either to help us or just for him to look at later—and we move to the next table. It's all more of the same. In fact, all these tables look like insurance for farm equipment, the occasional land deed, and a barn plan every once in awhile, all copies of each other.

There is one table in the back, however, that's different than the others. For starters, the table itself is probably as old as the Princess Alice, unlike the composite tables on wheels scattered around the rest of the room. It also has the most paper. Jacob's already investigating; he eventually says, "Skylar, come see this."

I flip through the papers. "They're genetically engineering soybeans?"

"Looks like it."

"But why?"

"No idea." He reads a couple more. "They're trying to make the soybeans stronger and more resistant to diseases, from what I can tell. This is, like, Eradicator-level genetic creeping."

"I mean, judging by their poor excuse for a harvest last season, it doesn't necessarily surprise me that they would want more reliable soybeans," I say. "But this, all of this, is going to awfully extreme levels to ensure a good harvest."

"Yeah," he says. "I think we should fix the Brazil thing and then come back to this and see if anything fishy's going on in Redway."

"Something fishy is definitely going on in Redway."

"Which I wouldn't expect from Redway."

"I wouldn't expect our island to be the home of several certifiable super geniuses, but the world has the infinite capacity to surprise us."

"Fair point."

I move to the next table. "Jacob, look." I hold up a flash drive in the shape of an ear of corn. "Corn flash drive."

"Corny," he says. "Think all this stuff is on it?"

"I'd hope so," I say. "I'd also hope no one would notice it missing."

"In this mess? It'll take a few days at least. I don't—"

"Shh," I cut him off. It sounds like footsteps—footsteps coming awfully close to the ballroom, in the direction where we came in. *Shit.*

I look around for somewhere to hide, but it's a freaking ballroom. They're built to be wide open spaces, gilded indoor prairies. Other than the alcove up front, there aren't any nooks or crannies that could fit something bigger than a baby capybara, and they would see us as soon as they turned into the room, anyway. We could try to go out that other exit, the one that the group in here before used, but I have no idea where it leads, and it could get us in more trouble if we walked right into another secret meeting.

Who knows what these people are up to, or if they're dangerous, or how illegal this operation is? Who knows *what* this operation is in the first place?

Fix Brazil, then fix Redway. And to fix Brazil, we need to get out of Redway at least mostly alive.

I look to Jacob, take a breath, and say, "This means absolutely nothing." Then I take him by the shoulders and kiss him.

Don't get distracted don't get distracted this is for a secret mission it doesn't mean anything it's just giving you an alibi don't get distracted. That is *not* as easy as my conscious makes it sound. Especially when his shock wears off and he kisses me back. God, if only he were worse at this. He isn't, which is a problem, the rational part of my brain believes. The other part is *kerplut*. Utter mush.

His hands wrap around my back and I don't exactly *mean* to pull him a bit closer and kiss him a bit harder but I do anyway. *Do NOT get distracted.* I slip the corn flash drive into his pocket before the bubbles in my chest completely take over. *Clear head. Alibi.* My hands, now free of the corn flash drive, tangle into his hair without listening to everything my brain has been telling them. His find my face and wrap around my waist; his fingers trace little streams down my cheek. *Don't play into the electricity. It isn't anything but a performance.* It's like playing a song that I haven't played in years—my heart knows every note without any help from my mind. I don't need any help from my mind. It only gets in the way. The whole thing should be mush. It would be if I were any more reckless than I appear to be now. I blame the red.

God, Skylar. You are still so in love with him, it's nearly laughable.

"Oh, hello," a voice says.

Could you have not taken an hour longer to walk down that hallway? I pull away from him like a horseshoe magnet pulls away from a wall of pure nickel, and I look to our visitor: a man with sun-cracked skin, mousy brown hair, pointy chin, gangly frame, like one of those crooks you tie to your fence with green twine and hang a plant with a hook off of.

I force out a giggle. (It isn't that hard, what with all those bubbles in my chest.) "Oh my gosh, we are so sorry." I hug Jacob's arm for good measure. He seems stunned, not that I blame him. He gives me a look, and I give his hand a squeeze.

"Yeah, we're sorry," he says. "We didn't mean to intrude. It was just empty, and . . ." I punctuate this for him with another giggle.

"No need to be sorry," the man says with a temperate smile. "Children in love. I completely understand."

This is usually where one of us would start arguing with him, saying that we hate each other if need be, but it works here. I giggle again and rest my head against Jacob's shoulder. "Thank you, Mr. . . ." I trail off, hoping he'll fill in the blank.

"Winston," he says. "Joachim Winston. I run the Princess Alice."

"Oh, goodness!" I throw my other hand to my heart and shy behind Jacob. "We are so, *so* sorry to bother you. You have such a lovely hotel. The details are just so beautiful. Never seen a building quite like it in my whole life."

"Thank you," Joachim says.

"All the molding—it's just beautiful! And is this another ballroom?"

"Used as a conference center nowadays," Joachim says.

"Is there a conference going on now?" Jacob asks.

"A small one," Joachim replies.

"For what?"

"Oh, for one thing or another. I never know." I can tell by his voice now, by the way he says that, that he's the one who led everyone out. Makes sense—if he owns the hotel, he would know all the back entrances. I would assume, then, that he knows exactly what this conference is, if it's for a conference at all.

"Well, we will get out of your hair, Mr. Winston." I drag Jacob towards the exit. "We are so sorry again for intruding. Have a wonderful night!"

Before he can respond, I pull Jacob down the hall, borderline running until I find another hallway for us to turn down. It's only a row of wooden doors and gold-leaf frames of oil-painted gardens.

"I am so sorry," I say.

"It's totally fine," he says.

"It didn't mean anything," I say.

"I know," he says. "Just good quick thinking."

"We needed an alibi."

"And that one made sense."

"Perfect sense."

Neither of us really knows what to say next, and to make matters worse, I realize I'm still holding his hand. And it's the hardcore hand-holding—our hands make a little basket. Good God. I have never hated myself more than I do in this moment. I let go.

"Hold on." I reach out and try to wipe my red lipstick off his face.

"What are you doing?"

"You didn't bring a baby wipe, did you?"

"Why would I bring a baby wipe?" At least I *think* that's what he says. Since I'm aggressively rubbing his mouth with the heel of my hand, I can't really tell.

"You always have weird things in your pocket."

"If I needed a baby wipe, I'd ask you."

I stop and look. "It's pretty much gone."

"Okay, good."

"Good."

"Yes."

"So we can just . . ." I trail off, unsure of where I'm going with that.

"Pretend nothing happened?" he finishes.

"That sounds perfect."

"Okay, cool."

"Cool."

"Do you still have the flash drive?" he asks.

"Check your left pocket."

He withdraws the silicone corn. "Clever."

"Thank you." I start off in the direction of the main ballroom, and he follows me, and neither of us say another word to each other.

We probably won't for a very long time.

Chapter Fifteen

About forty-three times a day, I find myself wishing that life had a control-Z feature. I always think that's so handy while doing yearbook things on InDesign: Made a mistake? All you have to do is hit two keys in tandem and it's like it never happened! Now that text box is gone, your border hasn't been moved, and you never kissed him and ruined your friendship yet again. Life goes back to normal. Everything stays lined up.

"You should go find Lexie and Hunter," I tell Jacob. "I'll look for Hallie and Alex."

"I thought we were doing all reporting on the way home," he says. "To stay away from prying ears."

"Just to check in," I say. "Not to report. I'll see you later." Before he can say anything else, I turn faster than a ballerina and dive into the crowd.

The three inches added to my height work wonders. I don't feel as if I'm underwater—I'm part of the current. When I look to either side, I see people's faces rather than their chests. This makes it much easier to look out for my friends, and to subsequently avoid them. Fortunately, I don't see any of them. I see Luciana for a second, who gives me a smile before turning back to the conversation Everett holds with some men in suits. I don't have to fight my way through this crowd; rather, it parts for me as if it were fluid. It can read my mind. *That girl wants out*, it knows, *so we can make it easier for her*. I thank it for being so considerate.

I step out into the lobby of the Princess Alice, but there are still so many people out here, talking and laughing because the ballroom wasn't a good enough venue for their talks or their laughs. I shouldn't be annoyed, but I am. I fully know that it's cold out, and I know that my coat is in coatcheck somewhere and very inaccessible, but I step outside anyway. I just need to clear my head and come up with my next few moves and not be around Jacob, lest I try to kiss him again. Which, presently, isn't far from the front of my mind.

A wraparound porch curls all the way around the Princess Alice, breaking only once in the back for what I think are the service entrances. Because it can't be warmer than the mid-thirties, I would seem to be the only person out here, which is exactly what I need. I pace around a bit, looking at the Princess Alice's surroundings. There is not a lot to observe, especially since it's nearly pitch black beyond the lights of the hotel. I speak from experience: Businesses in small towns close early because everyone's asleep or pretending to be asleep by nine. So it's quiet. Cars putter past every few minutes, but none are in a hurry. A dog will bark every so often, or a door will slam, but besides those aberrations, Redway is fast asleep or carrying on its charade flawlessly.

I try to organize everything I've seen tonight inside my mind, but it doesn't want to think about anything but Jacob. Typical. Though I suppose it has an excuse tonight. My hand flies to my mouth—did I *really* kiss him? Or was it just a very vivid daydream? It would have been a daydream I've had before, admittedly—come on, is it *that* strange to think about kissing the leader of the universe while wearing a beautiful gown at a very fancy gala before solving world hunger and abolishing the police force? I didn't think so.

Surely there were other ways we could have gotten out of that, but my brain, thinking it was being helpful, blocked every other option. It was *not* being helpful. Just as we finally, *finally* started to be able to talk again after six months of torture, we have found ourselves rid of all our experience points, as if the video game deleted itself and all its data completely disappeared. We'll have to start over. Back to level one.

No, I won't cry about this. I cried once in September, after I told him that we should pretend nothing happened and go about life as normal. I then told myself I would never cry over Jacob Connelly again. It would do absolutely nothing but mess up the eye makeup Lexie so strenuously painted on me and gives me an excuse to self-pity. Self-pitying makes me nauseous. I have better things to expend my energy on than myself. Or Jacob. Or any part of that incurable debacle.

Like Brazil. Like whatever the hell's happening in Redway, which I still can't wrap my head around. I can only hope that one of our other friends has found something interesting, since Jacob and I ended up asking more questions than we answered. Very little information, no funding, perhaps a new conspiracy on top of our previous one—was it even worth coming here? Did I make a mistake by dragging everyone all the way here, to the middle of a field surrounded by more fields, insisting they all lie to their parents and steal their siblings' clothes and play whatever part it is that we've found ourselves playing? We would be better off in Hunter's attic, making phone calls that end in static and sending emails that bounce off the language barrier.

Maybe tomorrow, we can get in touch with that Brazilian wildlife group. See if they've figured out why the bats are dying, or get them to expedite their research. We have connections if they need supplies, or we can intervene in Brazilian government if they lack approval. We don't need anyone here. We never did.

There's a clatter and the slam of a door at the back of the building by the service entrances. I set off in the opposite direction until I hear the unmistakable voice of Cécile Kettering holler, "I shut you up once, and I can do it again."

I find that too intriguing to ignore. Carefully, as if I were onstage, balanced on the balls of my feet so my shoes don't make any sound, I move closer to the service entrances. I stop right before turning the corner so they can't see me.

Someone else says something, but it's so quiet, I can't make out the voice or what it says. Just a rustle of fabric, the crunch of gravel, a sharp inhale, and the unmistakable cock of a gun.

I peer around the corner just in time to watch someone, silhouetted by nighttime, push Cécile against the wall and shoot her in the chest.

I bite my hand to keep from screaming.

Last year, on the Fourth of July, I attempted to deafen myself.

I barricaded myself in the basement with a stack of American Girl Felicity books (in keeping with the spirit of the holiday), every stuffed animal I could find, my phone, and my earbuds. I told my parents I had a headache before I gave myself one: I played Vivaldi at the highest my phone would play through my earbuds. But I could still hear the fireworks. It was impossible not to hear them. They put on the spectacle at the park, not too far from my house, over the river, so it could don a sheath of patriotic color and avoid being itself for another night.

Every time a firework shot up into the sky and burst into a shower of light, without fail, Harlow would collapse against the basement floor, and I would watch the stardust bleed out of her body.

They went on for days, seemingly. It never got better. I must have watched her die maybe a hundred times in one night. It didn't get easier. She bled more each time. The basement flooded.

The consistent spiraling made me dizzy. Seismic quaking racked my body. My lungs were riddled with holes and couldn't take in any air, and my hands were laden in bite marks since I would shove them in my mouth to keep myself from screaming. I wouldn't want to worry my parents with something that never happened.

I stayed in the basement all night. People were supposed to be done with fireworks by eleven, but they had no reason to abide by the rules. I slept maybe forty-five minutes, curled up in a pile of stuffed animals next to our Christmas decorations. The shaking didn't stop for another three days after that. It still hasn't really stopped, I suppose. It just takes breaks sometimes.

It never gets any better or feels any less real. I never feel any less helpless. It's the same thing every single time. Every firework. Every thunderstorm. Every time someone slams the door too loudly or pops a balloon or doesn't pop the spout cover on the kettle so it screeches when it boils. It sounds just like her.

It will never get better. I've come to terms with that. I think I've gotten better at hiding it and coming up with excuses, but it hasn't gotten better.

Especially not right now, as Harlow's starlight seeps across the porch of the Princess Alice Hotel, dripping between the gaps in the floorboards, tearing a thousandth black hole in the universe.

Chapter Sixteen

If you just hold in your breath
till you come back up in full,
hold in your breath
till you thought it through.

"Genius Next Door"
Regina Spektor

In, out. In, out. You're okay. Harlow's okay. You're okay. Harlow's okay. I repeat this a few hundred times before turning the corner and moving towards the end of the porch. I float, I think—this all has the eerie shroud of a nightmare, not of something actually happening. This has to be a dream. Just a dream. The edges of things are too blurred and the sounds are too muffled and the colors are too saturated and too pale to be real.

Cécile slumps against the back wall, blood oozing from the bullet hole in her chest.

I don't have a lot of control over my body, seeing as though I'm definitely just caught in a nightmare. Just a nightmare. I don't know how to make decisions, especially not good ones. I inch closer to her body as if she might jump up and strangle me at any moment. She won't. She's just a mirage. A very dead mirage.

Her eyes are open, mouth slightly agape as if the gun caught her just before she screamed, hands limp at her sides, diaphanous dress fanned out around her like a washed-up jellyfish. Her curls are still perfect, draped down her shoulders like streamers from rafters at the end of the party—pretty but worn. She is a prop in a horror movie, not something that breathed a few minutes ago.

She didn't struggle like Harlow did. Her killer must have known right where to find her heart.

I try not to throw up as I move closer. It's too dark to see anything, like footprints on the cracked concrete or an opportunity for someone to leave a set of fingerprints. Her head lolls to the left, almost touching her shoulder. Does that mean anything? It can't mean anything. Just that she tilts her head to the left when she stands. Tilted, actually. Since she's dead.

Two people watched this woman die. One killed her, and the other was me.

I think I start moving back inside. I don't know. Everything is coated in peach fuzz—not soft, just imprecise. Misleading. Doesn't belong on a fruit. I make it into the ballroom without seeing any part of my journey. One of my friends has to be around here. It isn't that big. Hazily, without walking towards them, I find myself in front of Hallie and Alex.

"What's up?" Hallie asks. "You look half frozen to death."

I don't know if I answer. I can't tell.

"Skylar?" Alex says. "You okay?"

"Cécile got shot," I say.

"What? Cécile Kettering?"

"Yes. She got shot. Now she's dead. Someone killed her."

"Here?" Hallie asks.

"Back door. She's there. I saw. I left her there. Her eyes are still open."

"Oh my God, Skylar." She takes me into her arms. "Jesus, you're cold." To Alex, she says, "Go find Jacob."

"On it," Alex says before the crowd absorbs him.

"Don't talk," Hallie tells me. "You don't have to talk. Just take some deep breaths. You're okay."

"She was fighting with someone," I say. "I don't know who. They were fighting. Then she died."

She ushers me into a chair at a table and sits next to me. "Do you want some water?"

"No," I say. What good would water do? "She's still dead."

"I know," Hallie says. "But you should hydrate."

"Not now."

"Skylar?" Jacob appears and kneels next to my chair, already concerned. "What's wrong? Are you okay?"

"I don't think I'm okay," I say. "Someone killed Cécile."

"What?"

"I went outside. Someone had a gun and shot Cécile and now she's dead. I saw it."

His eyes darken to nearly black as a thousand thoughts race through his head. "Bubble, I'm so sorry."

"And—" Now my breathing starts to get weird. "And then Harlow—"

"Harlow's okay," he says. "She's safe at home. Nowhere near here."

"I know, but—" I take his hand. It's steady, unlike any part of my body.

"Hallie," Jacob says, "could you please text everyone and tell them it's time to go?"

"Yep," Hallie says. "I'll get our coats, Skylar."

"Why did they kill her?" I ask.

"I don't know," Jacob replies. "I really don't know. But we can talk about that later."

"Someone here killed her. We might have talked to them."

"We're going to get out of here, okay? And go to Hunter's house, and we'll be completely safe."

"My head feels full."

He doesn't say anything; he just gives my hand a squeeze. "Are you ready, or do you want to sit here a bit longer?"

"I'm okay," I say. When I stand up, the world moves around a bit, but Jacob doesn't let go of my hand. "Can we go? Now?"

"Yes," he says.

By the time we get to the front of the ballroom, Lexie, Hunter, and Orion have joined Alex and Hallie. I don't say anything to any of them because my head is too full. Orion says something about going to get the car, and Hallie tells Lexie and Hunter that something bad happened and I'm not in the mood to talk about it, and my eyelids feel like they're made of lead. Cécile's eyes are still open.

Jacob helps me put my coat on, and I let him. I somehow get outside and to the car. Orion's already put his sea shanties on. I nearly trip over my dress while climbing into the car, but I manage to regain my balance. Maybe I shouldn't be three inches taller.

"Should we have said goodbye to Everett and Luciana?" I ask.

"Hunter and I did," Lexie assures me. "So don't worry about that."

"Did you get any funding?"

"Skylar, we can worry about all that later," Hallie says. "Let's just go home and get some sleep and figure that out tomorrow."

"Okay."

"Orion, turn off the sea shanties," Hallie says.

"Hunter, I have Vivaldi's 'Winter' movement on my phone, if you would like to put it on," Orion says.

"You guys don't like Vivaldi," I say.

"I find Vivaldi quite wonderful," Orion says.

As the violins embark on the staccato of the opening chords, I rest my head on Jacob's shoulder, and he wraps his arm around me. I let him hold me close and absentmindedly trace circles on my forearm like a little spirograph. I concentrate on his breathing, pushing everything out of my mind, save the rise and fall of his chest.

"Bubble," Jacob says through the viscous mist that hangs around my head. He rubs my shoulder. "We're home."

Disoriented, I sit up. Sure enough, we've just parked outside the Athan house. I must have fallen asleep. Which means I slept on Jacob's shoulder for at least an hour. If I had any more energy, I'd be mortified, but I'm tempted to settle back in before he unbuckles his seatbelt. I know him. He wouldn't move until morning if I did.

"Okay," I say. My eyes burn, probably because of my contacts. You're not supposed to sleep in contacts. The world blurs like a broken camera lens when I stand up, but once it straightens itself out, I follow everyone inside.

Lauren waits in the parlor, crossword puzzle half-completed on her lap. "Good. You all look alive."

"Mostly," Hunter says.

"Thank you for waiting up for us," Orion says, breaching the parlor threshold to give her a kiss on the cheek.

"You always have me so worried." She pats Orion's shoulder and stands up. "I will make you all some tea and start a fire in the back room. No snacks this late unless you want to be up all night."

"*Efcharisto*, Lauren," Hunter says, and Orion repeats him.

"Go get your pajamas on, all of you," she says as she glides into the kitchen. Because of her long skirt, I don't know if she has feet. She might not.

I still have trouble registering everything going on, but I must follow Hallie and Lexie into the purple bedroom upstairs. We help each other slip out of our gowns, and Hallie hangs all three in the closet while Lexie helps pull pins from my hair.

"Did you count them when you put them in?" I ask.

"No," she says. "Why?"

"I want to make sure that I didn't leave a pin at the crime scene."

"I'm sure you didn't," Lexie says. "And even if you did, there's no way they could have tracked it back to you. Everyone with long hair had bobby pins in."

"Okay."

Once the last pin is out, she brushes through my hair and braids it for me. Then she hands me a makeup wipe. "Use this to get your makeup off. Maybe take out your contacts first."

It takes several minutes to fish my contacts out of my eyes, and by the time I finally throw them in the garbage can, my eyes are raw and red. I use three wipes to get all my makeup off, and when I put my glasses back on, I can tell my contacts were the wrong prescription by the way my head swims and pulses. I slip on my beluga pajamas and sit on a bottom bunkbed and politely ask the world to stop writhing until Hallie and Lexie are ready. Maybe it will listen if I'm polite.

"Do you want to go downstairs, or do you want us to bring you some tea?" Hallie asks, pulling her strawberry curls into a messy bun.

"I can go downstairs," I say. "I'm fine."

"You don't have to be fine," Lexie says.

"I know." I stand up and pretend the world doesn't shudder like a Magic 8 Ball. "But I am."

"Want one of your whales?" Hallie asks.

"Yes, maybe Mortimer," I say. Hallie goes over to my bag and pulls out one of the whales. She hands him to me. "Thank you."

We go downstairs and have to follow the boys' voices until we find them in a back room, a living room that looks like it's actually used for living. The sofas are cushy and covered by layers of fluffy blankets, and art and a few tapestries and some wooden masks obscure the walls. A fire crackles in the fireplace. Next to it, Pickle sits on a pillow on the floor. From the windows that take up the entire back wall, paned in an even black grid, the river peeks in through the darkness. I hadn't realized it was so close—it's practically his backyard, except for a few yards of perfectly manicured grass and a covered porch. There's a dock, too, extending into the river, lights blinking at the end so boats don't crash into it. The stars would be inches away out there.

"Are we going to discuss our findings?" I ask.

"We can do that tomorrow," Hallie says. She sits on the couch next to Alex.

"We can do it tonight," I say. "We'll forget by morning."

"Would it be wise to relive tonight while still experiencing it?" Orion says. He wears matching red-striped button-down pajamas like a Norman Rockwell illustration. I would judge him if I didn't have a pair in purple.

"We can talk about it if Skylar wants to," Alex says.

"We can," I assure everyone. "I'm okay." Whether this is true or not is up for debate.

Hunter scoots over so I can sit between him and Jacob. He hands Hallie and Lexie mugs, each with a painted bird on it—robin and cardinal, respectively. "Peppermint for Hallie, lemon ginger for Lexie."

"Ooo, thank you," Lexie says. She takes a big gulp but spits it back out into her mug. "Way too hot. Don't drink it yet."

Hunter hands me a warm mug next, bluebird painted on the side. "Chamomile," he says. "With blueberry and anise."

"That sounds like the world's most perfect bedtime tea," I say.

"Jacob picked it out for you."

I look to him. "Your favorite nighttime tea and your favorite berry, together at last," he says by way of explanation.

"Thank you," I say. I'm grateful for my fatigue, or else I would smile at him involuntarily. "So, does anyone have anything interesting to share?"

"We really don't have to do this now, Skylar," Lexie says.

"Guys. I'm fine. Really." The lies come so easily to me now. I take a sip of tea. It's still too hot, but I take another sip anyway. "Hallie and Alex, let's start with you."

Chapter Seventeen

"Breathe"
Dom Fera

I try my best to pay attention as Hallie and Alex share their findings, but I find it very hard to focus. My mind doesn't wander anywhere in particular—just anywhere that is not here. It will land on Cécile, or find its way to Harlow, and I'll force them away with another sip of tea. I'm lucky I need both hands to hold my bluebird mug, or else everyone would see them shaking. Either that, or I'd have taken Jacob's hand by now and let him draw little circles on the back, which would be even worse.

"So most of the people you talked to *knew* about the soybean problems in Brazil?" Lexie asks.

"Yeah," Hallie says. "Except for, like, three people, and only one of them was actually a farmer. Other than that, everyone knew. Farmers, people who knew farmers, people who said they were about to start farming. They all said they had to up production to avoid the shortage getting any worse. They'll plant more crops than usual this planting season."

"But it hasn't been in the news," I say. "I even checked the local news of all the towns in the district, and no one mentioned it."

Alex shrugs. "I guess soy people have their own communication methods."

"That's so strange," I say. "Because Cécile Kettering didn't even know, and her district is full of soy farmers." I don't want to say her name, but it's information. That's all her name can be right now. Information. Pollen without a flower behind it.

"At least she *claimed* not to know," Jacob says. "Whether she knew or not is up for debate, judging by how she acted when we asked her, and by—" He stops himself.

"I suppose you're right." I replay the interaction in my head. "Does it really surprise you, though? Politicians are liars by nature. They have to be, or they wouldn't have a job."

"We know what that's like," Lexie says.

"What about Darcy, then?" I ask Jacob. "She didn't seem to know, and her reaction seemed pretty genuine."

"It did," he says. "We should have asked Luciana, too. I didn't even think of it."

"Luciana?" Hallie asks. "Who's that?"

"Everett's wife," I say. "In the pretty purple dress."

"Oh, I thought she was a visiting queen," Lexie says.

"They must have the most beautiful children," Hallie says.

"That's creepy," Alex says.

"What? It's true."

"Back on track," I say. "So neither Cécile nor Darcy knew about what's happening in Brazil. Did anyone ask Everett?"

"I did," Orion says. "I, of course, went to thank him for the invitation to his splendid soirée. He had absolutely no idea whom I was, yet he received me graciously all the same. We chatted lightly about immigration and capital punishment, and then I asked him if he happened to be aware of the horrendous situation transpiring in our friends to the south. He said he had heard something about it. His wife had mentioned it to him over dinner. He did not find it an urgent matter and began to talk about his own district instead. That was the extent of our conversation on the matter."

"Well, that makes sense that he would know, and now we know that Luciana does, too," Hallie says. "It *doesn't* make sense that Darcy or Cécile wouldn't. Especially Darcy, since soybeans are, like, her thing."

"We talked to Everett, too," Lexie says, gesturing to herself and Hunter. "Only for, like, three minutes. We had to find someone with kids and a lot of money to fund Redway art programs for Carson Sloane."

"Got that done in four minutes," Hunter says. "I showed them some of my drawings of horses and said they were from a Redway kindergartener who wouldn't be able to take art next year unless we had their help. Got a nice chunk of funding from this rich banker man who regrets not going to art school."

"And how did fundraising for our project go?" I ask.

"Pretty well, if you have loose morals," Hunter says. "The horse pictures worked on just about everyone."

"If I did the math right," Lexie says, "we should be fine." She tells us exactly how much they raised.

"Good God," Hallie says. "That's a shit ton."

"We might need it," I say. "Depending on our next course of action. Does anyone else have anything to share?"

"Skylar," Jacob says so only I can hear, "what about our trip to the second ballroom?"

Since the first thing I think of when he recalls that memory is kissing him, I almost say no, nothing interesting happened there. Then I remember that a woman who was in that room is now no longer alive, and I say, "Right. Can you tell the story?"

"Of course." He turns to the rest of the group and says, "Skylar and I did have a mini adventure, though it's kind of unrelated." He explains how we followed Luciana and Joachim Winston to the other ballroom, how Cécile and a bunch of other voices were there, what they all said, and all the stuff we found in there, including the corn flash drive. He briefly mentions Joachim coming back in after leading everyone out, but thankfully leaves out exactly how we played off being somewhere we weren't supposed to be.

"And now Cécile Kettering is . . ." Lexie trails off, as if she remembers that she shouldn't mention it.

"Dead?" I finish. "Yes."

"That kind of seems like an issue," Alex says.

"We have too many issues right now," I say. "That one—" I stop myself from saying *That one doesn't matter*, because that is very not true. "That one isn't of our concern at the moment, if ever." Also not true. The issues are inextricable. I just can't think about that one at the moment. If ever. "They took the murder weapon back inside with them and they probably left fingerprints everywhere and I'm sure there were a thousand eye witnesses. Redway can solve its own murder. We have bigger things to worry about."

"I'm sorry," Lexie says quietly. "I shouldn't have brought it up."

"It's fine," I say. "It— it doesn't matter. They'll figure out it was someone we've never met because of some money owed or an insurance claim or whatever it is Agatha Christie writes her novels about, and everything will be fine."

Did Cécile have a family? Kids? A dog waiting by the front window for an owner that will never come home? I only spoke to her once, knew almost nothing about her, but still, she could not have been terrible enough to warrant murder. (Then again, I tend to believe no one is terrible enough to warrant murder—even the worst of us are not disposable.)

It's funny, though, how a woman I spoke to a few hours ago is now frozen in a morgue somewhere, if her body has even been recovered yet. I hope her hair still looks nice. And that her eyes have closed.

I hand Jacob my bluebird mug and stand up, taking Mortimer the whale with me. "I'm going to go to bed. Goodnight, everyone."

I go back to the purple bedroom and sit in a chair by the fireplace. The small bookshelf in here has a few books on it, albeit childish and all ones I've read, but I find *Coraline* by Neil Gaiman and try my best to read it. It doesn't work. My head sounds like static.

There's a knock at the door. "Come in," I say.

Jacob appears, holding my bluebird mug. "I thought you might want this."

"Thank you," I say.

He comes over and sets it on the table next to my chair. I can read his shirt now—it has a picture of a column and says, *It's kind of Ionic.* And his pajama pants have astronauts and planets on them. My God, that's annoying. So cute it's frustrating.

I'm kind of expecting him to say something else, but he doesn't. I hear him search for words, but he doesn't say any of them.

I decide to help him out. "Is everyone still awake?"

"Yeah," he says. "Talking about *Shrek.*"

"I'm not surprised."

"Are you okay?"

Something about the way he asks irritates me. I'm clearly not *okay.* I could provide an alphabetized list as to why. Does he even need to ask? Despite the true answer, I say, "I'm fine."

"Are you sure? Because—"

"Really. Thank you for the tea."

"Skylar, if you need—"

"Jacob, leave me alone. Please."

He seems a bit taken aback. His eyes turn to dark chocolate. "Okay. See you in the morning, then."

"Goodnight."

He slips out the door and closes it without making a sound.

My God, could I have made matters any worse? I slam the book shut and leave it next to my tea, which has gone cold. I take another sip regardless. He brought it all the way up for me.

I take my whales up the ladder with me, and we settle in the top right bunk. I take off my glasses and set them on the ledge, along with my phone, melatonin supplements, and three bobby pins. (You never know when you might need bobby pins.)

I try to fall asleep. I take twice my usual dose of melatonin (so four times the normal person's), and I listen to the *Jurassic Park* theme song a few times, which always calms me down, but I remain thoroughly exhausted yet hopelessly awake. That has to be the worst part about it—I want nothing more than to fall asleep.

Could I be of any help in the investigation of Cécile's murder? Probably, I suppose. I saw it happen. But I couldn't see the other person, hear their voice, or understand why they were talking in the first place. Though I was also in the second ballroom where I witnessed Cécile get into an argument with everyone in there, which could have created a motive, or exacerbated a pre-existing one.

Someone in that room killed her. I'm nearly certain of it. That entire situation was a motive waiting to happen. The problem is, of course, that I don't know exactly who was in that room or why they were there. Luciana, for sure, but it couldn't have been her. She seemed certain that Cécile would come around. Joachim, too, and I don't know enough about him to determine if he could be a murderer. Everett probably wasn't there, because they were talking about him, but I can't say for sure. I don't know about Darcy Brecken, either. Or Mary-Grace Carressy, my district's congresswoman, who was at the gala. Or Carson Sloane, Redway's town supervisor, or the hundred or so other people I don't know anything about.

I know nothing beyond the fact that I am missing something. I have all the materials and all the tools, but I don't have the construction plans. With a bit more direction, I could put everything together. But I have no direction.

When my mind moves away from Redway, it finds itself in Brazil. Then to Sharonsville. Back to Paraná. As if it were trapped in a game of pinball, bouncing between two rubber-banded pegs.

Two pegs in the same machine.

The world is an awfully small place, as large as everyone tries to make it feel. One microbial being starts a pandemic, one match causes a forest fire, one person makes a decision without a thought and ruins another person's life. With an invisible spiderweb, intricate and sticky and bothersome at times, everything connects to just about everything else. Redway is connected to Brazil, or vice versa. Because Brazil is struggling, Redway farmers will pick up the slack.

When spiders decide to make a web, they go through a very specific set of motions. First, they size up the area—will it bring them the flies they desire? Then they assess how much silk they have and see if they have enough to execute their design. And then they pick the anchor points. They decide what their webs will connect—an unruly branch to a fencepost, or the rafters of an attic to a sputtering pipe, or a precarious tangle of dead leaves and garden ornaments. Some even decorate their webs with silk that can't capture anything, called *stabilimenta,* for reasons unknown. Probably so they can connect more things. Weave the anchor points together in a more convoluted way. Convolution *is* more fun —I'll give them that. It also makes things messy. Leaves bigger gaps where you think you've left fewer.

Hallie and Lexie come in, and I pretend to be asleep. They whisper to each other, but I can't hear anything they say. Then Lexie climbs the ladder and Hallie hops into the bunk beneath me and my mind keeps dancing around itself like a horse welded to a carousel pole.

Chapter Eighteen

"Trade Mistakes"
Panic! At the Disco

I never fall asleep. I stay in the delirious hanging fire between consciousness and dreaming, drifting in and out of my head and the room around me. Every creak of the house wakes me up; whenever Hallie or Lexie stirs, I wake up once again. Cécile and Harlow stick to the inside of my forehead like stickers that come on fruit: When I peel them off, they just get stuck somewhere else that they belong even less.

Eventually, the sun seems to rise. I check my phone, and it's seven-twenty-seven. A palindrome time. Hallie and Lexie are still fast asleep, but I slip out of bed and down the ladder.

Usually, being the first to wake up at a sleepover gives me copious amounts of anxiety, so I just stay in one spot until someone else wakes up. This is why I usually bring homework or a book to sleepovers—I'm always the first awake. But I don't want to be in this room anymore, what with all the nervous colors and timid sounds that won't let me hear them, so I creep into the hall. I can hear people rustling in the kitchen, so I hold my breath and tiptoe downstairs and towards where I think the kitchen is—under the stairs and through a butler's pantry. I stop holding my breath when I see it's just Alex and Lauren sitting at the counter, but I stop breathing once again when I see the rest of the kitchen.

All the cabinetry is earthy reclaimed wood. Open shelves hold a library of cookbooks, myriads of mason jars, baskets, bottles, herbs, spices, pottery, pots, pans, glassware, and everything in between. The stainless-steel restaurant-grade appliances glimmer. The only kitchen I've ever seen that comes close to this one was in Freja Lundquist's 432 Park Avenue penthouse. I didn't know a kitchen of this urbanity could exist anywhere but there, perched upon a tower, blinking at Manhattan as if it were nothing more than an empty field. Then again, this one overlooks the river, who judges us from beyond the paned windows, calm and periwinkle this morning. The river may not be Manhattan, but it still moves past us without giving us much thought. It's just as indifferent to its human occupants.

"Good morning, Skylar," Alex says to me.

"Good morning," I reply. "Good morning, Lauren."

"Morning, Skylar. You slept okay?"

"Yes," I lie. It's not Lauren's fault that sleep never found me. "You're up early," I say to Alex.

"I'm up at four-thirty for hockey practice most mornings," he says. "It becomes kind of a habit. Great for Christmas morning, though. My family hates me."

Lauren pours some coffee for Alex and gives him the mug. This one has a chickadee on it. "Sugar or cream?"

"Both, please," Alex says. "Thank you, Lauren."

"Don't mention it." She looks to me next. "Coffee for you, Skylar?"

"No, thank you," I say. "I'm not a coffee person."

"She lives off of tea," Alex supplies as he pours so much milk in his coffee that it's basically a cup of milk with coffee flavoring.

Lauren's whole face lights up. "I will put a kettle on." As she rummages through a cabinet, she says, "I buy tea with the groceries and no one drinks it. Mrs. and Mr. Athan don't like it, Hunter only drinks black coffee, Orion's never here— It just sits in the cupboard and no one enjoys it. Skylar, you come over any time, and I'll have tea for you."

Her excitement is contagious; I can't help but smile as I say, "Thank you, Lauren."

"Of course." She goes into the butler's pantry.

Alex looks to me as soon as she's gone. "How are you?" he asks, nearly in a whisper.

"I'm okay," I say. "Really."

"That's good." He doesn't sound convinced, but he doesn't press. "You looked ravishing last night."

I smile and shake my head. "As did you."

"Orion's so much taller than me, I had to roll up the pant legs of his tux."

I laugh. "That's amazing. I didn't even notice."

"Good. Where did Jessamine find that dress?"

"Her friend made it," I say. "She's very talented."

Lauren comes back into the kitchen with a wooden box. She sets it down on the counter, gingerly lifts the lid, and says, "Any kind you want, Skylar."

I decide on earl grey with rose petals. Lauren plunks it into a mallard duck mug and pours boiling water over it. She makes a warbler mug for herself of the same tea. "You reminded me we had this one," Lauren tells me. "I forgot how good it is. You'll love it." She sets the kettle back onto the stove. "When you want tea, you tell me, and I'll make you tea any time."

"Thank you, Lauren." I've never smelled better tea than this. I try to take a sip, but *shit*, when will I learn that I can't drink boiling water? This happens nearly every morning.

Alex laughs at me. "You should've seen the look on your face."

"Alex, I swear—"

I falter when Jacob comes into the kitchen. *Fantastic.* Instinctively, I try to smooth my hair down—people who claim that they "woke up like this" are *liars*. I need eight bobby pins and an industrial-strength hairbrush to not look like a silkie chicken. Not that he would care, since his hair is a total mess. *Good God.* He rubs his eyes a bit, which does *not* make the situation any better. *Can you* please *not be adorable for just* one *minute? Is it really that hard?* "Good morning," he says. Clearly, he didn't receive my mental plea.

"Hi," I say.

"Hi," he says.

"Hi."

"Good morning, roomie," Alex says.

Lauren hands him a sparrow mug. "Black with an ungodly amount of sugar. I don't know how you drink this."

He takes it from her. "Lauren, you are the best human being to ever walk this earth."

"Shut up." She flicks her hand at him and disappears into the butler's pantry.

"You," Alex says to Jacob, "get up so often in the middle of the night."

"Sorry," Jacob replies. He sits on the other side of Alex (not next to me, but I try not to notice).

"Oh, no, it's totally okay," Alex continues. "I got used to it, but I couldn't tell if you were awake or sleep-pacing."

"I was awake," Jacob says. "Sorry. Bad habit."

"It's cool. I didn't mind." Alex takes a sip of coffee. "How much sugar is ungodly?"

"However much you're thinking, it's more."

Alex looks to me. "Do you put sugar in your tea?"

"No," I say.

"Too sweet for you?" Jacob asks me.

"I guess," I say.

"You could add a little less."

"Or I could not add any at all."

"Isn't it boring then?"

"At least it doesn't taste like a liquified cavity."

We sit in silence until Alex says, "So, the river's, like, right there. That's cool."

"Yeah," Jacob says.

"Very cool," I say.

The silence settles back in.

"I had a dream last night that Tom Holland and I went rock climbing."

"How did the climb go?" Jacob asks.

"Pretty well. There was a polar bear there."

I take another sip of tea.

We sit quietly until Lauren comes out, holding a bunch of Tupperwares. "Did you all fall asleep again? Why are you so quiet?" She points to Jacob with her elbow. "Especially you."

"Not awake yet," Jacob answers. He takes another gulp of sugar. "How was your night last night, Lauren?"

"Not as interesting as yours," Lauren replies. "How did your gala go?"

"It was fine," Jacob says.

"Did you talk to that congressman about the bats?"

The three of us must look at her in horror; she laughs.

"Relax. I'm like you, Alex." She sets down her containers. "I freeze when they tell me to, but Hunter and Orion tell me everything. I know about Knowers and Eradicators and all the stuff you get yourselves into."

"Such a world we live in, Lauren," Alex says.

"Don't I know it," she says. "I consider myself lucky that I'm just a spectator."

"Every single day." Alex shakes his head.

"I can keep secrets." Lauren shrugs. "And those boys can't lie to me."

"So you know about the Eminence thing, then," Jacob says.

"Why do you think I always have *loukoumades* when you come over? Because I like you?"

Jacob smiles. "I know I'm your favorite."

Lauren points to me. "She is now. She drinks my tea."

"Thank you, Lauren," I say. "Sorry, Jacob."

"It's well-deserved," he says quietly. He doesn't look at me when he says it.

"Pancakes?" Lauren says from inside a cabinet.

"Your pancakes rival God's," Jacob says. He hops off his stool. "Need help?"

"Eggs from the fridge."

"I can help, too," I say. "Do you need anything else?"

"Me, too," Alex says.

"Butter, Skylar, on the counter opposite the stove," Lauren says. "Alex, you get the chocolate chips. Cabinet two to my left, middle shelf."

By the time we've gotten Lauren all the ingredients, Lexie and Hunter have come down. Lauren lets Lexie wake up with some coffee, but she puts Hunter right to work greasing pans. They bicker in Greek before she shoves the butter dish into his hands and points him towards a cabinet.

"Hallie's still asleep?" I ask Lexie.

"She sleeps like a hibernating bear," Lexie replies. "I would have woken her up, but I might have gotten eaten. How did you sleep?"

"Fine," I lie. "Did you like having a top bunk?"

"It was everything I dreamed and more," she says with a smirk.

Hunter joins us at the counter. "So, what's on the agenda for today?"

I pondered this question all night, and I don't really have an answer. I asked more questions than I answered at that gala, and quite honestly, I don't really want to think about anything (*anything*) that happened there. But I say, "Come up with a logical next step and take it."

"And what's the next logical step?"

"Call the wildlife group, I guess," I reply, though I'm not so sure. I decide to say that, in case someone else has a better idea of what should come next. "Though I don't know. It feels— I don't know. Like the answer should be easier to obtain."

"I know how you feel," Lexie says. "I feel the same exact way."

"Then we're definitely missing something," Hunter says.

"Where's Orion?" I ask.

"Still asleep, I guess," Hunter says. "He'll sleep until it's dark out again if no one wakes him up."

“You should go wake him up,” Lauren says.

“He hates when I wake him up,” Hunter replies.

I drink the last bit of my tea. “I can go with you,” I say.

“Okay,” Hunter says. He looks to Lexie. “Plan our joint funeral while we’re away.”

It’s a full workout to get to the third floor of Hunter’s house from the kitchen. I follow him up two flights of stairs, starting in the butler’s pantry, not the grand staircase out in the hall. We emerge in another storage room-type situation on the second floor, which seems to be used primarily to store fake flowers and vases.

“My mother has horrible allergies,” Hunter explains. “We can’t bring real flowers into any room she goes into unless we want her to sneeze. Though, sometimes, that’s what we want.”

“When?”

“Orion and I got super mad at her once, like a year ago, about something stupid, and we teamed up and replaced all the fake flowers with real ones. We felt too guilty, though, so by the time she got home from a meeting in the city, we’d already put all the fake ones back.”

“Diabolical.”

“She still sneezed a little.”

We get to the third floor after another hike, and Hunter marches straight to the door at the end of the hall. He doesn’t bother knocking and goes right in.

I’ve never spent any time imagining Orion’s room, since I have much more interesting things to worry about, but I can safely say that this would not have been my expectation. The walls are pale indigo, like the other half of the sky when the sun starts to rise, and one of them is completely taken up by a bookshelf. It isn’t overcrowded—it seems like he’s spent a lot of time organizing and curating the odd collection of things that occupy it in a perfect grid, vertical lines merely implied but somehow stronger than the horizontal ones. Some action figures (mostly Star Trek), big rocks, a blown-glass fish, three tea cups, a family of origami frogs, a light-saber (Sith—no surprise there), a pumpkin-shaped pot with a dead succulent, a jar of dirt, a wound-up string of Christmas lights, a Lego model of the Eiffel Tower, an old-fashioned hand mixer, and perhaps four hundred books. The rest of the room is just as orderly: His desk is pristine, the pillows on the window seats are plump and straight, and his bed is perfectly made. He is not inside of it.

Hunter sighs and turns around. I follow him down a flight of stairs and across the second floor, to a door at the end. This must be his parents' room, judging by the four-poster bed and lavish furnishings. He walks briskly through it to a set of French doors, which open to a balcony overlooking the bend of the river. From here, it seems to stretch nearly infinitely. Orion sits criss-cross-applesauce on the ground, woven blanket draped over his shoulders.

"It's freezing out," Hunter says to his brother.

"I find the cold quite invigorating." Orion doesn't turn around.

"You didn't come down for coffee first."

"I'm awake enough." He turns to face us. "Oh, good morning, Skylar, dear. I trust you slept terribly."

"You could say that," I say. "How are you?"

"Oh, you know."

"I don't know. That's why I asked."

"I am dandy."

"Lauren's making pancakes," Hunter says. "Do you want any?"

"Not particularly," Orion says. "I don't have much of an appetite this morning."

"We'll save you some for later."

"I'll come down in a spell." He turns back to the river.

Hunter doesn't leave, though that reads as a dismissal to me. With a critical eye, slightly narrowed, he studies Orion. Analyzes him like a set of lab results. Then he says, "You should eat something."

"I will. At some point."

"Now's a good point. You're gonna freeze out here."

"That's why I have a blanket."

Hunter rolls his eyes. "Fine. You can be like this if you want."

"Thank you. I quite enjoy being like this."

"We'll be downstairs."

"That sounds delightful."

We leave him on the balcony and go back inside.

"He is so annoying," Hunter says.

"He is," I agree, though I agree just to agree. Yes, he's undoubtedly annoying, but he seems . . . solemn, almost, though that doesn't seem like the right word. He exudes an energy I never knew him to be capable of exuding.

"At least breakfast will be enjoyable, then," Hunter says.

"Is he okay?" I ask.

"Is he ever?"

Chapter Nineteen

"You & I"
Colony House

After Lauren's pancakes, which are made out of magic and butter, we go get ready for the day. Lexie unbraids my hair and brushes it through for me, chattering about her cats. I let her play around with it until she decides on some twisty half-up thing that takes three hair ties. It's a little flouncy for me, especially paired with my black jeans and turquoise sweater with a raccoon on it. I'm better off than Hallie, though—Lexie's already spent a half-hour on her hair, and she kind of looks like a poodle since her curls from the gala last night haven't washed out.

"Are you feeling okay?" Hallie asks me while Lexie tugs at her curls.

"Yes," I say. "I'm fine."

"You're quiet."

"I watched a woman get shot yesterday. I'm sorry if I'm not in the mood for talking." I realize how rude that sounded. "I'm sorry. That was mean."

"It's okay," Hallie says. "I'm sorry I asked."

"The dresses last night were so beautiful," Lexie says, quickly changing the subject. "I would wear a ballgown every day if I could. No wonder people did for hundreds of years. They should have never gone out of style. Did you see that woman in the electric blue one? Interesting color choice, but the neckline was sooo pretty. I can show you the picture later. I took so many pictures of all the pretty dresses. I know, kind of questionable, but they were just so pretty!"

"I saw the one you're talking about," Hallie says. "It was pretty. I think my favorite was Darcy Brecken's, though. That was beautiful."

"Oh, I loved Darcy's dress!" Lexie agrees. "She looked like a sunbeam."

"Or Everett's wife's dress," Hallie says. "The shiny midnight purple? So pretty."

Lexie sighs. "I wish I were wearing a ballgown right now."

"You can go put one on," Hallie says.

She laughs. "Maybe I should. It makes me so much more motivated, you know? I feel like I'm a queen who's gotta go rule over her kingdom. I see why they wore them every day. All that *power*. The way it makes you feel taller, the way the fabric moves when *you* move—"

"The way the fabric moves," I say. I go over to Hallie's dress, hanging on the back of the bathroom door, take it by the hanger, and swish it around.

It's a different rustle than the one I heard right before the gunshot, but the killer's ballgown was made of a different material. Something stiffer. Cécile's gown was thin, quiet chiffon. It couldn't have been hers. There was another, stiffer fabric there.

"You okay, Sky?" Lexie asks.

"Just thinking," I say. "Lexie, could you show me all those pictures of ballgowns from the gala?"

She unlocks her phone and hands it to me. "I already made a special album with all of them in it."

"There are two hundred pictures in here."

"I have a big memory on my phone. Why not use it?"

I scroll through picture after picture as Hallie and Lexie talk, trying to envision what type of fabric could have made that sound. I go rustle Lexie's dress—it sounds like an ice storm because of all the sparkles—and then mine, which sounds just a little too weak. It was a thicker material than satin, it would seem. But not too much thicker. I look at the time stamps, too, to see if anyone was in the main ballroom at the time of the murder, but Lexie took these all pretty early into the night, so none of them coincide with Cécile's final moments.

I make a new folder containing all people wearing ballgowns of material thicker than satin, at least from what I can tell by the pictures. This includes Luciana Caldwell, Mary-Grace Carressy, Darcy Brecken, and eighteen other women. So I basically determined that it was not one of us, not one of eleven women wearing chiffon or organza, and not someone wearing a tuxedo.

And that's if my memory serves me correctly. But I think I can trust it. If I close my eyes, every single detail plays out right in front of me, and I undoubtedly heard the rustle of fabric. I wish there were a way to write down a sound so I won't forget what it sounds like.

But this recollection doesn't help me understand why she was murdered, or help me shake the feeling that there's still something I'm missing. Well, of *course* there is something I'm missing, since I can't answer any of the imperative questions. But this is more like a not knowing the picture the puzzle will create, rather than just missing a few pieces. I have no picture on the box to guide me. I'm not quite sure there's a picture at all.

There's a knock at the door. "Come in," Lexie says.

Alex comes in. "Damn, your room is cool."

"I know, right?"

"We're going up to the third floor to work on some stuff, if you guys are ready."

"This is the last pin," Lexie says, sticking one into the conglomeration of Hallie's hair.

"Thank God," Hallie replies. "I can't remember a time you weren't pulling at my hair."

I give Lexie her phone back, and we head up to the third floor. Jacob and Hunter are already there, but Orion is still nowhere to be seen. We sit in a circle on the floor.

"Where's Orion?" Hallie asks.

"Don't know," Hunter answers. "He's not on the balcony or in his room or with Lauren."

"Where else does he hide?" I ask.

"Don't know," Hunter repeats. "We'll start without him."

"And where, exactly, are we starting?" Lexie asks.

"Darcy Brecken gave me three phone numbers," I say, flipping to that page in my narwhal notebook. "Hers is first, then a man at a nature reserve, whom Darcy claims knows a lot about bats. Cécile Kettering's is the last, though it clearly would be no use to us now."

"At least she's out of Congress," Lexie says. She covers her mouth with both of her hands. "Oh my God. Sorry. It's too soon."

"It's okay," Hallie says. "We were all thinking it."

"I just mean that we don't have to worry about the embezzlement stuff now," Lexie says. "We can focus on this without worrying about that."

"Did Cécile say anything else to you?" Hallie asks Jacob and me.

"Some stuff about cows," Jacob says. "And how the farmers are doing pretty well and planting a bunch of crops. And as soon as we brought up Brazil, she got weird and left."

"Wait, Jacob," I say. "She mentioned planting more crops."

"Yeah, she did," he says. "More than ever before." As he says it aloud, I watch the realization dawn on him. He looks to me. "You don't think—"

"I *do* think."

"But she said she didn't know."

"Has someone never lied?"

"You'd think she'd have been easier to read."

"We weren't looking for the answers to a question we didn't ask."

"Hello?" Hallie interrupts. "Stop speaking in code. What are you talking about?"

"Cécile claimed not to know anything about what was happening in Brazil, but that's impossible," I say. "She must have if she's aware of all the new crops being planted, since all her farmers seem to know that's why they're doing what they're doing."

"Go through everything in the second ballroom again," Hunter says.

We do, this time going into even more depth about all the documents and things that we found, only leaving out the one detail that should be left out. Then it hits me. "Jacob! Where's the corn flash drive?"

"On the desk in the blue bedroom," he says. "Should we see what's on it?"

"If we're lucky, it will have all the documents."

"I'll get my laptop," Hunter says, and the two of them go downstairs.

When they come back, Hunter plugs in the flash drive, and we crowd around his laptop. Hunter flips through the files.

"Building plans," he says. "Land deeds, I think."

"For land in New York?" Lexie asks.

"Seems like it," Hallie says, reading one over. "Land near Redway."

"And Sharonsville?" I ask.

"What's Sharonsville?"

"Another town in Everett's district. Where he grew up."

"Yeah, land around there," Hunter says. "Sold to a bunch of different people."

"Are those contracts you were talking about on there?" Alex asks.

"I think so." Hunter shows Jacob one of the documents. "Is this it?"

"Same horrible font," Jacob says. "I can't read it."

"We'll probe it later." Hunter keeps flipping through the documents. "More building plans, and receipts, maybe. And insurance documents? Weird."

In a corner of my mind, I start planting some soybeans.

I know absolutely nothing about soybeans. Hold up pictures of different beans and ask me to identify the soy, and I could not do it. I am not up on my bean knowledge. But I've learned over the past few days that soybeans are not horribly picky. They like warmer weather, but not outrageously warm. They prefer fertile soil, but they aren't entirely opposed to drier soil, either. It isn't even that common for pests to munch on them, though it's been known to happen. It's happening right now, after all. No bats means more bugs and more bugs means fewer crops. The same three-link chain has been rolling around my head for days, yet it hasn't found another link. Where are they? Somewhere in Brazil? Or under the dirty snowdrifts of Redway?

I think I've found the answer in the latter.

Redway and Sharonsville and the farmers in between them are perfectly aware of the troubles in Brazil, or at least the results of them. That's why they're planting more crops, starting more farms, and building more barns. Increasing production. They know they will have to pick up the slack, and maybe they are, just a bit. Then again, farmers like high prices because it means what they're growing is worth more, so perhaps they won't.

Not only that, but those new soybeans we found in the second ballroom? The ones engineered to be more resistant? Should whatever's affecting the bats find itself near Redway, they would be ready. Hell, they might even take in more revenue by selling them elsewhere, to other places that could be prone to strife like this.

The ethics are fishy. If they know there's a problem in Brazil, shouldn't they do something about it? They can claim that they can't, but isn't there always something you can do? I know, I have more resources on hand than the average teenager, but everyone is capable of helping in one way or another. But if they keep the issue out of the public eye, no one feels guilty. It's like taking the last cookie from the jar without knowing that it's the last one. Someone else will be miffed, and it's totally your fault, but you don't know it. Or, at the very least, you convince yourself that you had no idea.

"They definitely know," I say, "and they've increased their own production, but not enough to fully compensate, because farmers benefit when prices rise."

"Oh, that's a yikes," Lexie says.

"Major yikes," Alex adds with a nod.

"So what do we do about it?" Jacob asks. "We can't really call them and tell them to stop what they've done to increase production, since soy prices are already on the rise as it is. I don't know how we would force them to grow more, especially when they seem to be increasing production as it is. And we can't make them help us in Brazil, since I don't really think it's their problem."

"Of course it's their problem," I say. "It's something happening in their industry. They should work to rectify it."

"They are," Jacob says. "By planting more crops."

"But that's not the right way to do it."

"It's *a* way to do it. Whether it's right or not—that's up for debate. But I can't say I really blame them for not intervening. How would they even go about doing that? *We* barely have an idea, and we have more resources and connections than the average person."

"Look how many resources and connections they have. All those land deeds and barn plans, and we didn't even go through half of that room. They certainly have the capital to intervene."

"But it's not just about having the resources," he says. "It's also about getting them there. It's thousands of miles away, in a different country with a different government. We're lucky since we have people there and ways to find more. Not everyone can get things there or get people to use them."

"There are ways to find ways." I try not to get aggravated with him, but that proves to be difficult. "We do it all the time, and we are sixteen and full-time students. I don't think they have an excuse beyond apathy."

"Look, I agree, I'm just saying that I understand why they didn't."

"Well, now *we* have to do something because they didn't. Imagine what might have happened if they *had*. We might not be in as much of a mess."

"But we *might* be."

"But we might *not* be."

"But we can't say for sure."

"We can't say *anything* for sure, Jacob. That's exactly what I'm saying."

"I'm aware, Skylar, that we can never say anything for sure."

"Things can happen at a moment's notice. You of all people should understand that."

"Um, guys," Hallie cuts in. My God, I forgot everyone else was here. My face spontaneously combusts. "Do you want to take a break?"

"We don't have time," I say. "I have to be home by one-thirty for Obligatory Family Dinner Night."

"And I have my piano lesson at four and a math test tomorrow I've barely studied for," Jacob says.

"Okay, then," Hallie says. "Can we be productive, then, if we have so little time?"

"We need a plan," I say, moving past Hallie's inquiry (or criticism). "A next step. Does anyone have an idea for a next step?"

"The second number that Darcy gave you," Lexie says. "The man who knows about bats. Let's call him and see what he would do in this situation. Or see if he knows anything about what's going on and can give us some insight."

"I'll do it," Hunter says. "I have nothing else to do today once you all go home."

"And I'll look into the increase in Redway's crops," Hallie says. "Check out the numbers and see when it all started. Maybe that can help us figure out how long this has been going on."

"Have I missed something?" Orion traipses into the room, fully dressed but still with his blanket over his shoulders, clutching a swallowtail mug with both hands.

"A shit ton," Hunter says. "Where were you?"

"Lost in the depths of my own mind," Orion replies, joining our circle between Hunter and Jacob. "I apologize for missing important Knower time."

"It's fine," I say. "Hunter, can you catch him up on the minutia later?"

"I guess," Hunter says with a sigh. "I'll go call Bat Man now. Orion, come with me."

"Right on, dear brother." The Athan boys go to Orion's room at the end of the hall.

Chapter Twenty

"Good for You"
Castro

    I close my eyes for what I think is not even a full second, just to wipe my mind like a chalkboard and clap the dust from the eraser, but when I open my eyes again, Lexie and Hallie are gone. "Where did they go?" I ask.

    "To get water," Alex says. "Like, a minute ago." He's no longer surprised by our brains acting like this. It was amusing when he first joined our friend group, since he didn't quite know how to react when we asked people to repeat things four times, or when we tried to count out thirty seconds but couldn't do it in thirty seconds or we did it in three, or when we zoned out and came back and a half-hour had disappeared. He's gotten used to his weird friends, even if he struggles to understand what it's like when time has no effect on you. It's a very difficult thing to understand.

    "Oh," I say. "Thanks."

    Since it's just him, Jacob, and me, the Awkwardness settles in. Maybe if I close my eyes again, it will go away. I try, and it doesn't work. The Awkwardness sticks like industrial-strength glue.

    "This is a pretty cool room," Alex says.

    "It is," Jacob says.

    "Yes," I agree.

    That's the end of that conversation. Alex tries again: "We have global tomorrow. That's cool. Probably gonna talk about World War I."

    "That should be exciting," I say.

    "Yes," Jacob agrees.

    Alex gives up. "I'm going to go get water. Would you like any?"

"No, thank you," Jacob says, and I repeat him.

"Okay." Alex practically sprints down the stairs. He was smart. I should have gone with him.

Jacob and I don't speak. He fiddles with a twist tie he definitely had in his pocket, and I aimlessly flip through my narwhal notebook, though there isn't anything interesting in here. I wrote it all, so I know what it all is. I stare at it to keep me from glancing over at him. He's wearing a stupid sweater and button-down, and I can't stand it. Boys should not be allowed to wear sweaters, especially if they're already endearing. It isn't fair to those of us with boys-wearing-sweaters weaknesses and better things to worry about.

Part of me thinks I should say something to him, but the much more rational part of me knows that will do much more harm than good. Besides, it's definitely his turn to initiate conversation first if he feels so inclined. Not that he should. Not that I even want to talk to him.

But after a few hours pass, he says, "Skylar."

I love the way he says my name. I don't know why. It sounds exactly the same as everyone else says it. Same emphasis, same cadence, same euphony. Only his voice is different, as everyone's is, but that's not even it. His intention, perhaps, how every time he says my name, he means it. He says it like a promise—it makes something at the bottom of my chest glow.

"Jacob," I reply, wondering if he feels anything even close to that when I say his name.

"Never mind," he says.

My God, why are boys the most stupid creatures in the universe? Even the smart ones are complete idiots. I can't help but sound a little aggravated when I say, "Never mind?"

"Yeah, it's . . . unimportant."

"Unimportant."

"Yeah."

I turn back to my narwhal notebook and pretend to ignore him. He goes back to his twist tie.

Fortunately for us, the door to Orion's bedroom swings open, and the Athan brothers return, arguing with each other in Greek.

"I take it your phone call went well," Jacob says.

"No." Hunter plops on the ground. "It went terribly."

"It certainly did not go as we had expected or hoped," Orion says. He sits on the sectional like a father watching his children play. "I do believe Darcy Brecken made a mistake."

"How so?" I ask.

"The man was certainly a wildlife enthusiast, but he didn't know much of anything about bats," Orion explains.

"He was a freaking fisherman," Hunter says. "Said we could ask him bat questions anyway, but he didn't know any of the answers. We asked if he knew of any sicknesses that could affect bats, and he said he didn't think bats could get sick."

"Did Darcy miswrite the number?" I wonder. "Or mix up her wildlife friends?"

"Whatever she did, she gave us a dead end," Hunter says with a curt shake of his head. "Sorry, guys. We tried."

"It's okay," I say. "We just need a new next step, then, seeing as though that one took us nowhere."

"I believe we should focus on determining the exact pathogen ailing the bats," Orion recommends. "And then decide the best course of action for combating the illness."

"Okay," I say. "Orion, could you do that tonight, since you don't have any homework?"

"I would be happy to oblige, Skylar, dear," Orion says. "I shall get in touch with some Brazilian news outlets and research centers and see what they have discovered."

"And I'll do my chem homework," Hunter says.

It seems that we've lost all motivation after the botched phone call with the Non-Bat Man, so we decide to call it for the day so we can work on our homework and get a reasonable amount of sleep before school tomorrow. We pack up our things (which takes Lexie a million years), thank Lauren for having us, and head back home. I walk with Hallie, going the long way around the Northern Tip, past the Rathcliffe Manor, so that we can enter our street from the other side so it looks like we're coming from Lexie's house, just in case our parents happen to see us approach our houses.

"Are you feeling okay?" Hallie asks me.

"Yes," I say, and I try to mean it. "Are *you* feeling okay?"

"Of course," she says. "So, can I ask you something?"

"If you feel so inclined."

"Are you and Jacob—"

"Never mind," I say. "You can't ask me something."

"You two were, like, extra tense today, even by your usual standards. Did something happen, or—"

"Nothing happened," I say. "He's horribly annoying and argumentative and he bothers me."

"Right," Hallie says. "Then I'll just come out and ask it. Why aren't either of you doing anything about the thing going on be-tween you?"

"Hallie."

"I'm serious. We all have to live with your weird tension, too, and it's agonizing."

"It shouldn't be, because there is no *thing*. There never was."

"Skylar. He told a room of the world's smartest people that he was in love with you."

Exasperated, I stop walking. "First of all, that isn't what he said. Second of all, it isn't like he had much of a choice. And third of all, there is no reason for us to talk about something incon-sequential that happened six months ago when there are many more pressing issues that are far more urgent and far more in-teresting."

She stops right next to me and crosses her arms. "Look. I know you don't talk about stuff like this, like feelings and stuff. And that's fine. You don't have to tell me any details or specifics or anything, but God, Skylar, if you don't talk about it, you might ex-plode. And you clearly haven't talked to him about any of this."

"Yes, I have," I say, almost without my own permission. "A few days after The Thing happened."

"Oh," Hallie says. "And how did it go?"

I sigh. There is no way I am getting out of this. "Come on." I pull her across the street and to a park bench that overlooks the river. We toss our overnight bags to our feet and pull our coats tighter around us to combat the wind. It's stronger near the river, as most things are. "It went how I wanted it to go, which is not actually how I wanted it to go."

"Okay," she says. She, of course, knows just what I mean by that—we've known each other long enough for her to translate my language. "And have you talked about it since then?"

"What is there to talk about?" I throw my hands up. "We decided that nothing else should happen. And almost nothing else did."

"Else?"

"You said no details."

"Fine. What about the *almost*?"

"That qualifies as a detail."

She dryly chuckles. "You're difficult."

"I know," I say. "Any more questions?"

"Do you still have feelings for him?"

"That's such a stupid phrase," I say. "You have feelings about everyone you meet, be them good or bad or completely indifferent."

"You know what I mean."

I don't respond.

She takes this as my answer. "So what are you going to do about it?"

"Nothing," I say. "It'll go away eventually. We're teenagers. We're flighty and fickle and our emotions change with the tides."

"Is that really the best thing to do?"

"Do you have a better idea?"

"Tell him."

"That is an absolutely horrible idea."

She laughs again. "Skylar, he looks at you like you built the Chrysler Building. It doesn't take a Knower to see that. So . . . look. Maybe it's not a terrible idea for you guys to be together."

"It's a fairly terrible idea."

"You work well together. You know that. Your brains are like inverses, and it makes you a good team. You don't have to play by all those stupid dating rules that would get in the way of the good things about what you already have. I think you both would be much happier."

"Until we inevitably break up and have to see each other once a year at the very least. Or we disagree over something and we argue and start to hate each other. Or we distract each other and start to mess everything up."

"You've handled much worse than running into an ex, and once a year is nothing, especially when it doesn't exist. You already fight like an old married couple, and you don't hate each other yet. And I think you distract each other more now than you would if you were dating."

I consider this. Maybe she's right. Or maybe she's wrong. She's definitely wrong, actually. I can't allow myself to think like that—that's how I get complacent. If you get complacent, you get caught. And—even worse—hope starts to seep in like hydrogen peroxide on a cotton ball, all fizzy and eccentric until it hits the open wound and burns like the thirty-thousand kelvins of a lightning bolt. Hope's just a prettier, more virtuous lie.

To save myself from whatever impact comes next, I push the thought as far away as I can and say, "Okay, that far surpassed enough emotional vulnerability for the month. And I have Obligatory Family Dinner in less than an hour.”

“Fine,” she says. “One more question.”

“If it’s really entirely necessary, then sure.”

She tosses me a devilish grin. “Is he a good kisser?”

“Hallie!” I swat her arm. “You said no details.” I stand up and throw my bag over my shoulder. “But, if you really must know, yes, he is.”

She laughs pretty much the entire way home.

Chapter Twenty One

"I'm Through"
Ingrid Michaelson

I try absolutely every approach I can think of to get out of going to Obligatory Family Dinner Night. I tell them I'm exhausted and my head hurts. That I just found out I have an essay due tomorrow and I haven't started it yet. That Hallie also found out she has an essay due tomorrow and now she's nervous (they see through this one immediately—the Great Hallie Giovia isn't afraid of an essay).

"Go get ready," my mom says, arms crossed, "or else you aren't going to another sleepover the night before family dinner."

I quit arguing and put my dress on—the blue one, the same one I wore to meet Everett at the laundromat. I choose not to fix my hair out of protest—which doesn't really work, since Lexie did it all fancy for me this morning, so it actually looks nicer than it has in awhile (disregarding the updo last night, which was the best my hair has ever looked ever).

My whole body feels as if it were made of lead, and everything annoys me. The song on the car radio is terrible, my parents' voices sound like nails on a chalkboard, and Evan won't stop tapping out a beat on the car door. I need to cry, I think. I feel like a dam with a crack in it trying to hold back a rising tide. There aren't any tears in my eyes yet, but there so easily could be. If I see one animal by the side of the road, that'll do me in.

"What did you do at Lexie's last night?" Dad asks as we cross the bridge.

"Oh, you know," I say. "Gossiped about people in our class, watched *Clueless* for the thousandth time, baked cinnamon rolls and ate every single one. The usual."

"That sounds nice," Mom says. "What's in the tote bag you brought?"

I glance at the bag at my feet, where I've carefully folded Jessamine's gown. "Something Aunt Jessamine let me borrow awhile ago. I've kept forgetting to return it to her."

"Good thing you remembered," she says. Thank goodness she didn't ask what it was.

Then Evan asks, "What is it?"

"A dress I thought I would wear," I say. "I never wore it."

"Yeah, I didn't think you'd want to wear that," he says, peering into the bag. "It's red."

"Exactly," I say. "I don't wear red."

When we get to Grandma and Grandpa's house, the Rainers haven't arrived yet, which is strange. They usually beat us. Of course, this makes me horribly nervous. What if something happened to Harlow and they had to take her to the hospital or call an ambulance or she's already—

Their car pulls in right behind ours. I feel the tension in my shoulders ease a bit—not entirely—but then Harlow climbs out of the car.

Slams the door.

She splatters across the ground, starlight oozing from her chest, collapsing next to the corpse of Cécile Kettering.

I could scream. I do, somewhere in my head. My feet would run if they could on their own, and my lungs give up. But I am not around people who just watched what I saw. To them, Harlow's still standing and Cécile doesn't exist. If I react to something they can't see, then they learn something. Whether it's about me or what I know is up for debate, but I would rather not have anyone learn anything. So I shut my eyes, clutch the ends of my sleeves, swallow the stomach acid that's crept up the back of my throat, and imagine roots growing out of my feet and attaching me to the driveway like a tree.

"You look like you stepped on a dead rat with your bare foot," Harlow says.

I hug her.

"I know, you missed me a ton."

"I did," I say. "It's been too long, Harlow June. Are you okay? How are you?"

"Fine," she says. "Nothing's happened in my life. It's been so *boring*."

"Mine, too."

She grabs my hand, and we escape upstairs to Jessamine's old bedroom before anyone can intercept us. She gently closes the door behind us so it doesn't alert anyone to our location, and she jumps onto the bed. "So, what's shaking?"

I spend an extra second looking her over. Her sapphire eyes glimmer, hair like a chocolate waterfall, rosy color in her cheeks, no hole in her chest. Ten fingers, looks like ten toes under her panda socks, same height, same proportions, no hole in her chest.

"Hello?" she says.

"Oh," I say. "Sorry. I zoned out." I join her on the bed. "Lots of things are shaking."

"Are you in a bad mood?"

"No," I say. "I'm just tired. Sleepover last night. With Hallie and Lexie."

"Ooo," she says. "That sounds fun."

"Yes."

We're quiet for a bit, and then she says, "Okay. What's up?"

"Nothing's up," I say. "I'm fine."

"I know you too well to believe that."

"I'm just—" *God, Skylar, if you don't talk about it, you might explode.* The tears start then, letting a little air out of the balloon in my head. "I feel like . . . like I'm trapped."

"Trapped?"

"I'm supposed to be one thing because that's what everyone has to be, but I also have to be this other thing."

"You have another part in the musical now?" she asks.

"Sort of," I say. "I— So it's, like, well, there are the leads. And I'm very good friends with one of the leads. I would find a way to stop the world from turning if he asked me to do so. But some of the ensemble members think we should do this scene-type thing without most of the leads, except for two of them. And it's like . . . the scene would be much better with all the leads playing. But it's too late now to work them in. They would be upset that they weren't involved in the first place, or they would be angry that we couldn't do it ourselves, or they'd try to dismantle everything we're already completed, which isn't bad, even without their help."

"Ah, okay."

"But, it's— it's so hard having to be two different people. Three, almost, depending on whom I'm around. I'm exhausted. I have to remember so many lines and keep millions of secrets so the people in the audience aren't aware of everything onstage.

That ruins it. If everyone knows, the theater combusts. It would be utter chaos.”

“It’s supposed to be fun,” Harlow says. “You do the show because you love performing. If it’s not perfect, then it’s not perfect. If there’s a smile on your face—and there usually is—the audience will love it.”

“It *has* to be perfect, though,” I say. “There is more at stake than I could even comprehend. I have to keep track of every little detail, know every person’s next move, anticipate things that I don’t know because I should be seven steps ahead of everyone else, just by nature of my part.”

“Well, Skylar Amelia, here’s my advice, and you can take it or leave it.” Harlow grips my hand, and it shimmers a bit, golden like the rest of her. “Take a break. Breathe a bit. Toss the sky away from your shoulders and give yourself a minute. There are a lot of other people in the musical. And I know you think that they can’t carry it without you—and you’re probably right—but they can handle it for the night.”

“What did you say? About the sky on my shoulders?”

“Like Atlas, that Greek dude.”

“But I don’t realize that I do it,” I say.

She smiles. “Hell no, you don’t.”

She said that to me not an hour before she died last April. We were in the Smithsonian Castle, right after we’d learned the Knowers weren’t whom they’d made themselves out to be, kicked out of the tower by Margaret. There’s no way she remembers, but regardless of time, she believes it. It’s immutable.

“Are you going to stop crying now?” Harlow asks.

“I haven’t decided,” I say. “Maybe not yet.”

“We can watch *Titanic* if you want, and then I’ll cry, too,” she says.

I laugh. “If you want.”

Eventually, there’s a knock at the door, and Jessamine pokes her head in. “Hello, darlings.”

“Hi, Aunt Jessamine,” Harlow says. “We’re hiding.”

“I can see that.” She smiles. “Grandma would like some help peeling potatoes, though.”

Harlow looks to me. “I’ll go. You stay here for a bit and I’ll tell everyone that we were watching sad puppy videos.”

“Thank you,” I say.

“Everything alright, Skylar?” Jessamine asks me.

“Just some sad puppy videos,” I say.

I actually do go downstairs a few minutes later, after staring at the mirror in Jessamine's room for far too long to see if I look like I've been crying. And yes. I do. Very much so. I look like that meme of the cat with tears in its eyes. And my eyes are stuck at their darkest setting: wet concrete. I try thinking about happy whales, but they don't change. I try baby otters, and still nothing. Then I try Jacob, and they manage to darken even more. That is not a good sign. Usually they look like an overcast sky when I think about Jacob. (And yes, I know this from hours of studying my eyes in my bathroom mirror, thinking about different things and cataloguing the colors they become. You would do the same thing if your eyes changed color. Don't pretend that you wouldn't.)

My family greets me but doesn't say much else. Judging by their whispers and glances in my direction, Harlow asked them not to ask me what's wrong.

"I brought your dress back," I tell Jessamine as we help Grandma set the table. "Mrs. Darner cut the ball scene."

"Oh no, I'm sorry," Jessamine says. "I would have loved to have seen you onstage in that dress."

"It did make me feel like a princess," I tell her.

We sit at the table, and it's a shame I'm not hungry. Grandma's food is edible heaven. I try my best to eat enough to not raise suspicion, but the pasta reminds me of Cécile's blood and the spinach looks like her unblinking eyes, so it makes me queasy.

"I was grocery shopping the other day," Aunt Clara says to my dad, "and all the produce prices were through the roof. You should have seen the prices on some of the fruit. I mean, three dollars a pound for apples! And ShopSmart raised the tofu prices *again*. We've been trying to cut down our meat intake, but it's impossible when they charge so much."

I'm not really supposed to talk at the table, since my grandfather still believes in the ancient seen-and-not-heard rule for children, but I risk it and ask, "Aunt Clara, how much did the tofu cost?"

"Four-eighty-something," she says. "It's usually three at the most."

"I wonder if there's some sort of soy shortage," I say.

"There can't be," Aunt Clara says. "My friend Polly—you remember Polly, Edward, from Sunday school—her sister's in the soy business a few miles from Syracuse, and she says that her sister says that they're getting ready to expand their crops this year."

"Do you know why?" I ask. "Why now?"

"I don't know anything about farming," Aunt Clara says. "Just that they were told that this would be a good year to plant more. And all the land around her has been sold up. A bunch of new farmers are coming in."

"New farmers?"

"That's what she says." Aunt Clara shrugs. "I don't know, Skylar. I didn't know you were so interested in soy. If you're looking at studying agriculture in college, I'd be happy to put you in touch with Polly who could get you in touch with her sister."

"May I be excused?"

"You okay?" Harlow asks.

"Totally fine. I'll be right back." I don't wait for permission. I run back upstairs and lock myself in Jessamine's bedroom.

It's six-thirty-four now; I should be back to the table by six-forty. Since I can't be gone for too long, I will my brain to work fast in a fruitless attempt to get time to side with me. *Please, time, work with me a bit here.* I pace around the tiny room, letting my mind search for the things it needs to find.

More crops. More farmers. Buying up land. If the US soybean industry is as booming as Aunt Clara claims, why are prices still skyrocketing?

I pull my phone from my pocket and see if there's anything in the Central New York news about soy, flipping through articles as I keep pacing around the room. There is absolutely nothing. Nothing about rising prices, initiatives to plant more crops, or the influx of new farms. The only pertinent article that comes up is about Cécile. I take a breath and open it.

They ruled her death to be a suicide. How, I have absolutely no idea. I *did* actually witness the shooting, so I know for a fact that it's false, but even if you weren't present, it was so clearly a murder. I saw where she was shot, and her arm would have had to been abnormally bendy and unnervingly long to reach that part of her chest. Besides, there was no weapon at the scene, unless someone went back after I'd evacuated and planted one.

Don't think about it. Push it away. Back to soybeans.

Not even the NYCSGA website has a public call to plant more crops or an advertisement seeking new farmers. It makes no sense. You'd think that to combat a shortage of something, you would need to reach out to strangers. Are there no strangers in New York's twentieth congressional district? It's small enough that it wouldn't surprise me.

But, still, that's unrealistic. That makes no sense. If they were expecting a shortage, then, sure, I suppose, they were prepared in theory. But their preparations didn't work. Prices are still high. A few extra farmers in Central New York can't make up for the entire state of Paraná's industry.

But how would they *anticipate* a shortage in the first place? How could they know that bats were going to get sick and die out and stop eating the pests?

I drop my phone.

They would know if they intended it.

They find a way to get the bats sick. Covert enough of an approach that the crops don't fail immediately, and it doesn't look as if anything was sabotaged. If all the crops died at once and there didn't seem to be a good reason, then that would raise suspicions, but bats? No one thinks about bats. Bats are spooky. The general public doesn't know or care a lot about them. People won't want to read articles or watch news reports about droves of dead bats because bats are gross and dead ones are worse.

So then, knowing that soybean farming is about to become a lucrative business, they plan on starting new farms—hence the land deeds and plans for farm buildings—and encourage Central New Yorkers to get involved. They could knock Brazil out as the only competitor for owning the soybean market. All those building plans—extra-convoluted and time-consuming—creates new jobs for construction workers. The population increases. The economy gets back on track.

And their constituents would love them.

I almost text my friends immediately, but it will have to wait until after dinner. I look at my phone, and it's— well, it's still six-thirty-four. Only a few seconds have passed.

I go back downstairs and spend the rest of dinner silent, building a new plan in my head.

There is no way in hell that I will allow Everett Caldwell to steamroll Brazilian farmers for his own political gain.

Chapter Twenty Two

"The Way It Was"
Coast Modern

As soon as I get home from Obligatory Family Dinner Night, I tell everyone to meet me at the Café on Dove Street as soon as possible. Once we've all gotten our hot chocolate (black coffee for Hunter) and they're all sitting down, I tell them of my discovery.

"That can't be true," Alex says. "Stuff like that doesn't happen."

"I think it's true," I say. "And stuff like that *does* happen. The Knowers just try their best to keep it underground when it does."

"I agree," Hallie says. "But— My God, people are the worst. How sick do you have to be to think that's a good idea?"

"What are we gonna do about it?" Lexie asks, eyes wide, ripping apart a paper napkin, making a little snowdrift on the table. "Like, where do you even turn a person like this in? Who do we even go to?"

"I don't know," I say. "At this point, we might have to get other Knowers involved. Especially if my theory that they're planning on expanding beyond Paraná proves to be true."

"I'm sorry, but I wholeheartedly disagree," Orion says. "We have gotten this far on our own. To engage other people now would be to admit that we did not engage them sooner, and that would make them detest us even more than they already do, especially once we admit that we've broken some rules."

"Technically, though," Jacob says, "we didn't do anything we weren't supposed to do. Nothing we did requires approval from anyone but the Eminences, and we certainly had their approval."

"Jacob, my friend," Orion says, "we did not go through Treasury for anything."

He's right—we acquired and distributed funding for Redway elementary school art programs without going through Treasury, which is in direct violation of *Practices and Rituals*. The other Knowers—especially Eula—would be furious that we didn't follow proper procedures, and Miss Felding would be horribly disappointed that we didn't ask her for help.

"Oh, right," Jacob says. "Well, shit."

"Precisely my point," Orion says.

"So we continue to handle this by ourselves." Hunter shrugs. "We've been doing it this long."

"So what do we do next, then?" Hallie asks.

"I have a few ideas," I say.

"Of course you do."

"First, we need a toxicology report and a virology panel."

"Oh, I'll do that!" Lexie raises her hand as if this were a classroom. "I can call Glaucia Alejo Bardo. Last I talked to her, when I helped Hallie get that list of protocols, she loved talking about her cats with me. I'm sure I can get the toxicology report and a virology panel from her, and maybe some kitten pictures."

"Perfect," I say. "Thank you, Lexie."

"Then what?" Hallie asks.

"I think we need to figure out who killed Cécile."

"Are you okay to do that?" Hallie asks. "Because—"

"I can handle it," I interrupt. This time, I'm pretty sure I mean it. "Whoever murdered Cécile is part of this whole operation. I think the second ballroom was the headquarters or hub of it. And Cécile found out about them moving forward with the plan during the gala, and she threatened to speak out against it or turn people in or something of that nature, so they killed her."

"It was probably Everett, then," Hallie says.

"I don't think so," I say. "I might have misheard, but I seem to remember every moment astonishingly clearly. I definitely heard the rustle of a ballgown. And Cécile wore chiffon that night, which is soundless, so it wasn't her dress. Whoever killed her was wearing a ballgown made of a material heavier than satin. So it was Darcy Brecken, Luciana Caldwell, Mary-Grace Carressy, or one of eighteen other women, judging from the obsessive amount of unsolicited photos Lexie took."

"Hey, they came in handy," she defends.

"Who seems the most likely suspect?" Hunter asks. "Not Mary-Grace Carressy, that's for sure. Lexie and I talked to her for, like, fifteen minutes, and she looked like she was going to cry the whole time.”

“Yeah,” Lexie agrees. “She volunteers at the hospital rocking the newborn babies and her voice sounds like a whisper all the time. I’m surprised she’s in politics, let alone a murderer. Not that there’s too much of a difference.”

“She was also one of Cécile’s super close friends,” Jacob says. “Cécile said she was the only one at the gala she genuinely liked. Loved, even, in her words.”

I think for a second, and then I ask, “Jacob, do you have any idea who else was in the second ballroom?”

“I don’t know everyone in there,” he says. “For certain, Luciana, Cécile, Joachim Winston, and at least four-ish other people, but I don’t know who. And then Joachim Winston came back when— before we left. But who knows who came in after that?”

“But who were the other ones in there when you were in there, then?” Hallie wonders. “There could have been other women with noisy dresses, too, and one of them could have killed Cécile.”

“Is there a way to find that out?” Lexie asks.

“There might be,” Hunter says. “Do you think the Princess Alice has security cameras?”

“Maybe,” Hallie says. “It’s a super old building, but they must have something.”

“If they do, Orion and I can get into them,” Hunter says. “That’s, like, day one Eradicator stuff. Our parents had us doing that at the museums in the city by the time we were six.”

“It is true,” Orion says. “Both of us are quite adept in the ways of reaping the rewards from technology.”

“Don’t phrase it like that,” Hunter says. “It’s weird.”

“Right on, brother.”

“Would we have to go back to Redway?” Lexie asks.

“We wouldn’t have time before the musical runs,” Alex says. “Tech week starts tomorrow. So we have rehearsal until five-thirty every night until opening night on Friday. And Darner wouldn’t be happy if any of us skipped.”

“I could go on my lonesome,” Orion says. “I would love to explore more of Redway.”

“What is there to explore in Redway?” Hallie asks. “Corn and concrete buildings?”

“When researching our favorite town in Central New York, I discovered a nifty little hiking trail adjacent to the town,” Orion says. “There is a crick and a waterfall.”

"A what?" Jacob asks.

"A crick and a waterfall."

"A creek?"

"There is no semantic difference between the pronunciations, my dear fellow Eminence."

Jacob almost continues arguing, but he stops himself. "So you'll go to Redway and hike the crick and somehow get security camera footage?"

"It will be a wonderful small vacation for myself," Orion says. "I, of course, will have to stay overnight at the wonderful Princess Alice, but I suspect that it will be quite an experience."

"Why do you have to stay overnight?" Lexie asks.

"I don't believe I would be able to obtain the footage in broad daylight. It's best I complete the mission under the shroud of nighttime. Besides, I would like ample time to spend at the crick and the waterfall."

"Stay as long as you need," Hunter says. "You could even stay two or three days if you wanted."

"Please halt your joshing, brother."

"Never."

"Then I'll work on a Plan B in case something goes awry," I say.

"I assure you, Skylar, dear, that nothing will go wrong."

"It's always good to have a backup. Especially if you get lost in the woods. In the meantime, Darcy gave me her number, so I'm going to call her tonight and offer my condolences and see if she has anything else to say."

"I'll do some digging on Joachim Winston," Hallie says. "I'm sure the Internet has something about him."

"I can find some stuff on the other women who were there," Lexie says.

"I would love to help out, but I have a math test tomorrow," Jacob says. "On derivatives. Power rule, chain rule, all that fun stuff." Jacob takes extremely advanced math classes since he's legitimately a math genius, and sometimes he forgets that we're all in geometry or trig and usually have no idea what he's talking about.

"It's okay," I say. "Good luck on your derivatives."

"I hope you derive some fun," Alex says.

"Alex, that was horrible," Jacob says, "but thank you."

"And we'll start from here tomorrow morning with more information?" Hallie recommends.

"Definitely," I say. "Try to be at school early if possible with new information. The longer this goes on, the more bats die, the more crops fail, and the harder it will be to fix everything. Can you be there by six-thirty?"

"Fuck no," Hunter says. "That's disgusting. No."

"It's only an hour before school starts," I say.

"I get up at seven-twenty."

"School starts at seven-thirty," Lexie says.

"And have I been late yet?"

We all say, "Yes." Even Orion says it, and he doesn't go to school with us.

"Be there at six-thirty," I tell him. "Or else."

"Or else what?"

"You don't want to find out," Hallie says.

It's approaching nine o'clock at night, which would ordinarily be too late to call someone, but a woman was killed, so I think it's okay. At least this time. (Though I find myself saying that most, if not every, time.) I climb up the stairs to my little glass room with my phone and my mini narwhal notebook. I find the page where Darcy scribbled the three phone numbers and her address.

Cécile's phone number catches my eye first. Pristinely written, the area code one number off from Darcy's, squiggly dashes between the three and four digits.

She and Darcy must have been close if Darcy were able to recall her phone number off the top of her head. She must have also been close with the fisherman.

But not close enough to realize that he knows nothing about bats.

She didn't pull out her phone or anything when she wrote them down for us, and who can remember phone numbers? Off the top of my head, I can only do mine, my parents', Harlow's, and Hallie's (after that unfortunate incident with my phone dying last April when she and Lexie were in Eradicator headquarters). How was she supposed to know each of the ten numbers of someone's phone number without realizing that this person was not a bat person?

How could she have even assumed she knew?

Despite any part of my better judgment, I dial Cécile's number.

The phone is answered by a man who sounds like he eats gravel. "Hello?"

I jump a bit. "Hi, I'm looking for the family of Cécile Kettering."

"Who?"

"Cécile Kettering." I pretend I think she's still alive. "I was given this number for her."

"Wrong number."

"Oh. I'm sorry to bother you." Surely, this must be someone else of interest. "May I ask your name?"

"No, you may not." He mocks my tone a bit. I hate when people do that. "Who are you?"

"Matilda Greenwald," I say, finally able to use my fake name. This is the perfect opportunity. "Do you know Cécile Kettering?"

"Never heard of her."

"Really?"

"Do I need to say it twice? Never heard that name in my life."

"May I ask how long you've had this phone number?"

"About five or six years."

"And you've never heard the name Cécile Kettering?"

"Good God. I won't say it again. Never heard of her. This isn't her number. Goodnight." He hangs up.

I see where this is going.

I try the first number Darcy gave me—the one she claimed to be her own. It rings and rings until someone answers, "Marco's Pizzeria, how may I help you?"

I close my eyes. "I have the wrong number," I say. "*Spiacente. Ciao.*"

"What?"

I hang up, retrieve my laptop, and look up the address she gave me and said was her own. According to both Google Maps and Zillow, it does not exist.

In my head, I replay all the voices I heard in the second ballroom, but I can't remember them well enough. I bite the bullet and text Jacob, *Do you remember a voice that sounded like Darcy Brecken's in the second ballroom?*

He responds a few minutes later. *Maybe. I can't say for sure. Wouldn't surprise me, though.*

All three numbers that Darcy gave us were incorrect, and the address doesn't exist.

He calls me immediately. "What do you mean, they were all incorrect?"

"Hunter and Orion tried the middle one and got a fisherman. I tried Cécile's and got a very scary man who had never heard of her. Then I tried Darcy's and got a pizza place. And there is no 178 on Tersia Street in Sharonsville. It starts at 240, and it doesn't look like a residential street. She purposely gave us false information."

"Why would she do that?"

"To ensure that we would never speak to her again," I say.

"Do you think she killed Cécile?"

"I don't know," I say. "She could have, judging by the material of her ballgown, but I don't know. Cécile claimed that they were friends."

"So? That doesn't mean she wouldn't murder her. Daniel, we're talking about a book for English. I'll tell you later. She definitely could have murdered her, even if one of them claimed to be friends with the other. She sounded like she didn't agree with the plan."

"What sane person would?"

"I don't know," he says. "Everett was going to lose his district, and maybe this was the only way he could think to keep it. The bus garage wasn't enough."

"I liked your bus garage."

"Thank you."

"I guess I just have trouble imagining that a person could be that cruel."

"I used to, but not since Freja," he says. "She desensitized me to bad people. She might be the worst of them all."

"Funny that—" I stop myself. *Funny that it was actually all Orion's idea*, I almost say, but then I remember that he still doesn't know that Orion managed to convince Freja to kill Stellan and alter the Winther strain's vaccine to start a pandemic which would subsequently lead to the Knowers and Eradicators merging.

My stomach twists.

"Funny that what?" he asks.

"That we deal with a lot of terrible people, but none could possibly surpass her," I say. "I'll let you get back to your derivatives. See you tomorrow."

"See you tomorrow," he repeats. It would seem we're not back to Bubble territory yet, but that doesn't surprise me. I have a feeling it will take quite a bit for us to get back to Bubble territory, if we find ourselves there at all.

I almost call him back and tell him about the Orion thing.

I'd planned on telling him as soon as I came downstairs from the fourth floor of Cooper Hewitt, but that did *not* go according to plan. (Read: I slipped up and accidentally told him that I was in love with him.) It's probably better that I didn't mention the Orion thing anyway, anyway, since he didn't need another thing on his mind that night. (Granted, I *did* give him another thing on his mind that night, but I stand by the fact that it really was unintentional. I have yet to intentionally tell him however it is I feel about him.)

We had only one conversation about The Thing that had happened, and it didn't touch on Orion at all. I caught him on his way to math class, pulled him into the empty classroom before his teacher got there, and told him that whatever was going on with us couldn't go on anymore. He agreed. We said we'd stay friends. I'm not sure if that happened. I nearly mentioned the Orion thing then, but my brain was too fuzzy and I might have started crying sooner if I had to keep talking to him after breaking my own heart like that, so I wished him a good math class and left him in the empty classroom.

Every minute I go without telling him will make it much harder for me to tell him one day. I'll have to at some point, I know. There's no escaping it, and there shouldn't be. But it never seems like the right time. I can never figure out how to do it. Besides, what he doesn't know can't hurt him. He always has so much on his mind—he doesn't need anything else. I can handle this thing on my own, as I have been.

I'm very good at finding new excuses to avoid him.

It's now far past nine, and I still have nearly all my homework to finish. I sigh and retreat to my desk.

Chapter Twenty Three

"Elevate"
St. Lucia

We meet at our table in the library before school starts the next morning. No one is very happy that I asked that we meet an hour early and in the library instead of the Main Classes Building, but we have a lot to cover and want as few prying ears as possible.

"Okay," Hunter says as soon as he sits down. "Orion left for Redway before I even got up this morning, so I didn't see him, so I don't know any of the specifics of his plan. Just his stupid crick hike. I have no idea when he'll get home tomorrow. If any of you are brave enough to call him and talk to him willingly, be my guest."

"No, thank you," I say. "Let's just hope he's back by tomorrow evening so we can watch it after rehearsal tomorrow."

"Rehearsal goes until five-thirty all this week," Alex reminds us.

"And the musical still sucks," Hunter says.

"We can still find the time to watch it," I say.

"I have a surprise!" Lexie claps her hands and pulls something from her backpack. "Glaucia Alejo Bardo and I had a fantastic conversation last night about fostering kittens, and she loved my stories so much that she gave me this!" She holds up what I assume is the toxicology report and maybe the virology panel. I've never seen either before. I should have at least Google-Imaged it to make sure I knew what I was talking about. "I can't read either of them, since they use some weird typewriter font and there are, like, millions of long words, but here it is!"

"That's awesome, Lexie." Hallie takes it from her and looks it over. "We just need to find someone who actually knows what this means, and we're good."

Lexie beams. "Happy to help. Did anyone else find anything exciting last night?"

"I made a discovery about Darcy Brecken." I explain the whole thing with the phone numbers and the address.

"Well, that's sketchy," Lexie says. "She's a suspect now."

"She's the president of NYCSGA," Hallie says. "She knows all the soybean happenings in the state. She's definitely involved, if not running the show."

"How closely does she work with Everett?" Alex asks.

"I don't know," I say. "She seemed pretty close with Luciana, so she must know Everett. Then again, Luciana did all the inviting for the gala, according to Cécile, so maybe not."

"Did you learn anything about Joachim Winston during your research, Hallie?" Lexie asks.

"Nothing, really," Hallie says. "He was kind of a boring dude. Grew up on a corn farm, no significant other, has owned the Princess Alice for sixteen years. That's about all I could find." She looks back to Lexie. "Anything on anyone else there?"

"No," Lexie says. "I can tell you where Cécile and Darcy and Luciana all went to college and their kids' names, but nothing more than that. I found the names of a few other women that were there, but not much about them, either. One of them wrote a picture book about cows, and the art was really cute, but that's about it."

"Okay," I say. "Okay. They all must be in on it, right? An operation of this size—Everett would need a lot of people working with him."

"I would guess," Hallie says. "I mean, getting all those bats sick? How else could they do it?"

"We have to confront Everett," I say. "It's the only way we can answer these questions. We have so much leverage on him, it'll be easy to get information from him. Jacob, do we have Eminence approval?"

Jacob isn't paying attention—he's doing a math problem.

"Jacob." Hallie jabs him in the shoulder. "Eminence."

"The Eminence has a math test today," Jacob says. "I approve whatever Skylar thinks will work. If she says it will work, then it will."

"Thank you," I say. "I'll call Everett tonight and see if we can meet sometime this week."

"It's tech week," Alex reminds us.

"We would have to do it in the middle of the night, anyway," Hallie says. "So we wouldn't miss rehearsal."

"Just a few hours of sleep," Alex grumbles.

"It isn't ideal," I say, "but neither is a global food shortage."

We walk back to Main. I have to go put my violin in the music wing, so I divert from the rest of the group and head that way. After I set it into its little cage, I have to cut through the math wing to get to homeroom. As if she were waiting for me, Miss Felding pops her head out of her classroom. "Skylar, could I see you for a moment?"

"Of course, Miss Felding," I say, but my heart starts beating double-time. She knows we're doing something behind her back, or she found out about Orion being behind Stellan's murder and the pandemic, or I failed my last geometry test and Mrs. Flaker would rather have her tell me now than me cry in front of the whole class later. I follow her into her classroom. "What's wrong?"

"How is Jacob doing?" she asks me.

"Fine," I say, a bit perplexed that she would ask me. "Why do you ask?"

"Mr. Seydin and I were doing his progress report for his math program, and he mentioned that it was extra difficult for him to focus last week, and that he seemed more distracted than usual. I was just wondering if you knew of any extra responsibilities someone had given him, or if there's an issue going on that I don't know about."

"There shouldn't be," I say. The lie comes so easily. I don't even have to try. "Being distracted isn't all that unusual for him."

"I know," she says. "I just wanted to make sure there wasn't something that we could help with. I mean, if it's a personal thing, then—"

"I'll let him know that he can come to you if he has any concerns or if anyone gets on his nerves," I say. "But I think he's fine right now."

"Thank you, Skylar," she says. "You're a good friend."

"I try my best to be. Have a wonderful day, Miss Felding."

I have to put my locker combination in seven times to get it to open, since my mind is far too preoccupied with the notion that I just completely, irredeemably lied to Miss Felding. It was one thing when we just weren't telling her things, but now telling her *untrue* things? That's so, so much worse. At least I know for a fact now that she doesn't know about what we're doing, but in a way, that makes it even worse.

Just for now, I tell myself. *It's impermanent.*

Hallie, Alex, and I attempt to do homework in Hallie's bedroom after rehearsal. Alex keeps throwing paper airplanes at us from the top of Hallie's loft bed, so I don't know how much he's gotten done, but he seems to be enjoying himself.

"That's a waste of looseleaf, Alex," Hallie says without looking up from her laptop after one hits her in the side of the head.

"Paper's becoming obsolete, anyway," Alex says.

"Then save it for a museum."

He throws another one at her.

"Alex, I swear to God."

I chuckle and turn back to my math problem. It, of course, is vastly uninteresting. I do much prefer word problems over straight numbers, though, since they tell a little story, but I would rather not do math at all if given an actual choice.

This one's about a swimming pool. We've been doing volume since fifth grade—do we really need to keep relearning it? Multiply three numbers. It isn't that difficult.

A swimming pool.

Of course. I should have thought of him days ago.

I might solve the problem.

I will admit—we have all gotten caught up in Redway's sketchiness as of late. I don't like admitting this fact, but I think we find it more interesting. It's a word problem instead of straight algebra. Or we find it easier, since it's easier to fight against other people than it is to fight against nature. Whatever the reason, we have been somewhat neglecting our responsibility to address the sick bats and get the farmers in Paraná back on track for at least a semi-plentiful harvest. And since Redway seems very, very against helping Brazil (so much so that they're the reason they need the help), then we will need to find an alternate path.

Being a Knower certainly has its caveats, and the benefits certainly do not outweigh the downfalls, but one of the good things about Knowerism is our built-in wealth of resources. The rumor about how everyone is six degrees from everyone else doesn't apply to us—we're usually about two or three. We know people we don't know we know. We can obtain things we don't know exist until they are at our disposal. Just call someone. Pick a number and call.

Thomas Redding does not remember meeting me—in his mind, it never happened. That Day did not exist to him. He never helped Margaret White create a plant-based explosive that detonated inside a Smithsonian, nor did he create a poison gas released in a different Smithsonian, set to kill every Eradicator in their headquarters. That also means the promise that he made to all those kids treading water in his girlfriend's swim class is still valid, because, in his memory, I never cashed in the favor he claimed to owe me. Not that I need that flimsy promise anymore. Since I'm much more connected than I was eleven months ago, I don't have to rely solely on a promise. If he wants something in return, I'll find it.

I grab my laptop from my backpack and search up Thomas Redding. To be expected, his phone number is nowhere to be found. People who work for the US Department of Homeland Security don't exactly post their phone number at every opportunity. I could always email him, since I've found his @dhs.gov email, but I would like a response immediately. So I text Jacob: *Is Thomas Redding's phone number in Margaret's cursed contact notebook?*

He replies a few minutes later. *I don't know. I can check, but I don't know how well that'll go.* Right—he can't read Margaret's notebook, so he wouldn't know. But he texts back a minute later, *I know what a T looks like so I'll send you T names.*

Sure enough, he sends pictures of names and contact information of people that clearly start with a T. The fourth picture he sends definitely says, *Thomas Redding DHS plants.*

That's it, I text Jacob. *Thank you.*

No problem, followed by a whale emoji. The cute one, with the water coming from its blowhole.

"What did Jacob say?" Hallie asks.

"He sent me Thomas Redding's phone number," I say. "Since— wait, what?"

Hallie and Alex both laugh. "Why else would you be smiling at your phone?"

"I— lots of reasons."

They laugh again. "Why do you need Thomas Redding's phone number?" Hallie asks.

"Who's Thomas Redding?" Alex follows.

"He's a botanist who probably knows how to read a toxicology report and perhaps a virology panel and might have an idea on how to stop a potential food shortage."

"Skylar, you're a genius," Hallie says.

"Don't speak too soon," I say.

"You think this botanist dude will know something about soy?" Alex asks.

"It's worth a shot. If he doesn't, he might know someone who does."

Alex throws a paper airplane at me, which hits my glasses with a *thonk.*

I rip a sheet of paper from my notebook, crumple it into a ball, and chuck it at him. It misses him by a foot or two.

He laughs and throws another one at me. I have no idea how he makes them this quickly. And they're all so perfect, too. Like a little paper Air Force.

Alex has an infectious laugh. I usually laugh when any of my friends laugh because I love when they're happy, but Alex's laugh could coax a grumpy old stranger into joining him. It's almost the laugh of a toddler: completely carefree, no ulterior motives, all-encompassing, fearless. Sounds like he gets a lot of practice, which he does.

"You have terrible aim," he tells me.

"Really? I wasn't aware."

Hallie smirks. "I didn't know Jacob's sarcasm could spread through osmosis."

"Hallie." I form another paper ball and hurl it at her. "It would be diffusion, anyway. Sarcasm isn't a solvent."

"If it were diffusion, we all would've gotten it."

Alex laughs even harder.

A paper ball isn't enough; I throw an entire pillow at her. She catches it and launches it straight back in my direction, and it hits me right in the face.

To Hallie, I say, "I'll fight you."

"You'd last maybe three minutes."

"But what a glorious three minutes they would be."

Chapter Twenty Four

Well, I took someone's advice.
With a roll of each eye, she told me to sit down twice.
What do you want from me tonight?
Now I'm stuck losing my mind
while everyone else just thinks that I'm really shy.
What do you want from me tonight?
'Cause I'm invited but I'm terrifying, too,
and I'll sit here for a million years
just staring across the room.

"What Do You Want from Me Tonight?"
Sidney Gish

I patiently wait until my sixth period orchestra lesson to call Thomas Redding. I knew he wouldn't pick up if I'd tried to call him last night, and I'm wary calling anyone before seven-thirty lest they're grumpy in the morning, so I knew I'd have to wait until my first free period of the day. Unfortunately, my only free period today is taken up by my orchestra lesson. Fortunately for me, it's tech week, so there are more important things than orchestra.

I don't bother taking my violin from its cage before going into the orchestra classroom. Mrs. Darner tunes a freshman's cello. "Hi, Mrs. Darner."

"Hello, Skylar," she says. "We're doing 'Scherzo' first."

"Actually, I was wondering if I could use this period to work on the sets for the musical," I say. "I was talking to Jacob yesterday, and he was concerned about finishing that one wall for the Niagara Falls scenes—you know, the one with the wallpaper? I thought I could help finish it. I'm very good at wallpapering. I wallpapered my grandmother's dining room just last year."

"Oh, that's a great idea," Mrs. Darner says. "We're rehearsing the Niagara Falls scenes before we start the run-through, so that would be awesome if we could have that."

"Of course, Mrs. Darner. I'd be happy to help. Could I have a pass for the auditorium please?"

She sends me on my way across campus with a little yellow hall pass. Thank goodness she didn't check the progress on the sets before leaving yesterday. That wall was finished by the time we got onstage.

I triple-check the auditorium to make sure it's completely empty, and then I go backstage, sit on Edison's fancy velvet chair, and call Thomas Redding.

"This is Thomas Redding," he says.

"Hello, Mr. Redding," I say. "I hope you're having a wonderful day. My name is Skylar Rawlings, and I think you would be a great help in an issue we've been seeing."

"I'm sorry, who are you?"

"Skylar Rawlings."

"I'm sorry, but that means nothing to me."

He's much more animate when he isn't catatonic. "I work with Margaret White."

He's quiet for a second until he places the name. "Oh. Ms. White."

"Yes. You helped her with some biohazard containment in Serbia about a year ago."

"Right."

"Since you handled that issue so wonderfully, we would like to request your help with another issue."

"I mean, I kind of have a lot on my plate right now," he says.

"Hear me out."

"If I must."

I explain our problems in Paraná, leaving out our problems in Redway.

"Well, that's a doozy," he says.

"A doozy," I repeat.

"And you think I can help with this?"

"I have a toxicology report and a virology panel," I say. "I'm fairly certain the bats have been exposed to a communicative illness, as it keeps spreading and more bats keep dying. I need to know exactly what it is, based on these studies, and how to counteract it. You also have a myriad of connections to other people in Homeland Security and the departments around it, so if you're unable to do this, you can help me find someone who can."

He thinks this over. "I think I can do that."

"Really?" I was so ready to launch every persuasion tactic I know, and I had a list of bribes ready. I might have even pulled out that favor he owes me from Delaney Mallonski's swim lesson if he were really intransigent.

"Really," he says. "Do you know what a soybean shortage would do to the global economy?"

"I do," I say. "Which is why I think we need to take action. And I knew you would be willing to help as soon as the issue was brought to your attention."

"I'm happy to help. Send me the toxicology report and the virology panel when you get the chance, and I'll see what I can do."

"Thank you, Mr. Redding. I'll have them over to you immediately."

"No problem. I'll keep you updated on what I find and what I think can be done. We've dealt with things like this before."

"Thank you, Mr. Redding," I say. "I'm sure every farmer in Paraná will greatly appreciate your help."

"That's good to hear, Ms. Rawlings."

Ooo, I like Ms. Rawlings. I usually don't get a lot of that because I look and sound like a child. "We'll be in touch."

"Certainly. Have a great day."

"You too."

He hangs up, and I wait a minute to see if he calls back and retracts his help; I wasn't expecting him to acquiesce so quickly, if at all. But I suppose it worked. At least for now. I can always go back in with bribes and blackmail later.

Or maybe, just maybe, he's just a good person who wants to help people. I suppose I'm just not used to working with good people, at least those who don't go to high school with me. Everyone has an ulterior motive. They are good people when it is in their best interest to be good people. It becomes another performance, another role to add to their repertoire. I am Good Person Number Four. Two lines to memorize and a few ad-libbed exclamations of gratitude when something goes my way. But it would seem that Thomas Redding is not like this. At least now, at least with me, he isn't acting.

That makes me much happier than it should.

I borderline obsessively check my email the rest of the day. Whenever I have my laptop open during class, I keep my email tab open and keep refreshing it. When I don't have my laptop in class, I check it on my phone as soon as the bell rings and pray that no teacher will see me and send my phone to the office.

At lunch, I turn my email notifications on—which Andrea advises us not to do, lest someone see an email from someone a sixteen-year-old wouldn't typically email—and put it next to me on the table in case he emails me during lunch.

"Nothing yet?" Lexie asks.

"No," I say. "How long could it possibly take to read a toxicology report and a virology panel?"

"You saw those things," Lexie says. "Not only did they use those godawful fonts, but all those words were so damn *long*. I'd need three days."

"We don't *have* three days," I say.

"Three days for what?" Meredith Pandey scoots closer to Lexie. "Oh my God, are you talking about the musical? I heard it's, like, not good, but I'm sure it is! I can't wait to see it!"

"It's not *terrible*," Sofia says. "It's really bad, but not terrible. Your line's really good, Skylar."

"Thank you," I say.

"Oh my God, Skylar, you have a line!" Meredith reaches across Lexie and grabs my arm. "That's so exciting!"

"Thank you, Mery."

"It *was* mine," Sofia says, "but Skylar is so so *so* much better at it. Wait till you hear it. She sounds like if adolescent Laura Dreyfuss were a true soprano."

"Um, thank you?" I say.

"I heard that Alex Summerheld is, like, the best singer in the show!" Meredith says. "Which makes him so much cuter!"

"He is really good," I say. It always makes me uncomfortable when the girls at my lunch table talk about Alex and how cute/hot/"much of a snack" he is, which is actually quite a common topic of conversation around here. Not that they're wrong—he *is* pretty cute—but he's one of my best friends, so it's just a little weird. But we only have maybe sixty boys in our class and about two hundred or so in the entire school, so it's not like there are too many options when it comes to cute boys. Meredith and Sofia tend to talk about the same seven, and Alex is usually the top contender.

"He's the *best*," Sofia says. "And *so* cute. Especially in his costume. It's *so* cute."

"Oh my God, I can't wait!" Meredith claps her hands a bit. "I'll bet he looks adorable."

Sofia nods. "And he sounds like if Mike Faist and Jordan Fisher had a baby who learned to sing where they train Disney Channel kids."

"Is that a good thing?" Meredith asks.

"Hell yeah it's a good thing."

"It's, like, so funny that you three are friends with him,"
Meredith says to Hallie, Lexie, and me. "He, like, completely aban-
doned Garrett Walaski and Will Harding and that whole friend
group."

"Because they're freaking annoying," Hallie says.

"They are annoying," Meredith agrees with a nod.

"Hallie, you two should date," Sofia says.

"Absolutely not," Hallie replies. "That'd be weird. He's one
of my best friends."

"So? People who are best friends first can date later. Look
at Skylar and Jacob."

"We aren't dating," I say.

"You're not?" Meredith's eyes go wide, and Lexie doesn't
even try to stifle a laugh.

"No. Never were. Also never will."

"I really thought you were dating." Sofia looks like I told
her the sky isn't blue. "Well, bad example, then. But you can still
date Alex, Hallie."

"No, it'll never happen," Hallie says. "Skylar and Jacob,
though . . ."

I don't get upset with her for deflecting the conversation
back to me because none of these girls know that Alex identifies as
asexual and aromantic. He's not attracted to people like that, and
he doesn't want a romantic relationship. Since he isn't completely
out yet, not everyone knows that he's not in the island dating pool,
but it doesn't seem to bother him too much. "I know, I'm terribly
adorable," he'll say with a laugh whenever Hallie tells him Sofia
brought him up at lunch yet again.

When he came out to us last November, he smiled after-
wards and said, "None of you told me I just haven't met the right
person yet."

"Well, yeah," Hunter said, "since that's not how it works. I
have yet to meet a girl that made me want to date one." (That's
how Hunter came out to us, too, though he claimed he thought we
already knew he was "like, really gay.")

"So, Skylar," Meredith asks, "what's stopping you from
asking him out?"

"Lots of things." True. "Mostly disinterest." Not true.

"Well, he's super cute," Sofia says. It's just a fact, but still. I
didn't know I was the jealous type until she says that.

"I guess," I say.

"Oh, he is," Meredith says. "Those big brown eyes, and his hair—he's *adorable*." Good God. He has the type of eyes that people write sonnets about. We get it.

"Not cuter than Alex, though," Sofia says.

"A close second, maybe."

"No, Will Harding is second. Maybe third."

I thank every God there is when my phone lights up with an email from Thomas Redding. I excuse myself, take my jacket from the back of my chair, and head outside.

Whatever conversation I'm about to have with him will certainly be easier than that one.

Chapter Twenty Five

"The Key to Life on Earth"
Declan McKenna

Our cafeteria is in its own building—part of the ploy, Hallie believes, to spread everything out so we have to cross the quad six times a day and make up for only having PE twice a week. There isn't another smaller, quieter room in the cafeteria building—just the giant lunchroom, kitchen and staff areas, and bathrooms—but there is a nice area outside. Since it's only in the low forties, the picnic tables outside are practically empty, save a few people studying or talking in whispers. I take the one furthest from everyone else and read Thomas's email.

It's only sixteen words: *I think I know what to do. Please call me at your earliest convenience. Best, Thomas.*

I don't hesitate to call him.

"Ms. Rawlings," he answers. "Thank you for calling me."

"Thank you for reading the reports," I say.

"Of course. So, it seems the bats have been exposed to a communicative virus. I won't bore you with all the specifications. I have no idea *how* they were exposed, since this isn't a virus natural to bats. It's not something they could have developed themselves, if that makes sense. They were introduced to it."

I almost tell him I know, but I don't. "I see. How strange."

"It's uncommon, that's for sure. It's been known to happen, though. It's nothing we can't work with. So I talked to a friend of mine at the CDC, and he has a few ideas of where we can go next. The problem is that this is in Brazil, not the US, so if anyone here were to intervene, we'd need to work with their government in addition to ours. That goes above my head, and, I'm assuming, above yours."

"Mr. Redding, nothing goes above my head."

He chuckles. "I've gotten that impression. But seriously, there will be things that we can't do from here."

"Some of my associates have been in contact with some members of Paraná's officials, so whatever we come up with, I'll find a way to make sure it can happen there."

"Okay," he says. "Since we're already kind of bypassing some channels as it is, I'll just leave that to you. So, anyway, we're thinking we need a tracer program."

"A tracer program," I repeat. "So we start tracking which individual animals have the disease, and begin to limit their interactions with healthy animals to lower the infection rate."

"Exactly," he says. "Bats don't fly over to the doctor when they're under the weather, so this is the most efficient way to start combating it."

"What do we do with the bats that are already sick?"

"With the tracing program, we'll start to find sick bats, and we'll quarantine them," he continues. "That's about all we can do for now until the virus is better researched. Then maybe we'll come up with a treatment. For now, our best bet is to stop the spread and to hopefully reintroduce the sick bats back into the ecosystem as they recover and as more research is conducted."

"This is a good short-term solution, though," I say. "Thank you."

"How did you find out about this issue?"

"I often find myself in the midst of terrible people," I say.

"I should advise you to turn whoever did this in to the proper authorities."

"I'll worry about the people, Mr. Redding, and you just worry about their actions."

"Can I trust you to do that?"

"Have I given you reason not to trust me?"

"No, you haven't. If you can find out how and where and when this poison was dispatched, and my hypotheses are correct and the lab sends me the results I want, then we can fix this by the next planting season. There's only one more problem, and that's the cost."

"How high is this cost, exactly?"

He gives me an exceedingly large number that makes me a little dizzy.

"Yikes."

"It's a yikes, that's for sure. I don't know how much I can get from the government. Really, I don't. DHS won't give much of anything for an international problem, but I could try a different department. I don't know how much leverage I would have in Paraná's government, but I can see what I can do."

"Thank you," I say. "Let me see what I can do with funding. I appreciate everything you've already done."

"Any time, Ms. Rawlings."

"Though, if I may ask, why are you being so helpful? I'm not sure you have a lot to gain by helping."

"I don't," he says. "But that doesn't mean it's not worth doing."

I smile. I don't hear that nearly enough. "I agree. Thank you, Mr. Redding."

"Any time, Ms. Rawlings. You're so much easier to work with than Ms. White."

I laugh. "That's the highest compliment I could possibly receive."

The world is a very small place. People seem to forget that because it appears to be huge, but it isn't, not really. We think it's big because we know nothing bigger. We think there are a lot of people because we've never known a larger population. We think humans are cool and can do cool things because we spend too much time thinking about humans.

Knowers have a different perspective of the size of our planet because we manage to hold it in our hands as if it were nothing more than a large watermelon. We can find anyone, obtain anything, reach anywhere. The world isn't a ball of yarn so much as a broomstick handle someone used to tear cobwebs down from the rafters—everything is stuck in a haphazard connection to everything else. Everyone knows everyone and touches everything and has been everywhere. We're both the everyone and their observers. Both the nouns and their modifiers. The Easter eggs we hunt for and the bunnies that hid them.

The only reason we know how to solve problems is because we're very good at creating them. We can fix the glass vases we threw against the wall since we know how they broke. Find the eggs we hid. End a pandemic we started or reverse a food shortage we allowed to happen. Watch it fracture now so you can fix it later.

The world, since it's a very small place, doesn't have a wide variety of problems. We can fit them into six subcategories of a Type B Meeting. Humans do not diverge from the paths that they've set themselves on. Those that do should be commended and surveilled. You wouldn't want to miss the moment that they become something different.

Knowers need two Meeting Types and eight subcategories to deal with our own problems—problems, of course, that we have created. Problems might not exist if we didn't. The world might not try to deviate from its axis if we stopped trying to keep it from spinning.

Maybe that's why Knowers are so bitter. We aren't commended or surveilled. We operate when your eyes are closed, the lights are out, the sun is down, and no one else is around. In the dark. People can't venerate the meteorites they never see fall to Earth. They overlook those that masquerade as raindrops and take cover in the storm clouds. Raindrops are small, so to them, the world is big. Knowers pretend to be small though we know that we are not, and we pretend the world is big though we know that it isn't. We lie to everyone we know—including ourselves—for our own sanity. There is more for us to do on a bigger planet. More ground for us to hurl ourselves into on a bigger planet. More room for caverns and eruptions and tsunamis.

I will give the Earth this: Our collisions are always far more seismic when the planet is so easy to rock. That's what makes it so fun, after all.

Chapter Twenty Six

You want to make up for lost time,
act like the last time was nothing at all.
You think I waited up all night,
you're out of your damn mind.
Don't lie to yourself.
Nothing you can say
is gonna change the way
I hate your guts right now.

"Way With Words"
The Wrecks

We run through the entire show twice during rehearsal that afternoon, and by the end, I am ready to curl up in a folding faux-velvet auditorium seat and go to sleep. My legs hurt from all the dancing, and my throat is raw from all the signing. But alas, the world stops messing up for no one, even those who know how to stop it from turning.

"That might have been the worst run-through yet," Alex says as we put our costumes away. He's still wearing his old-timey hat, though. He wears it as long as he can during rehearsal. "I don't think a single person got a line right in the Niagara Falls scene."

"They definitely didn't," Lexie says. "You'd think being in costume would make people better at the whole acting thing. It's impossible not to be excited wearing an old-timey dress like this!" She swishes the hanger that holds her dress.

Alex shakes his head. "It makes no difference, I guess. The show is a flop."

"It isn't a complete flop," I say. "We still have 'Parisian', which you and Wyatt and Rachel nail every time. And the costumes *look* pretty nice, even if their owners can't act, sing, or dance. And all the sets are wonderful."

"I still don't know how Jacob managed to design and help build eight sets while running the planet," Alex says.

"I know. He's incredible." That's not what I meant to say. "I mean the sets. They're incredible."

"Yeah, that's what you meant." Alex gives me a look that I choose to ignore.

Hunter comes over and throws his suit onto the costume rack. "Orion's back from Redway if you want to see what he found on the Princess Alice's security tapes."

"Careful with your costume," Alex says.

"Believe me, nothing worse could happen to this suit. I'm surprised no one's been buried in it yet." He readjusts the suit coat on the hanger anyway. "Are you guys coming over?"

"If you'll have us," I say.

"Unfortunately, I will," he says. "I don't know how I got roped into having people over all the time."

"Because an Eminence lives there and your house is giant and there isn't anyone else who lives there at the moment that isn't aware of what we're doing?"

"Fair enough." He shrugs. "Are you guys ready?"

Alex takes his hat off and sets it on the shelf. "Now I am."

The brink of the sunset joins us on our walk to Hunter's house. Somehow, I ended up walking next to Jacob, a little behind the rest of the group, which I did not intend. Thanks, subconscious, I guess. I decide to ask, "How was your math test?"

"Pretty okay," he says. "Thank you for asking."

"No problem. I'm glad it was pretty okay."

"Thank you."

That's all we say. I should tell him about my conversation with Miss Felding earlier, but it's clear that conversation isn't exactly working right now, and he seems to be preoccupied. I mean, he usually is, but still. (It gives me a lot of opportunities to use it as an excuse.)

Orion waits for us on the front porch. "Hello, friends! It has been far too long!"

"No, it hasn't been," Hallie says.

"How was your crick hike?" Hunter asks.

"Oh, purely magnificent," Orion says. "I shall show you some photos I took in a spell. We should review the security camera footage first. I could not wait for you all to watch the footage from the security cameras. I know I should have, but I did not. But I could get a clear view of everyone in the second ballroom, so we now know that my endeavors were worth it." He opens the front door. "Lauren has made some snacks, so we shall convene in the kitchen. I've already set my laptop up at the counter."

"Okay," Hunter says, leading everyone through the vestibule.

Orion stops Jacob and me before we go inside. "I suppose it's a good thing I previewed the footage," he says under his breath. "I edited a portion out, one that I did not believe you would have wanted shared with your friends."

I feel my face burn, as does Jacob's. "Thank you," I say.

"Of course," Orion says, and we go inside.

"Well, that's not awkward at all," Jacob whispers to me.

"It could have been a lot, lot worse," I whisper back.

"We would have never heard the end of that."

"Eternal damnation."

Orion hands us all mugs of hot chocolate with whipped cream, and he opens his laptop, which is covered in neat rows of bear stickers. Like, grizzly bears, polar bears, a panda or two. I did not know Orion Athan was a fan of bears.

"Do you like bears?" Alex asks.

"Yes, I really enjoy how bears exist," Orion replies.

"Huh. Cool."

"The receptionists at the Princess Alice were most accommodating when I told them I had lost a cufflink at Mr. Everett Caldwell's gala," Orion explains as he finds the videos in his files. "That allowed everything to go quite swimmingly. I could only get footage from an hour before the event started until the next morning, since I only had the time to download one segment. And, quite unfortunately, there is no audio, so we will not be able to hear any conversation. Nevertheless, I do hope this will give us just a bit more information than we currently possess."

He hits play.

We were right—when Joachim and Luciana walk in, there are five other people in there. Cécile, Darcy, Carson Sloane from Redway, and another man and woman that I don't recognize. (I can't discern the material of her dress, since everything is fuzzy black-and-white.) Everett is nowhere to be seen. They talk for awhile, and then Cécile storms out. Luciana follows a few minutes later. Everyone else follows Joachim out the other door at the back a few minutes after that.

"Then Skylar and Jacob come in, so I took that bit out so we don't have to waste time watching them rummage through papers," Orion says. "Then in comes Joachim Winston. A few minutes later, Mary-Grace Carressy joins him."

The two of them walk around the room, and then stop in the center and talk for awhile. They leave. Orion skips ahead another hour, when Carson Sloane, Joachim, and Darcy come into the room. They look agitated, and they have a heated conversation surrounding the table where Jacob and I found the corn flash drive. Fortunately, it doesn't look like anyone really notices something on the table is missing. Luciana joins them a few minutes later. They talk for a bit, then the three of them leave and the light clicks off.

"The light remains off until the end of the footage," Orion says.

I close my eyes and replay the conversation from the ballroom. I look around the room, put everything into its place, and land upon the oldest table in the back.

This might start in Brazil, but it isn't going to end there.

New, heartier soybeans, ones that can better withstand bad weather and bug infestations and diseases. Imagine the profit one could make from selling those in the midst of disaster. First in Paraná, then . . . well, who knows? Devastate the crops, then offer people a way to ensure their crops aren't devastated again. Redway picks up the slack in the meantime. Their district flourishes.

One should think I am no longer surprised by terrible people, but this has yet to be proven factual.

I open my eyes. "I'm calling Everett. We need to talk to him tonight."

"Tonight?" Hallie crosses her arms. "That's a little short notice. We don't have time to get more Broadway tickets."

"We can get him to come the other way," I say. "The bad way." I pull out my phone and call him.

"Hello, Skylar." Everett already sounds bored with this conversation when he picks up the phone.

"We need to meet. Tonight."

"Tonight? Another one of your middle-of-the-night things? No. Hell no. Not tonight. Not ever again."

"This is non-negotiable," I say. "Meet us, or I'm going over your head with the things I know."

"And what is it, exactly, that you know?"

"Cécile Kettering's death was a far cry from a suicide."

I hear his blood run cold through the phone. "Fine. Fine. If you want to be like that, then *fine*. Same place as last time. I'll be there at three AM."

"Sounds wonderful, Mr. Caldwell. I look forward to seeing you."

"Always a pleasure, Skylar." He hangs up.

I turn to the rest of the group. "It would seem that we're going on an expedition tonight."

"Skylar, I swear to God," Hallie says. "I'm still behind on sleep from the last four expeditions."

"I shall go nap now so I am in prime condition for driving you all tonight," Orion says.

"I can drive," Hunter says.

"No, you cannot."

"You already did so much driving today, though," Hunter says. "And I'm a really good driver."

"No, you are not."

"This might be the first and only time I actually agree with you, Orion," Jacob says.

"Splendid." Orion smirks a little. "Which means Hunter does not have Eminence approval to drive."

"I detest you both," Hunter says.

"Plan A should work," I tell the group once we're in the parking lot of the Wash N' Fold Laundromat at approximately two-fifty-six AM. "If Plan A fails, we try Plan A-point-five, which *really* should work. Plan B is worse-case-scenario. And in case everything goes awry, we have the contingency plan."

"Two contingency plans," Hunter says. He doesn't hold up the tiny silver handgun because I told him before we left that I trusted that he and Orion both had their contingency plans and did not need any visual proof.

Hallie and Alex take a basket of laundry inside. Not a minute later, the black Lincoln pulls into the parking lot, and Everett Caldwell emerges. He nearly runs into the building. Another three minutes after that, Hallie texts, *The bee is in the hive.*

"Good luck, guys," Lexie says. "Please be careful."

"We will be," I tell her, giving her hand a squeeze.

Jacob, Hunter, Orion, and I climb out of the car. Hunter stays at the front door, keeping watch. The rest of us go inside and follow the grumbling machines and flailing fluorescent light rods to Everett, who stands in exactly the same place, wearing exactly the same outfit.

"Hello, Mr. Caldwell," I say.

"What do you want?" he asks. "And how do you know about Cécile? *What* do you know about Cécile?"

"That was too many questions for me to answer at once," I say. "We'll start with Cécile, since you were so gracious to adjust your schedule to accommodate us."

"I don't have a lot of time, Skylar. Out with it."

"I know Cécile was shot by someone," I say. "I know that she was in a tussle and the other person had a weapon and discharged it and ended her life. I do not know who. Do you?"

"No clue," he says. Thank goodness he's been a terrible liar in the past—it's easy for me to tell that he really has no clue.

"Then why do you want to hide it, if not to protect someone?"

"Do you know how much bad publicity a *murder* at your fundraiser is? I mean, a suicide isn't great either, but at least that can't be connected back to me. Look, I'm not proud. I'm really not. I met Cécile a few times. She was always so kind. Not outwardly, or effusively, but where it counted, when people weren't looking at her, she was kind. My wife is very bent up about it, since they were friends, and I'm even keeping from *her* that it wasn't a suicide. That alone is killing me. If anyone finds out about this—"

"Don't worry," I say. "We don't use information like this against people unless they give us reason to do so."

"Do you have a reason?"

"Not right now. That isn't to say that I wouldn't have one in the future."

"How did you even know?" He shakes his head.

"I witnessed it," I tell him. I don't know why. I don't *have* to tell him that. I can think of four other answers that I could have given, but for some reason, it feels right to tell him the truth. "I only heard a muffled argument and the shot, and then I saw the aftermath. I don't know who killed her, and I'm very sorry that something like that had to occur on a special night for you."

"Thank you," he says. "I'm sorry you had to see that."

"Thank you. Now, about the reason I wanted to see you."

"And so urgently, too," he says with a slight, perhaps involuntary eye roll.

"Are you aware of the soybean shortage in Brazil?"

"Yes," he says. "It's horrible for Brazilian farmers, but it's pretty good for my district."

"Do you know how it started?"

"Something with the bats," he says. "They're sick and dying out, so they don't eat the bugs that eat the soybeans, so the bugs eat up the crops."

"Do you know how the bats got sick?"

"No," he says. "I'm guessing there's a disease that affects bats. Could have come from anywhere."

"Do you think this was done intentionally?"

"Intentionally?" He tilts his head a bit and looks confused. "Probably not?"

I study him. Flouncy hair far less detained by gel than usual, striking eyes ringed with consistent lack of sleep, the scar on his cheek evinced by his unaltered posture, the thread unraveling on his second button. One hand clutching the sleeve of his jacket, the other propping him up against the cesspool the laundromat calls a table, feet planted firmly as if he were expecting a strong wind.

Everett Caldwell is not lying.

"You don't know," I say.

"About what?"

"How close are you with the people in NYCSGA?"

"You mean Darcy Brecken and her farmer friends?" he says. "Not very, except for Darcy. She and my wife are close. They went all through school together, and I knew her in high school. I could take her or leave her, but she's almost Luciana's sister."

"I had the pleasure of meeting Luciana at the gala," I say. "She seems wonderful."

"She is," he says. "A great wife and mother."

"And campaign partner, I bet."

"She's the best," he says. "Helps me set up the fundraisers. Does all the inviting, finds the venues, all that stuff. I'm so lucky." Despite the circumstances, talking about her invokes a smile.

"We can all only hope to have a Luciana in our lives," I say. "But, Mr. Caldwell, you really aren't aware of the intentional harming of the bats in Paraná, Brazil?"

"No," he says. "You think they were harmed intentionally? Where is this coming from?"

I don't want to tell him because I don't trust him not to tell other people, including his wife. "That isn't information I would like to share until I have proof. Talking to you was part of our search for proof."

"And did you find any?"

"Yes, actually, I think we did."

"Anything I can do to help?" he asks. Though I know this is because he doesn't want to upset us, what with our knowledge of Cécile's death, I do appreciate the sentiment.

"As of right now, I don't think so," I say. "That is subject to change, however."

"Just let me know," he says.

I give him a smile. "Though I know you work in your own self-preservation and to ensure that what I know doesn't find its way into common knowledge, I do appreciate your help."

He holds back a sigh. "Always a pleasure, Skylar."

Chapter Twenty Seven

"Pretender"
AJR

"It's like the whole cast only has left feet!" Mrs. Darner calls from the front row of the auditorium. "More pizzaz! More *passion*! I feel like I'm watching a funeral!"

"We will *not* be ready by Friday," Lexie whispers to me.

"Oh, there is no way," I whisper back.

Mrs. Darner keeps re-running the "Budapest Telephone Exchange" dance because every time they do it, it looks like they learned it yesterday while wearing blindfolds. We're watching from the left wing of the stage, where the view is skewed and people dance in and out of our lines of sight, so I can only imagine how atrocious this looks from the house of the auditorium, where one can see everything. I know I'm only in five dances, which is far fewer dances than some of the featured dancers have, but how difficult is it really to memorize a few kicks and jazz hands? It's been two months of doing the same thing nearly every day. If Lexie, Alex, Hunter, and I can manage it while keeping the world from spinning off its axis, then everyone else has no excuse.

"Why can't Casey Whitten lift her arms above her waist?" Lexie asks.

"She's as flexible as uncooked spaghetti," I say. "How is she a featured dancer?"

"No clue."

"No! Cut!" Mrs. Darner hollers. "From the top. Again. And for the love of Gwen Verdon, get it *right*!"

"Well, there goes another fifteen minutes of our lives." Lexie rolls her eyes.

"When she calls upon the ghost of Gwen Verdon, she means business," I say. "We need a little brains and a little talent. Emphasis on the latter, of course."

Lexie laughs. "Whatever Lola wants, I guess. I have fruit snacks in my backpack. They're shaped like Paw Patrol characters. Want some?"

"Definitely." We leave the wing and head backstage, where we left our backpacks. She digs out two packs of fruit snacks, and we wander around backstage.

Jacob and Hallie work on a set piece in the hall. "You've been fighting with that desk since February," Lexie says.

"And it still won't cooperate," Jacob says. He wiggles it, and the whole thing shakes. "We've put at least twenty screws in this thing. What more does it want from us?"

"Well, it's an essential set item," Hallie says. "Tesla mentions his desk in six songs, and Wyatt's blocking has him sitting at it in four of those scenes and gesturing to it in the other two."

"Yet you pay no attention to rehearsal," I say. "Do you want my purple fruit snacks?"

"Even Casey Whitten knows that, Skylar." She takes all three purple fruit snacks and eats them at once. "It's common knowledge."

Jacob adds another screw. "Okay, try it now."

Lexie gives it a shake. "Well, it's *better*, but still squirmy."

"Squirmy," I repeat with a nod.

"I'm almost ready to take it apart and rebuild it," Jacob says. "There's something wrong with it."

"Don't we need it for the next scene?" Hallie says.

"If they ever get past this one," I say. "They're on their sixth run-through."

"We can help with sets in the meantime," Lexie says. She takes my wrapper and hands both to Jacob. "Can you put these in your pocket?"

"Okay, but why?"

"The garbage can is too far away," Lexie says. "Can I use the drill?"

"No," the three of us say at once.

"Fine, I'll just use this." Lexie picks up a hammer. "What can I do?"

"If you want to use a hammer, you can work on the turbine for the Niagara Falls scene," Jacob says.

"The freshmen messed it up," Hallie says. "None of them know what a nail is. I'll show you. It's on stage right."

When they leave, I know I should follow them. But instead, I ask Jacob, "What can I help with?"

"We still have to add another coat of paint to the hull of the ship," he says. "Darner said it wasn't dark enough. She said she could see through it."

"Okay," I say. "Where is the ghost boat?"

"Stage left," he says. "When do you have to go on?"

"At this rate, not until tomorrow's rehearsal. I enter stage left anyway, so I'll be prepared."

"And you won't get paint on your dress?" He gestures to my costume, a browning lavender frilly thing that looks like a pincushion and smells like death.

"That wouldn't be the worst thing to happen to this dress."

He does a terrible job of holding back a smile and leads me to the boat. Or half a boat, I should say. Since it sticks out from backstage during the scenes in which we need it, it's only the front. (The bow? I'm not good at ship speak.) It's nearly pitch black backstage because we're rehearsing with lighting today, so I take my steps carefully lest I trip over something I can't see.

"We only have to paint the side that faces the audience," he whispers, staying quiet so they don't hear us onstage.

"Okay," I reply.

He maneuvers perfectly in the dark, knowing exactly where everything is without having to feel for it. He finds two paintbrushes and a can of paint, and without saying a word, we get to work. I'm very careful not to let the parts of my dress that poof out brush against the paint, but it's so dark, I can't tell how successful I am.

"Are we going to Hunter's house after rehearsal?" Jacob asks me.

"Yes, I think so," I say. "Unless he's suddenly decided he wants none of us over."

"That wouldn't surprise me," he replies. I can tell by his voice and his silhouetted face that he's smiling his unsure smile that's usually involuntary.

My God, the things I wish I could unlearn. Living with him would be so much easier if I could get my memory wiped and forget all his nuances that I've unwittingly learned to read and inadvertently memorized. When I can tell that he's drawing a building in his head by the color of his eyes, or that he's stressed by the way his fingers will play with anything they can reach, or that his mind is in overdrive by a bite of his lip, then I know him too well. Life would be much, much easier if we were strangers.

"How is that side of the boat?" he asks me.

"Fine," I answer, avoiding a glance in his direction. "How is your side?"

"Also fine."

"Cool."

"Cool."

"Jacob."

"Yes?"

Are we okay? I almost ask, but that would be such a stupid question. It would almost be better if we *weren't* okay. After working with both him and Orion for the past few months, I've determined that it is much easier working with someone that you can openly hate than someone for whom you hide your feelings. At least I can complain without hesitation to Orion about how annoying he is or that he uses words that are too large for even me to handle, because he knows that I don't like him in any sense of the word. It isn't that easy with Jacob. I can't tell him that he has pretty eyes or the heart of a mother goose without it getting weird.

The universe must feel slightly apologetic for what it's put me through these past few weeks—"Budapest Telephone Exchange" ends and "*Bienvenue à Paris*" begins.

"I have to go." I hand him my paintbrush.

"Good luck," he says.

"Jacob! You don't say good luck to someone going onstage. You say *break a leg*."

"That sounds mean."

"It's not, though, since we're in a theater. There are different rules in a theater."

"Are there, now?"

Thank every God there is that it's so dark in here. "Don't make me miss my entrance."

I can hear his smile over the orchestra.

"*Bienvenue à Paris*" is a mess, but that surprises no one. I'm lucky that I'm in the back until the modulation near the end— no one can see me when I mess up.

We surprisingly make it to the modulation without substantial catastrophe, and I move up to my second place at the front of the stage.

The auditorium's house is not empty. Mrs. Darner and some of the other teachers that help with the musical are in the front row, there's Hallie in her spot in the ninth row, a few costume stage crew members on the left, and nearly at the back, two women.

They look different when not in their ballgowns, but not different enough.

I forget I'm supposed to be dancing.

"Cut!" Mrs. Darner calls. "Skylar! You froze like a macaw at a penguin party. And you were one of the last hopes I had."

"I— I'm not feeling great. I'll just—" I run offstage. After a second, just to make sure no one followed me, I slip out from backstage and into the house. I creep against the wall, where the spotlights can't hit me, until I find them. Eighteenth row, seats J and K. They notice me as I cross seat G.

"Oh, sweetie, you can finish rehearsal first," Darcy Brecken says to me.

"We wouldn't want to interrupt," Luciana Caldwell adds. "The show looks so wonderful. Excellent job up there."

"Thank you," I say. "What are you doing here?"

"Well, we just wanted to speak to you," Darcy says. "But we know you go until five-thirty, so we can wait."

"You're awfully well-informed."

"Your cast list is online," Luciana says, as if she were divulging a secret. "As is your rehearsal schedule. And we found an article you wrote for your school newspaper about the orchestra's winter concert. You're a very talented writer."

"Thank you," I say. "We can talk now. But not in here. We aren't supposed to talk in the house during rehearsal."

"That's such a nice dress," Luciana says. "Very in tune with the time of the show, I would say. Whoever's done costume design has done a remarkable job."

"Truly. Are we talking or not?"

They follow me out into the harsh light of the near sunset— everything is either brash gold or shrouded in shadow, there is no in between. Difficult to look at either way.

I take them to the gazebo on the quad. Usually, this is senior territory, but it's late enough and cold enough that no one else will want to be here. "Oh, how cute is this!" Darcy cries.

"You have a very nice school," Luciana tells me. "It looks like such a great community."

"Thank you," I say. "Why are you here?"

"Well, there's something we have to talk to you about." Darcy looks at me with pity. "You know I don't like getting upset with people, so we'd rather just talk to you and get it all out in the open instead of get upset with you, if that's alright with you, honey."

"Fine," I say. "What is it that you would like to discuss?"

"Everett told me that you two had a meeting the other night," Luciana says.

"Oh." I didn't expect Everett to break like that, but I guess you become a different person when someone gets killed at your fundraiser. "What did he say?"

"Well, you see, Skylar," she begins, her knowing smile inching across her face, "if I told you what he told me, then you would just confirm his story rather than tell me your own."

"I suppose you're right," I say. "I wanted to meet with him to see if he knew of any trouble happening in Brazil."

This sentence does not evince a reaction from either of them. Little do they know, that's all I needed. The faces people *don't* make are sometimes more telling than the ones that they do. It's like observing where a painter chose to leave the canvas blank, or why the author inserted a page break. Their unfazed expressions are the black parts of a crossword puzzle that tell me where the letters need to go.

"I asked you at the gala, Mrs. Brecken, but I do have a feeling that your answer has changed: Are either of you aware of the misfortunes befalling Brazilian soybean farmers?" I only ask this question because I already know the answer.

"Yes, we are," Luciana says. "We pray for them every day. Can you even imagine, your livelihood on the line like that?"

"I can't," I say. "I really can't. But there are things even more difficult for me to imagine."

"Like what, honey?" Darcy asks.

"Like intentionally destroying someone's livelihood," I reply.

"That would be horrible." Luciana shakes her head.

"It would be even worse if I didn't tell my husband."

I watch both of their faces shift as the realization dawns on them. I bite back a smile.

"I agree, that would be cruel," Luciana says. "Why do you bring it up, though?"

"Just a hypothetical situation," I say. "If I were to purposely disrupt the economy of a state, especially one not in the United States, I would probably run it by my significant other first. Maybe involve them. Just as, I suppose, a courtesy. Would you agree?"

"Wholeheartedly." Darcy throws a hand to her heart just to show how wholeheartedly she means it.

Luciana isn't as convincing. "Of course."

"Then, if I may ask, why did you not tell Everett that you got the bats sick in Paraná?"

"That's quite the accusation, honey," Darcy says. "Now, why on Earth would you think two ladies from Central New York would care about something so far away?"

"It's okay, Mrs. Brecken," I say. "You don't have to keep pretending. I already know. You encouraged people in Redway to start dozens of new farms. New farms that, of course, would take lots of people to build and therefore create a lot of new jobs, as they weren't designed as efficiently as they should have been. Though, I suppose the design was efficient in its purpose to prolong a project and employ more people than needed. And, once you see how this plan plays out in Paraná, you'll be ready to move to other places and sell them your new resistant soybeans. Lots of revenue for your district, and lots of revenue for you. Sounds like a win-win to me, if you forget about all the farms you ruin and livelihoods you destroy."

"You have no idea what you're talking about," Luciana says.

"I will admit, Mrs. Caldwell, that it was a nearly airtight plan. The problem is that I only need a very, very small hole to slip through. Had you not murdered Cécile Kettering, I would not have bothered getting involved."

"That's enough," Luciana says, her voice sharpening into something I hadn't thought it capable of becoming.

"How dare you accuse her like that," Darcy says.

"I have no reason to accuse you, Luciana. I'm already quite certain that you did it."

"You can't be serious." The color drains from her face.

"Taffeta makes such a lovely sound when you move."

Luciana stands up. "I will not sit here and have these false accusations thrown at me by a child."

"You're right," I say. "Because they are not false, and I am not a child, and you did just stand up, so you are no longer sitting."

"Accuse me all you want," Luciana says. "No one would listen to you. You're a child."

"As I've said, I am not a child, and I have a very good talent for making people listen to me. If I didn't, you wouldn't have come to find me in the first place."

Luciana grabs Darcy's wrist and pulls her to stand with her. "We don't owe you anything."

"You owe Cécile something," I say. "You owe all those farmers in Brazil something. Hell, you owe your constituents something because what you've given them is dripping in blood.

What you owe *me* can be questioned, but what you owe any of them is elementary understanding."

"I'm glad we listened to the other one," Darcy says to Luciana. "He offered us a much better deal."

"Who did?" I ask.

"One of your friends," Darcy says. "Tall, dark hair, very pretty eyes."

"Brown?" I ask. "Or green?"

"Green."

"What did he offer you?"

"He'd handle fixing the situation with the bats in another twelve weeks," Darcy says, "once we've set up a few new farms for some Redway folks. It would be too late to salvage any of the crops in Paraná, but they'd have a chance at bouncing back next year if the bats' virus were gotten under control. Then he told us exactly who he wants as Cécile Kettering's replacement."

"And who would that be?"

"A woman named Eleanor Parkins."

My God, he wants an Eradicator in the US government. Not a bad idea—I should have thought of that months ago—but this also isn't the way to do it. And certainly not Eleanor Parkins. And *certainly* not in the House. "What else did he say?"

"He would find a way to support Everett's senatorial campaign."

So Everett *is* running for Senate. That would explain the weird mail we've been getting outside his district. But why would Orion care? Why does it matter to him what Everett does?

Oh. He's learned something from Luciana.

Everett is a very nice puppet. Handsome, likable, a myriad of strings that control everything else. It doesn't take very much to get him to do what you would like him to do. And Orion has an endless supply to Broadway tickets and an architect for bus garages.

"This boy with pretty eyes," I say. "You spoke to him at the gala?"

"He was in Redway yesterday," Luciana says. "Met us at the Princess Alice for dinner."

"And you took this poor excuse for a deal that he offered you?"

"Of course we did, honey," Darcy says. "We'd be fools not to. He doesn't want a lot in return."

I exhale, close my eyes, force my brain to stay in the gazebo. "Why come here, then, if you've already spoken to Orion?"

"We met with Orion before your midnight meeting with Everett," Darcy says. "We wanted to make sure that nothing has changed."

"Why not find Orion again?"

"You are easier to find."

My chest tightens with a type of anger I hadn't known I could feel. I bite my lip and try to restrain myself. "I shouldn't be."

"Ask your high school to remove their rehearsal schedule, then," Luciana mutters.

I stand up. "This conversation is not over. Our musical opens this Friday, and I expect you both to be there."

"It would be our pleasure," Luciana says, not a hint of pleasure in her voice.

"Excellent. Don't kill anyone in the meantime."

I leave them both on the gazebo.

Chapter Twenty Eight

For love is but a fleeting friend.
We'll end up both alone,
oh, we know
how easy it is to pretend.

"Eventually, Darling"
Declan McKenna

I have not been this angry with someone since Kinlan Jarver killed Harlow. My vision is fuzzy as I rush back to the auditorium. Rehearsal's been over for awhile now, so it's completely empty. There's a text on my phone from Hallie saying that I can meet them at Hunter's if I'm feeling okay.

I nearly run all the way to Hunter's house, my entire body on fire. I pound on the front door until Hunter opens it.

"Where is Orion?" I ask.

"Kitchen," Hunter says. "What's—"

I push past him, leave my coat and backpack in the corner of the hall, and go into the kitchen.

Sure enough, there he is, standing by the window. "Hello, Skylar, dear," he says. "I do hope you're feeling better."

"Shut up," I say. "You made a deal with Luciana and Darcy yesterday, and you didn't think to tell us?"

"I'm sorry?"

"Luciana and Darcy came to rehearsal to talk to me, and they mentioned that during your trip to Redway, you met with them. Completely behind our backs."

He's obnoxiously good at hiding his emotions. "I can explain that."

"Explain, then."

"But don't you already know?"

"If I told you what they told me, then you would just confirm their story rather than tell me your own."

"I was not entirely sure it would work, and there was no sense in my explanation of a plan that seemed so likely to fail," he says. "I'd hoped to tell you last night, but I didn't have a chance."

"An hour-and-a-half car ride wasn't a *chance*?"

"You had to explain *your* plan."

"And the way home?"

"Everyone was so tired already."

"You are just making absolutely ludicrous excuses," I say.

"I would not call them ludicrous," he says. "For what it's worth, I was certainly going to tell you all tonight."

"You should have told us *before* you did something like that," I say. "We are in this together, and we all have to know exactly what's going on. You can't go off and do your own thing and expect us all to be okay with it when you finally enlighten us. That isn't how it works."

"I would be careful of throwing stones in a glass house," he says. "Your conscience isn't entirely clean when it comes to transparency."

"Don't go there," I say. "You know that isn't on me. And it isn't like you've been upfront about it, either. Which is precisely why I haven't been."

"I know," he says, "but at least I don't get upset about others doing the same thing."

"At least I don't have a habit of doing things without consulting anyone else first! Not that this is even on the same *plane* as the Freja thing. The Freja thing was above and beyond, Orion."

"What Freja thing?"

I didn't even notice Jacob sitting at the other half of the kitchen counter.

Shit.

Hello, worst case scenario.

"Jacob, my dear fellow Eminence," Orion says. "There is perhaps something you should know."

"Okay?" Jacob looks wary. He stands up and joins us by the window.

"Everything that happened in September was my idea." To Orion's credit, the words physically pain him to voice. He can't hide it. "I constructed the plan to start the pandemic to create a problem that would need both Knower and Eradicator efforts to rectify, in order to coerce the two groups into a merge. The murder of Stellan, the tweaking of the virus and vaccines—"

"You can't be serious."

"It was my idea to reach out to Freja."

"No, that— that can't be true." Jacob shakes his head.

"I knew that the murder of Stellan Winther would get the Knowers' attention."

"You started the pandemic intentionally."

"Yes," Orion says. "I did. And I regret it every day. It was not my proudest moment. But look where it brought us."

"So you're telling me that everything is your fault."

"Jacob, you have to know that I never intended for any of you to get involved—"

"But that doesn't change the fact that we're pretty involved now, though, does it?"

"I did not think Margaret would break in the way she did, that an induction of two new Eminences would be the immediate outcome—"

"But she did, and it was, and it's completely your fault."

Orion takes a breath, his patience unwavering. "I know you must be upset."

"My God, you're perceptive."

"And I should have told you immediately."

"You think so? Orion, what you did— you— it ruined my life." He looks to me. "And you knew?"

"I sort of figured it out," I admit.

"And you didn't tell me."

"I— No. I didn't."

"I asked her," Orion cuts in. "I requested that she did not tell you. She only meant to keep a promise to me, not to hurt you."

Jacob's quiet for a bit. Then he says, "Orion, could you give us a minute?"

"Jacob," I begin, but I can't explain myself. There's nothing to explain. "I'm so, so sorry."

"Why didn't you tell me Orion started a pandemic?" He looks far more hurt than angry, which drives a knife straight through my chest. It pokes out the other side.

"I don't know," I say. How do I even apologize for this? "I should have told you. I should have said something that night."

"But you didn't," he says.

"You already had so much going on then," I say. It's not an excuse, but the truth. (Maybe the truth used as an excuse.) "I couldn't put anything else on you that night."

"Or in the six months that followed?"

"It isn't like we've been really good at *talking* these past six months." It slips out. I don't mean to say it.

"So it's *my* fault."

"No," I say quickly. *Don't find a way to make this worse.* "Not at all. I don't mean it like that. Just— Just that we haven't been able to talk normally in a long time."

"I still tell you everything, though," he says. "Especially Knower things. Even more especially Knower things that involve you."

"I know," I say. "And I usually do. You're usually the first person I go to, and not just because you're the Eminence."

"Then why not about this? What changed?"

"What do you mean, *what changed*?" I know that I should not be getting upset, since I'm certainly the one in the wrong here, but he can't seriously be asking that. "Jacob, literally everything changed. I would be hard pressed to name something that didn't."

"Something changed to the point where you couldn't tell me that the other Eminence—that *you* nominated—started a pandemic on purpose?"

"We stopped speaking!" I cross my arms. "I don't think I said another word to you until October, at least. Though I know the answer is yes, I was supposed to approach you out of nowhere and explain that your co-Eminence started a pandemic?"

"Yes!" he says. "That seems like a pretty good reason to set anything else aside."

"You know it wasn't that easy," I say. "You couldn't exactly talk to me, either."

"I would have found a way if I'd known something like that."

"How do you know that, though? It wasn't that simple of a decision."

"It seems pretty simple to me."

"Well, it wasn't," I say. "Maybe it should have been, but it wasn't. And I should have made it anyway, but I didn't."

"Skylar. You nominated him to lead the universe with me. We will have to work together for the rest of our lives. Forget the fact that you knew I hated him, but you knew he started a pandemic and therefore killed hundreds of people, including Stellan. And I know you had a reason, because you always do, but you didn't tell me your reasoning. You didn't tell me *anything*."

"I came downstairs to find you right after nominating him with the intention of explaining everything. But you seemed so upset and preoccupied—and rightly so—that I resolved to tell you later. But then—"

"But then you told me that you were in love with me."

Hearing it out loud in his voice makes me nauseous. Something out of a daydream or a nightmare, depending on the context. (This is the nightmare context.) "That was a mistake."

"A mistake." He looks like I slapped him.

"Not like that," I say. "I just— I didn't mean it. No, I meant it, I just didn't— I shouldn't have said it. Not like that."

"So, what? You should have told me *after* telling me you doomed me to working with a complete madman for the rest of my life?"

"Maybe I should have told you in front of the world's smartest people while under oath." *Shit shit shit.* I should sew my mouth shut.

"That was *not* my fault," he says. "How was I supposed to know they would ask me something like that?"

"There wasn't anyone else you could have said?"

"You were the first person to pop into my mind. Per usual."

"And the second person?"

"They said I was lying. And I was. I didn't want to find out what they did to liars. What else was I supposed to do? At least I wasn't hiding anything else from you."

"I was going to tell you that night!" I say. "Then everything got weird with us. And I forgot how to talk to you, and I kept ignoring it and putting it off. It was in no way *okay*, but it might at least make sense. You forgot how to talk to me, too."

"About buildings. Or chem homework. Or anything that might make you laugh. But Knower stuff is different. It's so much bigger than us."

"And how was I supposed to tell you I nominated someone who purposely started a pandemic when I couldn't ask you what we had for homework? You ignored me just as much as I ignored you, if not more."

"Because you told me when we got back home that whatever happened should never happen again, and I couldn't look at you without wanting to kiss you again."

"Exactly," I say. "That's why I didn't tell you."

"Because you couldn't talk to me, I get it."

"Because I knew that the second I told you, you would stop looking at me like I built the Chrysler Building."

As soon as I say it, I know it's true. It might be the most true thing I've said in a year. Everything else is fodder, pointless lies I told myself more than I told him or anyone else on the planet. A mask I held up, a disguise I put on, a sequence of flashes to pretend the nighttime wasn't there. The lightning storm stops as soon as I tell it to stop. It's of no use to me anymore. The nighttime's already here. It's been here for awhile now.

"The moment I told you that I willingly played into Orion's game and made you another piece, you would never want to speak to me again, and rightly so. That would be it. And— And I know how you feel, and I know you know how *I* feel, because honestly, Jacob, we might think we're good at hiding it, or pretending it's not there, or that we don't feel it, but we aren't. We really, really aren't. I didn't want that to stop."

"Maybe it should," he says, so quietly that I almost think I imagine it. "Because, clearly, we're not getting anywhere. Not that we *should* get anywhere. Learning that you kept that whole thing from me just reinforces the idea that this would never work."

It hurt less when I actually got shot. "You're right," I say. "I can't believe I ever thought it would."

He's quiet, looking out the window, hands fidgeting with a dead leaf from the plant on the windowsill. "Me either. But I think that's on you."

"No, it isn't," I say. "Yes, I should have told you. I should have told you months ago. But you can't claim that there aren't things you should have done differently."

"Like what?"

"Like, I don't know, not telling me exactly how you became the Eminence?"

"You were there."

"That doesn't mean I know what happened."

"I thought she was going to kill you. I had no idea she was going to say the Latin thing. And you didn't, either."

"Of course, I didn't," I say. "Or else I would have stopped her. But you never told me. I figured it out, but you never told me. And don't you resent me, just a little bit, because it's my fault?"

"Of course not," he says. "Neither of us could have known that was coming. I don't blame you at all."

"Then why didn't you say that?"

"I never thought you needed to hear it."

"Jacob, of course I needed to hear it!"

"Before or after telling me about Orion starting a pandemic?"

I have never been more frustrated with someone. "I get it. I should have told you. I completely understand that. It would be difficult not to at this point."

He closes his eyes for a second, and when they open again, they're almost petroleum. "Skylar, it— it feels like I can't trust you anymore. Like I don't know how to talk to you." Tears burn in my eyes. "If you could keep that from me for six months, what else are you hiding?"

"Nothing."

"And how do I know that?"

"I have no reason to keep anything from you." I could leave it at that, but he stabbed me and I want to stab him back harder. "I have no motivation to think I could ever contemplate being with you ever again, so there's no reason for me to think that holding onto some trivial piece of information could fix anything so far beyond any semblance of repair."

"You can't turn this around on me," he says. "You fucked up this time."

"I did. And so did you."

"Maybe we should have kept that whole *not talking to each other* thing going."

"There's still time."

Without another word, I leave him standing by the kitchen window.

On my walk home, my heart breaks and the rest of me follows.

A jagged crack right down the middle.

Chapter Twenty Nine

Stranger, that's all I see,
when I look into your eyes,
a soulmate who wasn't meant to be.
Stranger, who knows all my secrets
can pull me apart and break my heart.

"A Soulmate Who Wasn't Meant to Be"
Jess Benko

The entire world was an oven that night. I was only seven or eight, so I don't remember a lot, but I don't have to. What matter is the day of the week, the pajamas I wore, what was for dinner, what happened before the clouds came? It was summer, but the crickets and the fireflies weren't out. The trees should have whispered to each other, but they didn't. The sensors on the streetlights weren't used to being bothered so early in the evening at this point in July, so they just languidly flickered and called themselves lit.

It was pitch black by seven PM. No sunset that night. No transition. As if God Himself had used a light switch to turn off the sun, or had left a big, trembling oil spill where the sky should have been. The house was too still, like a horror film before a jump scare. The whole island held its breath. When the first roll of thunder groaned from somewhere across the river, I understood why. Instead of exhaling, the island inhaled again.

A few minutes later, a flash. And another. And another. All those rules about counting between crashes of thunder and flickers of lightning were rendered useless. Count all you want, but the next sequence would hit before you'd reached two.

The incessant lightning masqueraded as a caustic daylight. Usually, the sky cracks and something peeks out from behind it, but now, the sky fractured itself. Shattered into a thousand pieces yet asked itself why.

I will admit—it beguiled me at first. I slipped out of my bed, crept up my spiral staircase, hugged a stuffed whale to my chest as the sky pulsed in front of me, close enough to grasp. I thought it was cool. I didn't see a sky in agony. Just a summer storm. Something to talk about at breakfast the next morning, make an appearance during a lull in conversation at some family get-together, or become a second-grader's daily journal entry because it's something they haven't written about before. It becomes a memory as it happens.

There was no rain. No distraction. Thunder played a song like a child with pots and pans and a wooden spoon, but there was no rain. Outdoor gatherings had relented and relocated, but there was no rain. We closed our windows and bolted our shutters and collapsed our umbrellas and shrouded our outdoor furniture, but the rain never came. The island inhaled again.

Then it exhaled.

A few hundred jet-engined airplanes took off. A volcano erupted. Something fell out of the sky and broke a hole through the ground. A mountain crumbled or a city caved in or everyone on the planet jumped at the same time. Too much to be thunder, too little for a heartbeat. The earth shuddered, kicked like a soccer ball and sent tumbling towards some unseen goal. The sound had something in mind, but we weren't privy to such divine information.

I leapt down the spiral staircase and into my bed and buried myself under all my blankets despite the fact I could feel myself melting in the summer heat. I didn't move until sunrise. I wasn't convinced there would be one.

The next morning, once the island had forgotten or ignored its prior evening, Hallie knocked on my front door just a few minutes after breakfast. "Stephen and Xavier found something super duper cool at the Delligans' house," she told me, hands on her hips. "Can you come see?"

"Okay." I put my shoes on and told my parents I was going to play with Hallie and her brothers and followed them to the end of our street.

There'd been an oak tree there. Only yesterday, when my mom had walked Hallie and me to the playground, there had been a tree there. Every day, when we walked to school or drove by on the bus, a tree had waved to us. Now there was only a mess and a grave.

What I assumed had once been the oak tree at the edge of the Delligans' yard had been reduced to a pile of splinters. They trickled out from a shell, left standing out of mercy or conviction or sheer determination. It had thrown its limbs across the yard, into the street, through a window, mandating that the glass try to understand its pain. *This is what it's like to explode, glass. You're lucky you didn't have arms.*

"What happened to it?" I asked.

"Lightning hit it," Xavier said. "And it went *boom.*"

"Boom," I repeated.

Lightning is nothing but cruel deception. No corporeality or substance, just energy, mockery, a performance. How could something as intangible as a game of pretend destroy such stolidity? It was so clearly meant to stay intact. It endured thousands of storms before this one. Why was this one different? What made it different? The fact that it had never felt lightning so close to it before? It stood there and watched it as if it were some far-off game, never thinking that a piece would dare to come near it. Oh, but one did. It did and we all saw the aftermath.

Some things are bigger than us, though we act as if they aren't.

Aren't we sick of acting yet?

I try to get to my bedroom without anyone interacting with me, keeping my shoes and coat on so I don't have to spend any more time downstairs. But the goddamned floorboards creak and the tattling door squeals. Why must I live in a noisemaker?

"Hi, Skylar," my mom says.

I don't respond.

"What's wrong?"

"Leave me alone." I leap up the stairs and manage to make it into my room and under the pillows and whales on my bed before I completely break down. All the cuts and bruises from the things we both said bleed all over the covers. Every ounce of me hurts and I hate him and love him and plead with every God I know to let me take everything back or shout it all at him again. No one has ever hurt me that much. No one else could. Only Jacob Connelly, since I handed him the ammunition.

It's my fault, but it isn't. It's his, but it isn't. Could the Mechanism reverse the past six months? The past year? Back to the day I doused him in orange juice? We would need to start from scratch. Hell, I would reverse all sixteen years of my life if it meant I could unsay everything.

There's a knock at my door.

"Go away," I say.

"Skylar," my mom says, "you can talk to me."

"Please let me be."

"Did something happen?"

"Mom, I mean it."

"Skylar, honey—"

"Mom! Leave me alone!"

I'm somewhat expecting her to reprimand me, but her footsteps back away from my door without another word. This makes me cry harder.

It's quite amusing that I'm so upset. Really, it is. When you set your own home on fire, you have no one to blame but the person holding the torch and the gasoline tank. I've got the thirty-thousand kelvins of a lightning bolt in my hands, yet I wonder where the smoke has come from. I threw my own heart against the wall and watched it shatter, yet I blame him for breaking it. I ripped out my own nerves one by one and crushed them individually, yet I complain that they hurt.

Shattered into a thousand pieces yet asks herself why.

I only try to blame him because I wouldn't have been able to find myself with the knowledge to do such things before getting caught in his unabashed chaos. It takes a storm to learn how to destroy something in so few moves. I hid from storms until him. I tried hiding from him, too. It didn't work. I learned destruction and somehow managed to use it against him.

I send Evan away when he comes to get me for dinner. I send my dad away when he tells me he made pudding that should have set by now. I send my mom away again when she tries to ask me once again why I seem to think the world is ending.

Once the sun has set and I have yet to move from my bed, there's a fourth knock at my door. "Please leave me alone," I say.

"I didn't come all the way here to leave you alone, Skylar Amelia."

"Harlow?"

The door creaks open, just a little bit. "Your mom called my mom with an SOS," Harlow says. "Said you wouldn't eat or talk to anyone. She thought you might talk to me. Now, I'm fully prepared to tell everyone you failed a math test if you don't want them to know the real reason you're upset, but I'm also ready to sit and listen if you want to talk. Which I would highly recommend you do."

I consider this, and then I say, "Come in."

She does, closing the door behind her. She says hi to Naussie, giving the back of her shell a quick pet. Then she climbs into my bed with me, and she sets one of my whales in her lap. "Who is this?" she asks.

"That's Jeffery," I say.

"Hello, Jeffery," she says, giving the whale a pat on his head. "So, Skylar Amelia, what's got you so bothered?"

I have two options here: I could tell her I'm hormonal, had a rough day at school, got called on in global and didn't know the answer, broke a plate in the cafeteria in front of everyone, lost a library book, or failed a math test, or I could tell her the truth. It's not the middle of the day, and I don't feel like pretending that it isn't pitch black outside.

I take a deep breath that ends up being quite shaky. "Jacob and I got into an argument."

"About what?"

"I messed up," I say. "It was entirely my fault. I was supposed to tell him something, and I didn't. And then we both got upset, and— And he is never going to speak to me again. Not after this. Not after everything I said to him and everything he said to me. I never want to see him again, and I take it he feels the same way."

"Skylar, it can't be *that* bad," she says.

"Oh, it's that bad."

"What didn't you tell him?"

"It pertains to him more than it pertains to me, so I don't think it's my place to tell you."

"I get it," she says. "But whatever it was, he knows now. You guys will heal and move on. It hurts like hell now, but it'll get better. You can't stay mad at each other forever. That gets boring."

I take another breath. There can't be a single charged particle left in the air, or another strike could work its way out. "Harlow, I love him."

"I know. You're really bad at keeping secrets."

"I don't know if I'd agree with that."

She reaches over the pile of stuffed whales and takes my hand. "Look at it this way. You two really, actually care about each other, at least from what I've heard, and people that really, actually care about each other don't let things like this break them apart."

"This is different," I mutter. "It's— it's just different."

"What makes it different?"

"I kept something from him for months," I say. "He will never trust me again, and he has good reason to withhold his trust. I didn't tell him that thing, and I still haven't told him that— Okay, well, I told him once, but it was an accident. And— Good Lord,

Harlow, I said I should have never told him I'm in love with him. What the ever-loving hell was I *thinking*?"

"You were upset," she says. "People say things they don't mean when they're upset. It doesn't mean you don't care about him, or that he doesn't care about you. Loving someone and being super pissed at them aren't mutually exclusive."

"It would be so much easier if they were. It's actually easier to hate him, which doesn't make any sense. Why doesn't any of this make sense?" I crawl deeper into my blankets.

Harlow comes with me, burying her head under my covers along with me. "Look, Skylar. Maybe I'm only fourteen, but I know some stuff. And I know for a fact that love is super, super messy. It's not all fluffy rainbows and butterflies. It hurts a lot. Drives you insane. I mean, sometimes you have to fight off the entire universe to make something work. Doesn't mean it's not worth it just because it's hard."

"I don't think he thinks that it's worth it."

"Have you asked him?"

"Not exactly."

"And you haven't told him how you feel."

"Well— okay, for our purposes, we'll say no, not on purpose."

"That's a really confusing answer."

"The whole goddamned thing is confusing!" I try to crawl further down, but Harlow grabs my shoulder.

"You're gonna suffocate yourself," she says.

"That's the goal."

"Would it be better if I stopped trying to make you feel better and just let you be upset?"

"Yes, actually," I say. "That would be better."

She lets me cry into her lap until Evan comes to get her because Aunt Clara said it was time for them to leave. I'm too numb to cry after that.

They say that love is a conscious choice, prompted but not made by emotion. I hid behind indecision, and now it would seem that the choice has been made for me. So even if I ever finally come to terms with the way I want things to be, and the things I might be willing to do to get there, never mind. The storm has arrived, and I have no umbrella. The cards have been dealt, but I still haven't played the last hand.

I blame the Knowers for forcing us into unideal circumstances and I blame Margaret for dropping the world onto his shoulders and I blame the island for its constraints and his smile for making him so difficult to ignore. But maybe the problem isn't anything but me. I've got lightning in my hands and clouds in my eyes. Hell, I have time itself under my control.

So it's not like I'm not enough.

I look at the sand dune. Shifty and erratic, sure, but at least it isn't fragile. It won't shatter on impact should it tumble from a few feet in the air. At least it's predictable, since no amount of wind could change its chemical composition or its tendency to settle back into its same undulation when the storm passes. At least it lay close to the ground, visible only to those who crawl to the desert to find it.

A sand dune is safe. Certain. Sheltered by a cloudless sky. Once you heat it up, give it more attention, and start to shape it into something that it wasn't before, then it becomes breakable. Precarious. The broken pieces get stuck in your hands when you try to pick them up and lodge in your feet when you try to walk away. Just leave it as sand. It's far less dangerous.

Okay, sure, I've taken more risks and done more dangerous things in the past year than I did in the fifteen that came before them. But something about this one . . . It shouldn't be more frightening than calling out the Eminence of the universe, fighting off a sociopathic pathologist, or constantly lying to my parents about what I do when I hang out with my friends. It just *shouldn't* be. There is no logical explanation, except for this: Margaret and Freja and everyone in between them really have no effect on me. Jacob does. Sure, they could shoot me in the arm or infect me with the Winther strain, but that hurts less. They don't have the capacity to hurt me like he does, since my heart is not invested in them like it is in him.

I find myself here quite often: Is it worth it? I then convince myself that it isn't. It never was, never has been, certainly is not right now. But this time, I won't force the blame onto something else's shoulders. I won't tell myself that it's something else's fault. It's mine. Entirely mine.

Just a pile of splinters that used to be a tree.

Chapter Thirty

"Guiltless"
dodie

"Skylar." Evan comes into my bedroom and pokes me in the shoulder, thinking I'm asleep. I, of course, haven't slept a second all night, but I still don't respond. He pokes me again, harder. "Skylar!"

"Tell Mom I'm sick," I say. "I'm not going to school."

"You know that won't work." He grabs my arm and tries to drag me.

I whack his shoulder. "Tell her I have a sore throat and my head hurts and it's flu season so I should probably stay home."

"She will never, ever believe you," he says. "But I can try."

"Thank you."

Sure enough, she doesn't believe me. "Skylar, you're going to school."

"No, I'm not," I tell her.

"It was just a math test, honey," she says. "And you'll make it worse by not going and asking Mrs. Flaker questions about what you got wrong so you can learn how to do the problems."

"I can ask her tomorrow."

"Skylar Rawlings, you are going to school. End of discussion."

By the time I'm ready, Hallie's waiting on my front porch. "Good morning," she says.

"Hi," I reply.

Though it is by no means warm outside and we could have taken the bus, we walk to school in silence.

Not a single charged particle left in the air. "Orion started the pandemic intentionally," I say.

"I know," she replies. "He told us last night."

"He did?"

"Yeah," she says. "Also about the deal he made with Luciana Caldwell and Darcy Brecken. And some promise he made to the head curator of the MoMA about an Edward Hopper painting."

"I didn't even know about that one."

"Me either," she says. "But he came clean about all of it. He said you already knew about the pandemic but promised not to tell anyone, so it wasn't your fault. He took responsibility for all of it, and he even offered to come clean to the rest of the Knowers. We said that would do way more harm than good and that we'd keep it between us, but he seemed genuinely sorry, which was both weird and refreshing. Like guava juice."

"I'm sorry I didn't tell you I knew about the pandemic," I say.

"I don't blame you," she says with a shrug. "Orion asked you not to. And you keep promises better than anyone I know. I can say with kind of a lot of certainty that I would have probably done the same thing."

We walk quietly for a few more blocks.

"Jacob wasn't there," she says.

I don't respond.

"So, can I ask, or—"

"No," I cut her off. "You can't."

"Then I won't."

"Thank you."

But when we get to school and start heading towards homeroom, my heart beats so quickly that I'm sure it'll explode, and my hands tremble so much that I have to grip the ends of the sleeves of my sweater. Hallie notices and says, "You good?"

"I'm fine."

I spend a very long time at my locker, dawdling by arranging my schoolbooks for the day and adjusting the magnets on the inside. Hallie waits for me.

When we walk into homeroom, Alex and Jacob are already there. Jacob looks up from his sketchbook for a second before looking back down without saying a word. Instead of taking my usual seat next to him, I sit next to Alex instead, and Hallie takes my usual seat.

"Good morning," Hallie says.

"Good morning, Hallie," Alex replies. "How are you on this fine Wednesday?"

"Just grand," Hallie says. "You?"

"Grand seems appropriate."

They must not be able to think of anything else to say to each other—the silence settles in and goes through deposition and tears a hole in the floor and drops all the way to the basement of the school. I pull out the first book in my backpack—my French textbook—and pretend to read it. I mean, that was probably not the best idea, seeing as though both Hallie and Jacob take French with me and know that we don't have anything to study for right now, but I've committed to the page on *l'impératif*.

"So," Alex says, "opening night is tomorrow."

"That's pretty cool," Hallie says. "Dress rehearsal tonight, and you guys get out of class to do the second dress rehearsal tomorrow."

"I'll bet you're upset now that you didn't join," Alex says with a smirk.

"I might just tell all my teachers I'm in the musical and not go to class," Hallie says with a shrug. "Darner can vouch for me. I've been at more rehearsals than some of the cast members."

I try to see what Jacob's drawing, but I can't tell. It just looks like a bunch of straight lines from here. I turn back to my textbook before anyone notices.

"Skylar," Alex says, "Your line sounded beautiful yesterday."

"Thank you." My voice doesn't sound like mine.

"And Jacob, the sets looked great," Alex continues.

"Thank you." His voice doesn't sound like his, either, and he doesn't look up from his sketchbook.

Alex stops trying with the two of us after that and talks to Hallie about something that sounds like static.

A conversation three desks ahead of me catches my ear instead.

"I'm telling you, we need to go back to the tiefling in the cave in Taritus Mountain," Caleb Maradi says to Blake Kingston. "He cast Moonbeam, which only druids can cast, so he probably has a high wisdom score." They're talking about their Dungeons and Dragons campaign that Kyle Connors has been DMing since sixth grade.

"So?" Blake says. "Why does it matter? I don't want next session to be another crawl."

"Because a high wisdom score means a high passive perception," Caleb says. "So he knows some shit. We have to insight check the hell out of him. We find his weakness, and we use it against him. But since we don't want the Dornima Guard to catch on, we have to play it so it looks like the tiefling did it to himself."

It would seem that Caleb Maradi/Fittiger the Gnome is a genius.

"Did anyone ever read the contract?" I ask.

"The one on the corn flash drive?" Hallie asks. "I didn't."

"Me, either," Jacob says. "They did it in a medieval serf's handwriting on purpose so no one would read it."

I look to Alex, the only one of my friends who doesn't have an attention deficit disorder, since people who don't understand time also don't have enough neurotransmitters. His neurotransmitters might be able to handle the contract better than ours can. (Sure, Knowers might have some cool abilities, but sometimes our brains make things harder, too.) "Do you have a problem reading difficult fonts?"

"No," Alex says. "I prefer serif to sans-serif since I'm no heathen, but I can read anything."

"This one is overly serifed," Hallie says. "Like, the whole letter is a serif."

"Sounds like the dream to me. Where is this buddy?"

"I have it on my laptop." Jacob pulls his laptop out of his backpack and pulls it up.

Alex goes over to Jacob's desk and reads over his shoulder. "What am I looking for, exactly?"

"Anything we can use," I say. "I have an idea, but for it to work, this contract will have to say something I'd like it to say."

"What do you want it to say?" Hallie asks.

"I'm not horribly picky. I just hope Luciana Caldwell has a low passive perception."

Alex and I have lunch at a picnic table outside so he can explain the contract to me. He types up some bullet points in Times New Roman so I can remember everything he tells me.

"So, the main gist of it is that they couldn't discuss anything pertaining to poisoning the soybeans in Paraná to someone whose name wasn't on the contract."

"That's it?"

"Well, that's the main part," Alex says. "Word for word, it says, 'Revealing information as outlined in this document is in violation of this contract, and any guilty party will be held accountable.'"

"Oh," I say. "Could you tell who signed it?"

"Yes, actually. All their names were somewhere in the contract because each of them had a different thing to do as part of it. The number of names specifically mentioned matches the number of signers."

"Who signed it, then?"

"Luciana Caldwell, Darcy Brecken, and Joachim Winston."

"That's it?"

"That's it."

"There were more people in that ballroom, including Mary-Grace Carressy and Carson Sloane and another man and another woman. And what about Cécile? Luciana murdered her, and she wasn't even part of the contract?"

"Wait, Luciana killed Cécile? Really? How did you forget to tell us that?"

I become very interested in a set of initials carved into the wood. "I had quite the night."

"Oh," he says. "Sorry."

Eager to change the subject, I ask, "What happens if the contract is broken?"

"I'll paraphrase it because this thing sounds like Orion talking," Alex says. "Basically, by signing the contract, they're insuring they won't back out of the deal. The whole thing's compromised if someone backs out. Case in point: Cécile. And she didn't even sign it."

"Yikes."

"If someone gets caught, they take the entire fall for it, leave the others completely out of it, and take full responsibility themselves."

"That's a lot to ask of someone," I say. "What else do you get out of signing it?"

"Well, you're a part of any future deals and get any of the revenue from them."

"Is this elaborated?" I ask, though I'm already certain I know what he means.

"Judging from what I read," Alex starts, "Paraná was the first step. They're planning on expanding their endeavors if Paraná works in the way they want it to. They even somehow acquired genetically engineered soybeans that they're planning on producing and selling to the districts that they've gotten sick."

"Dear God." Even though I already knew, it's worse hearing it out loud. "Anything else?"

"Two-percent each of Redway's farmer tax."

"Farmer tax?"

"In Redway, as of a year ago, farmers pay a local business tax."

"That sounds extremely illegal."

"Yeah, honestly," he says. "It seems pretty fishy. New York City pulls shit like that because, well, they can, but somewhere in the middle of the cornfields? *That's* sketchy."

"Clearly, it is," I say, "since six percent is going to these people."

"Right."

"So how would I go about breaking this contract?"

"Tell someone about the sketchiness in Paraná, I guess. Or don't complete the thing you're supposed to do, though all those things were already done."

"What would happen if I broke it?"

"You'd face the wrath of the other two."

"Is the contract voided once someone breaks it?"

"Only for the person who broke it. The rest are still in it."

I toss this over in my brain.

"So, was any of that what you wanted to find in there?" Alex asks.

I close my eyes, and something comes to me. It's morally reprehensible, borderline manipulative, and exactly what we need to do. "Yes. I think so."

"What can I do to help, then?"

I smile at him. "Alex, how do you do this?"

"Do what?"

"You're here by choice. At any moment, you could walk away from all this and be normal."

"I tried being normal," he says. "Wasn't for me."

"You're far too enigmatic for normalcy," I agree.

"Besides, who else would read your weirdly-fonted documents?" He smirks.

"Good point," I say. "Thank you."

"Any time. What else can I do?"

"If you really want to help and won't hate me for asking," I say, "could you please call Orion and let him know he'll be returning to the Wash N' Fold Laundromat on his own tonight? We all have a performance tomorrow and can't stay up all night, and no one wants to be around him right now, anyway."

"Sounds good," Alex says. "I'll let him know."

"Thank you."

He gives me a smile before moving to another picnic table to call Orion. I make a few calls myself. We both get off the phone just in time for the bell to ring and class to begin.

Not that I pay any attention in class for the rest of the day. I pore over Alex's simplified contract notes, dissect them, and obtain what I need. I research legalities, read past court cases, and ensure that whatever I am about to do, it does not involve lying to anyone. That hasn't gotten me much of anywhere as of late.

Between classes at one point, Miss Felding once again pulls me into her classroom. "Mr. Seydin came to me this afternoon and said that Jacob didn't do very well in class today. Much worse than normal. Do you know of anything—"

"It isn't a Knower thing," I interrupt. "It's entirely my fault, and entirely normal teenager stuff."

"Oh." She seems surprised by this answer. "Okay. Thank you for letting me know."

"Of course, Miss Felding." It's almost true, at least.

The plan starts with a series of bullet points down the side of my geometry notes. I delineate the demands and results of the deal Orion made with Luciana and Darcy behind our backs, what the contract entails, the information we need to get to Thomas Redding before he can help, the amount of money we need to get it done, how much we currently have. What I have, what I need, how I can use one to get the other.

Down the side of my geometry notes, something starts to form.

By the time rehearsal begins, I have a rudimentary plan. When I'm not onstage, I hide backstage with my laptop and my narwhal notebook and work out every last kink. I stay as far away from the set production people as I can, though Jacob does pass me at one point. There is a very, *very* serious instance of Awkward Eye Contact, but we pretend the other doesn't exist and go about our days. He still finds his way between my thoughts and still manages to distract me, but I force him away every time. I'll find a way to fix that next, but of course, that seems much harder than this.

The run-through of the musical manages to be the worst yet, even though the show is mere hours away, but I have a new part to learn, different lines to rehearse, and another performance to perfect. Besides, I did my job and learned my role for this per-formance back in January. This surpasses my problem.

After rehearsal, we meet Orion in the gazebo on the quad, and I hand out the scripts. I tell everyone what they need to do, whom they need to call, where they need to go, what we should expect. I run through the seven scenarios for which I've got Plans A through G perfectly oiled and ready to go. I then go over the twenty-three scenarios for which the plans are amorphous at best and nonexistent at worst (Plans H through Delta). For each possible occurrence, I give everyone their lines, blocking, and characters. When they ask questions, I answer. They answer some of mine. By the time I think I'm through everything, the sky is hazy orange.

"And all of this is completely legal?" Hallie seems dubious.

"To my understanding, yes," I answer. "I triple-checked with state and federal governments, read every source I could find, and as long as we execute the plans exactly as I've lined out, we will be completely within the bounds of the law. It goes against at least three rules in *Practices and Rituals*, but I don't think those matter. They haven't mattered since we found ourselves in this debacle."

"No, they don't," Hunter says. "And Eradicators don't even have rules like that, so we're in the clear, anyway."

"Alright, then," Hallie says. "That's awesome."

"Skylar, dear," Orion says, "you might have outdone yourself this time."

"Don't say that yet," I say. "The plan has yet to work."

"It'll work," Lexie says. "How could it not?"

"In lots of ways," I say. "A million things could go wrong. I mean, I have amorphous solutions to twenty-eight ways something could go wrong, but nothing is set in stone."

"Skylar, relax," Hallie says. "It'll be fine."

I ignore her and look to Jacob. "Do I have Eminence approval?"

"Of course you do," he replies.

"I wholeheartedly give you Eminence approval," Orion says.

"Okay, thank you," I say. "So everyone knows what things they need to do tonight?"

Everyone nods.

"Then get them done and get some sleep. We have a show to put on tomorrow."

Chapter Thirty One

Would you look at the space
just next to your feet?
The wood is warping,
the lines distorting.

"Easy"
Troye Sivan

"You look nervous," Hallie says as she wraps my hair around a curling iron.

"What else is new?" I ask.

She shakes her head. "Too much osmosis."

I let her comment slide because I don't feel like dealing with anything beyond the performance and whatever comes after. Judging by our run-through during the school day, the musical will be an abject embarrassment. My entire family is here, including all the Rainers and Jessamine and my grandparents. My grandparents only come to the island for birthdays and the occasional Christmas Eve, so this is a big deal. I told my parents not to invite them because no one else needed to witness this travesty, but did they take my advice? No, of course not.

To make matters worse, my mother texted me just as I started to change into my costume: *We're right next to Jacob's family! Small world.* I don't know if she was trying to be funny. It's a damn *minuscule* town. The odds were like one-in-four that she would land next to Jacob's family. Maybe higher than that because the universe wants to mess with me. It loves to do that.

"Is my hair supposed to be smoking like that?" I ask Hallie.

"It's just steam," she responds. "I'm not singeing your hair off, I promise."

"It would be a lot more smoke if she were burning your hair off," Lexie supplies. Her face is right up against the mirror as she applies dark eyeshadow. Stage makeup is intense. I thought I had too much makeup on for Everett's gala, but this is at least six layers more. It's like face paint.

"Relax," Hallie tells me. "It's supposed to be fun, remember? Not that you know what fun is."

"Hey!"

She and Lexie chuckle.

"I think it'll be awesome," Lexie says. "We don't have to worry about it being *good*, since that's a lost cause, so we can just have fun with it!"

"I suppose you're right," I say.

"Are you nervous about the other thing, too?" Hallie asks.

"Somehow, less so than I am about the musical."

"Your hair's done," Hallie says. "What do you think?"

I look in the mirror and see Cécile Kettering's perfect curls. Hers were a lot darker, and she had no childish ribbons to pull them from her face, but these still aren't mine. My stomach twists for a second, but my eyes adjust and my face turns back into my face and I say, "They look nice."

Once Lexie and I have finished our makeup and have our costumes on, we leave the dressing room. Just in time, too, it would seem—whoever's on the aux cord has started blasting *Hairspray*, and I don't really want to wish Baltimore a good morning. (I will admit that I sang every word I knew when we listened to *Hamilton*. Not that I know all the words. I'm smart, but not *that* smart.)

"Oh, you both look *lovely*." Alex comes out of the boys' dressing room in his Victorian suit, hair done like George Bailey in *It's a Wonderful Life*, a devilish smile adorning his face, and for a second, I understand why half our class is infatuated with him.

"Both?" Hallie puts her hands on her hips.

"You're, of course, the loveliest of them all, Hallie." He kisses her hand, and she swats him away.

"Thank you, Mr. Batchelor." Lexie twirls in her dress. It's so stiff and moth-eaten that it doesn't quite move with her, but she seems to love it nonetheless.

"Is the stage fright hitting yet?" Hallie asks.

"Hallie, you can't ask people if they have stage fright," I tell her. "It gives them stage fright."

"Surprisingly, I'm fine," Alex says. "Better than fine. I'm hyped. Super hyped. Jittery, but in a happy way. You know?"

"Like before a game," Hallie says.

"Exactly," Alex says. "I'm pumped up and ready to go."

"Have you seen Hunter or Jacob?" Lexie asks.

"Hunter's getting his makeup done still, and Jacob's helping people get their mics on and lecturing freshmen about proper set movement."

"Not surprised," Hallie says. "I'm on my way to the audience to see if our special guests actually made it."

"We'd best hope they did," I say.

"I'll let you know." She slips out the door to the house.

"I promised I'd do Sofia's eye makeup, so I'll see you later," Lexie says, and she disappears back into the girls' dressing room.

"I'm about to get my mic," Alex says. "Want to come?"

"No," I say. "I don't."

"Don't make me go alone," he says.

"I don't have a mic," I say. "And—"

"You know I don't like to meddle," Alex says, "but it's been two days."

"Fine," I say before he can say anything else. "Fine. Let's go."

I follow him past the dressing rooms and to the left side of the stage, where the tech people and Jacob help the leads put their mics on. Jacob helps Rachel Kwan put on her mic. She's in a suit since she's playing Edison, though she pulls it off better than most of the boys in the cast.

Jacob sees us, and whatever he's saying to Rachel falters. He starts over, and after she's all set, he says, "Alex, I have your mic over here."

"Thank you," Alex says. "Am I the last one?"

"We haven't seen Wyatt yet," Jacob says, "which is slightly concerning."

"I'm sure he's just making some poor freshman costume kid redo his eyeliner," Alex mutters.

"Or reminding the ensemble that every part is an important part," I say.

Jacob looks to me for just a second, turns back to Alex's mic, and says, "I like your curls."

"Thank you," I say. "I feel like a thrift store china doll."

"Pretty in a dated way?"

"I was going to say musty and disheveled, but pretty works, too."

He blushes, just a little bit, and says, "Alex, make sure the green light stays on, and don't touch any of the other buttons."

"Red light and play with all the buttons," Alex says. "Got it."

"Do you need any help backstage?" I ask Jacob.

"Unless something tragic happened to the sets or the freshmen played with the props again, we should be good," he says. "Thank you, though."

"No problem," I say.

Once Alex's mic is all ready to go, I follow him back towards the dressing rooms. "Well, that went well," he says.

"Please shut up," I say.

"What? I think it went well."

"Alex."

He smirks. "Okay, well, it could have gone worse."

I nudge him with my shoulder.

We find Hallie, Lexie, and Hunter in the hall, and we stay there until Mrs. Darner runs out of some invisible portal and calls us into the blackbox. The auditorium has a random room in the back that alternates between extra rehearsal space, storage for unused sets, and the temple for Secret Cast Rituals. It isn't ever used as a blackbox theater, but someone painted the walls black, so the name isn't completely unwarranted. The entire cast, crew, and orchestra squeezes into the room, and we form an amoeba-like circle.

"Well, I never thought we would get here alive," Mrs. Darner says. "And I don't want to jinx it, since the show's not over yet. But here we go. We don't have much, but let's show them what we've got."

"Was that supposed to be a pep talk?" Lexie whispers to me.

"I guess?"

Mrs. Darner leads us in a few vocal warmups, then a school cheer, then a prayer, which must mean she has absolutely no hope for earthly success and must reach out to a higher power. Then it's five minutes to places. We flood to the stage. Maybe everyone will actually make their entrance this time, though it seems unlikely.

They keep the lights on behind the curtain while we find our spots, but then, somewhere beyond the velvet wall, the crowd hushes. The stage goes black.

I know what Alex was talking about now. The happy jitters. Which would seem to be an external phenomenon, since everyone onstage must be feeling it. Electricity bounces between us as if we were metal rods in a mad scientists' lab. I close my eyes and absorb it. It twirls down my veins and through my stomach and around my shoulders like a feather boa, tickling and luscious. By the time it reaches my head and dances around it like a tiara, I'm not Skylar anymore. I'm Girl Ensemble Member. Maybe more than that.

The curtain opens, revealing nothing but an oil spill and a few blinding spotlights, but I have no problem smiling.

Miracle of all miracles, the show doesn't suck. For the first time ever, the opening number goes without a single mistake. The streak unfortunately doesn't last into the second scene, when Tesla's father forgets a line and Tesla needs to improvise, but out of all the things that have happened in scene two during rehearsal, that's not even close to being the worst.

"I don't even believe it," Lexie says when scene three passes with nothing more than Marica Tesla being consistently off-key (which we all saw coming). "This is, like, lowkey a normal show."

"Don't jinx it," I say. "We haven't even hit intermission."

When we take our places for "Mountain Time," my heart does take the opportunity to thump so loudly I can hear it over the orchestra. I count out each note in the intro, wait for the first few people to sing, then Karina Bepal's line, which means—

"He will go and explore the mountains," I sing.

I don't want to brag, but I do it perfectly. I hit every note (even the D) and smile without reminding myself that people are watching me. In fact, I don't quite care that people are watching me. It isn't really anything new, and this is so much more benign than what I'm used to. The audience doesn't despise me or want to kill me. It's refreshing.

I really am a fantastic actor, if I may say so. I'm so good that people don't actually know how good I am because they don't know I'm acting. Despite any circumstance I might find myself at present, it does feel really nice to be appreciated for something that has become a constant in my life.

Once we exit after "Mountain Time," Lexie grabs my arm. "Sky, that was *amazing*! You were the best one in the whole song!"

"Thank you," I say. "I don't know if I was the *best*, but I do think I did quite well."

She grabs both my hands and squeezes them. "You were the best and you killed it."

"Thank you, Lexie."

We stumble towards intermission with little more than off-key notes or misplaced lines. "Parisian" takes us into intermission, and of course, "Parisian" is never a problem. Tonight is the opposite of an exception. Lexie and I crowd with half the ensemble and crew backstage to hear Alex, Wyatt, and Rachel, and this is perhaps the best time they've ever sung it. Every note is spot-on, and they show emotion they'd neglected during rehearsal.

The curtain falls as they belt the last note, and I feel someone grab my hand. It's Sofia. "You need to be branded. You too, Lexie."

"What?" I don't have time to question anything because everyone in sight rushes towards the blackbox. I don't remember this being determined beforehand, but I go with it. Surely, something must happen.

I can't go into the details of the Secret Cast Ritual. I'm told by a group of seniors that I will be ostracized and quite possibly expelled if I release the details of The Intermission, and I fear them more than I fear any Knower or Eradicator. Besides, this is a much more interesting secret for me to keep than those I usually do. (If you aren't privy to such information, it's imperative that you know: Theater kids are even weirder than you think they are.)

Once the Ritual has concluded, we only have a matter of minutes to get back to our places for the start of act two. And by my count, every single person makes it for the rise of the curtain. A true miracle.

In fact, nearly the entire second act moves all but seamlessly. People are still off-key and still don't know all their lines exactly, but something about the energy makes the show better. It's the audience, I think. They make us better. They give us a reason to try to be good.

Once we take our final bow and the curtain falls, we erupt into cheers. Mrs. Darner told us not to do that because it's "unprofessional," but we've so far surpassed unprofessional that it doesn't matter. Lexie grabs my arm and says, "No one died!"

"Not yet," I say. "That was only the first performance."

We follow the current out through the doors and into the house, where the audience waits for us. I don't even have to look before I feel my ribs being crushed.

"Oh my *God*, Skylar Amelia! You were *awesome!*"

"Thank you, Harlow," I manage to get out. "You're squishing me."

She lets up on her hug a bit. "You were awesome. Really. Best singer in the show."

"Thank you," I say.

The rest of my family comes over, and I'll be honest, it's a little overwhelming having that many people congratulate me at once over singing seven words. I keep peering over my shoulder, hoping to find Darcy or Luciana, but there is too much of everything going on for me to pay attention. It doesn't help that Jacob's entire family is right next to us, congratulating him on the sets. Mr. Connelly then comes up to me and tells me I have a wonderful voice, and it is so awkward that I can barely thank him. Jacob looks as if he'll spontaneously combust, which simultaneously makes it worse and better. He's cute when he's embarrassed.

"Skylar, you really should curl your hair more often," Aunt Clara tells me. "It looks darling on you."

"Thank you," I say.

"I didn't know you had a voice like that," Grandpa says. "It really is something."

I smile. "Thank you, Grandpa."

I catch a glimpse of Luciana and Darcy hovering at the back of the auditorium, trying to survey the crowd without making it obvious but making it blatantly obvious in turn. My chest buzzes—seeing them makes it real. The plan isn't hypothetical, a daydream on my geometry notes. Time to see it through. I turned in the construction documents, and now we break the ground. Build the whole freaking building if everything goes right.

I put on my hard hat.

Guiltily, I find a way to tell my family I have to take my costume off and set my props for tomorrow's performance. I remind my parents that I'm going to Hunter's house tonight for a post-opening night celebration but I will be sure to be home by curfew, and I thank them all for coming. They all hug me and congratulate me again.

Harlow squeezes me until I hear a rib crack and says quietly, so no one else can hear, "I could have sworn you used to have stage fright."

"Me, too," I say. "Things change, though."

"And it's not a bad thing, is it?" She gives me a look.

I reluctantly smile at her. "No. It's not a bad thing."

Conspicuously, she looks towards Jacob.

"Stop. I'll figure it out."

"You always do." She hugs me again and then follows her family towards the exit.

I wait until I'm sure they're out of the auditorium before making my way towards Luciana and Darcy. I don't know why they seem surprised to see me—they did come here at my request. "Hello," I say.

"Skylar, I must say, you are extremely talented," Luciana says. "What a strong voice you have."

"Thank you," I say.

"It truly was something," Darcy says. "Great show, honey."

"As much as I loved the show," Luciana says, "there certainly must be another reason you invited us."

"Of course there is," I say. "Excursions that have only one *raison d'être* are a waste of time. I have a few things to do to prepare for tomorrow's performance, but could you both meet me on the stage in fifteen minutes' time?"

"Sure thing," Darcy says.

"Excellent. Thank you again for coming." I give them a smile before heading backstage.

Chapter Thirty Two

Walking in the darkness,
pointing flashlights to the sky.
See 'em disappear in the shadow of the night.
And you're talking, hearing nothing
in your broken paradise.
So let it go to lose my security in a lie.
Send me away on a rocket to space,
so maybe I'll see who we really are.
Send me down to the depths of the sea,
so maybe I'll find what we're standing on.

"Send Me Away"
Truslow

Before the show, we resolved to meet in the blackbox after we'd seen our families and after we'd reset our props and costumes for tomorrow's performance. Lexie and I help each other out of our costumes before meeting everyone else in the blackbox. I think the stage makeup is too much and almost take a makeup wipe to it, but Lexie says it makes me look more powerful. I take off the red lipstick, but I leave my contacts in. I triple-check that my glasses are in my bag just in case I get too dizzy.

When we get to the blackbox, Jacob, Hallie, Alex, Hunter, and Orion, who unsurprisingly wore a full suit to the performance, are already there. "Great job, everyone!" Lexie says. She gives a round of hugs to everyone, even Orion. "Alex, Hunter, your performances were spot on. Jacob, the sets looked beautiful. Hallie, you made Skylar's hair look great."

"The most important job of all," I say. "Is everyone ready?"

They all nod.

"Alex, Hunter, how's Joachim?"

Alex pulls his phone from his pocket. "Outside the auditorium, according to his last text."

"Hallie, is Mary-Grace here yet?"

"Texted me maybe three minutes ago," she says. "She's in the parking lot."

"I have yet to hear from Everett," Orion says.

"And I made sure Mrs. Darner left," Lexie says. "Convinced her we'd all check our own props and wouldn't need her to stay, and that she really should get some rest before tomorrow's show."

"Perfect," I say. "Luciana and Darcy will be on the stage in fewer than ten minutes now." I mentally flip through my narwhal notebook, and when I land upon what I intend to find, I say, "We are going with Plan G."

"Plan G?" Lexie asks. "Isn't that when all the continents were stuck together?"

"That's Plangaea," Hunter says.

"That's *Pan*gaea," Jacob says. "It's also irrelevant. Skylar, that's the one where we split up, right?"

"Yes," I say. "Take your person—by the hand, if necessary—and run through Base Plan One. Use any means necessary to get them to stay with you. Promise them anything, and we can find a way to make it happen. Then the rest will fall into place. Does everyone remember where to go next? Lexie, you have your phone ready? Orion, call Everett if you haven't heard from him yet, and make sure you have the contingency plan ready in case everything goes awry. We are dealing with some pretty dangerous people, one of whom is a murderer. Jacob, you know the stage better than anyone, but Lexie can go with you if you need help securing it. Alex, Joachim has to finish his popcorn before he comes into the auditorium, since there's no food allowed inside. Does anyone have any final questions? We only have a few minutes."

"There's no way anyone could have any questions," Jacob says. "You've done everything perfectly."

"I've tried, at least," I say. "So, let's go, then."

"We need a team cheer," Lexie says.

"No," Hunter says. "No cheer."

"Write one for next time, Lexie," Hallie tells her.

"No cheer," Hunter says.

"Lexie, you have Eminence approval to write a cheer," Jacob says.

"I second the approval," Orion adds.

Lexie smiles and claps her hands. "I'll work on it for next time." She takes her phone from her pocket and moves into the hall.

Everyone else begins to follow her, going to their pre-determined spots, but I hang back for a second.

There are a bunch of things that could go wrong. I think I know how to deal with anything that comes up, but I always run the risk of my mind going blank. It is *not* trustworthy. Fortunately for me, I tend to work well under pressure, and this situation far surpasses STP.

As he's leaving, Jacob notices me not following everyone else. "You okay?" he asks.

"I think so," I say. "Just—" I check to make sure he doesn't want to leave. I'm surprised he wants to talk to me at all. But judging by the sepia of his eyes and the slight tilt of his head, he's not going anywhere. "Something can always go wrong."

"And you'll fix it, Bubble," he says. "You always do."

My heart warms up like I just drank way too hot tea, but in a good way. I unintentionally smile, my nerves momentarily subsiding. "You're right."

"Did Skylar Rawlings just tell me I'm *right*?"

"Maybe I spoke too soon."

Seemingly despite himself, he smiles. "Let's go save the soybean industry."

I follow Jacob to my spot backstage, in the left wing. Here, I'll wait for a minute until I see Luciana and Darcy. They aren't here yet, but I know they're coming. I know how to tell if they're lying now since I've watched them do it so many times.

Lexie's at the other end of the left wing, fiddling with her phone. She'll use the extensive memory on her phone to record the entire encounter for legal reasons. We aren't breaking a single law, and in case these people are ludicrous enough to sue a bunch of sixteen-year-olds, we need to be able to prove that we were within the bounds of the law. Besides, it'll document any information we learn, especially the information we need to send to Thomas Redding.

Across the stage, in the right wing, I see Hallie and Mary-Grace Carressy. Mary-Grace didn't sign the contract and therefore is under no obligation to uphold it.

Hallie took on the harrowing responsibility of enlightening Mary-Grace as to how her best friend died. No, it wasn't suicide, and Hallie's own best friend watched it happen. Mary-Grace cried over the phone, hung up, and called Hallie back an hour later.

"What can I do?" she asked as soon as Hallie picked up.

"Come to a school musical," Hallie replied.

Alex and Hunter should be with Joachim Winston in the lobby of the auditorium. Jacob's double-checking that the building is completely empty aside from us, since he can get around every inch of the place without being seen or bumping into anything with the lights off. Immediately after the show, Orion disabled the auditorium's security cameras, and now—hopefully—he's found Everett. If we don't have Everett, we don't have a plan.

Jacob comes back to the left wing once he's made sure the auditorium is empty. He'll stay here and text Alex and Hunter when they're needed, and respond to any other texts from anyone else if they need anything during the plan's execution. "Completely empty," he says quietly. "I saw three spiders, but no humans."

"Spiders might pose a liability issue," I say.

"I know. They're such gossips."

I chuckle, but it falters once I see Luciana and Darcy climb the stairs onto the stage. They stand down-center, which doesn't surprise me. They think they're the stars.

My hands start to shake.

"I'll go with you," Jacob says.

"No, it's okay," I say. "You're the communications manager. We can stick to the plan."

"I'll veer from the plan if you want me to," he says.

"I know," I say. "You'd stop time from progressing if I wanted you to."

"That really isn't that hard. I just need my phone and login ID."

"Jacob."

"I'm serious. If you need an extra second, I've got you."

I shake my head. "You are so annoying. I love you, but—" I stop myself, feel the dread set in like a raw egg cracked into my hair, and say, "My God, I did it again, didn't I?"

"You did," he says.

I dare to look up at him, eyes pure brown, a shy smile he tries and fails to subdue. *And it's not a bad thing, is it?* I grab the first fistful of sand. "I'll intentionally tell you one day, I promise."

I don't know how I expect him to respond to that, but I certainly don't expect him to kiss me.

I revel in the darkness. No light tries to fool us. There are no fires or atom bombs or even the blinking light of an overhead airplane, let alone any lightning. Nothing but his hand on my face, the fabric of his sweater, a faint air of lavender, and my feet on solid ground. Not shifty. Not erratic. Solid.

When we part, my brain isn't fuzzy, since it never went *kerplut*. No, all the angles I see are sharper. It's like putting my glasses on in the morning, or slipping into hyper-focus during an exam. I'm calm. Alert. No bubbles clog my chest. My periphery is clear.

"I'll be right back," I tell him.

"I'll be here if you need me."

"You always are."

I step out onto the stage.

"Hello, again. Thank you for being so patient."

Chapter Thirty Three

*But I am
a carefully laid plan.*

"Ballad of a Politician"
Regina Spektor

"Oh, there you are," Darcy says. "We were wondering what was taking you so long."

"I had to reset my props and costume for tomorrow," I explain. "So, do I have to ask you if you enjoyed the show, or could we skip that part?"

"Please," Luciana says. "Though we did enjoy the show."

"Thank you," I say. "So, I requested that you come here because I have a counter-proposition for you, and it's much safer to talk in person. No prying ears, and we've double-checked that fact to be sure."

"I appreciate that," Darcy says. "What's this proposition?"

"So, I understand that you talked to Orion Athan about potentially rectifying the damage done to Paraná's soybean farms in twelve weeks' time," I say.

"Right," Luciana says. "Which we're fine with doing. Everett's senatorial campaign will be up and running by then."

"Well, I have a different idea," I say. "We expedite that, start working with some members of Homeland Security, the CDC, and members of the Brazilian government tomorrow morning, and you fund it. Everett withdraws from the senatorial campaign, Darcy steps down from NYCSGA, you reimburse the Redway farmers you've been extorting with your farmer tax, you cancel any plans you may have in the works to expand your endeavors beyond Paraná, and, if you're feeling decently humane, you come forward with the information you have about Cécile Kettering's death, including the fact that you were the cause."

Luciana answers immediately. "No."

"You didn't even consider," I say.

"Why on God's green earth would we consider that?" Darcy says.

"Surely, you must know why," I say. "You've broken your contract."

"What contract?" Luciana asks.

"Luciana, really," I say. "You should stop trying to throw me off. It won't work. It never does. You two, along with Joachim Winston, signed a contract. And you two are in violation."

"How so?"

"Well, here you are, discussing the contents of the contract with someone who did not sign it. You've discussed it with me before, and with Mary-Grace Carressy, Cécile Kettering, and Carson Sloane, plus a few others, I'm sure. That alone is a violation, but of course, you needed more people involved, or it never would have worked."

"We decided verbally that it was okay to discuss with Mary-Grace, Cécile, and Carson, among others," Luciana says. "It was never written down, but it was agreed upon."

"Okay," I say. "I don't know about the legality of that, but I can give you the benefit of the doubt if you'd like."

"It's certainly legal," Luciana says.

"Well, considering the things you've done, I would say that is probably one of your more legal endeavors. That doesn't, however, change the fact that it was most likely never agreed upon that you can discuss it with me. Or Orion Athan, which you've done."

"What do you want from us, Skylar?" Luciana's getting impatient now.

"I told you," I say. "Forget Orion's deal, and take this one instead."

"No."

"Okay," I say. "I asked nicely, and that didn't work, so I won't ask nicely this time. Jacob, could you ask Joachim to come in?"

A few seconds later, Alex and Hunter lead Joachim down the center aisle and onto the stage. "What in the heavens are you doing here?" Darcy asks.

"I came to see the show." Joachim shrugs. "But I heard from these young men—" he gestures to Alex and Hunter, "—that someone broke their contract."

"That's a lie," Luciana says. "I don't even know how he *knew* about the contract."

"In all fairness," Joachim says, "I broke mine, too."

"He did," Alex says. "I asked him if he'd ever been to Brazil, and he took that as an opportunity to tell me the whole story. It's a good story, though it seems too awful to be true."

"Joachim," Luciana says like a disappointed mother.

"To be fair," Hunter says, "we did already know."

"I'm sorry, Luciana," Joachim says. "Really, I am. I didn't tell them about you and Cécile, though."

"You just did," Alex says. "Thank you."

Joachim sighs and shakes his head.

"It's okay, Joachim," I say. "I know you didn't mean to."

"It's a lot, okay?" he says. Perfect. His fissures start to show through his clothing. "It's a lot to keep from people. My wife, my kids, my whole family—I can't tell them why I can suddenly buy a new car or get them a playground for the backyard. I can't, so I lie, and I can't lie, so I avoid them. And it doesn't work. It does *not* work. And don't you two feel any ounce of remorse? For what we did to those families in Paraná? What we might do to other families in other places? That when Everett finally gets to office, it's not because he deserves it, but because you bribed his way there for him?"

"How dare you," Luciana says. "You act like this hasn't been hard for any of us, either. You think I *wanted* to do that to Cécile? That I want to lie to everyone?"

"Yes, actually, I do," Joachim says. "It was all your idea. It always has been."

Luciana's hand flies to her heart. She sputters for a second before she changes the subject altogether. "So, you broke the contract," she says. "You owe us for that."

"What a shame," I say. "This was so long in the making. I mean, how long ago did you place that virus in the fields?"

"It wasn't in the fields," Joachim said. "We found the bat dens and released the virus in there."

"Oh, clever," I say. "And when did you do that?"

"Stop," Darcy says. "She's just trying to get you to spill, Joachim."

"It's okay," I say. "I already know. Three months ago."

"Probably four," Joachim says. "It was before the new year started."

"Joachim!" Darcy scolds.

"My God." Luciana shakes her head.

"Thank you, Joachim," I say.

"I'm out." Joachim moves to leave the stage, but Hunter stops him.

"Not yet," he says. "Hold on a second."

"This is ridiculous," Luciana says. "You both realize these are kids, right? And we don't have to listen to them? They have no power over us."

"Luciana, please," I say. "You don't actually believe that."

Joachim backs me up. "Yeah, really. I mean, look at what they've managed to do already." He looks to me. "I, for one, am scared of you."

"Thank you, Joachim." I give him a smile. "Okay, Luciana and Darcy, if we could return to my proposition, that would be great. We don't have all night. We have another performance tomorrow."

"I don't want to hear your proposition," Luciana says.

"Listen to her proposition." Mary-Grace Carressy steps out of the right wing, Hallie right behind her. "I already signed the new contract."

"What new contract?" Darcy says. "Mary-Grace, what on Earth—"

Mary-Grace's gaze doesn't veer from Luciana. "I knew there was something wrong with you."

"Mary-Grace," Luciana says, "I can't begin to apologize."

"You don't have to apologize to me," Mary-Grace replies. "I wouldn't accept it, anyway. What you can do is sign the new contract and get away from me as soon as possible."

"What does this new contract entail?" Darcy asks.

"I would be happy to tell you," I say. "First off, upon signing the contract, you recuse yourself from any dealings in Paraná. Darcy, you step down from your position in NYCSGA and pass it onto someone more deserving. You allow my associates and me to enlist the help of the US Department of Homeland Security to correct your mistakes. You give us any and all information necessary to aid Homeland Security in stopping the spread of the virus and helping the sick animals. Everett withdraws from the senatorial race, and we'll help him stay in office for at least another term as a congressman, if he chooses to accept our help. You get rid of Redway's farmer tax immediately, reimburse them, and fund anything and everything you are asked to fund."

"You can't be serious," Luciana says. "That's asking so much of us. And for what?"

"As I said, we guarantee Everett serves another term in the House, if he chooses to accept our help, which we don't require. That is his decision, and his decision alone. And when we supply this information to our friend at Homeland Security, we leave your names out of it. And we don't tell the Redway police department about what happened to Cécile, either. Mrs. Carressy is free to do what she will with the information she's learned tonight, but I won't testify as a witness."

"That's blackmail," Luciana says.

"Actually, it isn't," I say. "It's called a nondisclosure agreement. It's completely legal. You should know, since you've already signed one."

"Ours was a lot different than yours." Darcy crosses her arms. "I don't know how on Earth yours is legal."

"Well, it wasn't that different at all," I say. "I ask you to do some things for me, and I do something for you in return. In this case, my agreement to you is that I won't disclose information. That's exactly what you all agreed to do when you signed the contract with Joachim. So that, Darcy, is how it is legal on Earth. I'm not familiar with space's legalities."

"My God," Luciana says. "Well, I'm not signing. Everett's dropping out of that race over my dead body."

"Actually, I withdrew this morning."

Everyone turns to see Everett Caldwell and Orion sitting in the first row of the auditorium. Both his legs and arms are crossed, like pipe cleaners that a child weaved together. His face betrays just how stunned he is, though Orion did brief him last night at the Wash N' Fold Laundromat. Poor Orion had to divulge the secrets of Redway's princess to her husband, but I don't really pity him. It's just the beginning of his atonement if I have any say. Besides, the blacklight smile beaming up at me from the audience seems to be enjoying this performance too much to call his presence a sacrifice.

"How long have you been there?" Luciana's face loses all its color.

"Longer than you've been there, actually," Everett says. "I got to hear it all."

"Everett, I can explain," Luciana says.

"Please, don't," he says. "I already know how much faith you have in me if you went through such lengths to get me elected. Did you meddle with my first election, too? Plow down all the cornfields in Ohio so Sharonsville could grow more corn and thank me for it?"

"Don't be silly," Luciana says.

"I signed that contract last night," Everett says. "Agreed to every term. Donated all the money we raised for my senatorial campaign at that godforsaken gala to these kids so they can clean up the mess you made, except for the money I set aside to pay for Cécile's funeral and her headstone. You'll sign that contract, or I'll go to the police. Nothing in the contract says that *I* can't turn you in."

"It would ruin you," Luciana says.

"No, you already did that."

Next thing I know, Luciana tears the contract from my hands, crumples it, and throws it across the stage. Then a gun materializes in her hands and she points it right at me.

It's a Glock, I think. I remember reading about one in a book once. Black plastic, looks fake, like a prop from a James Bond movie. Eradicator handguns are far more interesting. And somehow less menacing.

It hasn't fired yet, but my entire body convulses at once as if a bullet had already ripped through it. My arm sears, just like when Andrea Jennings shot at me during Eradicator training. Cécile lies a few feet away from me, her hair still in perfect ringlets, just like mine. Stage hair for two different productions.

Harlow lies at my feet.

Stagnant sapphire eyes stare back at me from the pool of liquid starlight that oozes from her chest. The puddle expands as if she were a leaky gutter over a concrete driveway, soaks into my Converse, turns them gold. Beads up and runs across the stage, chasing something I can't see. A constellation my mind can't connect the dots to find.

"Nobody move!" Luciana shouts. No one does.

Except for Jacob.

He runs towards me, a flurry of storm clouds, and I wish I could read his mind. Know his next move, so I could make mine in accordance with it. And maybe figure out if he's just impulsive or the most selfless person on the planet. If he loves to a fault or to a strength.

Luciana takes the gun off of me and redirects it towards him.

Time, I need you on my side here.

Luciana's muscles ripple, revealing her plan to me. How she'll move next, where her aim will fall, if it will serve her. She blinks, just once, before her face shifts away from me and follows her arms towards him. Her finger wraps around the trigger.

I'm seven steps ahead of her.

Human reaction time is about a quarter of a second. I have no idea what a quarter of a second is, and therefore, I don't abide by those rules. Luciana is bound to them like moss to a boulder. She plays by rules my brain can't comprehend. In this case, incomprehension is a superpower.

I reach out, grab her wrist, and twist it. When the gun fires, the bullet tears through the yellow-wallpapered set piece and lodges itself in the back wall, yards away from Jacob. Harlow and Cécile evaporate. The crackle hangs in the air; everyone holds their breaths. Her hand falters, and the gun clatters to the floor.

Then Luciana says, "What the ever-loving fuck?"

"Please sign the contract," I tell her.

"How did you do that?"

"I won't ask you again."

Gingerly, as if the stage were a minefield, Darcy goes over to where Luciana threw the contract. She picks it up, tries her best to smooth it out, and asks, "Does anyone have a pen I could borrow?"

"I do." Hunter jumps up onto the stage and hands Darcy a chewed plastic pen with no cap. "Here."

"Thank you, honey." Darcy scribbles her signature on a line at the bottom and holds it out to Luciana. "One more blank line, sweetie."

Luciana looks down at the mangled piece of printer paper, the contract etched atop it in the point-five millimeter lead of a mechanical pencil, names scrawled at the bottom in chunky blue ballpoint ink. It looks like a joke, I'll give her that.

"Luci," Everett says, gently, as if she were a sick puppy, "you should sign it. Then we can find a way to fix this and move on."

"Everything will be ruined," she murmurs.

"Everything is already ruined," I tell her. "This just codifies it."

"I hate you," she says.

"That's okay," I say. "I don't mind."

Luciana takes the contract from Darcy and signs it.

"Thank you," I say.

"Thank you," Everett repeats.

"I did it for you," Luciana says to him. "I set this all up for you."

"I don't think that's true."

"Of course it's true."

"Let's go home," Everett says. "And we'll talk about this in the morning."

Though he's twenty feet away, I can still tell by his eyes—he loves her. It's so easy to see. Regardless of every mistake she's made and all the ways she's destroyed so many things, he still sees something in her and loves her for it. Not a sand dune in sight.

She looks to Darcy. "I'm sorry."

Darcy shrugs. "I had low expectations, sweetie."

She looks to Joachim but doesn't say anything.

"I'll take that as an apology," Joachim says.

Her gaze finally shifts to Mary-Grace.

"Don't start with me." Her voice is hardly more than an exhale. "Go to Hell, Luciana."

"See you there," Luciana replies.

She descends the stairs and makes her way towards Everett.

"We'll be in touch," Everett says to Orion.

"I look forward to it," Orion says. "I also would be happy to recommend a marriage counselor should the need arise."

Everett looks up to me. "Fare thee well, Skylar."

"Thank you, Everett," I say.

He gives me a nod, takes Luciana by the hand, and marches her towards the exit.

Darcy and Joachim stagger out behind them without saying a single word to us.

Mary-Grace is the only one who stops in front of Jacob and me and says, "Did you get the chance to meet Cécile?"

"We did," I say. "Only briefly, but she's the type of person of which people paint portraits."

Mary-Grace smiles. "I'm sure she would have loved you."

"I can only hope," I say. "Let us know if you ever need anything, Mrs. Carressy. And though we're all too young to vote, you have our symbolic votes next election."

She chuckles. "I appreciate that." She takes my hand in both of hers for a second before turning to leave. "I don't know how you kids got mixed up in this, but maybe try a calmer hobby."

"Anything calmer than this is too calm," I say.

The door slams behind her, and once it finishes reverberating through the auditorium, we're left in total silence.

"What next?" I ask Jacob.

He takes my hand. I let him. "Bubble. Just breathe for a second."

"Sounds like a waste of time to me."

Alex hops onto the stage and meets us center. "Sorry about your wall, Jacob."

"Yeah, I don't know what we're gonna do about that," Jacob says. "Or about the bullet stuck in the back wall. Mrs. Darner is not gonna like that."

"I'm just glad it didn't rip the backdrop," Hallie says. "Darner would be *pissed.*"

"Guys, the video looks *awesome*," Lexie says, skipping out from the left wing. "Skylar, you're scary."

"Me? Scary?" I say. "I don't know about that."

"It's like you've never met yourself," Hallie says.

"Want to go to my house now?" Hunter says. "Lauren can make hot chocolate. Maybe we can play spies."

"I'd be down for spies," Lexie says. "I'm all hyped up now. Gotta use this energy for something." They climb down the stairs and make their way up the center aisle.

"You okay?" Jacob asks me.

"For now, I think so," I say. "I'll let you know if that changes. How are you?"

"I haven't decided yet. I'll let you know when I do."

"Sorry you almost died."

"Sorry *you* almost died."

I shake my head. "Been there, done that."

Chapter Thirty Four

Take my hand,
let's see if you can dance.

"Simon and Mary"
Noah Floersch

Though it's nearly ten o'clock, Thomas Redding answers his phone when I call him on the walk to Hunter's house. I trail a bit behind the rest of the group and stop beneath a flickering streetlight. "Hello, Ms. Rawlings," he says.

"Hello, Mr. Redding," I say. "I'm sorry to call so late, but I have the information you requested."

"Excellent. Thank you."

"So, according to my sources, the virus was released directly in the bat dens," I tell him.

"Ah," he says. "Okay. We'll need to get a bat expert on board, then."

"I can put you in touch with a wildlife expert in Paraná who might be able to help you," I say. "You also might need to get in touch with some people in Paraná's government, but I can forward on those contacts to you, too."

"Thank you," he says. "And were you able to figure out how long the virus has been in the bat dens?"

"Between three and four months," I say. "Which is quite some time, I know."

"It is," he says. "But it's still manageable. Everything is manageable."

"And you will be able to enact the solution in Paraná?" I clarify. "My associates and I wouldn't be able to get all the way to Brazil."

"We can handle all that," he says. "What we need help with is funding this project. I can apply for government funding, but I'm not sure it would get approved, and if it did, it could take months to actually receive it. And I'm sure there would be caveats attached, anyway."

Between the funds we obtained at Everett's gala, plus the funds Everett donated, plus the money Joachim gave us, and the small but kind donation from Mary-Grace Carressy, we should be fine. I tell him exactly how much I think we can supply.

"Oh my God," he says. "Yeah, that should do it."

I smile. "Excellent. I'll have one of my associates get that to you by the beginning of next week. We have a prior commitment this weekend."

"Perfect," he says. "So, were you able to find out who did this?"

"Yes," I say, "but I am under legal obligation not to disclose that information."

"Oh," he says. "I mean, as a government official, I'm obligated to encourage you to—"

"I know," I interrupt. "But trust me. These people won't try something like this again. I can assure you."

"Well," he says, "as you've said, you've given me no reason not to trust you."

"Thank you, Mr. Redding. For everything you've done. I don't get a chance to work with a lot of good people."

"Honestly, me either." He chuckles. "You're refreshing."

"You're from a strong community, aren't you?" I ask.

"Yeah, I am," he says. "A super small town. On an island, actually."

"An island?" I smile. "That sounds like an adventure."

"It was stifling at times, but yes, it was a very strong community."

"Love thy neighbor?"

"You get it. Send Ms. White my well-wishes, too, if you get the chance."

"I—" I nearly lie, but it doesn't feel right. "I wish I could. I haven't heard from her in months."

"Oh," he says. "That's too bad."

"I don't know about that."

I hear him smile. "I can understand that. I'll be in touch when we start the tracing."

"And I'll have your funding to you as soon as I can."

"Have a wonderful night, Ms. Rawlings."

"You too, Mr. Redding."

I wonder if some part of Thomas Redding, even a subconscious part, knows I'm from his island. Regardless of how far you stray from our river, the current brings you back home in one way or another. We can find each other blinded and deafened, with our hands tied behind our backs. Maybe that's the status quo for small towns. Maybe we're different. Or it could be some combination of both.

As I walk back towards Hunter's house, I take a breath. That's it, then, at least I think. Farmers in Paraná won't have nearly as successful of a harvest as they deserve, but at least acting now will stop it from getting worse. And Everett has his eye on Redway, so we can leave it be for now.

And we managed to do it without alerting a single other Knower.

I'll admit, it still feels deceitful to me. So what if we had Eminence approval, which is all we really need? A lot of the Knowers—especially Miss Felding—have been there every step of the way in other situations. They've taught us how to read legal documents, edit treaties, talk on the phone and sound like an aristocrat, and—most importantly—how to lie seamlessly. It feels like I've just pointed my sword at my fencing instructor.

We'll tell Miss Felding one day, I'm sure of it. Maybe even Eula. Coira would send an assassin after us if she ever found out, but she deserves to know, too. Just not yet. For now, it's our victory, and so long as we have Eminence approval, we don't have to share it with the people who have had them before.

Though I really should mention to someone what happened with the gunshot.

I would say I don't know how I managed to reach for Luciana's gun just as she shot it, but I think I do. It isn't the first time I've begged with time to let me have control over it just for a moment, or for what everyone else perceives to be one. And, so far, it's managed to work. I don't know what to make of it. Maybe it's just luck, but I'm not sure I believe in luck. Everything takes a little human interference.

I ignore it for now. Jacob's right—I should just breathe for a moment.

So before I meet everyone else inside Hunter's house, that's what I do.

It might be considered trespassing because I don't receive explicit permission from an Athan or from Lauren, but I step out onto the dock at the edge of the Athan's yard. I go to the very end and sit on the splintering wood, feet dangling over the side. Fortunately, I'm too short to reach the river, so my shoes won't get wet. I do kind of wish I were wearing pants instead of a dress and thin microfiber tights that will certainly snag on the wood, but it doesn't bother me enough to justify going inside with the stars only inches away.

Like the balcony where Orion likes to hide, the dock is right at the tip of the island, so the river stretches out towards some vanishing point in a one-point perspective drawing. I don't know how long our river is off the top of my head, but it isn't very short. Of course, from here, it appears to move with the curvature of the earth and wrap all the way around it like a necklace, our island the pendant in the middle.

At night, the river doesn't really have a true color, since it mirrors the sky and whatever light it can find. The stars, however bright they may be, don't find themselves in the river, since they know better than to mess with something that deceptive. They're safer in the sky than they would ever be down here.

It's funny—the river seems calmer at night, though I know that couldn't be true. It doesn't sleep. The undertow and the rip currents don't want to rest, lest they miss the opportunity to tear something limb from limb, shrouded by the tranquility of moonlight. Maybe, like most things, it's more fun in the dark.

I've just found Cassiopeia when I hear someone step onto the dock.

"Sorry, did I scare you?" Jacob says.

"No, you're fine," I say.

He holds up a mug—I can't see what bird it is in the dark. "Lauren sent you some tea. Blueberry chamomile. It's really hot still."

"Thank you." I take the bluebird mug from him and take a sip. It burns my tongue to a crisp. "Okay, it's a little hot."

He smiles. "We're inside if you need us. There's a pretty intense game of spies going on."

"I'll be inside in a minute."

"Don't stay out too long. It's freezing out here," he says. "On the bright side, your tea should be cool in no time." He gives me another smile, slightly unsure, and turns to leave.

"Jacob, wait," I say. "Stay. Just for a minute."

"Okay." He sits with me at the edge of the dock. "Is that Polaris?"

"I think so," I say. "It's the tip of Ursa Minor, see?"

"I see," he says.

"It's easier to see the stars in the winter," I say. "Something regarding the amount of moisture in the air, combined with the amount of stars we can see because of the Earth's angle this time of year. We aren't facing the Milky Way in the winter months, so the few stars we can see aren't obscured by the light of all those we can't."

"So the sky's less complicated," he says.

"Basically," I say. "That one's Cassiopeia. She was a bitch."

He laughs. "What did she do?"

"Chained her daughter Andromeda to a rock and let a sea monster come for her."

"Yeah, that's pretty bad."

"She was rescued by him." I point to the constellation next to Cassiopeia. "Perseus. He was smart. He used his problems to solve each other."

"So that's where you learned it."

I look to him, constellations flecking his eyes, jealous of the storms that get to live there full-time. I take a breath, pull every stray charge from the air, and dispel them. Nothing left. "I think we should talk about some things."

"Yeah, we should," he says.

"We haven't really done that."

"I don't think we know how."

"We should learn."

"We really should."

"I shouldn't have kept Orion's secret from you," I say. "Really. You should have been the first person I told, and I should have told you that night. All those other things, all the excuses as to why I didn't— None of it matters, really. I should have told you."

"I get it," he says. "Really, I get it. I don't know what I would have done in that situation. I mean, I like to think I would have told you, but how do I know? You're right—things were really messy. I shouldn't have gotten that upset."

"You had every right," I say. "And I— My God, I said some horrible things to you. That was unwarranted."

"None of it was nearly as bad as what I said to you," he says. "Seriously, telling you I didn't want to talk to you anymore? That's so far from the truth. Everything I said was so far from the truth."

"Me, too," I say. "And I blamed you. I'll be completely honest with you—I blamed you as if you did something wrong. But—" I sigh. "Jacob, I'm not good at feelings."

He laughs a little. "What do you mean?"

"Everything I do has reasoning behind it," I tell him. "Each move I make is calculated, and I think through every possible outcome before I go through with something. I mean, you've seen the plans I make. I account for everything. I do that in my head, too, with day-to-day affairs. Name something, and I've already established exactly how I'll handle it and keep everything else around me intact. But feelings and emotions are completely different. They don't follow the plans that I make for them."

"Only you, Skylar."

"I mean it," I say. "They won't work with me. And you . . . All logic points away from you. Everything about you is not a good decision for either of us to make. Too many things can go wrong and end badly, yet I don't seem to care."

"I don't, either," he says. "I'm fully aware of everything bad that could happen, but . . . but is any of it really that bad?"

"That's what I've been thinking," I say. "I don't think it is. I think I convinced myself that it was so I wouldn't have to deal with you."

He laughs.

"That came out wrong," I say. "Not you, so much as myself. You scare me."

"I scare *you*?"

"You terrify me," I say. "You're a hurricane. Unpredictable. Chaotic. You fearlessly make decisions in half a second, and you follow through with them. I mean, God, you nearly took a bullet for me today without any hesitation or premeditation. I can't do that, and I can't fathom how you are able to. You astound me. And it freaks me out."

"I think you're the most intimidating person I've ever met."

I laugh. "That's impossible."

"Seriously," he says. "You're an absolute genius, and you have a stronger moral compass than most saints, and everything you say is so eloquent and perfectly phrased, and people are drawn to you because you're just magnetic somehow, in a way I don't even really understand, and you're stunningly beautiful, which might be part of it."

"Jacob."

"I mean it," he says. "You're alluring. And you're terrifying. So it's not just you, being scared. It's scary. I mean, just saying it out loud, knowing you know how I feel about you, even though I've never been good at hiding it, and I've almost never wanted to hide it . . . It freaks me out. Like, a lot."

"Well, you know how I feel, too," I say. "I keep accidentally telling you."

He laughs. "I've accidentally said things I only meant to think before, but Bubble, you've reached a new level."

I laugh with him and nudge him with my shoulder. "Come on, you probably knew without me telling you."

"Well, kind of," he says. "You have a very particular eye color when I talk about buildings."

"Overcast sky?" I supply.

"Exactly."

"Yours go full chocolate."

"For buildings or for you?"

"For both," I say. "Darling, you look at me like I built the Chrysler Building."

"You're way prettier than William Van Alen."

"From what I know, that's kind of a low bar."

He laughs again, but then he's quiet for a bit, lost in the stars.

After a moment of silence that is far from awkward, I ask, "What's on your mind?"

"I can be entirely honest?"

"Please be entirely honest."

He looks back to me. "I want to be with you. I always have. Nothing has ever changed that. I don't think anything could."

"Let's do it, then." I don't think about it before I say it, yet it's completely intentional. "I'm irreversibly in love with you, and I'm very much over pretending that I'm not. I am. And I want to be. I'm committing to it. Saying it intentionally. I love you. Logic be damned."

"Really?"

"That's what I want, at least. What about you?"

"That's exactly what I want. But only if you do."

"Forget about me for a moment."

"Then yes. I don't want to pretend I'm not in love with you, either. It's exhausting. I tell so many lies, but that's the hardest one."

I feel a smile spread across my face. "You're intentionally saying it, then?"

"I don't mean to brag, Bubble, but I've always intentionally loved you. I love being in love with you."

My God, I think I melt. Into an actual puddle. "So we're doing this."

"Yeah, I think so."

"Okay."

"Okay."

"So . . . what now?" I ask. "Am I supposed to put a heart emoji next to your name in my phone? Do I have to tell Harlow she was right all along? Or—"

"Skylar." He gestures to Cassiopeia. "Isn't it easier to see the stars when the sky is less complicated?"

"You drive me insane."

He brushes my hair from my face. "You might need to get used to that."

I pull him closer to me, caught between the stars in his eyes, but I stop right before I kiss him, close enough that my nose bumps into his and I can feel his heartbeat in my chest. "If I kiss you now, there's no going back."

"Fine by me. I love you. Logic be damned."

When I kiss him, every false pretense I've ever held up clatters to the ground. I don't need any of them. Besides, he could see through all of them, anyway. Maybe he would pretend not to for my sake, but there's no pretending anymore. It's all there. It's been there all along.

People aren't afraid of the dark, not really. We just don't like the mystery of it. So we replace it with surrogate sunlight, rely on electricity to alleviate our anxieties, force ourselves to marvel at lightning storms because so what if it's just a performance? At least it isn't nighttime. It's fine when we choose to burn ourselves, even when our half of the planet doesn't face the sun, because at least we know the pain is coming. At least we know something. It's easier when we know something.

But that gets so boring, all that certainty.

We part for a second; I rest my forehead against his as I try to catch my breath. "Am I supposed to breathe through my nose?"

"I think so," he says. "That's what I've been trying to do, and I haven't suffocated yet."

I laugh, and he kisses me again. And again. And again after that. I smile against his lips as I take his face in my hands, allowing myself to remember everything I'd forced myself to forget. (Not that I ever succeeded. It's impossible to look at him and not want to get closer.) His face, his neck, the slight curl of his hair behind his ears—it comes back like the finger patterns for a song I haven't played in awhile but remember as soon as I see my violin. His hand runs through my hair—carefully, as if he doesn't want to mess it up, as if that matters, as if anything matters beyond him and me and a few of the stars.

Pollute the night sky with your fraudulent sunlight. Turn on your lamps, point your flashlights towards the rafters, but what will it do? Make things clearer, or only ignore the fact than some things aren't meant for you to see until you're meant to see them? Wait until sunrise. Or wander through the dark until you find the sunrise yourself. There is no room for wonder if life is all answers, and nothing keeps us from finding the answers ourselves except for the fear of what they may be.

As he pulls me closer and traces the side of my face as he were memorizing it with his fingers, and as I wrap my arms tighter around him as if he were a sentient daydream, I see nothing but stars. Certainty in our movement through them, invisible lines that tie them into constellations, tentative space between them. Infinite darkness doesn't faze me because I am okay with the stars I cannot see. Perhaps it's reckless, stumbling in the dark towards a light you can't see yet. Or perhaps that is only what the darkness wants you to think so you won't challenge it.

With my hands in his hair and his heartbeat in my chest, I challenge it.

Logic be damned.

Chapter Thirty Five

"I Don't Pick the Music"
Noah Floersch

Orion's flight back to Rhode Island boarding school is set to depart at eight AM on Saturday morning. I'm up early anyway, so I make my way to the Athan house to see him off.

I patiently wait on the swing on the front porch until the door opens and he steps out with his suitcase and a backpack. "Oh, Skylar," he says. "You startled me. What brings you here so bright and early?"

"I'm sorry to come unannounced," I say. "I wanted to wish you safe travels."

"Thank you." He tosses me a blacklight smile and starts descending the porch steps.

"I wasn't finished, Orion."

He turns back to me just in time for me to watch his eyes morph from their usually comical cellophane green to a more sub-dued jade. "I should have known that."

"You certainly should have."

He sheds his backpack and rests it atop his suitcase, and he joins me on the porch swing. "How can I be of service, Skylar, dear?"

"Your deal with Luciana and Darcy fell through," I say.

"I'm aware," he says. "And you've come to offer your con-dolences?"

"Absolutely not," I say. "In fact, the contract that I wrote for them ensures it. Once Thomas Redding receives his funding, the problem disappears. Darcy's out of NYCSGA, Everett's out of the Senate, and we leave Redway behind us. That *we* includes you."

"Of course it does," he says. "I have no reason to keep myself familiar with Redway."

"Really."

"I swear to you," he says. "I've already visited the crick, and it was underwhelming at best."

"You understand why I have reason not to trust you, right?"

"Of course I do," he says quietly. "But I will do my best to abstain from giving you another."

"Good," I say. "Because I don't know what part of you thought that you could get away with something like that, but it won't fly. If you want to keep other Knowers out of your dealings, I won't stop you. Miss Felding wasn't your algebra teacher, and you see Eula as nothing more than someone who tells you what to do, and I won't bother trying to change your mind. It would be a waste of both of our time. But leave *us* out of one of your plans, and we'll have a problem."

"I understand," he says. "It won't happen again."

"You're right," I say. "It won't." I withdraw a piece of folded looseleaf paper from my purse. "So this is just a formality."

He takes it from me, unfolds it, and reads it at least twice. "A contract."

"You didn't sign the first one I wrote."

"I was never asked to do so."

"I know," I say. "It didn't occur to me until later to request that you sign it. So here's your very own."

"Does Jacob know about this?"

"He helped me write it." I gesture to a line. "See, it has both of our handwritings. His is the messier one."

"And what does this contract entail?"

"You read it," I say. "You forgo your quest to get Ms. Parkins into a government office, which would never happen, anyway. If we ever decide to put someone from our rankings into US government, it won't be her, and it certainly won't be in the House of Representatives. Besides, that would be a decision for all of us to make."

"I see."

"You also promise not to make deals with people without alerting the rest of our group. And if you have any Knower-oriented secrets that have yet to be divulged at the time of signing, you have forty-eight hours to enlighten us."

"And what am I granted in return?"

"I don't take my phone out of my purse and call Eula right now and tell her why Stellan really died."

"I don't believe you would do that."

"I am much easier to forgive than you are."

"We are both at fault there."

"Why? Because I nominated you as Eminence while fully knowing what you did to get there? No one would believe you. I would say I didn't know at the time. Which is true, actually. I had a strongly backed hypothesis, but I had yet to receive a confession from you. And all my friends would back me up. Including your co-Eminence."

"You are not sinless, here, Skylar." He sits up a bit straighter on the porch swing.

"Oh, I know," I say. "But I've already repented."

He looks to me. The dying leaves in his eyes betray him. "Could I trouble you for a pen?"

I hand him a pen, and he signs the contract.

"Are you satisfied now?"

"Almost," I say.

He looks to me, tilts his head just a bit, tries to hide his annoyance and fails because he can no longer mislead me. "Please, let me know what I can do."

"One day, I might find it in myself to forgive you," I say, "but Jacob never will."

"I know," he says. "But I won't stop trying to earn his trust back."

"You never had it."

He doesn't say anything.

"Look, Orion, I won't sugarcoat it," I say. "Given the choice between protecting you or protecting Jacob, I will choose Jacob over and over and over again. There is nothing you could do that could ever change my mind."

"Nor would I ever expect your mind to change," he says. "You are invested in him."

"Then we have a mutual understanding."

"Of course."

"Because, so help me God, if you ever do anything to hurt him ever again, I will find a way to destroy you. I won't wait any longer for the weight of the world to crush you. I'll stand on your shoulders and do it myself."

There it is—the first crack. It skips down his arm like the ground once a meteorite strikes. "I would expect nothing less of you, Skylar."

"That's in your best interest."

The front door opens. Lauren and Delia Athan step out. "Oh, hello," Delia says.

"Hello, Mrs. Athan." I give her a smile. "I'm so sorry to intrude. I just wanted to wish Orion safe travels."

"How sweet," Delia replies, hand on her heart. She looks to Orion. "You have such kind friends."

"I surely do." Orion shoves the contract into his pocket.

"Are you ready?"

He smiles, but it's empty. "As ready as ever, Mother."

Orion Athan gives me one last look before he climbs into the passenger seat of his mother's minivan.

He looks so small.

"Skylar, come have tea," Lauren says. "Hunter is asleep and won't be up for awhile, but I will still make you tea. It's early. You need caffeine."

"Thank you, Lauren. That would be wonderful."

I follow her into the kitchen, stopping to pick up Pickle along the way. "Earl grey with rose petals?" Lauren asks.

"Yes, please." Pickle curls up at my feet while Lauren fills the kettle. "I never thanked you for the tea last night."

She smiles to herself. "That boy needed a little help."

I laugh. "You're devious."

"It worked, didn't it?"

"It worked perfectly," I say.

"Time might work for me like normal," she says, "but I'm still smart."

"You're very smart."

She taps her curl-covered head and turns back to the kettle. "He's a sweet boy."

"I know."

"And an incredibly lucky one if he has your affection."

I smile. "I consider myself pretty lucky, too."

She pours the boiling water into the sparrow mug. "If he ever messes up, you tell me, and I cut him off of *loukoumades* for life."

"Lauren, what did the universe do to deserve you?"

"Don't drink your tea right away. You'll burn your tongue."

Lightning in His Hands closes on Saturday night with a standing ovation. The seniors present Mrs. Darner with a bouquet of flowers and a signed photo, the audience cheers, the curtain closes, and we all cheer again.

The morning after the cast party in the cafeteria, the cast and crew sleepily stumbles back to the auditorium to strike the set. The stage needs to be clear by tomorrow so that the choirs can start rehearsing for their spring concert, and frankly, we left quite a mess last night. Since we had no reason to reset props or costumes, or put set pieces back in exactly the same spot, the entire auditorium is kind of chaotic.

The six of us dismantle some of the larger set pieces so they can be stored and saved for later productions. The helm of the ship needs to be completely taken apart before it can be stored in the auditorium's basement. Once we've taken the whole thing apart and put every screw into an old plastic pretzel container, we start bringing the pieces downstairs.

I've heard horror stories about the auditorium basement—everything from rats to ghosts to illegal substances—but it's kind of a wonderland. Racks of costumes, shelves of props, tables, chairs, white-picket fences, doors with no frames, frames with no doors, walls on wheels, and everything else that has appeared in a production in our school's history lines the walls and every inch of space between them.

"Look at this!" Lexie holds up an old rotary phone. She picks up the receiver. "Hello?"

"Looks like *Bye Bye Birdie* to me," Alex says.

"I hate that show," Hunter says.

"It's not that bad."

"Name one song that isn't annoying."

Alex thinks for a second. "Fair point."

Hallie finds a top hat and puts it on. "Good day to you, sir."

"Good day, Mr. Lincoln," I say.

"Good day, Miss Rawlings," Hallie replies in her President voice. (It isn't the first time I've heard her President voice.)

"How much do we have left to do?" Lexie groans.

"We still have the rest of the ship to bring down," I say. "And take down the backdrop, and pack up the props from the Niagara Falls scene, and figure out what to do about the bullet in the wall—"

"Aren't there, like, forty people here?"

"Yes, but still," I say. "It doesn't mean we don't have an obligation to help clean up."

"Look," Lexie says. "We just stopped a global food shortage from happening, we got a corrupt group of people to stop messing with shit they shouldn't mess with, and we crushed that musical. Don't we deserve a bit of a break?"

"Scavenger hunt!" Alex cheers.

"No scavenger hunt," I say. "The rest of the ship—"

"Come on, Skylar," Hunter says. "Lexie's right, and you know how rarely I say that."

"You should say it more often." Lexie puts her hands on her hips and raises her eyebrows at him.

I look to Jacob.

"A scavenger hunt sounds pretty fun," he admits.

"We have things to do."

"We always have things to do. And this time, we have other people to do them."

I sigh. "Fine. Scavenger hunt."

Lexie jumps a bit. "Okay. Everyone, find something red that can go on your head, something with pearls, something we could have used in this show and didn't, something that definitely has a ghost living in it, and something that's older than your oldest grandparent. On your mark, get set, go!"

We scatter in six different directions. I duck into an aisle of shelves filled with ancient typewriters, mirrors, scales, cash registers, and a super old Mac desktop. Behind the monitor is a masquerade mask, and sure enough, pearls adorn the eyes. I slip it on and wear it like a headband.

"No way, you found your pearl thing?" Alex says when he sees me. "I've been looking in the jewelry and still can't find anything."

"Sorry," I say with a shake of my head.

"Ha!" Hallie calls from inside a chest. She emerges from it with a red pioneer-style sunbonnet tied under her chin. "Boom."

"You look like Laura Ingalls," Jacob says from somewhere behind a rack of pantsuits from the sixties.

"Skylar," Hallie says, "that's the osmosis at work. It goes both ways."

"Fight me, Kirsten Larson," I say.

"Who is that?" Hunter says.

"One of the original three American Girl dolls," Alex replies. "God, Hunter. So uncultured."

"Alex, I am so proud," I tell him.

"See, I listen to you," he says. "Now tell me where you found that mask or I'll end you."

"Never." I disappear into another aisle.

From here, I can see all my friends fight over a red baseball cap and argue over possible years of their grandparents' birth. Lexie tries to pry a plastic lightbulb from Hunter's hands, Jacob tries to convince Hallie that a ghost would never live in a bread pan, and Alex tries to swipe Hallie's sunbonnet while she's distracted.

What did I do to deserve these idiots? I smile at them.

This is one of those moments that time can't reach. We stole it and claimed it as our own. Removed it from a timeline because no timeline in existence deserves to witness what we've created.

How many moments have I allowed time to usurp because I overthought how to shoo it away?

Yesterday, I didn't know that in twenty-four hours I'd be hiding behind Audrey II from *Little Shop of Horrors*, masquerade mask on my forehead, laughing at my friends fighting over junk from estate sales and dumpster dives. A few months ago, the idea would have seemed preposterous, and a year ago, I wouldn't have considered most of them my friends. It's not like I sat down and outlined our friendships. I didn't meet Alex and Hunter in kindergarten and choose not to talk to them until high school but then declare them two of my closest friends. I didn't avoid Lexie until my calendar said it was time for me to invite her over. Hallie's a little different, since I always knew she'd be my best friend, but still. Our adventures aren't scripted. And Jacob— everything about him is unpredictable. No amount of premonition would have told me how that would unfold.

Lightning doesn't always decide where it will strike. It doesn't calculate each crook of its gash, how much damage it will do, what it will destroy when it touches the Earth. It just does it. No orchestration. Pure spontaneity. Improv.

We write the rules that we force ourselves to follow. Always know your next move, the next stop on your journey, what the end destination will be. Plan it out. Know what happens next. If you see the lightning about to strike, it won't catch you by surprise.

I've found myself quite bored with that. Recklessness is so much more enchanting.

"Do you think there's a ghost in this?" Jacob comes over to me and shows me a porcelain doll with ragged curls and half her foot missing.

"Oh, definitely," I say. "That thing should be exorcised."

"I forgot my holy water at home."

"What kind of Catholic are you?"

"A really, really bad one." He pauses for a second, fiddling with the porcelain doll's sunhat. "Are you doing anything interesting later?"

"Aside from geometry homework, no," I say. "Why do you ask?"

"Well, it occurred to me that we have never been on a real date."

I look down at my arms to see if they glow like the tentacles of a bioluminescent squid. "No, we haven't."

"Yeah."

"So, are you going to do something about that?"

He's *nervous*. As if I'd possibly say no. I swear to God, he is too adorable for comprehension. "Bubble, will you go on a date with me?"

"I would love to."

He smiles. "Awesome. So, I've never been on a date before, so I don't know what people usually do, especially on the island since there isn't really a lot to do in the first place, but we could go to the café on Dove Street, or if you don't want to do that, we could go to the park, but it's kind of cold, so—"

"Jacob." I take the porcelain doll from him, set in on a shelf, and take both his hands in mine. "Don't worry. Fewer stars, right?"

"Right."

"Meet me at my house at seven, and whatever happens will happen."

"You strike me as the type of person who's been planning her first date since fourth grade."

"It doesn't seem perfect anymore," I say. "Besides, I don't think we'll be able to find a medieval castle in this part of the world or a field of daisies this time of year."

"I'll see what I can do."

"Hey!" Lexie calls to us. "I know you're all in love or whatever, but Hunter only needs a pearl and he can *not* win this thing."

"Victory will be mine," Hunter cries from somewhere in the costume racks.

Lexie looks to us, crosses her arms, the corner of her mouth turned up in her permanent smile. "You've waited *this* long. What's another ten minutes?"

I look back to Jacob. "I'll give you a pearl from my mask if you show me where you found that doll."

"Take that doll, and I'll get a different one. There are, like, forty, and they're all terrifying."

"Then what?"

He smiles, unintentionally biting his lip, hair unintentionally a disaster.

He is pure, unmitigated chaos, and I absolutely love it.

"Let's see what happens next."

ACKNOWLEDGMENTS

As always, I have no idea how to begin to thank everyone and everything that's brought this book to where it is now. This is, what, the third time I've done this, and it really doesn't get any easier putting all my gratitude on paper.

First, thank you to you! You've read (probably) three of my books now, and honestly, that's quite the accomplishment. I hope I was able to make the time you've spent with me worthwhile (though time isn't real anyway, so).

My parents are my rocks, and I would be nowhere without their constant love and encouragement. Thank you for enduring my rambles during dinner or when you're trying to do something else, my grumpy moods when a scene isn't working, and how loud I get (just in general). My dad has been my editor and my inspiration to start writing in the first place, and my mom has been the epitome of determination. I love you more than I could ever explain.

Max, my dearest brother, thank you for living with me (unexpectedly, too) and giving me idea after idea with your charm and your imagination. Love doesn't cut it, buddy.

Ella and Anna, my pseudo-sisters, you guys teach me things that I'd never realized I needed to learn. Ella, my star, don't yell at me this time. (I have a feeling you will, but whatever.) And Finn, nugget, your laughter keeps me going.

All my friends, Pratt or Nardin or somewhere in between, I wouldn't be who I am if you didn't help me figure out who that is, exactly. My love and appreciation for you knows no limits. Thank you for midnight excursions, singalongs, conversations in the city lights, laughter in the middle of the woods, and allowing me to unintentionally cut you off and write something down. Nastazja, my yee, thank you for watching me freak out over *The Eminence* not even three weeks in and staying with me regardless. It's just gonna get worse from here, I'm warning you. Asa, thanks for answering my weird farm questions. Lee, thanks for answering my other interesting questions. To my D&D group, thank you for jumpstarting my imagination and my charisma and for the contracts (though mine are in a much, much better font). And to Rep Night, my sleep schedule thanks you for teaching my brain to work so well at three AM.

Architecture school has given me (and Jacob) so much more than just being able to identify dormers. Thank you for bending my brain to the point of snapping and teaching me to see stories in every corner. Special thank yous to the Chrysler Building, 8 Spruce Street, Cooper Hewitt (as always), and Higgins (because I never thought I'd miss your weird vestibule or the way the stairs curve in).

Thank you to my Knowers artists (whose lyrics begin each chapter) for giving me a reason to dance while I write. Thank you to my time in theater for giving me lots of insight on how to write about it, and to Nikola Tesla for being so interesting to research (that's a real rabbit hole). Thank you to old houses for being so intriguing, and small towns for being so enchanting. Extra thank yous to scalding hot tea, excessive amounts of chocolate, manatees, Canada geese, *The West Wing*, *Parks and Rec*, flickering streetlights, and, of course, lightning storms.

To my own island, my *first* island, very different from the one I've built yet almost identical in all the ways that don't actually matter, it's about time I've spent more time with you. Daydreams don't have to stray too far.

ABOUT THE AUTHOR

Nina Martineck has been writing for pretty much all twenty years of her life. She published her first novel, *The Knowers*, at age seventeen, and has since published two more, *The Eminence* and *The Duplicity*. Her short story "The Bug Whisperer" was featured in the Western New York Young Writers' Anthology when she was just ten, and she's since published short fiction in *Just My Cup of Tea Magazine* and *Havoc*, which has featured her on its podcast. She writes and edits for *The Prattler* literary magazine and served as her high school literary magazine's editor-in-chief for two years. She currently studies architecture at Pratt Institute in Brooklyn, NY. In addition to writing, she loves buildings, manatees, singing too loudly, and very hot tea.

Instagram: @the.knowers
Website: https://ninammartineck.wixsite.com/mysite
Goodreads: Nina Martineck
Spotify: sugarbeet6

Other Works by Nina Martineck:

The Knowers
The Eminence
The Duplicity

Marvin the Manatee

www.ingramcontent.com/pod-product-compliance
Lightning Source LLC
Chambersburg PA
CBHW070548120726

47909CB00007B/2277